SUSPENDED

A Novel

Written By
Geraldine Davis

To JaVonna
Enjoy every word
2nd Chron 20:17

Published By

ZOË LIFE PUBLISHING
WORDS TO LIVE BY

Published by:
Zoë Life Publishing
P.O. Box 871066
Canton, MI 48187 USA
www.zoelifepub.com

Author: Geraldine Davis
Cover Design: Zoë Life Creative Team
Editor: Zoë Life Editorial Team

First U.S. Edition 2012

Publisher's Cataloging-In-Publication Data

Davis, Geraldine

Suspended - A Novel

Brief summary: Christian Urban Contemporary Fiction Novel

ISBN 978-1-938807-06-0 Softcover

1.   Contemporary Urban Fiction, Love Story, Mental Illness, Abandonment, Recovery, Inheritance.

For current information about releases by Geraldine Davis or other releases from Zoë Life Publishing, visit our web-site: http://www.zoelifepub.com

Printed in the United States of America

V7.2 07 09 2012

Dedication

First, I must thank God, my Heavenly Father for all of the help and patience He has used in getting me to this point in my life. I must also thank Him for that day in the car driving home and the thought of two words take off in my mind and I am blessed to build an entire story around them. And so yes, Lord, I'm "Truly Grateful" for the blessing of this and every book you have given me to write.

◆

Acknowledgements

To Jessica Johnson
I want you to know how very much I appreciate your kindness in helping just because it is the way you are. I needed someone to read my work and give me honest feedback and you without my even having to ask, offered your help. Little did we know that it would turn into such a big thing like it is today.
—Thanks again, Dear Friend

I want my daughter to know how much I appreciate you taking the time in the very beginning to read with me as you lay sick on the couch. There were many things that drew your interest but reading the next page or just listening to the story line seemed to be at the top of your list that summer.
—I love you

Thanks also to my son Emmanuel Jr., and my grandchildren Aaryn Joshua, William, Ebony, Christian, E.J., and Autumn for just being my family. And to all of my siblings for being my both family and friends, thanks so much.
—I love you all

SUSPENDED

A Novel

Written By
Geraldine Davis

TABLE OF CONTENTS

PRELUDE

Chapter One   13
Chapter Two   15
Chapter Three   25
Chapter Four   31
Chapter Five   39

MOVING ON...

Chapter Six   43
Chapter Seven   49
Chapter Eight   53
Chapter Nine   67
Chapter Ten   71
Chapter Eleven   75
Chapter Twelve   83
Chapter Thirteen   85
Chapter Fourteen   91
Chapter Fifteen   95
Chapter Sixteen   101
Chapter Seventeen   113
Chapter Eighteen   123
Chapter Nineteen   127
Chapter Twenty   129
Chapter Twenty-One   133
Chapter Twenty-Two   141
Chapter Twenty-Three   145
Chapter Twenty-Four   161
Chapter Twenty-Five   169
Chapter Twenty-Six   175
Chapter Twenty-Seven   181

TABLE OF CONTENTS (CONTINUED)

MOVING ON... (CONTINUED)

Chapter Twenty-Eight	187
Chapter Twenty-Nine	191
Chapter Thirty	193
Chapter Thirty-One	197
Chapter Thirty-Two	201
Chapter Thirty-Three	207
Chapter Thirty-Four	211
Chapter Thirty-Five	215
Chapter Thirty-Six	221
Chapter Thirty-Seven	229
Chapter Thirty-Eight	237
Chapter Thirty-Nine	241
Chapter Forty	247
Chapter Forty-One	251
Chapter Forty-Two	261
Chapter Forty-Three	269
Chapter Forty-Four	273
Chapter Forty-Five	277
Chapter Forty-Six	285

THE VOW

Chapter Forty-Seven	295
Chapter Forty-Eight	301
Chapter Fifty-Nine	307
Chapter Fifty	311
Chapter Fifty-One	315
Chapter Fifty-Two	319

TABLE OF CONTENTS (CONTINUED)

RESTORATION

Chapter Fifty-Three	327
Chapter Fifty-Four	333
Chapter Fifty-Five	335
Chapter Fifty-Six	339
Chapter Fifty-Seven	343
Chapter Fifty-Eight	353
Chapter Fifty-Nine	357
About the Author	363

PRELUDE

CHAPTER 1

Suspended high above the room with strings from nowhere that tie to my wrists and ankles, my head bobs back and forth continually and my mind is always in reset mode. That's how I feel every minute of every day. There is nothing there to catch me if the strings break. There's no one there to see me fall; no one who will care if I fall and certainly no one who will remember me if I never show up again anywhere. To depend on me, and only me, all of the time is stressful, to say the least. I want to marry, but what will that do for me? I want the big house with a white picket fence, two or three kids, a dog and a husband who will love me; you know I want the dream. And if I can't have it all, at least let me have some of it. So that's what I got, just some of it. A small apartment instead of the big house, a chain-link fence instead of the white picket fence I've always imagined and I got an extra, I got Kane. While he was lovable, he wasn't loving, and while he was there all the time physically he couldn't share his feelings like I needed. So I did for him and his return was alright, but not exactly what I longed for. But what was I expecting? After all, Kane ate his dinner on the floor, scratched the door to go to the bathroom, licked himself to get clean, and bit himself to get rid of fleas.

He never knew about the strings that held me suspended in mid-air. He didn't understand that he was all that I had and I needed so much more. Why I named him Kane, I'm not sure, but when I first saw him that name had already been on my mind for several weeks and that, I thought, was a great way to settle my mind with the word. I figured it was because I must have known subconsciously that I was getting him. Kane was always there until the day he decided to chase the squirrel without looking before crossing the street, and a truck hit him. The squirrel never looked back.

I have a few weeks to myself this month and I don't want to spend it with thoughts that could cause me unhappiness so I've turn my attention to my computer and the internet. I am hoping for a response to my search, but still there is nothing. It has been nine months since I started the search for my family and I am getting a little unhappy about it now; therefore, lunch will have to be something with ice cream.

CHAPTER 2

My mother died when I was six years old. At least that is what my Aunt Birdie told me. But my mother's mother, Grandma Lucy, told me that my mother left me and the family at church to go and pick up my brothers from their fathers' houses, one hot August day. For two years, we waited for Syvon to come back with my brothers, and to make sure that she could find us, we moved right next door to the church she left us at. It was a small church; with a very dark door is all I have ever been able to remember. The church resembled us in a way. I remember Aunt Birdie and Grandma Lucy as being small women, but they, too, were very dark just like the little church and its very dark door.

On her death bed, Grandma Lucy told me the story or at least her version of the story, about what happened to my mother when she left us. Grandma Lucy said my mother was sick is why she left. She left "us" Grandma Lucy always said, but I always felt that Syvon left *me*. My mother, Grandma Lucy told me, loved me and all of my sisters and brothers and that my mother would one day come back and get all of us kids and make us a real family. I was surprised to hear that I had a sister or maybe sisters and brothers. I wanted to know where they were and when could I meet them. I asked Grandma Lucy if I could meet them once, but with tears in her eyes and gray hair that circled her face from one corner of her eye to the other, she squeezed my hand and looked deep into my eyes as a tear ran out the corner of her left eye and slipped down her tiny cheek to the corner of her mouth and smiled slightly. She didn't have to say anything more at that moment; I knew I would probably never meet them because my mother would probably never return.

Before Grandma Lucy died, she told me lots of things that I couldn't understand at the time, and many things I didn't want to remember. But there were some things that have stuck with me and I've thought about almost every day since she told me. One of the things that has stayed with me is the fact that my father died the night I was born. My mother's boyfriend shot him when he was leaving the hospital. That story she told me one day as she peered out the window of the house we lived in right next to the church where my mother left us. My mother, I don't think, took commitment very seriously.

Grandma Lucy sat in the window everyday peering out onto an empty street. She couldn't see too far down the street to the left because the church was there. But when she sat down in her old tattered, green, faded and once called a recliner chair, that caused her to face to the right and into the sunset, Grandma Lucy could see to the end of the street. Not that was such a great view because it wasn't. There was more trash it seemed facing west than there was facing the sunrise. Then one day, in a heated argument between Aunt Birdie and Grandma Lucy, the real reason why Grandma Lucy always listened to her favorite television shows but never let her eyes leave the view from the window came out. Aunt Birdie yelled at Grandma Lucy and said she needed to get on with her life in-

Chapter Two

stead of watching and waiting for my mother to return. Aunt Birdie screeched the words out of her mouth with spit flying everywhere from her lips, "that selfish little Syvon will never come back here for those kids or to see you," declared Aunt Birdie. She said that Grandma Lucy would shrivel up and die right there in the green-faded, broken recliner before Syvon would show up at that house. It might have been what Grandma Lucy needed to hear because after that, Grandma Lucy started getting up early on Saturdays and going to the church to help give out food to the hungry, and on Sundays she went to morning church service. But always, without fail, she would be back home and in the window by two o'clock to keep watch over the McDonald's food wrappers and Bud Light beer cans that lined the cracked and broken sidewalks which lay out before the condemned houses, the charred, fire-burned properties and abandoned, boarded-up homes that sat alongside lovely three and four bedroom houses standing behind fenced-in yards on Bronson Street. Ever so often someone would pass by and Grandma Lucy would sit up a little straighter to see if perhaps it could be my mother. Once it was obvious that it wasn't Syvon Peoples, Grandma Lucy would alter her position to fit her mold in the chair again.

This went on for the next three years even after Grandma Lucy got sick, she had her bed moved over to the window. She said it was so that she could enjoy the sunshine, but even at a young age, I knew what she was really doing. It's funny; Grandma Lucy would never admit that she was looking, waiting, hoping for my mother's return. But the truth is she never liked looking out of the window before my mother left me. Grandma Lucy always said there was nothing but trouble out there on the street. I think she believed that the street took my mother away from her and that's why she always said that. But Grandma Lucy always believed even on her deathbed that my mother would come back some day. It just wasn't the day she died.

After Grandma Lucy died, while we were at the cemetery standing around the grave site, just before the preacher said his final words over Grandma Lucy's dead body, my Aunt Birdie, all five feet and one hundred pounds of her, and my Uncle Stew who stood a full foot taller than Aunt Birdie and weighted twice as much, argued over who would get to take me home. After all, I did come with a monthly check that would last until I was sixteen. Aunt Birdie lost the fight at the cemetery, but won the fight in court, at least for the first two years.

Life wasn't all that great at Aunt Birdie's, but as she said to me time and time again, "you're a lucky little girl to have so many people who love you and want you with them." Yes, Aunt Birdie told me that often to make sure that I remembered how lucky I was to be at her house. I was lucky to know that her daughters who were both going to be doctors because they were able to go to private school while I had to go to public. And yes, I was very lucky to learn how to cook at age nine when her daughters only spent time in the kitchen getting a drink of water as they passed through. Oh yeah, I always felt lucky with Aunt Birdie after Grandma Lucy died.

Finally, my luck changed just before my eleventh birthday when all of a sudden, one month, the checks stopped coming to Aunt Birdie and her daughters. And the next month, I was sent to live with Uncle Stew. I stayed with him until I was almost thirteen years old, but he died nineteen months after I got there. Those were some of the best months of my life. I got my first new coat ever that first winter I was with Uncle Stew, and I got as many toys and clothes for Christmas as Uncle Stew's kids. Since I was the only girl and Uncle Stew and Aunt Joyce had two boys, I had a room to myself. I found out that Uncle Stew and Aunt Joyce had put up some of the money they got for me each month so that when I turned eighteen I could have a good start. They had been saving for their boys, Russell and Clayton since they were born. Russell was ten years old when I came to live with them. He wanted to be an airplane pilot and to attend something called college. Clayton who was eight wanted to attend college too, but Clayton wanted to be a clown. Uncle Stew

Chapter Two

and Aunt Joyce were alright with the idea of Clayton being a clown as long as he was willing to go to college like his brother Russell. I think that is where I got the idea to go to college myself. I didn't know what college was at eleven, but if Uncle Stew wanted his boys to go, I thought it would be a good idea for me to go, as well. The month before Uncle Stew died, I asked him if I could go to college with the boys and he said it sounded like a good idea to him. Then I thought it would be a good idea to know what it was I was getting myself into so I asked him what college was. That was the last time we ever heard Uncle Stew really laugh. He died at the hospital a few weeks later and a few weeks after that I was up for sale again.

I understand that Ruth was my mother's cousin, and she and my mother were close at one time. So Ruth took me in after Uncle Stew's wife, Joyce, said she didn't want me, and if no one else would take me, she would have me put into foster care. I guess she got a pretty large check from an insurance company for Uncle Stew's death, so she didn't need the money that came with me. She never told Cousin Ruth that there was money attached to me.

Cousin Ruth, her three kids, and me were put out of Ruth's house twice before a friend told her she should be able to get money for taking care of me because of my father's death.

I was fourteen just five months short of my fifteenth birthday when I had to leave Cousin Ruth's house because of her boyfriend. Rayford Moore was a pig. He even squealed like a pig when he laughed. Rayford wasn't a bad-looking man; he was just stupid and lazy. All he did all day long was lie on the couch and eat. Me and my cousins Andre, Andrea, and Raymond, were constantly going to the refrigerator and the corner store to keep him supplied with snacks, drinks, and cigarettes while Cousin Ruth slaved away in the kitchen or ran to the grocery store for Rayford. On the rare occasion that Rayford left the house, he would go the corner store and hang out with the low life there. I saw him there once, with another woman and they were kissing, but I never told Cousin Ruth.

Suspended

Cousin Ruth and Rayford had dated many years ago when Cousin Ruth was ten years younger and thirty-five pounds thinner and her hair didn't need to have so much weave in it. Back in the good old days when Cousin Ruth had a full set of teeth and her eyes weren't so red, Ruth had been a very pretty woman. I saw the pictures of her around her house and she looks like a completely different person. I saw some pictures of Rayford from the same time and he still looks the same...he still looked like a pig. Rayford might have been the father of one of Ruth's children, but Rayford said it wasn't possible and Cousin Ruth never said anymore about it.

The night he put his hand down my pants and said he had lost something and was looking for it was the same night I wanted to move out of Cousin Ruth's house, I just didn't have any place else to go. When Ruth's son Raymond told Cousin Ruth what he saw Rayford do to me, she yelled at Rayford and told him not to try it again. Then she told him he couldn't handle a real woman like her. She was really angry with him so she grabbed his hand and led him up to her bedroom. The thought of what could have happened in that room made me shiver. I can still remember the moans and screams coming down the stairs. That was the very first time in years, since I was five or six years old that I drifted up to the ceiling. I stayed suspended there for what felt like hours, I couldn't speak or talk. I don't remember anything else until I saw Cousin Ruth again and she had a very pleasant look on her face. It wasn't until that next day when I was telling the only friend I ever had named Deborah Lincoln, what little I could remember about what happened with Cousin Ruth and Rayford that I was made to understand that I had to leave Cousin Ruth's house. The next morning, Cousin Ruth told me that Rayford told her everything that had happened and that I shouldn't keep flaunting myself in front of him. She informed me that two women couldn't live in the same house especially when a man is involved so I needed to find a place to go for a few days until she could figure out what to do with me.

Chapter Two

I was only supposed to stay with the Lincolns for a couple of nights but after eight months the Lincolns were pretty sure that Ruth wasn't coming back to get me. They never asked why I didn't go back or why Ruth never came to get me. They were Christian people and didn't want to put me out onto the streets, but when Mr. Lincoln's job transferred him to another state they didn't want to get into any trouble by taking me with them so the Lincolns gave me five hundred dollars for my new life. Two days later, I turned sixteen and I was completely on my own.

◆

I decide to try to find Aunt Birdie to see if I can stay with her until I turn eighteen. I'm willing to get a job and pay her for letting me stay with her. But when I step off the bus a block from where I last knew Aunt Birdie had lived, the car that rounds the corner and almost hits me, turns out to be Aunt Joyce and her boys. I hadn't noticed it was her, but she stops, reverses the car and gets out of it in the middle of the street. I think it could be trouble so I pick up my pace. It takes me a few steps to remember her voice before I stop walking and turn around.

Aunt Joyce looks good. She wasn't a bad looking woman before, but now she looks good, she isn't plain but pretty. She let her hair grow longer and she has changed the color of it. Aunt Joyce even lost weight; about twenty pounds and she's had her teeth fixed. She's also driving around town in a pretty new car. That must have been some check she got when Uncle Stew died.

We stand facing each other for a couple of seconds before Aunt Joyce speaks. When she does I notice her new teeth.

"Hi, Naturallee, how have you been?" She seems nervous when she speaks. With the car keys in hand she traces the key ring between her index finger and thumb. It makes me remember how nervous she would get when she had something important to talk over with Uncle Stew. I can still see her sitting at the kitchen table in front of a cup of coffee with steam rising up out of the cup. And again, with her index finger as she'd trace the lip of a cup, she'd carefully tell Uncle Stew about a car accident she'd had with the garage at her mother's house.

"Hello, Aunt Joyce. How have you and the boys been doing?" I can't think of anything else to say so I wait to get her answer.

"We've been good. The boys have adjusted to the loss of their father and we have moved from the house on Grant Street. We live on the west side of town now on Grander Boulevard. But how are you? What have you been up to? Where are you staying now?"

With so many questions at once I wondered if she was in a hurry and needed to leave. "Well again, I'm good, I can't do much, I'm still in school and I am staying with a friend right now." Of course, she didn't need to know that friend and her family had just left a few days ago moving to another state, probably to get away from me. After all, I promised Deborah's mother that I would only stay a night or two and ended up staying for eight months.

"Look, Naturallee, I must apologize to you for the way I treated you when your uncle died. I shouldn't have just put you out just because my life had been turned inside out. But I would like to help you now, if I could."

"What are you talking about? Help me how?" Now it is my turn to be nervous and caught off guard. Why would Aunt Joyce say that she wanted to help me? She owed me nothing. Aunt Joyce was my aunt only by marriage, we weren't blood related so what could she owe me? I wasn't hers to take care of or help. I was only in her house because of my mother's brother, Stewart Peoples, and after he died I knew I would have to leave.

As my thoughts are in the past, Aunt Joyce grabs my hand and shakes me back to the side of the street where we are standing. "Naturallee, I owe you an apology, but I owe you what your Uncle Stew left you, too." Aunt Joyce has a more serious than nervous look on her face now and I notice that she also has soft brown contact lenses in her already soft brown eyes, giving her eyes the look of a younger woman. "Naturallee, first, your uncle and I had started a saving account for you when you lived with us. Each month your check came, your uncle put away half of the money for you for your future. He said that you would need some money to get your life started when you turned eighteen even if you didn't go to college. We saved it for eighteen of the nineteen months you were with us." Then she looks away as if there is something she has to say that is shameful for her to speak. Aunt Joyce looks down at her hands still playing with her keys. The horn blows from inside her car and both of us look at the car to see the boys beckoning her to come back to the car. Aunt Joyce glances quickly at me and asks that I wait one minute.

I wonder how much money she and Uncle Stew have saved for me. I could really use that money now. I still had three hundred twenty-seven dollars of the money the Lincolns gave me, but over the last several days I have already spent almost two hundred of the five hundred dollars just trying to eat and keep dry from the past three rainy nights. As I think of what I have spent the money on, Aunt Joyce returns and is speaking to me again.

"As I was saying, Naturallee, we had put away the money for you, but probably because your uncle always dealt with the accounts for you, I didn't think about it when I turned you over to your Cousin Ruth. As a matter of fact, it wasn't until I went to the bank to open up new accounts for the boys that it was brought to my attention by the bank teller that Stew had opened the accounts for you. I need to get you the money, Naturallee. I feel horrible having that money set all these years when your cousin and you could have been using it. Are you still with Ruth?" Aunt Joyce looks concerned when she asks about Ruth.

"No. Cousin Ruth asked me to leave when her boyfriend tried to get interested in me. Ruth told me I had to get out more than eight months ago."

Aunt Joyce looks horrified at my words. She puts her hands over her mouth and her eyes get as big as half dollars. "Where have you been living, child?" Aunt Joyce whispers from behind her thin fingers that covered her full lips.

"I had for the last seven months been staying with a girlfriend from school and her family. They let me stay even though I had nothing to give for staying there. They were really good to me, the Lincolns gave me money to take care of myself before their family left town," I told Aunt Joyce and right away I wished I hadn't said the last part. What if she decides not to give me the money she says is mine.

"Well, where are you staying *now*? Aunt Joyce asks as she slides her hand away from her mouth overcoming her initial shock of what I have told her.

"I have a place to stay, but I am running out of money for the rent," I thought I should say that to get her back on track if she was thinking about not giving me the money.

"Oh, then as usual God has brought us together at the right time because I have money to give to you. And I can give it to you right now if you have the time to go to the bank with me."

I'm too shocked to move. Did this woman just say that she had money for me? Could Uncle Stew have been onto something with this God thing? Boy, I haven't thought about God in years, since I left Uncle Stew and Aunt Joyce's house. Uncle Stew would always tell me things like God would always take care of me. He would provide for me. All I have to do is trust in Him. I never really knew what that meant. Actually, since I left their house I haven't spent much time thinking about God; frankly I didn't think He was thinking about me.

"Let's go then, the bank will close in an hour and if we go now I can get you the money, or maybe get the money transferred into your name. It might be more that you want to walk around with in your purse," Aunt Joyce says with a smile as she walks fast to her car and I kind of shuffle along, trying not to stumble over what's happening right now. I have just gone from rags to riches, so to speak, in a matter of minutes. I decide I had better walk a little faster.

CHAPTER 3

Waiting in line at the bank, I wonder how much money there is. Aunt Joyce gave me a lot of information in the car, but she hasn't said just how much money there is yet. She told me that not only did she and Uncle Stew save my money for me, they also started a college fund for me like the ones they had for their own boys. Aunt Joyce said that I was starting to feel like a daughter to her and that was the reason that she took me back to my uncle's family. She said that she was starting to love me like I was her own. She was afraid that if she tried to hold on to me that someone from Uncle Stew's family would fight her for me and that she knew she would lose, at least that's what a lawyer told her. So to save herself and me the pain of the whole thing she simply gave me back. Aunt Joyce also told me that she was getting married again. She and her new husband-to-be and the boys are going to move about seventy miles away and so she was very glad that she had found me before they had to leave.

Suspended

"Come on, Naturallee, it's our turn," Aunt Joyce urges as she pulls me to the bank counter with her and snaps me out of my daydream.

"Hi, Ms. Peoples. How are you today? Is everything alright? This isn't your usual day or time to stop in," the bank teller announces with a smile as she looks me over. I can see her pretty green eyes beneath her shaggy bangs that are in need of a new dye job. Her name tag says Lori Plainne but she is anything but plain. Her jacket is bright red and she has a yellow scarf around her neck. I think it's supposed to go with her blouse but the look is gaudy like her hair color. Fortunately, she is sitting down so I don't have to look at the rest of the outfit she's wearing. But I have to laugh to myself as I remember the way Aunt Joyce used to dress; wearing a green shirt with pink shorts and some brown high heel shoes.

Aunt Joyce has made a lot of physical changes, but who she is has stayed the same. I understood the teller's surprise with Aunt Joyce being in the bank at anytime of the week other than Monday morning at ten o'clock. And the fact that I (an adult or at least more than twelve years old) am here with her has probably caused the teller to consider putting her finger on the alarm button. When Aunt Joyce would come to the bank back when I lived with them, she would take me along with the boys, but only we kids could go with her; never any adults. If someone else needed to go to the bank, she would take them, but only after she did her banking alone or with us. Then she would go and pick them up and take them to the bank while she waited in the car for them.

"Hi Lori, I know I feel a little strange myself being here in the middle of the week, in the middle of the day, and having someone with me, but this is something I need to do. I have wanted to do this for several years but I couldn't find my niece. But as God would have it, today quite unexpectedly, we ran into each other. Oh, Lori, let me introduce her to you," Aunt Joyce says as she pulls me even closer to the counter. "Lori, this is my niece Naturallee Joy Peoples.

26

Chapter Three

Naturallee, this is my favorite bank teller and friend over the years. Lori, Lori, oh my goodness, Lori, what is your last name?

"It's Plainne, Lori Plainne," she says as she points to her chest. Her smile said she didn't take offense to the fact that Aunt Joyce didn't know her last name even though it is on her name tag.

"Sorry about that, but you know, Lori? I can't say that I have ever known your last name," Aunt Joyce says with a puzzled look on her face as she looks strangely at the name tags of all the tellers.

"You wouldn't have reason to know it. We just started wearing these new name tags yesterday. Besides, I need to know yours but you don't have to know mine," Lori said with a warm smile.

"That's true," Aunt Joyce agreed then continued, "And this is the reason why I'm here. Do you remember a few months ago I asked you about that account that Stew had opened up for the daughter we wished we had?" Aunt Joyce asked with a serious stare in her eyes.

"You mean the one that belongs to a child that once lived with you?"

"Yes, and this is that child. The account belongs to Naturallee Joy Peoples and I want her to have the money transferred over into her name today if you could do that for me," states Aunt Joyce.

The statement caught Lori by surprise. While the smile never leaves the teller's face she does make a bit of an adjustment to her face before returning to its usual position. It's clear that Lori wasn't sure what to do or say. Watching her face frozen in that position makes me smile a little. She simply stands there even when Aunt Joyce calls her name twice; Lori only comes back to herself when Aunt Joyce waves her hand in front of Lori's face.

"Mrs. Peoples, do you think that's a good idea to transfer all of that money at one time to someone as young as this child? I mean, she has to be sixteen to have the account in her own name. Is she sixteen?" The teller's question is more of an interrogation than a question. Her attitude makes me step back and I could tell that it made Aunt Joyce feel a little odd, as well.

"Well, Naturallee is sixteen, Lori," Aunt Joyce replies then looking at me she asks, "Aren't you Naturallee?

"As of a couple of weeks ago," I tell them both.

"Do you have any identification on you, Miss," the teller asked with a bit of distrust in her voice.

Aunt Joyce is becoming uneasy with Lori now.

"Lori, is there a problem with anything? I could go over to the desk and have it done if you're busy; it's no problem for us to do that. I just need to get Naturallee her money. I feel like I have been holding up her life for the last couple of years." Aunt Joyce gives me one of those soft, sorrowful looks that says she really does mean every word she said. Hugging my shoulder, Aunt Joyce returns her gaze to Lori, "I need to make this right for Naturallee, for Stew, and for myself. Can you do it or do we go to the desk?"

Lori's cheeks are no longer perky and her eyes have fear hidden behind them. I have no idea what is going on, but Aunt Joyce is figuring out that something's wrong and she is starting to press Lori with a whole litany of questions.

"Please, Mrs. Peoples, Joyce; I am just looking out for you. You don't know how many times our customers have been taken by someone ripping them off without the customer knowing it." It's a good thing that her fingers are connected to her hands or all ten of Lori's fingers would be laying on the counter in front of her. As Lori stumbles for her next words, the pleading look in her eyes causes Aunt Joyce to pull me back a step.

Aunt Joyce tells Lori that she would rather take care of the transfer at the desk and then she leads me over to some chairs and we sit down. After Aunt Joyce spends the better part of an hour at the desk with the bank manager, and with the bank being closed for the past seventeen minutes I am ready to leave, but Aunt Joyce is agitated about how they are handling the transfer, and us. Then, just when I think I can't take it any longer, the bank manager comes in with the paperwork and a little booklet in her hand. She has a pleading

Chapter Three

look on her face and a bank gift that she hands over to me. She and Aunt Joyce talk a little more. The whole savings account thing is explained to me and I am given the little book and some papers to sign. Finally, Aunt Joyce stands up to leave and I follow her lead. But the manager starts to talk again so I just tell Aunt Joyce I will wait at the car. I walk outside, glad to breathe fresh air.

While I am waiting for Aunt Joyce, I think about how glad the boys must be that they were left at the house while we are at the bank. Sitting on the curb in front of the bank I hear the bank door open behind me and I look back. My jaw drops when I see Lori Plainne being escorted out of the bank in handcuffs by a police officer in uniform and a guy in a suit. Lori looks down at me with tears in her eyes and a bright red nose. She tells them how sorry she is for what she has done and that she needed the money. The men don't respond to her statements they simply put her into the police car and after they got in the car, they slowly drive away. When Aunt Joyce comes out we get into her car and drive away, too.

For the first few minutes, Aunt Joyce says nothing. About half way to her house, she begins to open up. It would seem that Lori had been borrowing from Aunt Joyce's accounts for several years and the account that was set up for me was her favorite one to use. As a matter of fact, there were two accounts for me. One account had at one time a balance of over five thousand dollars in it, but Lori had borrowed all but eight hundred dollars of that. The other account had a beginning balance of fourteen hundred before Lori started borrowing from it. Aunt Joyce said the bank manager told her that all of the money would be put back into the accounts by the end of the week; she wanted to make sure that I received all of my interest and all the monies that had been deposited over the years. She is also going to put in the five thousand that Aunt Joyce put into the account when uncle Stew died. Lori had taken the cash from the deposit Aunt Joyce had given her but the computers were off line the day Aunt Joyce made the deposit so Lori never put the money into the account. There had been an investigation of sorts made but because Aunt Joyce had no receipt they convinced her she had not made the deposit. The bank manager always felt that Lori Plainne was behind much of the missing customer money but never had any proof, at least not until today.

CHAPTER

4

I spent that evening and the next four days and nights with Aunt Joyce and the boys. I enjoyed being with them when Uncle Stew was alive and I quickly realize that I still enjoy being with them now. Being here makes me remember what a family feels like. Aunt Joyce still has the boys say their prayers at the end of the night once homework, housework and dinner is over. The boys are still very respectful to their mother and they speak favorably about Lawrence, their stepfather-to-be. And even though things are very much the same, there is a lot that had changed. Most of the changes are with Aunt Joyce. She uses words that I never thought I would hear her say and I believe I heard her swear. I also notice right away that the word doesn't offend either of the boys. I accept the fact that she has made a lot of changes in herself though not all good changes but the new way of talking is what surprises me most. Her new language seems to roll naturally off of her tongue. I used to think it was Aunt Joyce who kept the family focused on God and Jesus, but now it seems that it was really Uncle Stew's doing. I wonder what her new husband-to-be is like. Is he one to use such language or could he be more like Uncle Stew? I'll find out tonight because Lawrence is on his way over for dinner and I will get to meet him then.

If Grandma Lucy were here she would have enjoyed watching this beautiful man about her age coming up the street. At sixteen a man of sixty is too old to consider. But for this stunning, six feet three inches, two hundred twenty pound specimen is definitely the exception to the rule. I would be so proud to call him granddad or even grandpa. I would love to be seen with him at a school function or even at the grocery store. His top lip is covered with a well shaped gray-black mustache that drapes over each corner of his mouth and with just enough chin hair to cover the tip of his chin he looks very professional with his mostly black hair and black eyes. He's dark enough to lose at midnight but worth straining my eyes to find at any hour of the day or night. In the summer heat, at the close of the day, this man had a light layer of sweat clearly visible at the base of his throat just above his open pink and green shirt that matched the green design stitching on the front left leg of his jeans. Yeah, if Grandma Lucy had been alive today and sitting in her window looking out for Syvon, I am sure if only for a few minutes, she would have taken her eyes away from searching the streets for her daughter to gaze upon the beauty of this man...who is now coming up to the door of this very house. This can't be Aunt Joyce's new...but the doorbell rings and he is the only one here.

I'm too surprised to move as Aunt Joyce answers the door. They exchange a few words but I can't hear what's being said because of the humming in my ears. I feel like I am drifting up. I'm leaving the room and I don't know why. I see him coming to me but with each of his steps I feel a greater distance between us. The room is getting smaller and I feel like I'm sweating more than he is. My eyes want to close in hopes of making things stop; to try to get my feet back on the floor; to stay in the room and meet this man, but I can't. I'm up against the window so tightly I feel I could break the glass.

Chapter Four

"Naturallee, this is Lawrence Young, my fiancé. Lawrence, this is my niece, Naturallee Joy Peoples."

There's quiet for what feels like hours before I can hear anything else.

"It is good to meet you, Naturallee. Your Aunt has told me so much about you these last few days until I feel I already know you," I hear Lawrence speaking and his words pull me back to the floor and into the room, and it pulls my hand into his extended hand and we shake.

"Oh. Oh, yes. Hello, I'm sorry," the words stumbled out of my mouth like a baby taking its first steps. My words and my voice sounded as if I was stuck in a window. "Lawrence, it is nice to meet you," I finally got the words out of my mouth without any funny looks from the others in the room.

"Naturallee. That's a different name. How'd you get it?"

I haven't been asked that question in a few years; most people take it as if it's common anymore. But the way Lawrence asks makes me feel like there is something behind the question, and it makes me feel a little uneasy. Now the gorgeous man who just walked up to the door has become more than just a stranger, he's strange. I wonder if I'm the only one in the room that has this feeling. Lawrence has not taken his eyes off of me since he entered the door. If not for the strange feeling I can't seem to shake, I would take it as a compliment, that he thought I was cute. I have known for a couple of years now that even at sixteen, I'm more interested in older men; maybe Lawrence has picked up on my interest. This is his way of letting me know that he knows how I feel and he wants to discourage me from getting interested in him because I am too young for him. Plus he's Aunt Joyce's fiancé.

"Is it a family name?" Lawrence asks, still studying me.

"No. My mother named me Naturallee because she said that I was born naturally, without any drugs." I haven't told that story in a long time but if it gets his eyes off me I'll tell it again.

"Let's sit down and discuss her name and any other names, but sit, the dinner is getting cold." Aunt Joyce is feeling left out and the boys are looking like they missed the beginning of a bad joke.

I notice again how much Aunt Joyce has changed. When Uncle Stew was alive, she would never have allowed something as obvious as Lawrence's interest in my name pass by and simply suggest that we sit down and eat.

The dinner is great and I'm glad that cooking is one of the things that Aunt Joyce hasn't changed about herself; she was and still is a great cook. The moment I put the chicken in my mouth, my mind falls back to the many chicken and hamburger meals eaten across the dinner table at six o'clock sharp for nineteen months while I lived with Aunt Joyce and Uncle Stew. The dining room in the old house was covered in soft blue and white wallpaper that had baseball size horseshoe wreaths with silver bells inside each one. The drapes were burgundy with very sheer panels behind them and a chandelier that hung too low over the table. And three times a week we ate chicken in this room. Uncle Stew loved both Aunt Joyce's chicken and that room and Aunt Joyce knew every way to cook chicken.

As the flavor of the crispy, hot chicken fills my mouth and my memories I forget about Lawrence, the bank teller, and the fact that I'm homeless. I feel safe and loved, and as I open my closed eyes and chew slowly I find that I am smiling, as well. Once I remember that I'm not alone, I look around the table and I have to laugh. The look on the faces of everyone else says that I love the chicken a little too much.

"Hey, girl, that's only chicken,"

"Yeah, and it's only fried...in the kitchen...in this house...by Mom's hands," is Russell's response to Clayton's funny little statement.

The evening is fun and allows me to talk about some of the past without feeling numb to the memories. Russell left around seven to go to a friend's house to study and Clayton wants to see a television

Chapter Four

special for a class he is taking. So I found myself with Aunt Joyce and Lawrence. We are still laughing about the past when Lawrence calls me Syvon unexpectedly. Aunt Joyce and I stop our laughter instantly and stare at Lawrence.

"How do you know that name?" Aunt Joyce is the first to find her voice which sounds like a ship horn lost in the fog. She must have thought so too because she clears her throat before she asks him again. "Where do you know that name from?"

Lawrence lost six feet of his height in that moment. He stands frozen, allowing only his eyes to move back and forth between me and Aunt Joyce. His right hand still holds the glass of ice cold coke while his left hand stays in his pocket. The sweat that was on his throat when he arrived has now returned. He seems fragile and almost like a waxed statue.

"Lawrence," Aunt Joyce calls his name once more.

Lawrence lowers the glass of pop then moves over to the coffee table and places it down before sitting on the couch. Looking at Aunt Joyce and then back at me he opens his mouth to speak but no words come out. We are all speechless for several minutes before he finally starts his explanation.

"You look just like your mother, I mean exactly like Syvon Peoples when she was your age. That's when I first met her before she got mixed up with all the wrong people and things. She was absolutely beautiful. Even when her life turned the wrong way she was still the most beautiful girl and woman I had ever seen."

Lawrence's words take me by surprise and I am still unable to say anything.

"Syvon was sixteen when I first met her. At sixteen it wasn't right for any girl to be that beautiful and sexy and desirable. And it wasn't possible for any man to simply know her and not want more of her, at least not for this man." I think a wave of shame came over Lawrence because he put his head down and stopped talking.

Suspended

"Go on, Lawrence," Aunt Joyce encouraged.

"Baby, she was so many years ago and I was a man without any self control," Lawrence says through pleading eyes to Aunt Joyce. "And if I had known that this was Syvon's daughter I would have said something the minute you told me about her," he continues with the same pleading look in his eyes.

"How well did you know Syvon, Lawrence?" Aunt Joyce's question is very direct and very blunt, so blunt that even I understand right away what she's asking. She never takes her eyes away from Lawrence's face as she waits for his answer.

Lowering his eyes to the floor as if the answers to all his problems are in the shag of the carpet, "I knew her well enough to father one of her children." Lawrence stands up and looks directly at Aunt Joyce. "Remember I told you that my fist daughter died just before her fourth birthday," Lawrence said slowly then he waits for Aunt Joyce's acknowledgement of his statement.

"Yes. You said she died needlessly due to the neglect of her mother." The second she said the words Aunt Joyce looked at me realizing she had just made a very negative comment about my mother. I couldn't really say too much because none of her words or Lawrence's words is a lie. Besides this is not the time to side track this conversation, I want to make sure this man wasn't my father, and so, I ask.

"How long ago did you know my mother?" It wasn't the same direct approach that Aunt Joyce used, but I am sure he understands my question.

"I knew your mother about twenty, twenty-one years ago. We were together about eighteen months or at least in my mind we were together about eighteen months. In that short period of time, Syvon had broken up with me several times. I had caught her with other men several times as well. When we met, she told me she was twenty-five years old Syvon always looked older. If you had known her then you would remember, too, how much older she always looked

Chapter Four

so I didn't think anything of it when she told me her age. I didn't find out how young she was until she told me the baby was sick and in the hospital. When I went to the hospital to see Lovely Girl, Syvon's mother told me I was too old for her daughter. Then she asked me what it was I thought I was really going to get from a woman that young who already had a bunch of kids. When Lucy Peoples said that her daughter wasn't twenty-five years old I thought she was saying that to get me away from Syvon. Lucy thought I was supplying Syvon with drugs. I explained to Lucy what had been going on and how I got involved with Syvon. Lucy said she could understand but that she wanted me to do right by my daughter, and I meant to. But Lovely Girl died five hours after I promised Lucy that I would be a good father to her." Lawrence drifted into the past which was an ugly past to relive.

There is so much pain inside Lawrence when he's telling the story that Aunt Joyce's living room became filled with Lawrence's painful memories. We all wait motionless for the next words that Lawrence forced out of his memory and through his lips loud enough for us to hear. When he says the next words his voice cracks and breaks and my eyes fill with tears for him. Remembering the last moments he spent with my sister, Lawrence speaks softly as he talks about Lovely Girl. Then he remembers how Syvon swayed up to him in a drunken state and asked him for money to buy more liquor. He said she was very flirtatious trying to entice him to give her some cash. After she saw that he wasn't interested in her advances, she spit on him and stumbled away. But before she left, she remembered their child and laughed when she told him that Lovely Girl was sick and in the hospital. She told him that she would probably die soon and he wouldn't get to see her again. Syvon also told him it was for the best that the child dies because she was sick of her mother taking care of the kid. Lawrence said he had wanted Syvon to give him Lovely Girl but Syvon wanted to keep the child to keep the relationship with him. Otherwise, Syvon told him, there was no real reason for the kid to be alive.

Suspended

When Lovely Girl got sick that last time, she was too weak to fight off pneumonia she had developed and she died after three days in the hospital. Lawrence was glad that Syvon had told him in time for him to see Lovely Girl before she passed away. Lovely Girl died at a quarter after three on a cool, early fall afternoon with her grandmother and Aunt Birdie at her side while she lay in her father's arms. Syvon wasn't there. As a matter of fact ,no one saw Syvon until the funeral. She arrived twenty -seven minutes after the funeral service started and had to be taken out because she screamed and carried on so badly until they had to stop the service due to the all of the noise she was making. Lawrence said that it took him ten years to get over hating Syvon.

I didn't know that I ever had a sister named Lovely Girl or that she had died at a young age. Just knowing caused a hurt inside of my soul and it makes me understand Lawrence better. I didn't know Syvon, but today, I hate her, too.

After a while, the evening gets back on track, somewhat, and it ends alright. Aunt Joyce and Lawrence still have their plans for the wedding and leaving town and I am actually happy for them both. After all, Lawrence had been through with Syvon, he deserved some happiness and so did Aunt Joyce.

Before the evening ends, Aunt Joyce and Lawrence ask me what my plans are and what I was going to do once the money ran out. They ask me to say in touch with them so they could know how I'm getting along. I tell them I will, but I let go of the words the minute I say them. I just can't believe that they or anyone else is that interested in my life. Although it feels good to think that someone cares. I do feel safe back here with the boys and Aunt Joyce. I know I will miss them and all of the family stuff when I leave.

CHAPTER
5

I somehow finished high school and stayed out of trouble and under the radar. With the money I got from Aunt Joyce and the full time job I got my sophomore year of high school, I was able to get my own place by the end of the first month of school. Aunt Joyce also helped to get me enrolled in school since I no longer had the Lincolns to help me with things like that.

I kept to myself and made no friends. I didn't want anyone to know what or who I was so for the next three years I did a good job of staying invisible. But it was now my senior year of high school and I was ready for graduation, but no one was there for me. I lied and said that my dad was diabetic and in the hospital. I told Cindy Long, the only person who seemed to notice that I had no one there, that my dad's blood sugar was too high and we had to rush him to the hospital in the early hours of the morning. I told her that my mom was with him and couldn't be at the graduation ceremony. Cindy bought the story because I heard her tell someone else the story right after the graduation ceremony. Cindy was sure I was not interested in going to any of the graduation parties because I would want to get to the hospital to see my father. My thoughts fell to him and who he could be, what he could look like, and if I was attending school with any of his other children but just didn't know them. I pretended to take the bus to the hospital to see my dad, but in reality I took the number ten bus to the apartment building across the street from the hospital where my apartment actually was.

I had made plans for celebrating my graduation at home alone. Before I left for the graduation ceremony I put up a banner and streamers and I had a cake and a party hat for myself. I didn't buy anything to drink other than pop. I had heard in my younger years that if my mother hadn't been a drunk she could have found her way back to the church to get me, so I wanted to be sober when she found me. Looking in the mirror, I want to see if that was really me who allowed those words to enter my mind. And that was the first time I ever cried about my mother or me or my situation.

Suddenly, I felt a string stretch me tight and high in air, and it frightened me. Even though I knew there was a floor beneath me, I felt like I was being pulled up and away from it. Then as the floor got farther and farther away from me I couldn't stop myself from drifting upward. There was panic inside of me but I couldn't scream, the room changed from a soft white and beige color to violent red and black, smoky, dull to brilliant shades. The few pieces of furniture I had are, all of a sudden, gone. With my arms stretched out and my feet being pulled down I was suspended again and this time I felt my ankle snap and things go black.

MOVING ON...

CHAPTER

6

I haven't remembered graduation in years. Just as I am about to ask myself, what brought that thought up? I feel a sharp pain in my right ankle and lean in hard to keep from falling and to keep the pain from being too much. Then I remember that's what brought back the memories of graduation. As I limp my first few steps over to the window, my ankle pain subsides and I feel like a young woman of twenty-six again and not like my grandmother.

Since graduation, I have changed jobs three times and I've started college again for the second time. I haven't been able to make friends at any of the past jobs. I think it is because I knew I wasn't going to be staying at the job for long and there was no reason to make friends for what was sure to be a short time and then leave them behind. That's what I'd tell myself anyway whenever I started something new, and that's what I told myself when I started college this time.

Suspended

College is different, in that, no one seems to care if I show up or not. No one asks my name or if I want to study with them. The instructors don't ask if I need help with the courses or why I'm late to class or anything else. I'm not sure if they even know who I am or that I am in one of their lectures. I say this because one late spring semester night after my last class my old Mercury refused to start. As I sat there trying to get my car started, pleading with it to get it started, one of my professors walked by and told me to have a good night as he continued walking to his car. I was too surprised to ask for his help, I just said thanks and watched him pull away. Finally, campus security came by and fiddled with something under the hood and it started. He told me to get it fixed before I came back to school because it would stop on me again soon. Of course, he was right, but I was able to get through exam week, which was the very next week. After that I quit school for a little while.

Returning to school this time, I realize I should have stayed in school the first time. Education is easy for me, but more than that I need a place to be. I need something to do. I need to know there are other people in my quiet, unnoticed world. After working all day at the museum, there is no place to rush off to. After dinner and dishes, there is nothing important to do like homework when I'm enrolled in school and studying something. What bothers me most is that there is no other face to look at but my own. No other voices, just mine, and no hope of breaking free of this seclusion I'm living in.

Sitting on the bay window, I watch the car lights race across the wall in front of me. Feeling a little like Grandma Lucy, I wonder where everyone is going in such a hurry. Are any of them as lonely as I am right now? I hear myself chuckle, "Did I just say I'm lonely?" I have to admit it, my life is lonely. Not boring, or a disaster, or too busy, or too anything else. It's just lonely, and I don't know what to do about it.

Chapter Six

Again, I'm crying. Over the last several months, I have cried twice. There must be something wrong with me, I don't usually cry. I have to figure it out before things get any worse. Just then the phone rings and I jump up as though someone has just kicked in the door. For a long moment I don't move, the phone has ringed as many times in the last several months as I had cried. I'm not sure what to do, at first. Then, pick it up, comes to mind.

"Hello?"

"Yes, hello, is Naturallee there please? Could I speak with her?" Someone on the other end of the line with a familiar and kind voice asks.

"This is Naturallee, who is this ....please" I am confused and curious. It is someone who knows my name and hopefully knows me. But it could be an insurance salesperson. At this moment though, I don't care, I need someone to know that I'm alive.

"Naturallee, this is Carl, Carl Morgan. We had a math class together two semesters ago. I don't know that you'd remember me but we shared the math table for the last six weeks of class. I'm the guy who was supposed to call you if I couldn't figure out the concepts for our team, remember. I needed to keep our team alive so we wouldn't have to take the second half of the final.

"Oh yeah, Carl, how are you?" Other than he was quieter than I was and he wasn't very good at math, that's all I remember, that and he was a pretty good-looking guy. He probably still is. But what did he want with me. "What can I do for you?" I ask.

"Well this is a little awkward, I don't usually do things like this but here goes. I've always wanted to ask you out when we were in class, but I never did. I thought there would be time that next semester. But you didn't return and so I waited for this semester to see if you were coming back. Since you didn't, and I still had your number, I thought...hoped it would be alright to give you a call to say hello, and ask you if you would consider having dinner with me this weekend and..."

But he finally runs out of breath, and I have a chance to say that I am at school this semester and to ask him why he wants to take me to dinner. After all, we hardly know each other.

"Then, how is it that I haven't seen you this semester? Are you still full time or," but I stop him to say that I am taking day classes this time.

"Well that explains that doesn't it. Look. Naturallee. I know that you're a quiet and reserved person, you're someone who respects others and you like your privacy. I know it's not important to you to have a lot of people around you all of the time and I know that I like the way Lever 2000 soap smells on you."

I had to smile at that. Who knew people noticed things like that?

"I also know that you just smiled at my last observation and ran your finger across you top lip," Carl pointed out.

I'm speechless at the observations Carl just made. How could he know so much about me from sitting in a math lab a couple of days a week for sixteen weeks? While I'm impressed, I'm also a little spooked by his words. Concern starts to grab hold of me and I feel myself starting to drift up. The telephone feels heavy in my hand and I feel sick to my stomach. My feet are feeling light, as if they are no longer underneath me. And then I heard Carl say, "Naturallee, would you like to go out sometime? I mean, like this weekend. There's this really great restaurant just east of town and I know the owner real well. I'd love it if you would be my date Saturday. It's my brother's birthday and we, my family and friends will be celebrating his birthday there and I want you to come with me as my date." I hear him suck in air finally.

It was enough to bring me back into the room. The words grab me like a one ton weight and I am back on the floor. I find my voice and stammer out, "I'd love to go." Then I immediately ask myself what am I *doing*. I just accepted my very first date with a man I hardly know. If he's not the guy with the dark-brown hair and one-sided smile who sat two rows in front of me in class, I'm going to be in big trouble.

We agree to finalize our plans on Friday, and then I hear the dial tone. I slide the receiver back into its cradle and smile.

Standing next to the table in front of the window, I notice an older couple outside on the street holding hands. I realize that's something I've never paid attention to before, people caring for one another and showing affection toward each other. I watch them walking and talking together until the trees get in the way, then pressing the side of my face against the glass, I continue to watch until I'm sure I can't see them any longer. I stand in the window for another half hour watching and waiting, I think, to see if they will return. I also want to see if other couples are out taking a stroll in the early night-time hours and just for a short moment I hope one day soon one of those couples will be me and a man who loves me. But as usual, by eight o'clock the street is quiet and empty, except for the red-haired older lady who walks her dog four times a day rain or shine, winter or summer, sick or well. What will she do, I wonder, when her dog dies and she no longer has a reason to walk the streets four times a day? Will she take the time to let someone into her life? Is she like me, I wonder? I always have a good excuse why I am alone. And until lately the excuses were enough. I was satisfied. What's wrong with me and what's wrong with the red-haired lady with the dog?

CHAPTER
7

My feet leave the floor and I'm not as frightened this time. And as quickly as I feel myself floating up to the ceiling, I find myself drifting back to the floor and then I feel the carpet under my bare feet. Twice in the same hour I've overcome being suspended in midair and suffering the sweating fear of having no control over myself. How I've overcome it both times I don't know, but I hope I will be able to overcome it more often. Car headlights beamed into my eyes and flooded the room with light, causing me to snap out of my mind-wondering trance. I go into the kitchen and make dinner for one again. Just thinking about eating with someone else is exciting to me. The thought keeps me company throughout dinner this time so it's like I didn't have to eat alone.

The next several days go by like ice cream melting in a freezer. Ice cream only melts in a freezer when the freezer door is left open for a long period of time. And the hours in a day only moved when I have something to help keep my mind off of Saturday, the birthday party, and of course, Carl himself. These days I feel a little like my feet aren't on the ground but the feeling is different from when I am suspended. I actually spoke to a woman at the grocery store who hadn't spoken to me first. I even got sick one day when I spent the afternoon thinking about "the date" for too long.

The telephone rings again. This is twice in one week. How many people know me and how many of them have my telephone number? "Hello," I said sharply because the ringing chased away my daydream.

"Hello," again, I snap then I wait for a response.

"Hello, is this the home of Naturallee J. Peoples?" A man asks.

"Yes, it is" After I answered so shapely I wished I hadn't, at least not until I knew who it was that was doing the asking.

"Who wants to know? Who's calling?" I ask as my mind races for the next words to say and brace for his answer at the same time.

"Ms. Peoples my name is Walter Mayfield. I was a friend of your stepfather, Nathan Grey, and I am also his attorney. Nathan was married to your mother Syvon Peoples for almost five years. About two years ago when Syvon just vanished and..."

"Excuse me, but who did you say you were and how did you find me?" I need to catch up with the words coming into my ear.

"Please, forgive me. I should give you a moment to digest what I am saying. My name is Walter Mayfield and I was and am both friend and attorney for your late stepfather Nathan Grey and your mother Syvon Peoples Grey. Nathan was married briefly to your mother Syvon. And you are Syvon's daughter Naturallee Joy Peoples, are you not?"

"Yes, Syvon is or was my mother, but what...." Walter Mayfield cuts me off before I can continue my line of questioning.

"I will explain further if you could come to my office sometime this week, Ms. Peoples. Nathan has passed away and you are listed as next of kin to his estate. So there are some things I need to discuss with you. Could we meet Friday perhaps around two o'clock?"

Chapter Seven

"I don't know a Nathan Grey, I barely knew my mother." I tell Mr. Mayfield. But he is persistent.

"I understand this is all confusing and a little unsettling for you. But if we could just meet I could clear everything up and give you some information about your mother."

I never thought about receiving information about my mother. It wasn't important until Walter Mayfield made the statement.

"Alright, Friday at two o'clock will have to work." After he gives me his address and phone number, the line goes dead, and slowly, I return my receiver to its cradle for the second time in as many days but this time there is no smile on my lips. "What could this be about?" If it has anything to do with my mother, I am pretty sure it can't be good, I tell myself, as I turn my thoughts back to dinner and an evening out. I don't want anything to mess up Saturday, and my mother could, so I leave all thoughts of her behind and go to kitchen for a soft drink.

CHAPTER
8

The week finally goes by but not before I get myself all worked up about the phone call, the date, and the meeting with the attorney. It's Friday and I'm late for the two o'clock appointment with Walter Mayfield. When I step off the bus, I believe I still smell of gas fumes from the previous bus I was on. The first bus broke down seven blocks from the attorney's office. The bus company sent another bus to finish the bus route but that took time. When I called Walter Mayfield's office to let him know about the trouble there was no answer so I left a message on the voice mail. I hope he is still there waiting for me. I get off the bus just around the corner from the Grey-Mayfield Building. Turning the corner, I face a large building with a rather daunting facade. Long white columns and endless steps, makes me wonder if the people inside are of the same type of structure. Once inside the coliseum-like building, I slow my pace a bit. I need to catch my breath, but after checking the time again, I rush to the elevators. Stepping in, I push the button for the seventeenth floor. When the doors close behind me, I lean against the back wall, took a deep breath, and held it for a long moment and ask myself again, what could this be *about*, but the bell dings and the elevator doors open and my thoughts change.

I am thirty-three minutes late, and I still have to wait in the outer office for twelve minutes once I enter suite seventeen hundred. But I have more of a chance to catch my breath and to look around the office. It is elegant and spacious, very light and airy. This is the kind of room that makes you relax, even if you don't want to. The light oak trim goes gracefully with the egg white walls, beige furniture and splashes of green from all the plants sitting around the office.

As relaxing as the office is, I feel out of place and uncomfortable in my jeans and sneakers. I feel like I should have gone to the salon at ten o'clock this morning instead of later this afternoon. And now, suddenly, I feel myself lift up off of the chair I'm seated on. Somehow, I left myself open to the unknown and fear has stepped in. I am floating. My feet are off the floor, but my right hand has a tight hold on the arm of the chair. My voice is inside of me unable to find my throat and therefore, unable to make a sound. I am leaving the room and no one seems to notice. High above the floor, fear takes me over. I feel myself sweating, and finally I cough, and feel water stinging in the corners of my eyes. My arm hurts at the shoulder from trying to hold onto the seat. My wrists and ankles are fiery hot from the rope burns that have me suspended and tightly stretched out.

"Miss, are you alright? Here let me get you some water," the secretary finally looks up from her work due to the sound of my coughing. Why she hadn't seen me looming high above her, I don't know, but I am thankful for the attention now. Rushing back, the secretary carries a bottle of spring water that has a picture on it from someplace out west where they have gushing springs flowing over large boulders and the sun glistening on the tops of each white

Chapter Eight

wave of water. The water bottle is like the office, it makes you want to relax and take a drink. I reach for the bottle, but she is nervous and drops it just before I can reach it. She looks as if she needs the water more than I do. I pick it up and quickly get the top off and take a long drink.

"I am so sorry, but are you alright now? What just happened?" The secretary looks as though she has seen something strange.

Maybe she had seen me suspended. Finally, there is someone who can verify that I'm not insane. This isn't my imagination; it really does happen to me. But before I can speak she asks if I am diabetic. And I know then she has seen nothing, and my heart drops. I shake my head and wave my hand as if to say I'm alright. Go away.

Just then, a door on the far side of the room opens and a distinguished gentleman steps into the waiting room. His suit says he is expensive, but his smile says he is friendly. The ring on his left hand says he is married. Yet something about him is unhappy. But when he speaks, the room comes alive, and the music that was barely noticeable playing in the background before comes up a little louder and I recognize the Isley Brothers music.

"Ms. Peoples, I am Walter Mayfield. Won't you come in please, and forgive me for expecting you to wait so long without any courtesy. Ms. Blair, would you get Ms. Peoples a glass with ice in it, please," Mr. Mayfield requests as he extends his hand and guides me into his office and then closes the door behind us. His office has three calming, restful, walls to it, and a forth wall that gives the illusion of the room opening up into the ocean. The mural behind the waterfall on half of the back wall has a three dimensional look to it, drawing in the water behind it as it pours into the room, and back out again.

Pulling out a chair for me at a table for eight and sitting down next to me, Mr. Mayfield draws in a deep breath, releases it slowly, then smiles nervously, "Are you comfortable," is all he can find to say for several long seconds. Then, finally he remembers his promise and speaks very professionally at first, but his nervousness quickly returns.

"As I promised you Ms. Peoples, I will tell you why you are here. But first I must tell you I have set aside a couple of hours for this meeting. There is someplace I need to take you, so do you have the time today?" Mr. Mayfield doesn't blink when he speaks, he keep his eyes staring straight into mine the whole time he is talking.

"Take me where?" I am beginning to regret coming to his office already.

"As I mentioned on the phone, Nathan Grey was married to your mother, Syvon Peoples, for nearly five years before she just packed up and left one day. But Nathan, I mean Mr. Grey couldn't get over her. He had fallen madly in love with Syvon but Syvon couldn't accept or return his love, at least not at first. She said she had too many ghosts in her past, and that one of them or all of them would catch up with her one day. She said she couldn't hurt anyone else who loved her. So, one day, she left without saying good-bye to Nathan. He spent a lot of time and money trying to find Syvon, but when a person doesn't want to be found, they aren't. Anyway, Nathan died last year, and I was his best friend and attorney. As his attorney, I have the responsibility to fulfill his final wishes."

"And how does fulfilling the wishes of a dead man whom I never knew fit into my life or me into his?" If for no more than curiosity sake, I want to know.

There's a knock at the door. Ms. Blair walks in with a tall glass of ice. The glass fit the room perfectly. It's a beautiful crystal glass with a thin gold trim at the lip. She sits it in front of me on the table, gives me a quick smile, and leaves without a word.

"Nathan met your mother when she was working on the streets. We were headed to a business meeting one evening when he saw her. Syvon had a beautiful smile, the same smile that you have." Mr. Mayfield says while still staring deep into me. I'm feeling a little uncomfortable.

Chapter Eight

"I am sorry. It's just that you look so much like your mother, it's a little unsettling."

This is the second time I've ever been told that I look a great deal like my mother. At least, now I had some idea of what Syvon Peoples looked like.

"Anyway, Nathan and I had to go around the corner and pick her up," Walter Mayfield continues, "Nathan actually took her with us to the meeting we were going to, he could do that, it was his company. He promised her he would pay her well if she would wait for him and stay with him for the entire night. He said he would pay her double if she was willing to wait for him to finish the meeting. She waited and they went to his place together. I made him promise to call me the next day. You see, Nathan was a bit older than your mother and I didn't want her to take advantage of him. Nathan called the next morning and said everything was great. They spent the night talking, and that Syvon would be staying with him for a few days so that she could try to get her life together. Then a couple of months later, they were married."

If it wasn't for the fact that Mr. Mayfield was talking about my mother, the story would have made for a great TV movie.

"But where do I fit in all of this, Mr. Mayfield?" As charming as the story is and as much as it has given me some insight about my mother, I still don't' know her nor do I really care.

"Ms. Peoples, Naturallee, please. Nathan couldn't find your mother at first, but he was able to find you."

"How did he find me? How does or did he know about me?"

"Your mother told him about you and your brothers and sisters that first night they met. Nathan had told her that if she told him about herself, where she was from, something about her family and her past that he would pay her one thousand dollars for every true story she told him. Syvon said she would, but that Nathan had to promise that he would never say a word in any way to those she told him about. They struck a deal and she told him thirteen thousand dollars worth of information. Syvon told him all about you, and how she left you at the church with your grandmother, and the fact that the two of you were probably still waiting for her to come back. Naturallee, you have six older brothers and three older sisters. Plus, you have three younger brothers, there are thirteen of you spread out across the country. I must say Syvon was creative with all of your names, or at least the names I know."

I have some brothers and sisters. I have a family, well sort of; I'm not alone in this world. I feel warm tears build up in my eyes and run down my face and a smile at each corner of my mouth.

While Mr. Mayfield is compassionate, he is also an opportunist. As he consoles me in my time of joy and confusion, he is also reaching for my purse and water bottle. Clearing his throat and standing up, he reminds me that we have someplace else we need to be. I stand up more mechanically than naturally and allow him to lead me to the door. I made a mental note when I came into his office that I wanted to take a final look at the room before I had to leave just to remember the beauty of it. But as I walk through the doorway, and into the waiting room, the beauty of the room is millions of miles from me. All I can think about is family. I have a family, someone to spend the holidays with and someone to talk to when I am home alone and lonely. I can tell someone about my date with Carl, my first date. In a matter of thirty-five minutes my whole life has changed, and I am happier than I have ever been.

It's not until after we had pull out of the parking garage and are on the street for several blocks that I come down out of the clouds, and remember I'm still with Mr. Mayfield, and he's driving me somewhere. The day is already beautiful, but now it has even more qualities that delight my eyes. Finally, we hit a pothole and I snap back to reality.

"Where are we going, again?" I ask.

"If you will trust me for a few more minutes we will be there and I think seeing is better than telling you. It's not much farther,

Chapter Eight

alright?" Mr. Mayfield gives a pleading pity look and returns his attention to the road. Not changing his focus from the road he makes small talk with me for the next several minutes, telling me a few more things about Nathan Grey and my mother. But before he can catch the words, they leave his mouth, he says and I quote, "I do understand now more than I ever have before why Nathan was unable to let your mother go. You are a beautiful woman and you look exactly like her," end quote. I notice the stress he put on the words "are beautiful" as if to say that he would challenge anyone who disagrees with him. Then Mr. Mayfield becomes a little embarrassed, stumbles over a couple of words and then clears his throat. We ride quietly the rest of the way there.

When the car stops we are in front of a beautiful home in one of the ritzier neighborhoods of the suburbs a few miles outside the city. The magnificent house reminds me of the office building we just left. I hope there will be good news inside of those walls, news as good as the news I got when I arrived at Mr. Mayfield's office. Walter Mayfield opens his car door, and comes over to me and opens mine. As he opens the car door, I look into Mr. Mayfield's face. For a man who's probably in his late fifties, he looks good. He also looks healthy. He looks as though he runs the beach every morning, eats right, listens to relaxing music every evening, and retires to bed with a glass of red wine each night. I find his look to be alluring for a moment. I smile up at him as he reaches for my hand to help me out of the car. We walk to the house silently. Before he reaches for the doorknob, he stops and turns to me. With the same bit of embarrassment on his face he had when he let the words out about how beautiful he thinks I am but he tries to stay professional with me. Again, he clears his throat and tries to begin.

"Naturallee, because this could take all night, I need to ask you to cancel your plans right now if there is someplace you need to be. When we walk into this house...your house...if you want it, but when we walk in, you are here for the night.

"I don't believe in ghosts and if Nathan Grey's body is still here I must ask why?" I really don't believe in ghosts, but I'm not staying even for one minute with a dead body. I step back away from the door and start to turn to leave. Mr. Mayfield catches my arm.

"No. It's nothing like that. But the problem is that I can't tell you what you want to know until you decide to go in."

"What if I leave?"

"Then this house and everything Nathan left you, and your siblings from your mother and him will be forfeited, and given to charity."

"What all is there?" I asked

"I can't tell you until you decide to come in and stay."

Mr. Mayfield looks to be in as much pain, as I am curious. This afternoon is turning out to be something straight out of a mystery movie. What is it that is so mysterious behind curtain number three, or in this case, the door, that I have to decide whether to walk away with nothing, or stay and have it all? I'm not sure what to do but for my own safety, I decide to go.

"Mr. Mayfield, I appreciate your trying to honor a dead man's last request but this is too much for me. I can't stay here all night alone in a strange house..." Before I could finish, he put up his hand and cut me off.

"Ms. Peoples, Naturallee, you won't be alone. There will be someone with you."

I think Mr. Mayfield is going to faint right here on the door step.

"I must say that Nathan has kept his word. He said even in his death he would have the last laugh on me, and he was certainly right." Mr. Mayfield says while having to sit in the chair in front of the window. He put his head in his hand and takes a deep breath.

"If I'm not alone, who's staying here with me?" I ask needing to sit in the chair next to Mr. Mayfield.

Looking right into my eyes he says, "I am," with a numb look on his face."

Chapter Eight

"What is really going on here?" I ask standing up and stepping away.

"If there is some way you could find it within yourself to trust me enough to just go inside I swear to you, I'll do my best to make this thing as right as I possibly can. Look," he says as he runs his hand into his pocket and comes out with a key. "This is the key to the first bedroom at the top of the stairs. If you want to run in, and up the stairs, you can lock the door behind you; I'll wait here at this door. The room is stocked with food and drinks for a week. I put a cell phone on the bed, or you can go to the car and get mine. Keep it with you all night. If at any time, you don't feel safe, you can call 911. You know where my office is and you have the address to this house, after I tell you what Nathan wanted, you can leave first thing in the morning if you would like. But first hear me out, please."

Mr. Mayfield is a great lawyer. He at least persuades me to go inside and to the bedroom. I take the key out of his hand. We walk back to the door and he reaches for the knob.

"We must both go inside, you understand and we must both stay tonight, correct." He confirms with me.

"Yes. I understand," is all I can say.

He opens the door and I step into the most beautiful palace I have ever seen. I forget right away about the bedroom and the key as my eyes take in the view. In the middle of the foyer is a mesmerizing fountain with water pouring from a pitcher. The stairs have that *Gone With the Wind* style to them and the woodwork is flawless. The floor has a shine to it that makes me glad I decided to wear jeans. On the wall opposite the door straight across from me is a picture of a woman with what looks like a dozen kids playing at her feet in a beautiful park. There are no faces to any of the children but one, and that child's face is familiar.

"Naturallee, would you like to go up stairs or could we talk now. But remember we are here for the night."

Mr. Mayfield's words bring me back to the here and now. I think about the bedroom but decide that there's something about him that says he can be trusted. I decide I want to hear the rest of the story.

"Please, tell me. I want to know what is really going on."

Mr. Mayfield takes my elbow and ushers me into another magnificent room. In this room, there's a waterfall, and brightly-colored flowers in one corner with what looks like a walkway leading to the outside. I walk over to see where it leads to.

"Naturallee, Nathan loved your mother more than anyone should love another, I thought. He did everything she ever mentioned that she thought she would like. That's why the waterfall, pond, and flowers are here. Syvon saw it in a book one day and mentioned it to Nathan. Three days later, work began on it in their own home. He added the walkway for her so that if it rained, and she still wanted to go for a walk, she could without getting wet.

"Mr. Mayfield, all of this is nice and their story is very romantic, but why am I here?" I just need to know what more all of this will cost me, after all, I'm giving up one night of my life to someone I don't know for someone else I don't know. I'm beginning to think that I'm losing my mind.

"I'm sorry. Let me start at the beginning. You see, Naturallee, Nathan wanted me to have something special all of mine and his life. Once he met your mother he said that he finally knew what he wanted me to have. He wanted me to have a love like his. And so, it would seem Nathan has set this meeting up between the two of us hoping that I could be as happy with you, as he had been with your mother. He was also hoping that you could finally smile a true smile at last."

The look on my face must have said it all. Mr. Mayfield launches off into some additional words, but I'm too overwhelmed with his first words to let anything more in. I remember hearing him say something about me and him being happy together and love and I

Chapter Eight

hear myself say out loud, "stop talking please!" I can't bare anymore information. I'm beginning to feel sick. I have to stay the night and hear more of this crazy talk from a mad man. I said I would stay, but he can't really make me. Then I remember the key in my hand. I clinch it tightly and run for the stairs. Mr. Mayfield doesn't try to stop me.

Once I reach the top of the stairs, I run through the bedroom door and close the door behind me. I see another open door and I hope it's the bathroom. It is, and I run for the toilet. After several minutes in the bathroom, my head stops spinning enough that I'm able to go out and sit on the bed. My thoughts are everywhere, so I don't realize in time that more than my lunch was coming up. I'm already suspended high above the bed and I feel the ropes on my ankles hurting. My left hand is free and I try to reach for something to hold onto. I feel little beads of sweat form on my back and upper lip. My head is hot, and my throat is dry. I can't get myself down. And it feels like the ceiling is fifty feet high. I'm leaving the room and for the first time ever, I know I wouldn't return if I don't get down now. Somehow, I find my voice. I hear my own voice come out from below me. Once I start to scream I can't stop.

Mr. Mayfield rushes into the bed room with the look of fear and dread on his face. I guess he wasn't sure what he would find. "Naturallee, Naturallee, what's wrong? What happened?" He yells looking around the room for some clue as to why all the screaming.

He reaches for my arm and I feel myself on the bed once more. Grateful to be back on something solid again, I reach for Mr. Mayfield. I grab his neck as if he is my husband and has been away at war for several years. I grab him and hold on tight for a few minutes before I realize what I'm doing. Regaining my senses, I let go and slide back on the bed.

"Oh, forgive me. I am sorry. I didn't mean to do that."

"It's alright, you were frightened. But I don't see what frightened you. What happened?"

Suspended

I have never told a soul about the things I go through. I always thought that it was my cross to bear and mine alone. I sit looking at Mr. Mayfield and wondering what to say. I have just moments before run away from this man, afraid of the things he was saying. If I tell him what I have been going through, the feeling of being suspended in midair, high above the floor, never sure if I will recover from each episode, how will he react? How could what he tells me compare to that? I turn to look away. Feeling hot tears on my checks, I find myself crying and not caring that anyone is with me. I can't remember the last time I let someone see me cry. The release feels good and I totally break down. I cry and sob so much I feel an out-of-body experience again, only this time I'm a huddled mass on the floor.

"You can leave. We can void this whole thing. Nathan had no idea what he was asking of you. I knew him, and so I understand what he was trying to do. But you didn't know him, and now, you must think only the worst of him. Please, you can go." Mr. Mayfield says as he points to the open door. But I can't move. I just stay on the floor crying. Mr. Mayfield sits on the bed and looks desperately at me. It takes me the better part of ten minutes to get myself together. When I speak, my voice sounds strange even to me.

"I don't know what to say. I'm not sure what happens. Something always causes me to return to where I am, but this time it felt different. I was afraid that I wouldn't come down. I was afraid that I could be suspended forever." Now he has to think I'm crazy. Maybe now he won't want to stay with me tonight, and tonight I need him. Still crumpled up on the floor like a bag of old clothes, I wait for him to run out screaming.

"Let me help you," Walter offers as he bends down to help me up from the floor. For the first time I notice he's wearing cologne and it has an intoxicating scent. His tie is a powerful red and black and the black suit is expensive. And for the first time, I think of him as Walter and not Mr. Mayfield.

Chapter Eight

He gently speaks, "Perhaps, you should rest. Here, lie down and I will get you something to drink." After he helps me to the bed, he rushes to another room that I hadn't noticed, and is back almost instantly with a bottle of chilled water. "Here, drink a little," he says as he shoves the bottle into my hand as if trying to get it down my throat as quickly as possible. Poor Walter looks like he should have been in a hospital emergency room. This entire day has been more than even he could have imagined.

Watching the color return to Walter Mayfield's face, somehow, makes me feel better. I don't know if he needs to talk more, or if he should get some rest. I suggest that the talking wait until morning and he agrees. We both just sit there, him in the chair and me on the bed, for several very long minutes before I speak up.

"How did you get into this room? I locked the door when I came in.

"The door wasn't completely closed when you put the lock on, so I just pushed it open. Sorry."

I look at the door and notice that my purse is on the floor at the door. I must have dropped it in my haste and it caused the door not to close. With the realization of how he got in the room, I ask Walter if I can see the rest of the house as I am looking for something to say.

"Oh yes, yes, of course. I can give you the one-dollar tour or you can explore on your own," he says, but I notice that he made no attempt to get up and neither did I.

CHAPTER 9

The sunlight on my eyelids causes me to rub my eyes, and for the first few minutes I forget where I am. The bed is like nothing I have ever slept in before, and it is nothing I want to leave in a hurry. I stretch and then remember where I am, and what happened the night before. Quickly, I turn to see if Mr. Mayfield is still in the room. The chair is empty, but I have a strong feeling that he spent most of the night sleeping right there.

I throw off the covers that he must have wrapped me in. I call out for him, but there is no answer so I slide off the bed and focus on the real beauty of the room. I notice things that I hadn't noticed the night before. There is a bouquet of live flowers on the table in front of the window, and another picture with no faces like the one downstairs. The room has a light, open look and feel to it. It makes me want to wake up here every morning, and end each day in here right in front of the sliding glass doors that lead to a spacious balcony overlooking the pond a little bit off in the distance. Moving around the three rooms I've been given, I think about how large and spacious these rooms are compared to my apartment with only one bedroom. Then, I remember I am owed an explanation and I need to find Mr. Mayfield to get it.

After showering and getting myself together, I go to the door and open it up. I find a captivating view of this newly built mansion that I believe I am one of the first to ever spend the night in. The view from the doorway causes me to pause for a minute and take it all in. The carpet under my feet is so plush; I lose the tops of my toes when I step into it. The beige color called *Alluring Beige*, or I think it's called *Alluring Beige*, is tempting to walk on. The walls are a pearl white, and I feel kind of like I am at the beach.

But I force myself to remember that I need to find Walter, so I follow the carpet to the next door which is open a bit. I knock, but there is no answer and I decide that Walter must be downstairs already. But I knock again just to be sure. Walking into this room is nice, but it isn't like the room I spent the night in. My room is larger and more elegant. There is a warmer, more inviting feel to my room. Then I have to smile as I realize that I am already calling it my room, and I am calling Mr. Mayfield, Walter. I think to myself how easily I've slipped into this situation or time or whatever this is. But there is a lot more house to explore while I am looking for Walter, so I go down this lavish hallway to the next room and then to the next and the next until I am at the last door. Not finding Walter in any of the other rooms I've stopped knocking and I just walk right in.

I find Walter on the bed still asleep. He fell asleep fully dressed and reading something that is still in his hand. I don't want to wake him; he seems so peaceful laying here, and after the day we both had, I think I will let him have his rest. I leave the room and go back to the stairway and down to the first floor. This morning, I feel a little like Scarlett O'Hara as I glide down the stairs with a more graceful step than the race I ran getting up them last night. I find the kitchen and make myself some coffee and something to eat. The refrigerator is stocked with plenty of food but I find the fresh fruit and juice more enticing than the eggs and bacon. I chose to eat at the counter looking out into the garden. I don't know if or when I will see such beauty again, so I want to take as much with me in memory as I can. Then I realize that I haven't changed my mind. I still have plans on not staying regardless of what Mr. Mayfield tells me.

Like cold water being thrown on me, I remember tonight and Carl. He was supposed to call me last night to make arrangements for tonight. Panic comes over me and I want to drift up, but before drifting up can happen, Walter is standing before me.

"I'm sorry. Did I startle you? My goodness, it seems that all I do is apologize to you. I have not handled any of this very well, Naturallee. Please, forgive me."

"Oh no, you didn't startle me. As a matter of fact, I am glad you're here. How did you sleep? My rest was the best I have had in years." I can't believe I had just told a perfect stranger something like that. But then I guess after spending the night in the same house a few unlocked bedroom doors away from each other we aren't perfect strangers anymore.

"Well good, then I guess something good came from all of that chaos. And the coffee smells like you know what you are doing in the kitchen, if you don't mind my saying." With the coffee pot in his hand, he motions to refill my cup and I hold it out for the top-off. "Well, shall we get right to it or do you need a little time?" he questions.

Carl comes back to mind and I ask for Walter's cell phone. Reaching it to me, he reminds me that I have a cell phone on the bed upstairs. He smiles a warm comforting smile and leaves the kitchen. He yells back over his shoulder that he will be on the front porch whenever I am ready. I can't believe this is my life at this moment. Two days ago, life was exactly what it had always been for me, uneventful, uncomplicated, and expected. Today, it is anything but that. I struggle to remember the number I saw on the phone the day Carl called.

I dial what I think I remember and what luck, I remembered right. When the man answers it is Carl's voice and I am relieved. "Carl, hi, it's me, Naturallee. How are you?"

"Relieved now that you've called, I was afraid you had forgotten about me and our date tonight." He did sound relieved.

"No. Nothing like that, but something did come up," and I held my breath.

"Do you have to cancel for tonight?"

"Oh no, nothing like that, I just had something happen yesterday that I wasn't expecting, but everything is fine now."

"Are you sure? You don't have to go tonight. I will just go alone after telling everyone I was bringing the most beautiful woman they would ever see with me."

Again there is that word "beautiful," and again, I am surprised it's the second time in as many days, someone has called me beautiful. I never thought of myself that way.

Then I hear Carl laugh and say "I'm just joking I didn't tell everyone that. I'm sure they will be able to see for themselves when we get there. That is if we are still on."

"Yes, we are. What time should I expect you?" I was glad for the stability of the plans continuing.

"I thought I would pick you up around eight if that's all right with you?"

"Eight would be fine. I will see you then."

"Not so fast. Where do you live?"

"That's right that was one of the reasons for last night's call." I give Carl my address and we hang the phones up. I feel that bit of happiness again. The happiness I felt the first time he called. I smile again at the thought of the evening and my first date. But I still have the situation at hand to deal with, so I go to find Walter.

CHAPTER 10

School break can't come fast enough this semester and Professor Peoples can't get away from the school fast enough to satisfy his need for freedom. At forty-two years old, he has only had one serious relationship until now and he finds himself off his game often and he is afraid that his students have noticed the change in him.

Seven weeks ago, he did something totally out of character for himself; Honestly Sweet Peoples had dinner at Macy's on the River on a Thursday night instead of eating at home on Thursday and eating out for dinner on Friday. Twice a week, Honestly Sweet allowed himself to splurge and spring for a cheap dinner out one night and a movie and dinner the other night. The most exciting thing Honestly does is to surprise himself and not choose, until Tuesday, if he will go to a movie and dinner then or if he will go to the movie and dinner on Friday.

But the week he went to dinner on Thursday instead of Friday is the week life changed for him. Eating at a new restaurant on the

other side of town on a different night of the week is living danger-
ously for Professor Peoples, but he has become so bored with his life
away from work that he now wants some excitement. That night, he
gets what he is looking for plus a whole lot more. While enjoying
his medium-well done steak and baked potato with sour cream, no
butter, and sea salt, Honestly Sweet catches a glimpse of a woman
he has seen only twice before. The first time, he saw her was on the
third anniversary of his divorce. She was leaving the dry cleaners
and he was going in. The second and last time he saw her was about
three months ago when, on a Tuesday morning, while on his way
to work she pulled up right behind him in her SUV at the red light.
Honestly couldn't take his eyes out of the rear view mirror; she had
to blow her horn at him and brought him back inside of his own car.
He felt foolish for looking at her so long and for getting caught staring at her. Honestly Sweet Peoples had never been so mesmerized
by anyone. For weeks after that last time he saw her, he couldn't
sleep, he couldn't eat, and at work he couldn't concentrate. He made
a mistake with three different students' grades. And one Friday, he
had forgotten that it was Friday and that he was supposed to drive
to work so that he could go to dinner right after work before he went
home. Because Honestly believed in being on schedule, he wouldn't
allow himself to leave the house once he got home telling himself
that he would be off schedule too badly for the rest of the day.

Honestly Sweet also knew he was out of sorts because he wanted
to speak to this woman as they passed through the door at the dry
cleaner, but for whatever reason, he couldn't. Honestly had always
been afraid of women for as long as he could remember, even when
he met his ex-wife Gail. A friend of his named Jake Early, a college buddy, introduced him to Gail. Jake and his girlfriend Brittney
were kind enough to double date with Honestly and Gail for the first
several dates so that Honestly could get comfortable with her. Honestly had not dated much before meeting Gail and after just nine
months, he asked Gail to marry him. The wedding took place six

Chapter Ten

months later and they stayed together for almost twelve years. Then one day Gail left her job early; rented a truck and a couple of men and had all of her things moved into the apartment she had rented three days before. When Honestly got home and went in to shower he found the note she had left him pinned to the shower curtain. Unable to digest the information; he continued with his routine of showering and reading the paper before he allowed himself to read the note again and let the words register in his head. That next morning Honestly waited an extra fifteen minutes before he left for work hoping his wife of twelve years would return. But she didn't, at least not in the allotted time and he really couldn't be late for work so Honestly left the house for the first time ever without a kiss on the cheek from his loving wife Gail Ann Peoples.

But after" running into this woman at the dry cleaners for the second time, he finally spoke to her. Honestly Sweet Peoples has his mind on a new life with hopes of starting a new relationship with this woman he simply can't get out of his mind. Tonight, at dinner he wants her to know how he feels about her. Beverly Young needs to know so that she can make up her mind as to whether she wants to run for the hills and get as far away from him as fast as possible or if she wants to stay around and see where things go from here. After all, he's not getting any younger, besides that, the days of being so shy to the point of being afraid of a woman need to end. This is how Honestly has spent all of his lonely adult life. These last seven weeks of dinners and movies and bowling and parties and laughter with Beverly have been something that he wants to continue. But he needs to know if there is the possibility of a bright future with her because if there isn't, Honestly has told himself that he will cut his losses and move on. Tonight, at Macy's Restaurant he will definitely tell her; this he promised himself. As he reaches for his office door knob and pats his pockets for his keys, Honestly remembers again that he forgot to drive to work. Slapping his forehead with the palm of his hand he also remembered, that is why he is leaving the school early today. *Even though he would now have to go all the way home to get his car before he can see Beverly,* he thought, even the extra time spent going home is worth it. "That's what you do for someone you love," he heard the words around him, and walking to the elevator he smiled. Yes. Honestly Sweet Peoples actually said it out loud to himself and to anyone around who was lucky enough to hear him say it. Nodding to those getting off the elevator, he politely put his hand up to hold the elevator doors open to let everyone off. Honestly gave each one a closed lip smile with the nod and got on the elevator when the last lady stepped out. With the thought of Beverly still on his mind, Honestly whistled all the way to his first lecture class.

CHAPTER 11

This morning has the promise of goodness for the day, and I think and hope that the things Mr. Mayfield has to tell me will be positive for me and for him. I find Mr. Mayfield sitting on the porch as he said he would be and I think he probably is a man of his word.

"Well, are you ready? Can we get into it? Will you tell me what is going on now?" I ask, standing before Walter. Walter stands up and offers me the chair. I'm afraid that what he is about to say is more than I can stand hearing on this beautiful morning, and I consider going back into the house. I must look that way too, because Walter asks me if I am feeling alright. We both need a moment to gather ourselves. Then with a deep sigh, his words begin to flow as he starts to release words that have been locked up inside of him for some time.

He is telling me something about Nathan Grey's way of thinking. "Nathan," he says, "Was sure I wasn't happy. He had been happiest when he was married to your mother. It may have only lasted a few years, but it kept him happy the balance of his days." Then I hear Walter say the words, "hoping we will marry," which unsettles me again.

"What did you say," I ask while standing up. "Who's getting married?" I step away from Walter Mayfield.

"Yes. That's what I said. Nathan was like a brother to me. He wanted me to be happy and he felt like I wasn't happy all the years I was married. When Nathan believed in something, he stopped at nothing to prove that he was right. While I knew he wanted me to marry again after my wife died fifteen years ago, he didn't let on that he wanted me to marry the woman of his choice. Nathan was a pretty easy man to read. He always wanted a person to know where he stood in most matters. But he did have his secrets and this is the first of several."

"What do you mean the first of several?" This beautiful morning is taking a terrible turn for the worse. They were more like brothers than Walter Mayfield knew; they were both crazy. Evidently, money caused them both to go insane. I have a date tonight with a man I'd like to get to know, and it *ain't* with Walter Mayfield. "I am going to leave now. Please don't call me again." I rush to the door, run through it, and then up the stairs. I dash into my bedroom from last night and stand motionless in the middle of the room. This has to be a bad joke someone's playing on me and the only way to get out of it is to leave the house. But I remember that Walter had driven us both up here. How am I supposed to get back to town? I can't face Walter at this moment, I need to think. I sit down on the chair next to the window and wonder what in the world I was thinking in the first place staying in this house all night long with a man I don't know. I move to the bed and lay down. Again, the bed is inviting almost intoxicating and before I know it, the fear and anger I feel, is drifting away.

◆

Chapter Eleven

I need to hear the rest of what I could be involved in before I definitely turn away from another night in this fabulous bed. I decide to try to talk with Walter one last time. Maybe the problem is that he's just a bad storyteller; he doesn't seem to be able to talk without sweating. How much worse can this Nathan Grey have been? What more could he possibly want? I get off the bed that I want to take home with me and go to find Walter once more.

I find him swinging in the yard swing in back of the house; he seems at peace with the whole thing. And I think, *why shouldn't he be at peace with everything, he would be getting an estate-ordered bride if I go along with this crazy plan.* To clear my head before I speak, I stand at the door and watch him swinging for a few minutes. I notice how strong Walter's arms are. He must workout, diligently or maybe he has a part-time job lifting furniture. Whichever, his arms look great for a man in his fifties or at least I think he could be in his fifties, and just for a second as I leave the doorway to talk with him, I even think about how great his legs might look.

"Excuse me, Walter. Let me start by apologizing this time. I shouldn't have run away like that. I'm afraid that your words frightened me. But when someone talks about marriage..." before I can finish speaking though, Walter puts his hand up to stop me from talking. He doesn't turn around to look at me, he just hands me some papers and tells me I should read the papers sitting on the swing. He thinks if I read it myself, in Nathan's own handwriting, I might understand things better. Plus he says the morning is slipping away, and before it gets too hot, I should enjoy the cool serenity of the yard. When he stands up to leave, he still doesn't look at me, but he does have a slight smile on his face. He is right, the morning is slipping away and I am missing it. I sit down and look at the first words on the page that's drafted in letter form.

"My dear friend Walter," it starts out. I know I should have let you or Naturallee Joy know what I was planning, but both of you would have had too long to think about it and could have decided not to try this. Walter, as you know, we have been best friends for all but three years of our lives. From the mechanic shop where our fathers worked, to the bar they went to after work and dragged us along. My being a businessman and you being an attorney has helped to keep us together. But I think in some ways, I had the upper hand on you, because of our professions. You have always had to work inside the law and live by the spirit of the law, but I've only had to work inside the legal system and I have learned that surprise is sometimes the best option. So here is what I am asking of you both. And here is what you will each receive. Naturallee, I have written things this way so that it will hopefully be very clear to you. Walter understands all the legal stuff, but I need you to want to do this for whatever reasons you choose.

First Naturallee, you both must live in this house for one full year, starting a week from the day you read this proposal. You must move in completely (although, you may keep your apartment. I have set up an account that will pay your rent for the next year if you should decide to do this).

Second, you and Walter must get to know each other. So you two must have dinner and spend the evening together once a week to help get to know each other better. Dinner and a movie or just watching television and talking are good. Or a walk along your mother's pathway could be enjoyable if you two wish. But you must start your evening by six o'clock.

Thirdly, you must honestly try to get to know each other. I believed that Syvon did try to get to know me, and I believe that is why she loved me. I also believe that you are like your mother in many ways Naturallee, in that you have a lot of love to give. And that your love is honest to you and to whomever you share it with. I also believe that you are like your mother in that you have a fear of loving. You don't want to ever be hurt like you were when you realized that your mother wasn't coming back for you. I know that living with your grandmother, then your aunt, next with your uncle, and then with your mother's cousin and finally with the Lincolns couldn't have been what you would have planned for your life, but it is what you have had. And if it had not been for your mother leaving you, things would have been very different. Life on your own at sixteen wasn't easy so to trust now is even harder.

I know Walter has a lot of work ahead of him, but you are both important to me for different reasons, and I hope you will give this a chance. If you will live here with Walter for the next year, Naturallee, I will have Walter release the title to this house, the car and thirty seven million dollars to you. This is for you and you alone. There is also one million dollars for each of your siblings. (If you can find them they, too, will get the million dollars). To be fair, I will also tell you what is in it for Walter. He gets a thirty seven million dollar donation in his name to colon cancer research. He also gets a hefty fee for managing my estate. The balance of my estate will be divided among the many different charities that have a special meaning to me as well as the orphanage in Jamaica. Several million will be given to the new psychiatric wing at the hospital in mine and Syvon's name.

There are a few other things that go along with this offer that are spelled out more in the actual estate papers for which Walter will explain, but you have the jest of it. Oh yes, and this is big, you need to know that the reason I am doing this is because I believe in love and happiness. Not just any love but true love and real happiness. By now you must know that Syvon brought me great and lasting happiness. We were only together for four years and four days, but each moment was worth the heartache I felt when she left. Syvon never lied to me or tried to be someone she wasn't. I knew I could trust her and she knew she could trust me. When I looked in her eyes, I saw myself better than I was the day before. She let me be myself. If I had lost all that I had, she would have loved me all the more. When she left, I searched for her for five months before I found her in a hospital in Maine under an assumed name. She left because she found out that she had a rare cancer that took her over quickly. Since she had never taken good care of herself, her system was unable to help fight the disease. She died six weeks after I found her. I was able to spend those last six weeks with her. She gave me information on you because she felt she was an even worse mother to you and your older brother than she was to the others kids. She hoped you would not hate her once you knew what she had suffered from when she was younger. She wanted you to have something special from her since you are the one that she tried to keep.

But she kept you for all the wrong reasons. You were worth money, drugs, and revenge to her, but as you may remember she was never very loving or kind to you. This is a big part of why I have decided to do this for you. Naturallee, your mother and I believe Walter will be able to give that missed love to you. You two just don't know it yet.

So in a way, both your mother and I want you to give this a try. Please take the time to think..."

I can't read anymore, I can't believe my mother even thought about me anymore after she left me at the church with my grandmother. When I was with her, she used to tell me how much she didn't like having me around. She disliked me so much so that she wouldn't even ask me to get her a drink of water. Syvon said that if my father hadn't come to the hospital to see her, her boyfriend would not have gotten angry and killed him. Which means her boyfriend would not have had to go to prison for life for killing him plus twenty- five years for other crimes he had committed.

The letter made me remember how she really felt about me. I never told my grandmother or anyone else how she really felt. And that let me know Nathan Grey knew her well. I close my eyes and cry.

After a few moments, I stop the tears from falling and I go into the house to talk with Walter. He is waiting in front of the television in the kitchen. He looks up from the game with a blank look on his face.

Chapter Eleven

"Did the letter help?" he asked.

"Yes." I answer in a weak voice.

"Did you decide what you want to do?

"Yes, I believe I have. But I need to know what you want to do Mr. Mayfield." I look at him to see what his reaction to my words will mean.

"I would like to have the thirty seven million for cancer research, but I can continue to give my annual pledge. I want to do whatever you are willing to do. I can take you back to town and give you a check for one hundred thousand dollars and never call or bother you again. It is completely up to you. But I will tell you that Nathan only asked that we live in the same house together for a year. We can still have our lives as they are for the most part. It's just once a week we have to spend any real time together. You seem to be a pleasant enough lady to spend an evening talking with or watching television with."

"I agree. We can do this if it is alright with you." The words came out of my mouth easier than I thought they would. "What do we do now?" I am ready to get this thing started. The sooner we start, the sooner the year will be over.

"I need to go and get some thing's settled at my house and with my family."

"Walter, I noticed that you are wearing a wedding ring, what's that about," I feel I have to ask I don't want to assume something and my assumptions be wrong.

"I was married about fifteen years ago and I guess I just never took it off after my wife died. It's, I think one of the reasons Nathan did this thing between us. And while it's not as much for you as it is for me, I do hope you will see some benefit in it for yourself," Walter states as if the only reason we are doing this is that it is a business arrangement.

"Anyway, I need to let them know where I will be for the next year, get some things from my house to bring out here and that's it. How about you? Can I help you get things together? You can go home tonight, then you can call me in a day or two and I will pick you up or send a car for you," Walter tells me. As he goes back to the game on the television, he wants to know what made me decide to do it. I tell him my mother wanted me to give it a try. I thought he might be a little surprised by my words but there is no change in Walter's demeanor. Then I tell him that I have no one to inform where I will be staying and there isn't that much to get so I could be moved in by tomorrow evening.

Later on, Walter drops me back at my apartment and I have a few hours to relax and to get myself together for the party tonight. I know what I'm wearing and I know how I want my hair to look, but I'm not sure if I want to try makeup. I don't think it will be too smart to put it on without wearing it for several hours before I go just to make sure I want to look that way. I decide that it won't be a good idea, so I don't have too much left to decide on.

I sit on my bed in my tiny apartment all by myself and think about how different it will be for me next week this time, and then I had a chill run through me. I will be living in that big, beautiful house, sleeping in a fabulously relaxing bed and there will be someone there in the house to talk with who will talk back to me. I'll have a person to respond to my questions instead of just licking my face like Kane did. Just thinking about the future made me happy and sick all at the same time. It also made me late for getting ready for my date with Carl.

CHAPTER 12

What will this new-old city bring to Reverend David (Baby Boy) Harris? It has been twenty years since he was last here. Although he knows he was born here and that somewhere in this city there is family, biological family that might remember him, Rev. Harris is hoping that none of them will. At thirty five years old, and married now for fifteen years, Reverend Harris has always felt sure of himself and of what God has planned for his life. It's not until he stops the car and turns off the engine that he realizes that he is questioning God's decision for his life for the first time. Why has God chosen to bring him back to this city and why has God chosen to have him accept the head pastor's position at a church too big for him to pastor. With five hundred active members and another three hundred names on the church roster, Reverend David B. Harris is feeling overwhelmed with things already.

It is hard for Grace Harris to leave her home of thirty three years and follow her husband, but she knows that it is put on him by God and she isn't about to get in the way of her husband's calling. Tall, with a full figure Grace knows she could have had the love of any man in Scottsdale, but not just any man would do for her. Grace has standards that she is not willing to compromise not even for a man of God. She is only interested in a man who will be his own man who is led by God. Yes, he needs to be a man of God, not necessarily a preacher, but someone who knows and loves God is number one on her list of qualifications. Grace believes that if the man loves God then she has a better than average chance that he would love her and treat her right. Her beauty and sex appeal are both gifts from God and something she has heard said about her for all of her life or at least as long as she could remember. Being watched, stared at and desired wherever she went is something she has become use to. Regardless of what Grace wears, the eyes of most men are on her, even women have a tendency to take note of her whenever she's around.

Reverend Harris has always felt blessed by God to be the man who won this woman's heart. He is well aware that his wife, while loved and desired by many, loves him.

CHAPTER
13

The doorbell rings and I jump. I start to wonder if I am doing the right thing. But the fact that my mother thought I could be happy if I give the arrangement a try is something I can't get out of my mind. My mother actually thought about me. She remembered me. She regretted the way she treated me, that had to be it. That's why she left those words for me. It makes me so happy, and I guess that's what really stays on my mind and encouraged me to do it. Keeping her and my past, off my mind, is the only way I could get through life, and now, here it is and I was inviting it into my thoughts.

I open the door and see a man I hardly recognize. Carl looks great and a lot taller than I remember. He actually has very nice eyes, a wide smile, and the brightest teeth I have ever seen. A clean mouth and a bright white smile have always been important to me for some strange reason. When he speaks, he sounds like a well-polished person and I think for a moment I'd better ask for identification.

Suspended

"Hello, Naturallee, it's been a while since we've seen each other and I must say that you look great. What have you been doing with yourself?"

"I haven't been doing anything too much, just trying to keep busy." I wasn't sure how to answer the question or if the question was supposed to be answered. I hate rhetorical questions. I also don't remember Carl looking this good.

The question also made my mood change a little. I start to regret accepting the invitation for the evening already. I decide that it is too late to back out or cry headache so I suggest we get started on our way. Carl is gracious enough to pick up on the hint and a few minutes later we are on the street going to his car. It feels a little strange being outside on my street after dark with someone, not that there was ever any problem in the neighborhood. Thinking about it, I realize that I don't usually have a reason to be out after dark. I feel like a grown up for the first time and smile.

The drive to the restaurant is chattier than I thought Carl and I would be for a first date. He told me about his family, his best friend and his college days before he dropped out the first time. He tells me about the surgery he had at age thirteen after he and some friends broke a neighbor's window on purpose and tried to run away. The friends got away but Carl caught his left hip on the fence as he was going over it and ended up needing sixty three stitches. He had to sleep on his stomach for several weeks until he healed. To make matters worse, Carl had to pay for the window and apologize to the neighbor for breaking it. It's something Carl has not gotten over completely; I can tell by the way he ended the story. Thank goodness we are at the restaurant.

Inside the restaurant, things are quite lively, the people are fun, and the cuisine is even better than what Carl said it would be. I can't believe I am having such a great time even though I don't spend much time with Carl. He is with his brother and the rest of the guys, so I'm on my own some of the time and at other times I talk with

Chapter Thirteen

his sisters and his mother Bethany Morgan. Beth as she prefers to be called could be Carl's older sister instead of his mother. I think her long, silky black hair adds even deeper color to her luscious, large, soft eyes. This entire family it seems is tall; Beth must be six foot three in those heels. Her body is so tight it makes my body look under appreciated and... I workout. Beth is the reason why Carl is so chatty; she too carries a conversation on only a few words on my part. I don't know if she even heard me answer her. I would walk away but she is an interesting woman but all of a sudden she states that she has monopolized all of my time and walks me over to her mother, Carl's grandmother.

I find his grandmother to be a fascinating lady to talk with as well. She was a single parent who raised her children to be good citizens after Carl's grandfather died. She finally remarried seven years ago to a man she had known for the past twenty-three years. Grandmother Gerri, or Gigi as she likes to be called, works out and it shows. I can see where Beth gets both her height and personality from. Gigi's tall and slender and everything about her is tight as well. Her arms had none of that jiggley fat hanging, her stomach is firm and flat and she's wearing three inch heels under a clinging black dress that accents her short, glossy red hair. I decide tonight at the party I am going to start taking better care of myself. I want to be Beth when I get older and Gigi when I grow up.

Finally, Carl and I find ourselves alone at a table and at first it feels a little weird. I came to the party with him, but after meeting so many interesting people, I forgot all about Carl and the fact that he brought me here. I think he forgot for a while that he was the one who had brought me here, too. We must have realized it at the same time and laugh.

"Are you having a good time, Naturallee?" Carl asks as he pats my hand and strangely enough the gesture makes me feel good.

"Yes...I am. I am so glad you asked me to come," and I mean that. After his irritating, rhetorical question back at my house, he's made up for it with this fun evening. "You know," I say, smiling back at Carl, "I could do this about once a week. It's better therapy than any doctor's couch." We spend the rest of the evening talking and laughing together and apart. His brother, Michael, for whom the party is for, leaves an hour before Carl and I do but we are having such a good time that I wasn't anxious to leave.

Finally, Carl returns me to my apartment just after midnight. The street is quiet and almost lonely, but I can't feel too bad for the night, after all, I'm just retuning from the best night I have ever had. But thinking about it makes me feel a little sad for myself. After all, here I am a grown woman and the best night of my life was spent at the birthday party for the brother of a college classmate I barely know. Nevertheless, I have enjoyed myself and I decide that is all that matters. I feel Carl squeeze my hand and I hear him ask me where am I with my thoughts and I come back to the moment. When I realize where I am, we were at my door. He says he will say good night here at the door because he is a little tired and wants to get to bed. If he sits down, he says, he will probably not get back up until morning. Carl also thanks me for being his date and he tells me that the guys all thought I was "hot." He says he already knows that but what he didn't know was that I can be so much fun. He also wants to know if we can try going out again, just the two of us. I give him a good night kiss on his cheek, and say, "yes," and then I slip inside my door.

I'm sure I'm living a dream. This time I am on the ceiling, but it feels different, and I am happy to be up here. I understand the old adage of "being on cloud nine."

In my own bed I sleep through the entire night, for the first time, since I can remember, and when I awake I'm still smiling. By late afternoon, I have come back to the place of reality that I'm not sure I want to be at. My mind is back on my mother, Nathan Grey, and Walter Mayfield. How am I going to explain all of this to Carl? Before last night, it didn't matter, I think that I thought it would

Chapter Thirteen

be one date and we would not see each other again unless it was at school. But I am both sad and glad about being wrong. Walter is expecting to pick me up at seven and I want Carl to call. I think about calling him, but after I say hello, and thank him again for asking me to go with him, what would I say. I don't want to seem desperate but at this very minute, I am. But the ring of the phone again brings me back to the moment.

"Hello," my heart races as I say the word. Waiting for the response to know who it is takes forever. But finally, Walter Mayfield's voice breaks the silence and I hear, "hello," and my heart drops a little. I still want to do what my mother wants, but I also want what I want now, and I wonder if I could have them both.

"Hi, Mr. Mayfield," is all I can say. I hope he can't tell the disappointment in my voice.

"Sorry, I guess you want someone else to be on this end of the line. But I want to find out if I can pick you up a little earlier. I need to go by my office and do a few things for a client that I didn't get to yesterday. Would leaving early be a problem for you?" I am waiting for another unrealistic request from Walter but he stopped talking. I want to yell at him. I want to tell him his friend Nathan Grey was completely right about him. I want Walter to know that he knew nothing about love. I have just had the best night of my life and I would wait for the next year if I had to, right there in my tiny apartment for the phone to ring and for it to be Carl on the other end of it.

"Naturallee, are you there? Hello. If this doesn't work for you, I can come back for you later," and again there is quiet on the line. "Naturallee, are you there?"

"I'm sorry, Mr. Mayfield how early are you wanting to leave?" I hope he will say six-thirty, but that's not what I hear.

"Well, I'm hoping for now. I can be there in about half an hour, if you can be ready about then."

"No, that will not work for me, but I could be ready in an hour."

"That will have to work for me. Also, will you mind stopping at the office with me. I will be a couple of hours there, but the mall is just a few blocks up and there are movie theaters there as well. And I have your charge card that Nathan had opened up for you at the time you accepted his arrangement. It has a ten thousand dollar a month limit to it. And tomorrow your car will be delivered to you around nine in the morning.

"Are you kidding!" Is all I can say. I think about Carl again and then about what I've just been told. Another old saying comes to mind, "money can't buy you love," is true. It caught my attention for a minute, but I still want to hear from Carl.

"No. There are many things that I have yet to tell you. Tonight, I have the pleasure of telling you a couple more. I'll see you in a hour." Then the phone goes dead.

I must be dreaming or having a nightmare and I just can't wake up from either of them. Carl is definitely the dream. Walter May-field and Nathan Grey are for sure the nightmare. I remember hearing my grandmother saying many times that the Bible says with blessings come curses. I want to thank her for letting me know this in advance. I look at the telephone one last time; then, I go to my bedroom and start to pack. I decide to pack for a few days instead of packing for a week or more. If I have a credit card with a ten thousand dollar monthly availability, I can get what I need at the mall. I've never had the opportunity to just go to the mall and spend as much as I want to. This is the best weekend I have ever had. Last night, a fun evening with Carl and tonight I get to shop until I'm tired. And, oh, I almost forgot, tomorrow morning I get a new car. I smiled and wonder what Tuesday will bring.

CHAPTER 14

The mall looks different tonight. The stores seemed busier, the restaurants bigger, the people friendlier, and I know I'm happier. Tonight, I can spend money until I get tired and dinner is the first thing on the list. I have always wanted to eat at Macy's on the River or even Morris Lang's Restaurant. Both are expensive and very elegant places to spend time and money. Of course, I won't eat at either tonight but I will soon and perhaps with Carl, but not tonight, I'm not dressed for it. As I walk by the entrance of Morris Lang's, I can smell the cuisine and it makes me smile at the thought that I could actually eat there one of these days soon. Instead, this time I will eat in the food court, shop in any store, and maybe take in a movie. Tonight Mr. Mayfield can work until the mall closes!

Walter gave me my cell phone that I had forgotten at the house, so we could keep in touch. Right away I understand why. After only thirty- five minutes, the phone rings and Mr. Mayfield says that something has happened and he will be about an hour longer than he originally thought. But if I don't want to wait for him I can come back to the office and take his car back to the house and he will take a taxi out to the house when he's finished. The thought of being out there all alone doesn't set well with me, so I tell him I would rather wait and then I asked him to try not to be too long and I also told him why.

I'm not used to spending without looking at the price and so shopping is what it had always been, light and somewhat disappointing. When Mr. Mayfield finally picks me up, the mall is about to close. He apologizes profusely, but I'm not interested. My mind has returned to Carl and I now hope he hasn't called. Mr. Mayfield has a lot on his mind because he doesn't say a word all the way out to the house and it's all right with me. I have my own thoughts to keep me company. Then without warning, I feel myself leaving the car. I can't feel the floor of the car and my head feels like it is being pressed against the top of the car. I feel sweaty all over my body and my teeth are clinched so tight I think I could crush them into tiny, ivory dust particles. I need to get out of the car before I explode. I can't speak or cry for help. Walter continues to drive as though nothing is happening in the car. And for the first time in days, I remember that this thing happens to me all too often and it is happening to me now.

Passing under a street light in a split-second, I see the floor-mat under my feet expand and then it disappears. I feel the blood leave my face and my head is light. I turn to look at Walter but through my hazy eyes, I'm not sure that he's still in the car. I try to scream and I reach out for him hoping that he is still in the car with me. Then I hear something that sounds like a voice down a deep well.

"Naturallee, Naturallee, what's wrong? What's going on? Oh my God, what's happening? Naturallee answer me. Talk to me."

I hear a distant, hollow voice and feel a light touch of a hand on my arm. But I am so far away now, I'm not sure I can get back. I keep going up and before I can scream, my head hits the top of the

Chapter Fourteen

car. Hitting the car seat again, I snap my head back on the head-rest.

"Naturallee, what is going on? What just happened? Are you all right?" I hear true panic in Walter's voice. I sit paralyzed while my eyes begin to adjust to the darkness in the car and I catch a glimpse of Walter's face. I know that someone has finally seen me and that I'm not crazy. This thing really does happen to me. I'm still rubbing my head and trying to get my voice, but Walter isn't waiting, he needs answers right away.

"Naturallee Joy, what is going on with you?" The stress in his voice makes me try to answer him.

"I'm alright. I don't know why it happens," is all I can manage to get the out of my mouth which feels like it is full of cotton.

"What did happen?" Walter still has to have answers but I just don't really have any answers to give him. I just sit paralyzed. Walter has stopped the car and is sitting there with his foot on the brake. "You need to talk to me, Naturallee Joy, please.

"It happens, but I don't know why it happens."

"This has happened *before*?" Walter asks in a genuinely surprised voice.

"Yes."

"How often does this...this...thing happen? What causes it? How long has this been going on?" There's still fear in Walter's voice.

I have no answers for him. All I can do is sit there with a number of emotions running through me. My hands are wet with sweat and I feel a hard lump in my throat. I have always wanted someone else to see me suspended above them. I want to know if they can see the ropes that stretch my arms and legs. I want someone to tell me what it all looks like, what I look like when I am suspended. But now all I want is to leave the car as fast as I can and run back to my tiny apartment. I feel sick and ashamed for drifting away. But I'm also glad that it's out in the open and Walter knows.

"Naturallee, you're scaring me."

"I'm all right, just give me a minute," I need to get myself together. After another few minutes, I find both my words and my
courage to speak. "Yes, this has happened before. As a matter of fact,
it happens a lot sometimes. I don't know why it happens. When I
was younger, I thought it happened to everyone until I noticed that
I was the only one above the room reaching for someone or something to hold onto." Then I wait for him to say something. The car is
quiet for what feels like hours before Walter says the next words.

"You need to get some help. We will call someone in the morning." Still looking at me, he lets his foot up off the brake pedal and
allows the car to roll a few feet before giving the road his full attention. We don't talk anymore that night. When we enter the house,
we go straight to our rooms like bad children sent to bed without
any supper. As I shower, I wonder what Walter thinks he can do in
the morning. I get into bed quietly and immediately the memory of
what had happened starts to fade as the bed begins to take me in
and comfort me. I snuggle the covers around me and close my eyes.
For a hot, July day this night has suddenly turned cold.

CHAPTER 15

For the next couple of days, there is no talk about the situation in the car. Walter and I are now having dinner together twice a week instead of just once a week like Nathan required. I find it's easy to talk with Walter. He's always interested in my life. Even though he knows a lot about me, it is obvious that there is still a lot about me he doesn't know. For instance, Walter doesn't know that I've never been kissed by a male over the age of six. I found out some interesting things about Walter though. Walter told me about his wife and his life with her, but he also told me something that he had never told another living soul, including Nathan. Walter had stopped loving Elaine years before their break-up. He said he didn't want to take her back after the break up but he did, and he had gotten a vasectomy while they were apart. He said he couldn't take a chance on having any children with her. Little did he know that they would never even kiss each other again.

Suspended

Everyday, Walter tells me more about my mother and Nathan Grey. Well, actually more about Nathan Grey than my mother, but I don't mind because ever so often he does tell me something about Syvon Peoples Grey. She, Walter said, must have loved Nathan because Syvon kept his name until the day she died. Syvon also told the nurses at the hospital that she left Nathan because she didn't want him to spend his life dying with her. She told them that Nathan was a giving, loving man who she didn't deserve, but was very grateful she had the opportunity to know and love him. When Nathan found her, and went to her, he stayed with her until she died, never leaving the hospital. In that time, he and Syvon spent their last weeks together putting together a series of letters for me and my brothers and sisters. Nathan believed she could find the peace she needed to have before she died by leaving the information for each of us. In this way, we could learn about her and each brother and sister that is a part of this family, if it can be called that. We could learn why she did what she did and how she regretted it.

Walter seems a little sad while he tells the things about Syvon and his best friend, Nathan Grey. Today is a day that he really misses Nathan, I can tell. Walter spends the day at the house; he doesn't go to the office, and except for when he is telling me about Nathan and Syvon, he has nothing to say. He just sits in the chair gazing out the window or at his hands folded in his lap.

◆

By evening, I'm ready to see Carl. I want to go back to my apartment and wait for the phone to ring, that is, if it hasn't already. I haven't been home in four days and if Carl has called, he could be feeling like I'm not interested anymore. I think about it and I decide that I will tell Walter I have to go. I could drive back to the apartment and wait there for a while to see if Carl will call again. I go to the doorway to speak with Walter but he's not in the chair. I walk

Chapter Fifteen

through the house looking for him. The house is nice and too large for just the two of us, especially when we don't know where the other one is. I spend the better part of ten minutes peeking in rooms I don't know are even in the house. The house has a set of rooms for a maid to live in and there is a lower floor (it's just too nice to call a basement) that seems to be large enough to live comfortably in, as well. I wonder if Walter realizes all of this is here. In the lower part of the house there are some beautiful paintings in the corner that are hidden behind plastic. They, too, have people in them that have no faces. The artist who drew them must have been a close friend of Nathan Greys' for him to purchase so many of the same type of paintings. Looking through the paintings, I find one that causes me to pause for a minute. It reminds me of a past time in my life, but I can't fully recall when. It's like déjà vu—when you feel like you have lived it before. The picture holds me longer than I intend to look. I'm supposed to be looking for Walter, but instead, I am so captivated by this painting that I don't hear the familiar voice that comes up behind me.

"I was beginning to think you didn't mean what you said the other night." The voice was the one I expected to hear on the phone. How did Carl get here? At the moment I really don't care how he got here all that matters is that he is here. I am so excited I can feel the smile on my face widen and I want to jump into his arms, but I stand stuck in the floor in front of him.

"Well, are you going to say something or would you prefer I leave?" Carl starts to turn to the door.

"No," I almost yell the word and before the one single word is out of my mouth I'm standing so close to Carl that I am able to feel his breath. "No. Please. Stay. I'm glad you're here. Please...stay." I plead with him. I need him to stay, and the need surprises me. I'm so glad to see him until I don't even ask how he found me. Carl gives me a hug and a smile as if he missed me too, and the frozen statue I was just seconds ago starts to melt into the thick carpet due to this man's touch.

Suspended

"I'm glad to see you," is all I can get out of my still surprised and fumbling lips. Then something bad starts to happen. I am leaving the floor. I can't catch myself. I'm already looking at the top of Carl's head. I need him to catch me...and he does. Suddenly, he touches my elbow and slides his hand down my arm to my hand and holds it.

"Don't look so frightened, I'm not leaving. I was just kidding. I didn't drive all the way out here for a three minute visit. I want to spend a little time with you...if that's alright." Carl could have stayed forever and right now I almost need him to, or at least I want him to.

"How did you find me out here?" I realize I haven't asked him yet.

"I called the phone number you called me from last week and Walter answered. I thought I had the wrong number, but he said it was your phone and you were out but was intending to call me when you returned. He thought it would be a nice surprise for you if I just came out, so here I am. I hope he was right," Carl says in an asking way.

After spending the last four days longing for this man to call, and then having the nerve to go looking for Walter to let him know I was going to go back to my apartment to sit and wait for the phone to ring, I wasn't about to let Carl leave. I finally get it together and I ask Carl to join me in the yard. I notice Walter heading back up the stairs. Walter notices me and gives me a nod and a smile as he raises his glass of wine and continues on his way.

Once Carl and I settle in the yard, I take a few minutes to think about what Walter did for me and why he did it. Certainly Walter knows why we are in this house together. He knows that Nathan Grey hoped that Walter and I will find love for each other, so this act of kindness for me is quite unexpected from Walter. But I can't spend too much time with these thoughts, after all, Carl is in front of me and I don't want to waste even a minute. I tell myself I will think about Walter and everything else later. I laugh with Carl and forget about Walter for the time being.

Chapter Fifteen

Carl leaves about three hours after he had arrived here, and I walk on cloud nine again until I fell asleep. I don't see Walter anymore tonight. I promise myself I will talk with him first thing in the morning. But as glad as I am that Carl came to see me and as much as I want to spend all of my thoughts on him, Walter continues to invade my thoughts. Walter presses into my thoughts so much so that I finally come down from the cloud I'm on and find myself at Walter's bedroom door. I raise my hand to knock, but I hear him talking through the slightly open door.

"I can't do that. You know I have a problem with doing something like that. No, I am not in love with her. I told you what this is about." There is silence as he listens to the person on the other end of the phone, and I wait trying to decide if I should knock or go away. I am about to leave when Walter yelled. "Stop it, Beth. I am not going to continue with this conversation. I am hanging up now." Then I hear him snap the phone shut and throw it across the room. Lowering my hand, I hit the door accidentally then I knock as if I was really going to, but truthfully, I was going back to bed and pretend I heard nothing.

"Yes. What is it," its obvious Walter isn't in a good mood. After having the depressed day he had, his night seems to be no better.

"Walter, I want to talk with you if you feel like it." I hope he will say no, and tell me to just go away, but instead he says I can come in and then he opens the door up completely. I notice right away that Walter has a bottle of wine sitting on the table next to his bed and I also notice that Walter has been crying. His eyes are red and wet and he tries to keep his face from me.

"Yes, Naturallee, what can I do for you? I think I hear him sniffle and then clear his throat. "I'm sorry, I'm a little tired. Could we talk in the morning? He still doesn't look at me.

"Walter, is everything alright? Is there anything I can do for you?" I don't know what I can do, but I feel I should try to do something. Walter is clearly upset. True enough I don't know him very well, but he is hurting and I am a sucker for a hurt animal. He doesn't answer and I walk closer to Walter. He puts his hand up and asked me to leave. Not sure what to do, I turn around leaving him to his emotions. As I wander aimlessly back to my room I wonder what happened to cause him to fall apart. Who or what brought Walter to this low point that he would break down? I think about the things I heard him saying as I was standing outside of his bedroom door. I want to know who he needs to explain our situation to. Is there a girlfriend who doesn't understand about this whole thing? I can understand it though. I mean trying to explain it to Carl wasn't the easiest thing to do in the yard tonight, and Walter had already explained some of it to him. I can just imagine how an existing girlfriend might feel. But is it enough to make Walter cry?

CHAPTER 16

Carl has called several times since the night he came out to the house and I couldn't be happier. We've had a couple of dates since the night of the party. Fortunately, he doesn't seem to mind the arrangement I'm in with Walter. Walter has gotten over his disappointment or whatever it was that upset him the other night. He also has not brought up the episode in the car that night a couple of weeks ago, so I am in great spirits.

I notice that Walter is spending more time at the office than when we first started this agreement. I don't mind it, but I don't want it to affect the stipulations of the agreement. Now that I am used to the idea, it isn't so bad. Already we have put in two months. Walter isn't bad to live with and the dinners we've shared each week are kind of pleasant. Walter is quite interesting. He knows all kinds of odd things that I never think about. I have no idea how many trees it takes to make the New York Times Newspaper for a Sunday morning addition, but Walter does. Walter also has a very pleasant way about him. He's a very loving and kind man. He told me about his childhood and how he and Nathan Grey met. He told me that his mother had died just after his father died after a long, anguishing, painful bout with cancer. As though that wasn't enough, four years to the date of his mother's death, his brother Richard died of the same cancer his father died of. Things continue to get worse for Walter when seven years later Walter's wife Elaine found love with a perfect stranger and left him. Five months after she left Walter, she was back. She moved back into their house as if she had never left. They never spoke about it he said. They went to a family wedding the next weekend and carried on like everything was fine. Then one day a few years later, Elaine was shopping in New York, not paying attention to what was going on around her, and was mugged by a young girl in desperate need of money for drugs. The woman was caught but Elaine lay in a hospital bed for three days before her head injury overtook her. Walter went to the hospital to be at her bedside, and he cried at the loss of life, but not for the loss of his wife. After that Nathan started in on him about finding true love. Actually, I understand more about Nathan Grey than I am willing to accept. Nathan was right, it would be better to love for only a few years and have to let go than it would be to be in a loveless marriage for twenty years. Yes, I understand Nathan Grey better than I want to admit.

I go into the kitchen for a cold drink from the refrigerator and a cookie from the cookie jar, but the papers on the counter catch my eyes first. Carl's name is on the third line with the words "still married," and I am sure I am reading about someone else. The paper goes on to say things like "father of two" and "nineteen months in jail." The first page is shocking, but I preferred those words compared to the words on the second page. Now I need more than a cold drink, but I really don't drink, so I just stand here looking at the papers for what feels like hours before I snap out of it. Maybe the papers are talking about someone Walter knows or who he rep-

Chapter Sixteen

resented as their attorney. Yes, that has to be it; after all, the name is common. Carl Morgan is a common name, the Carl Morgan on this paper could be any loser in this city because certainly it isn't the man I've been longing to spend all my time with, kissing on, and telling my dreams to. No, this can't be the same man. I go upstairs, I need to lie down. After several minutes, I know lying down won't give me the peace of mind that I need. I need to find Walter.

Sliding out of the bed, my mind is on overdrive. There has to be a simple explanation to all of this. I go back to the kitchen and get the letter before I leave the house. The shiny little red Chrysler that Nathan Grey has made available to me sits in the driveway. I haven't driven the car much. I mean, the car is more than I'm used to having, but today it is what will have to get me to Walter quickly. As I sit on the seat, I am reminded of the bed and how comforting it is. The car usually makes me want to relax and drive slowly taking my time, but I can't let that happen right now. I start the engine, put the car in drive, round the circle driveway in front of the house, and then drive away. I think about calling Carl instead of looking for Walter, but I don't want to accuse him, and I need to know what the paper is really saying and who it is saying "it" about.

I'm almost to Walter's office when my cell phone rings, "Hello," I say, but I can't take my eyes off the road to see who's calling so I wait for their response.

"Naturallee, where are you going in such a hurry?" I'm caught off guard and look hard at the phone.

"Who is this?" I hear a horn blow and my eyes quickly return to the road.

"Am I that easily forgotten?"

"Where are you," I ask, looking into the rear view mirror.

"You just blew past me in your little red car." I have the top down so he probably saw me with the look of steely determination on my face. When I get focused on something I don't get distracted easily. But that is beside the point. I don't want to talk with Carl before talking with Walter.

"I'm sorry, Carl but I can't talk right now, I have something important to take care of. I'll have to call you back." I think he is still talking, but I hang up, anyway. I can't call Walter to say that I am on my way because I don't want him asking questions like the attorney he is, so I keep driving the last three miles to get to town.

When I get to his office building, I remember the first time I was here. I thought it was the most beautiful, intimidating building I had ever seen. And I remember the first time I went into Walter's office with its soothing relaxing waterfall and up-scaled elegance, and I wanted to stay there for as long as I could. As I walk up the steps and into the lobby I think about how many times over the past few months I have come into this building, and how different I feel coming into it today. The security guard speaks to me and uses my name. The receptionist gives me a pleasant smile and says that Walter, as far as she knows, is still in the building and that he hasn't had lunch. I give a quick smile back, and walk quickly to the elevators. Once inside and the elevator doors close, I realize that I am going to see Walter as if I am his wife, angry with my husband. After thinking about it, I decide it would be best to wind it down a notch or two before I speak with Walter.

I step off the elevator and see Walter at the end of the hall speaking with a woman, who for a moment, I think I know. Before I can get a good look at her, she goes out the door that leads to the stairway. Walter drops his head to his chest and just stands there. He is clearly bothered by her visit. He turns to walk back to his office, and I can see the distress on his face. Walter doesn't notice me as he opens the private door to his office with his key. I decide to wait for a few minutes before going into his front office. I don't want him to know that I have seen them together; although, I not sure why not.

When I finally go into the office, I see that Ms. Blair isn't at her desk watching the door and being the good little gatekeeper she usually is. I take a seat and wait for her return. I have always waited for Ms. Blair to announce me to Walter; I've never just walked

Chapter Sixteen

into his office. Besides, this time I want to give Walter a few more minutes to get himself together. I also don't know if he has another appointment coming in. I usually enjoy sitting in the outer office, anyway. It's so warm and bright, and very comforting. I'm starting to relax a bit when I hear a loud noise in Walter's office. I stand up and run to his door. It is already slightly open so I push through it and find Walter on the floor passed out. I run to him and kneel down over him.

"Walter, Walter, what's wrong, what's happening," I know I'm yelling but I'm frightened. His eyes are closed and he says nothing, and then I scream for help. Ms. Blair had returned and was unaware of what has happened. She rushes in and yells out Walter's name before she picks up the phone and dials 911. When I look up again, the office is filled with people I don't really know and they all look scared.

It takes what feels like my entire lifetime before the paramedics arrive and start to work on Walter. I hear one of them say "I have a pulse," and someone else says, "Good." They continue to talk medical jargon as I stand there close to Walter still lying on the floor; they continue to work on him. After what feels like many more hours have passed by, the paramedics get him on the stretcher and prepare to take him out to the waiting ambulance. And then, as if they know I live with Walter, one of the paramedics looks at me and asks if I want to ride with him to the hospital, and for whatever reason, I think about Nathan Grey and the plans he has for Walter and me.

"Yes, I would," I answer without hesitation and follow them out of Walter's office toward the waiting ambulance. I hear Ms. Blair say that she will take care of things there and then follow in her car. I yell back over my shoulder, "alright," but I never stop speed walking with the stretcher that is carrying Walter out of the office and to the elevator.

In the ambulance, I am asked about Walter's medical history, and I feel strange not knowing anything detailed about him. Nathan

Suspended

Grey knew what he was doing when he had Walter and I enter the contract. I realize now that I care for Walter more than I thought I did. Seeing him lie there on the stretcher gives me a fear for him that I would have denied that I could have had just a few hours ago. But now looking at him, I want them to do everything possible for him. I need them to help him before it could be too late.

Once we get to the hospital, they rush Walter through the emergency room doors and into a room, all the while working on him, taking his vitals, and talking medical lingo that I don't fully understand. Once the doctors and nurses rush into the room, I'm rushed out and left standing at the other side of the door looking in. I start to wonder who the woman was that Walter was talking with before all of this happened. I wonder if she had stressed Walter to the point of collapse.

I feel an arm around my shoulder. I'm surprised to see Carl standing next to me. He looks concerned, but I'm too concerned about Walter to inquire as to why he is even here at the hospital.

"He's going to be alright," Carl says, and squeezes my shoulder. "Come on, let's sit down."

We walk slowly to the closest seats to the door in the waiting room. Several minutes pass before Carl speaks again and he is saying something about the party and his brother. I'm not really listening. I want to hear something about Walter. I did notice that Carl finally stopped talking, but I didn't notice when he got up and walked away. I find that this day holds a lot of surprises for me—the paper about Carl, the woman in the hall with Walter, Walter's collapse, Carl's somehow knowing about my being here and just showing up. But the biggest surprise to me is the way I am feeling about Walter and the fear I have for Walter's life. I need someone to come and talk to me and tell me everything is alright. Each time the doors open to the emergency room I hold my breath.

"Naturallee, do you know anything yet?" It is Ms. Blair and two men that I don't know running down the hall.

Chapter Sixteen

"No, no one has been out to talk to me and it has been hours since they brought him in."

Ms. Blair smiles and rubs my hand. Then she tells me that it has only been about an hour and fifteen minutes since the ambulance left the office. I thought she was lying. No wonder the doctors haven't told me anything. It must be too soon. Perhaps, they don't know anything yet.

"Naturallee, this is Ralph Donaldson and Peter Richards. Ralph is Walter's business partner and Peter is Walter's nephew. I called both of them. I didn't know if you and Walter have had a chance to really know enough about each other, you know, to know about each other's families and friends.

Ms. Blair is right; I don't know anything about Walter's family and friends. Walter knows more about my family than I do. Now that I think about it, Walter probably knows more about me than I do. We have lived together for several months now and I have never asked Walter about his real life. I've been watching time pass for the sake of my mother, but I never considered what Walter was giving up to do this. Maybe the woman in the hall was his girlfriend and she's not as understanding as Carl is about all of this. Maybe she's giving him a hard a time about the arrangement and it caused Walter to have a heart attack. Walter always came home and asked how my day was and if there is anything that I need, but I only answer his questions. I never ask about him about his day or if there was anything I can do for him. He tells me what he wants me to know about him when he wants me to know it. His medical history isn't something he talks a whole lot about. I do know that he had a surgery that no one else knew about, but that wasn't a life- and- death thing. I know he had his tonsils taken out when he was a kid. He and Nathan had it done at the same time. And I know that Walter hates hospitals. It would seem that every time someone he loved went into one, they didn't return home, or at the very least, they didn't return with good news. Now Walter is lying in a hospital room possibly dying.

"He'll be alright, Naturallee. Don't cry. Walter will be just fine. We have to believe that." I am crying, and so, here's another surprise for me today.

"I hope you're right, Ms. Blair. Walter is the first family I've had in a very long time, and I just realized I can't lose him now." I put my head on her shoulder and cry a little more.

Then, I start to drift up. My feet leave the floor and I cry out, "No."

Ms. Blair, Peter, and Ralph stare at me as if my head had separated from my body, but I can feel the floor under my feet again and I know I haven't drifted to the ceiling and I am glad about that.

"Sweetheart, you are going to have to get a hold of yourself. Walter wouldn't want you falling apart like this." Ms. Blair is right, but what she doesn't know is that my outburst isn't for Walter this time; it's for me.

It's another forty-seven minutes before anyone comes to talk to us, and when they do, they don't have anything encouraging to say. Walter had a heart attack plain and simple, the doctor said. It's a bad one, but Walter is in good hands and they are going to do all they can for him. They want to keep him comfortable and quiet for a while. Walter is resting, but wants a moment to speak with Ms. Blair. The doctor asks Ms. Blair to keep the visit to a minimum and suggest that the rest of us go home. It will be tomorrow before Walter can have any visitors. As the nurse takes Ms. Blair down the hall to Walter's room, the rest of us start to pick up our things, preparing to leave.

"Mrs. Mayfield, your husband asked if you could stay tonight. So when we get him into his room, we have a bed brought in for you. It's a roll-away bed. It's the best we can do on such short notice. I'm afraid we weren't expecting Mr. Mayfield to visit with us tonight."

Everyone stands silent, captured by the doctor's words. No one knows what to say.

Chapter Sixteen

"I do apologize for the crude accommodations, but really it's all we have for you at this time. The hospital is very grateful for…" the doctor continues before I snap back to reality and stop him.

"Oh, that will be fine; it's more than fine. If Walter wants me to stay I will sleep on the floor if need be," I say looking at Peter and Ralph. "Can I see him now?"

"If you don't mind waiting until Ms. Blair returns, it will be better for him…if you don't mind."

"Of course, I'll wait until she returns."

"Thank you," the doctor says as he extends his hand to me. "My name is Dr. Brown; if you need anything tonight, have the desk call me. I will make sure they know I am to be called if you need me. And may I say it is nice to meet you, Mrs. Mayfield. Walter has been unhappy for a long time, but when I spoke with him a couple of weeks ago, he seemed happier. I didn't realize he had married again. That explains his happiness." Dr. Brown smiles and walks away.

After the doctor leaves, I don't know what to say. I didn't want to say anything contrary to what Walter has said, but I'm not sure how Peter and Ralph feel about what just happened. I hadn't noticed that Carl has returned as well, and now there are three sets of confused eyes staring at me.

Peter clears his throat and sits down again. Ralph just stands there with his mouth open, and Carl is looking up at the ceiling as if there are answers to all of the world's problems up there. I wonder why Carl has stayed. I told him I'm staying until I know what is happening with Walter. Now that I know what is going on, and that I am staying at the hospital with Walter, I have to tell Carl and encourage him to go home. Before I can say anything to him, Ms. Blair returns, she too, is looking a bit puzzled. She announces that I will be staying with Walter and that Walter wants everyone else to just go home including her. I also notice that when she comes back to us she doesn't come alone. She has a police officer with her, and from the look on his face, he means business.

"Certainly he doesn't mean me," Peter speaks up with a horrified look on his face. "I'm his nephew for crying out loud. I'm the only true family standing around here. Why should I leave?" I've never met Walter's nephew, but Walter had warned me about him once over a cup of coffee and a slice of toast one morning. Walter never said his real name; he always called him Greedy Pete. He told me that if anything ever happened to him make sure that Greedy Pete was not allowed to make any decisions for him and not let him into our house or his other home. That statement was always followed with chuckling and head-shaking by Walter. I always thought it was one of those family joke things. I didn't take it serious, until now.

"Sir, you were asked to leave the hospital at the request of one of the patients here. Please get your things together and I will walk you out," the officer instructs Peter who is now standing firm in the floor.

"Sir, I will not be leaving this hospital or any other until I am good and ready. This is a public hospital and I have every right..." but Ms. Blair cuts him off.

"Peter, shut up. You well know that Walter and Nathan have almost paid for the entire wing of this hospital by themselves. If Walter doesn't want you here, you know you have to go. This isn't the first time you've been asked to leave this wing of the hospital, so just get your things and go." Up to this point I was under the impression Ms. Blair and Peter were friends. Obviously, I'm wrong.

"Rachel, you have no business speaking to me like..." His words are cut off by the officer this time, moving toward Peter. The officer grabs Peter's arm to walk him out of the building, but Peter snatches away. The officer grabs Peter with both hands, and before any of us know what is happening, Peter is wrapped up by the officer and pushed up against the wall. Peter's voice rings out in the hall as he continues to yell accusations at the officer, Ms. Blair, Ralph, and me. Then the officer leads him away.

Chapter Sixteen

After the officer takes Peter to the door and warns him not to return, the officer comes back up to Walter's room. He asks that everyone else leave except me, then he goes to find a chair.

Ms. Blair and Ralph began to gather their things and talk between themselves, and I turn to Carl. I not sure how he will take my words but I have to tell him.

"I am sorry, Carl, but Walter wants me to stay, and of course, I said that I will. Thank you for staying with me. I'll call you tomorrow," I say while reaching up to kiss his cheek good night, but Carl pulls away, and smiles shyly. I'm not sure what to make of his reaction, but I don't have the time to worry about it. I turn to go to Walter's room. Ms. Blair says she will walk with me and show me which room is Walter's. I think she wants to speak with me, after all, I can read numbers on a door. I've been reading them since I was in kindergarten.

◆

CHAPTER 17

"Naturallee, I need to tell you something before you see Walter. He doesn't handle his health issues very well. That may be why he still works out three times a week before he goes to his office. With that said, let me say this, he's afraid of sickness and hospitals and doctors and...well all of this. He wants you to stay because right now you are the closest thing to a family he has that is close at hand. He will probably say a lot of odd things to you tonight. I'm asking you to please be patient with him. He's just scared. Don't promise him anything tonight; he may want you to live up to it once he gets out of here." Ms. Blair never misses a step while she is speaking. She gives me some papers that she says I need to read, and one that I need to read very carefully, and then, I need to sign it. We are at the door to Walter's room now and Ms. Blair wants to say good night in the hallway because she doesn't want to get drawn into another disagreement with Walter. She actually hugs me and tells me she will call later to see how I am doing before she walks back to Ralph who is waiting for her alone, now that Carl has left.

Suspended

I need to take a deep breath at the door before I go into Walter's room. Walter looks so different lying in this hospital bed. The strong, powerful man I've spent the last couple of months with is not the same man lying here on this bed and I wonder where Walter Mayfield really is. I want to go out and ask a nurse what they have done with Walter Mayfield, the attorney who has donated so much money to this wing of the hospital. Standing here, unable to move and not sure what to do, I hear Walter call my name.

"Naturallee, are you there?" Walter asks in a very weak voice, and then he reaches out his hand for me.

"Yes, Walter, it's me," is all I can say. Even though his hand is reaching out for me, I just stand there looking at his weakened fingers, wondering what I should do.

"Naturallee, please, come closer and sit with me a while, please.

I walk a little closer to the bed and see that Walter has a washed-out look on his face. His strength is certainly not what it was this morning even for a man of his age. I'm not sure what I am expecting to see when I look at him. Certainly, he is in no shape to run around the room; neither is he in any shape to look his best. The man is in a hospital bed struggling for life. His eyes are barely open and he has dried drool at the corners of his mouth. He finally has disheveled hair and I see for the first time that Walter is vulnerable. Walter can come off as a little larger than life sometimes to me, but tonight he is almost childlike with his hand stretched out to me as if I can touch him and make it all better. I stand looking down at him, shocked at the man lying in the bed.

"Naturallee, are you still here with me?" Now Walter sounds whiny, almost wimpy, and I don't like it. I start to get upset, but before I can let it really get next to me, he drops his hand and closes his eyes completely. Then one of the machines that are hooked up to him starts to beep, and I'm at his bedside quickly.

"Walter, Walter, speak to me. Say something, please, say something. Don't die on me. Open your eyes Walter. Open them now," I am yelling at him now.

Suddenly, a nurse comes in the room. She doesn't seem to be as upset about what is happening as I am. I yell at her and her short thick legs stiffen as she reaches the foot of the bed. Allowing only her eyes to move, she looks at me as if I have lost my mind.

"Mrs. Mayfield, relax. Mr. Mayfield is just sleeping; he is under a lot of medication. He'll go in and out of consciousness all night, so you should try to get some rest yourself. The bed the doctor ordered for you will be here shortly. Is someone bringing you some things for the night? The nurse goes about her work checking the tubes that run from a machine to different parts of Walter's body.

I haven't thought about what to wear for the night. I was just planning to sleep in the chair in my clothes. "Oh no, I didn't think that far. I wanted to get in and see Walter for myself."

"I can understand that. Mr. Mayfield is a very nice man and for something like this to happen to him is just the worst. He has always been so full of life and encouraging to others. This hospital owes a lot to your husband and his best friend, Mr. Grey. Without the two of them, I think this hospital would have folded years ago."

"Did you know, Mr. Grey?" I only have Walter's version of Nathan Grey, but Nathan was Walter's best friend, so of course Walter would speak well of Nathan.

"I didn't meet Walter until after Nathan died. I know they were good friends and Walter loved Nathan and thought the world of him." But I would like to get someone else's opinion of larger than life Nathan Grey. Walter has always said nothing but good things about Nathan, and he has also been pretty open about the way he felt about Nathan's whole plan for his life and mine. While Walter wants the money for charity, I think he would have also wanted to have it the way he wanted to have it, without all the strings attached.

"Well, let me tell you, Nathan Grey was quite a man. He had a passion for the sick. Notice I said he had a passion not compassion, which he had as well, but his passion was greater. No one loved the sick as much as Nathan. He would stop in here at the hospital and help wherever he could. Did you know that Nathan Grey was a licensed surgeon? Yep, and he was brilliant at it too. He had to give up the life of a doctor twenty-five years ago when he lost the use of three fingers on his left hand after a simple fall here at the hospital." The nurse never stops what she is doing for Walter, still checking wires and tubes, fixing things around him on the bed, and straightening up the room.

"If it was a simple fall, what caused him to have to give up medicine?" This story has a lot more to it, it has to. No one who has a simple fall has to leave medicine.

"When Nathan fell off the curb in front of the hospital, the president of this hospital was chewing him out at the time for something the president's daughter had done. She was head of registration at the time. Carol Plascow was as dumb as her name was. She didn't have enough sense to keep her mouth shut or to take advice and help from anyone. She got offended by Nathan Grey when he tried to help her at the computer one day. She said Nathan was trying to show her up in front of the staff. She actually had wanted to date Nathan for several months but Nathan always said that dating co-workers was a bad idea. We figured that was the reason she lied and told her father that Nathan had changed a registration form for a patient.

"Did he do it?" I asked.

"No, Nathan wouldn't do anything like that. A few months later, the hospital found out that Carol had a bad habit of changing things for patients all the time. If she thought the patient didn't know how to spell their own name, she would fix it for them. Once a lady was admitted on a day that Carol wasn't working, the woman's name was spelled K-e-l-l-e-e B-r-o-w-n-e. At the time Carol Plascow had admitted another patient, a man whose name was Kelly Brown. Believing that someone had made a mistake she went up to the woman

Kellee's room to get her name and correct spelling; the woman gave it to Carol. Carol thought she was sure of how to spell it so she called the woman's husband for correct spelling. When he confirmed what the woman said, Carol tried to correct it for him. The man was so angry about the phone call until he had the woman transferred to another hospital the next day. He said that he didn't want anyone like Carol around his wife." Nurse Hilary said it was one of many, many stupid things this Carol Plascow had done over the five years that she had worked there.

"I'm sorry, I didn't mean to say all of that, but every time I think of Nathan Grey and his simple fall, I get upset all over again. I'm so glad that President Plascow is no longer here; they got rid of him the year after Nathan had to give up medicine."

"How did a fall cause Nathan to give up medicine?" Now I am really curious.

"Oh yeah, well, Nathan was headed to his car one afternoon and the president was on his way to his daughter's car, he and his daughter were going to lunch together. Carol was waiting for her father out front. President Plascow and Nathan were leaving at the same time, just not together. Carol jumped out of the car and started hitting Nathan saying that he had tried to embarrass her and steal her job by stepping in and helping Kellee Browne and her husband cool their anger toward the hospital and by trying to get Mr. Kelly Brown mixed up as to the day of his surgery. Carol had taken it upon herself to get the name right which caused a mix-up for Mr. Brown's surgery almost killing Mr. Kelly Brown. That part didn't come out until the day the hospital staff and Mr. Brown's family had to give their depositions. But before we knew that and when she was hitting Nathan, President Plascow pushed Nathan, while grabbing for his daughter, he said. It was just the wrong way to fall for Nathan because when he hit the payment, the bone just above his elbow came through his skin and his fingers were under him in the wrong position. It didn't help when Carol is kicking him while he's on the ground in agonizing pain at the hands of both her and her father. By the time her father got her off Nathan, she had kicked him one good time in the broken arm and the pain was so much that Nathan had passed out. After that, President Plascow fired his daughter, but it was too late. The board fired President Plascow.

"But Nathan has given so much to this hospital over the years. Why?" I couldn't wait to hear the rest of this story.

"There were plenty of eyewitnesses, including a board member on his way to a meeting here at the hospital and a news crew was here to do a story on the hospital's need for more funding. The whole thing was a disaster. Nathan had to have a seven hour operation to try to repair his arm and hand. They were able to save the arm but not the ability to use all of his fingers. Nathan was devastated by the news. He loved being a surgeon and had such great promise of being one of the best surgeons this hospital would ever have," Nurse Hilary says as she looks at Walter lying in the bed. I wait for her to remember whatever it is that had her mind for the moment. I think it is an enjoyable thought because she has a slight smile on her face.

"Anyway", she announces as she is ready to continue with the younger life of Nathan Grey, "Once the dust settled from all that followed, Nathan left the hospital with a severance package of just under fourteen million dollars and his dream of being a great doctor shattered. After a few years, the hospital called him to work for them in a teaching kind of position. He did it for about three years when he met some salespeople with a piece of new hospital equipment that was supposed to make tremendous strides in the medical world. Nathan saw a future for the equipment, but the hospital didn't. Nathan invested three and a half a million dollars of his own money to get it going. For the first two years, no hospital seemed interested in it. Then Nathan got this one hospital in the next town to take a chance with it and it turned out to be the best thing that hospital ever did. Long story short, the machine's suc-

Chapter Seventeen

cess got around quickly and Nathan became more than rich almost overnight. Nathan then bought into that company until eventually he owned fifty-five percent of it. I hear that he eventually owned the whole thing and died with a net worth of something crazy like one hundred million dollars, but you know how much people talk." The nurse takes her seat at Walter's bedside letting me know that she is here for the night.

Walter groans and tries to turn over, but drifts back off to sleep before he can really move. I am still standing when I hear Nurse Hilary speak again. She is on the phone asking where the bed is for me. She also tells the person on the phone to get a meal for me, some toiletries, as well as sleepwear from the gift shop, and a larger television. When she hangs up the phone, she smiles and introduces herself. Her name is Hilary Grant and she is the night nurse for Walter, and she is a wealth of information to me. Nurse Hilary has done a great job of keeping my mind off of Walter. Without having to ask for much, I'm getting more information than I even imagine. Once Nurse Hilary gets Walter settled and comfortable, she asks if I am interested in ordering take-out, the hospital will take care of having it delivered.

I understand why Nathan Grey, as a patient could command such attention, but why Walter. He is only a friend and attorney to Nathan. I decide that I will ask Nurse Hilary how Walter fits into all of this once she stops long enough to take a breath.

"...And wasn't Nathan handsome, so tall and good-looking with thick, black hair and hands like a real man? You know I always thought his hands were too big for a surgeon. And when he died, he still had a full head of hair. Did you know that Nathan was a runner? He ran marathons all over this country. I used to love talking to him, not just because of his good looks, but also because Nathan was a brilliant man. The business world was lucky to have him as was the medical field. Nathan was to business like Michael Jordan was to basketball. He had a very unique and creative mind."

Suspended

Nurse Hilary finally takes a break again and I have a chance to ask about Walter. When I ask how Walter fit into the importance of the hospital, she acted as if I had snakes on my head. She even stops what she is doing and put her hand on her forehead. She stands perfectly still for a long moment, then Hilary finds her voice. When she speaks, her voice has a husky tone to it, and her eyes never leave mine.

"Walter, Mr. Mayfield, is just as important to this hospital as Nathan Grey. Mr. Mayfield has been the attorney for this hospital for fifteen years or so. He has won some of the biggest law suits against this hospital brought on by greedy, fraudulent companies as well as people. Mr. Mayfield sued and won a very large case against a medical company that had been stealing from the hospital for years causing the hospital to pass the expense on to our patients. When Mr. Mayfield got involved with the case, he won seventy- three million dollars in that suit and got them to somehow pay it and not contest the judgment. He has, hand in hand with Nathan Grey done so many, many good things for the kids here at Christmas time and summer holidays. Mr. Mayfield has done far more than we could ever thank him for. And I am sure there is much more about Mr. Mayfield that I don't even know about." Nurse Hilary is stern in her praise for Walter, even more firm than she was when she spoke about Nathan Grey.

I'm pretty sure there is very little Nurse Hilary doesn't know about. But she has given me a new view of Walter and it makes me feel good that we are married.

Oh my goodness, I have mentally fallen into this charade. I need to get myself together and remember who I am and what I am really doing here.

Nurse Hilary leaves the room for a minute, but promises to return ASAP. I figure I have maybe five minutes to myself and I need these few minutes to think. Walter is someone I really do need to get to know. The things nurse Hilary has told me about Walter

Chapter Seventeen

I actually had no idea about. It makes me look at him differently, and then I hear myself say out loud "Lord, help this man," and it scares me. I have never said words like this before. Well, not really believing that I am speaking to someone who's real, but that I've never seen. I got my bed and things while nurse Hilary was out of the room so that moment to myself is lost. I am so tired. It doesn't matter now. All I want is to lay on the bed and listen to more of the things nurse Hilary has to say about Walter and Nathan. Sitting down on the bed, I know that it won't be as comfortable as my bed at home. Hopefully, it won't be for too many nights.

The rest of the night is filled with the sound of Nurse Hilary's voice. She never gets tired of hearing herself talk. But she did have other things to talk about. Nurse Hillary told me that the president of the hospital now was former President Plascow's roommate when they were in college. And I didn't know that the basement of the hospital was suppose to be haunted, and that the head nurse of the night shift was having an affair with the night guard. The hospital has had celebrities stay in its rooms, and about ten years ago there was a big fire that burned this wing badly and that was when Nathan and Walter stepped in and did what they did. Yes, Nurse Hilary knows it all. I actually fell asleep while she was talking.

I think I heard Walter calling my name in my sleep and I dream that Walter and I are at a basketball game and a nurse is playing on one of the teams. I am tired because, I think I hear Peter's voice just outside the door saying to someone, "She isn't even his wife I bet you. No one in the family went to the wedding or knows anything about this woman." I dream Peter is talking, but as I turn my head the dream goes away. As the dream ends, I can still hear Peter's voice, and the voice of the police officer in the hall.

"I said you will have to leave, sir," the officer tells Peter.

"I am not going anywhere. That is my uncle and I have a right to be here," Peter spit the words back to the officer.

Suspended

"Sir, I don't care if you are Mr. Mayfield's father, he said he doesn't want anyone here and you are not allowed to stay. So please, go home-- or at the very least leave this floor of the hospital, please," the officer is pleading with Peter, but Peter isn't smart enough to take the warning. He takes a swing at the officer and is pinned to the wall with his face pressed against a picture of flowers in a field.

I watch the whole thing through a crack in the open door. Peter's face is fire engine red and I think his ears have smoke coming out of them, and for a second I think his brain is on fire. Once the officer puts the handcuffs on Peter, he drops to the floor and just sits there. The police officer stands over him looking surprised and shaking his head. He asks Peter if he needs medical help then tries to get him up off the floor. I think the whole thing is a bit much for Peter because he can't get up. I know this isn't a dream; I'm wide awake and I understand better why Walter said some of the things that he did about his nephew. Walter also has a niece that he has warned me about. I wonder what surprising things I will find out about her if she shows up? Hopefully she won't show up here tonight. Peter has been escorted away by the officer and two security guards so the halls are quiet again. Maybe I can get back to sleep before nurse Hilary gets back.

CHAPTER 18

Day six of Walter's hospital stay and I feel like it's been a month already. Don't get me wrong. Everyone has been great to me and more than kind to Walter. Every day someone from the hospital administration comes in to see how he's doing and to make sure that I am comfortable. The nursing staff could not be better if I had handpicked them myself. Wonderful things like the children from the second floor have come up twice to see Walter and give him some cards they've made for him. Nurse Hilary has only taken one day off and that was because her husband had outpatient surgery and needed someone to spend the day with him. She wanted me to know if there was any way around it she would have been with Walter instead. Even though Nurse Hilary has three children, two girls both of them are in high school and the youngest, a son that's eight and diagnosed autistic. But Nurse Hilary makes me feel like Walter and I are most important in her life when she is here, not that she doesn't love her husband; she's just very dedicated to her patients as she hopes her husband's nurses will be to him while he is at Hopewell Community Hospital across town. The rest of her family is out of state so she is the only candidate for the stay at home job with her husband. Walking down the hall to Walter's room I can't help but think how important he is to this place. And I wonder if anyone here knows that Walter and I aren't married or would it not matter to anyone here.

Approaching Walter's room I can't help but think about Nathan Grey and his plans that have in a way caused this situation to be. After all, if it hadn't been for the arrangement that he put Walter and me into I would not know Walter and therefore Walter wouldn't have had to have the argument with the woman at his office, probably. And I wouldn't know anything about this part of Walter's heart or life or anything else.

Peeking into his room first, I see that Walter isn't in bed or in the room at all and I start to panic. The room has been cleaned, the bed made, and the many flowers, balloons and cards wishing him well are all collected together in bags in the corner. I'm afraid something has happened to him and no one has called me to let me know. But before my fears run away with me a kind hand on my shoulder grabs my attention and says, "He's at the end of the hall with an old friend of his who came out to visit today." It's Nurse Hilary out of uniform.

"Hi. What are you doing here? I thought you weren't here until seven tonight." Not that I'm not glad to see Nurse Hilary, she just caught me by surprise.

"I'm not able to work tonight; I can't find anyone to stay with my husband. He's not doing as well as we had hoped since the surgery and I'm afraid to have him stay by himself just yet. I have asked someone else to cover for me tonight. I hope you don't mind," Nurse Hilary says in a pleading voice.

"No, of course not, you need to be with your husband just like I need to be with Walter." I was careful not to say my husband. I need to keep things straight in my own mind. After all, if I don't pay attention to what is really going on, I will be overtaken by this whole thing and sucked into a relationship that is built on anything but love. I could marry this man just because of the situation with him right now.

I tell Nurse Hilary it will be alright Walter and I can get through the night without her one more time. She seems reluctant to go but her home situation pulls at her and she finally leaves. Before she leaves the floor though, Nurse Hilary stops at the nurse's station to give them last minute instructions for Walter. I smile and wave goodbye to her and head down the hall to where I find Walter and a man with gray hair and big eyes are seated. Walter is speaking and I can tell from his hand movements that Walter is adamant about his position, whatever it is he is speaking on. His back is to me but his posture says he is probably getting more excited than he should be right now. But because I don't know Walter well enough to simply step in and tell him to relax a bit, I just wait on the other side of the wall just out of the sight of either of them. I'm curious as to what it is they are discussing that is so important that it can't wait until Walter gets out of the hospital and is feeling better. I decide to see what it is that has Walter so engaged so I move closer to the door but stay out of sight.

"There is nothing like it Frank. I mean there is always going to be some kind of problem in our lives, it doesn't matter if it's emotional, physical, social, or spiritual there is always problems that we will face. The good thing is that we don't have to face our problems alone. We have someone who is always there to see us through these tough times."

The man seems interested in what Walter has to say because I hear the man say to Walter, "Please tell me more, Walter. I feel I'm at the end of this thing." The man's voice is shaking enough that I want to peek in and see what is going on, but I hear Walter continue with his belief in what he is saying. Walter is determined not to lose this patient so he continues with his same forceful, encouraging words, "Frank, have you tried to get through this all by yourself or have you let anyone other than me know what is going on?" Walter has a little stress in his voice and I start to have greater concern for him. His health needs to improve not decline. I now wonder if I really should step in and say something, but I don't know how Walter will respond to me stepping into his personal affairs. I think it is better to wait a little longer here behind the wall.

"Frank, this is too big for you to handle alone. I know Pastor Richard will be leaving in a month but he's here now and you need to talk with him. I'll tell Pastor Richard to expect your call and I mean for you to call him as soon as you get back to your hospital room. Will you do that please? If you won't do it for yourself, will you do it for me and for Katie? She's only twenty years old, what is she suppose to do without you?" Walter must be waiting for Frank to respond but the room is quiet. Frank doesn't give an answer fast enough for Walter because he urges Frank to give him his word that he will call this Pastor Richard. Then, finally, I hear Frank agree with Walter when he tells Walter that he will at least give the pastor a call.

CHAPTER 19

Finally Walter is released from the hospital and I am able to take him home, along with Nurse Hilary and a day nurse. Walter doesn't like the fuss that is being made over him but he has no choice, it is the only way the doctor would let him leave the hospital.

In the hospital, Walter had so many visitors that the doctor told him he would have to limit the amount of visitors per day. But the visitors were more business associates and church people than family. Church people; I had no clue Walter knew people who went to church until now.

His nephew Peter didn't try to visit any more at the hospital, but there are several messages on the phone when we get home. Walter also has a niece who is very cute and very personable. Sheila is at the house when we arrive from the hospital. She treats me with kindness and respect which is more than I expected. Sheila came to the hospital three times to see her uncle, and even though she never asked for anything of Walter, he asked me to make sure I restricted what I told her. He even grabbed my hand very firmly, looked deep into my eyes and stressed to me that I make sure that Nurse Hilary understands that she is there as his nurse and not a gossip columnist. If Walter wasn't so stern about his demand, I would have chuckled, but there was something in his eyes that said it was no laughing matter.

At home and away from all of the hospital personnel and hospital rules, I hope that life can get back to normal, whatever that is. I want to call Carl the first chance I get. I don't like the way things were left between us the last time I saw him. I have noticed that my cell phone hasn't rang one time with his number on it. Carl already knows that I share the house with Walter so my staying at the hospital shouldn't be a big surprise to him. Maybe, I will wait for a day or two. After all, Walter just got home today and there will be plenty of people in and out visiting. Walter doesn't need my attention split between he and Carl. I know Walter has around the clock nursing care but I want to be available, just in case.

CHAPTER 20

With so many foster children in her home, Regina (Babydoll) Peoples Whitham is happier than she has ever been. She has been a foster mom for nine years and she sees no reason for stopping now. Regina has a life that many women only dream of. She is married to a successful architect who has no clue she is the product of a drug-loving, drunken, street-walker or that she has many brothers and sisters that she hasn't seen in twenty years; seven siblings as far as Regina knows. Her husband knows the real reason why she doesn't know her father is because her mother didn't know who her father was either. Her husband, Markus, knows her true story; that she was put into foster care at the young, tender age of five and stayed in the system until she was old enough to ran away. Since her sixteenth birthday, Regina Peoples has always told people that her parents died while traveling through Canada. Regina also said that there were no other living relatives and that is why she was adopted when she was seven years old.

Suspended

Regina hated the foster homes she had stayed in, causing her to run away from one of the homes when the cousin of her foster mother continually raped her even when the foster mother was in the house. It was only when cousin Rickie started raping one of the boys that had been put into the same foster home with Babydoll that anyone took notice. His school called the authorities after noticing bruises on odd parts of his body. When the authorities questioned Daniel, he started rambling about sick disgusting things that were happening to him and others at home, forcing an investigation of the Graybar's foster home.

At thirteen years old, Babydoll knew the things that had been done to her could never be repaired or forgotten. After two years of such treatment, she had accepted what had happened to her but she also vowed that she would not let it happen to anyone else when she grew up.

One day, three years after she and Daniel had been taken away from the Graybar's foster home, and the Graybar's had lost their license to foster other children and been put in prison, Babydoll and Daniel found themselves together again in another foster home. Even though these foster care parents were nice and loving to all the kids in the home; Babydoll and Daniel weren't able to trust them. Finally, running away together, they left town and started their lives together as friends two states away.

In the beginning, neither she nor Daniel spoke of the things that happened with the Graybar foster family. But over time, they did open up to each other crying and hurting together for years before they were able to get counseling together and finally make peace with everything and begin to heal.

Sharing so much together; Daniel and Babydoll married at age twenty five and twenty- six. Daniel didn't want to be known by anyone from his past and neither did Babydoll so they both changed their names just before they married and that seemed to help both of them find peace with all that had happened to them. They felt

Chapter Twenty

the secrets that they had between them was something they wanted to keep that way. It was also something that they both understood as to why neither one had any interest in a physical relationship with each other or anyone else. They did agree though that if either one or the other ever changed their mind or met someone who they would be willing to share such an ugly past with, the other one would willingly step away and allow that one a chance at happiness and a more normal life. But it had been fourteen years and neither Markus, formally Daniel nor Regina, formally Babydoll had any desire to take that chance.

They both wanted to be foster parents; to be there the way foster parents were supposed to be for foster children. It felt a little strange at first coming back home to the city where it all happened, but Markus and Regina knew it was where they wanted to help. And after nine years of fostering to children neither of them have any interest in giving up the work they are doing.

CHAPTER 21

"Why don't you talk to her? Ask her if she's interested in you or Walter. I would hate to see you give up so early in this relationship. Carl, please it's the same mistake you always make," I hear Carl's mother say. She must have thought she hung up the phone. It's the third time I've called to talk with Carl. I was beginning to think he was avoiding me, and now I have the confirmation. Carl is avoiding me.

"Well, I'm not going to keep covering for you. If you don't talk to her soon, the next time she calls I will give you the phone." Then I hear them leave the room, still discussing me.

I think about what Carl's mother said and wonder if there is any truth to her words. Am I more interested in Walter than I am Carl? I am concerned about Walter. I want him to be well again, but me being more interested in him than I am Carl; of course not. Walter has many great qualities, I find myself thinking about Walter, but I want Carl. I really like Carl and I want to see more of him. But I can't leave Walter at this time. I hope Carl understands that, but maybe he can't. I mean, when I last saw him two weeks ago in the hospital, he was a little strange when I tried to kiss him good-bye. And the fact is, he hasn't tried to contact me one time, coupled with the fact that Carl isn't taking any of my calls causes me to think I may have misjudged his understanding. Maybe I had misjudged him altogether. Hanging up the phone, I decide to go and see Walter.

Walter is awake and watching ESPN again. For some reason, he likes to watch television in the kitchen. Walter does some strange things at times. He also likes to disappear on Sunday mornings and Tuesday nights; although, he hasn't been able to disappear lately. Then I think of something else. Walter had some visitors at the hospital that I didn't know and he didn't seem interested in introducing me to them or them to me. They were pleasant enough people, but it was clear that he didn't want them and me to meet.

"I guess you are feeling better now that you're home and able to move freely around the house. Being around familiar surroundings has done you a world of good, already," stating the obvious as I walk closer to the chair Walter is seated on. I, without thinking, stroke the back of Walter's head and panic the second my hand slides down his neck and off his shoulder. I just stand next to Walter for a long minute before I regain myself. Walter acts as if it was the most natural thing in the world for me to do. He simply smiles up at me and goes back to the television so I let the moment pass as well and sit down in the chair next to him.

I want to ask him why he told the doctor and the hospital that I was his wife. But after the mistake I had just made I decide that the answer can wait. We sit watching television for a long time before Walter speaks. Not looking away from the commercial, Walter asks, "Aren't you going to at least ask me why I did it."

His question catches me off guard, and I just stare at him.

"I didn't want to spend the night alone and I didn't want them to give you a hard time about staying, so I said that we were already married. I'm sorry if it has caused you any embarrassment or prob-

lems. I'll try to get it all straightened out as soon as I possibly can."
Then Walter turned to me with the saddest look in his eyes. I feel so
sorry for him and I hear myself say, "Oh no, I didn't mind that you
told them that. I wanted to be there and I am glad that you wanted
me to stay." And I think I have lost my mind. Maybe Carl's mother is
right, maybe I'm the one that doesn't know what is really going on.

◆

Week three has passed and still no call from Carl. I am sure that
he is busy and will return my last call soon. After all, there is no way
he can still be upset about the hospital and my staying with Walter.
Maybe he believed it when the doctor said that Walter and I were
married, but Carl has to know that I needed to be there with Walter.
I want to explain everything to Carl, and I will, the minute I get to
talk with him. I want to call him again, but after the last call, I think
it would be best to wait for his call. If his mother leaves the phone
open again and I hear something else I'm not ready for, I don't know
what I'll do. Maybe, I'll drive to Carl's house and teach her how to
hang up the phone. And then ask him what kind of problem is he
having that he can't return the last four calls I've made to him. Or is
it that I'm I just acting like a high school girl who's being dropped
by her first boyfriend and too immature to know it.

I still need to ask Walter about the letter on the counter that
sent me to his office the day he went to the hospital. I don't want to
upset him, but I need to know if the Carl on the paper is the same
Carl I want to call me back. What if I'm longing for a bad boy who
is going to hurt me? What if I'm longing for this guy who will be in
prison next month? What if I fall in love with him and he doesn't
love me back? What if...what if...I can't think about it anymore. I
need to find Walter.

◆

Suspended

Today I find the sun a little too warm, the wind a little too still, and me, a little too nervous but I have to get this over with. Walter is sitting in the sun and he looks sad or maybe he is just deep in thought. I don't know which he is today. With every step I take toward him, I feel I am being unfair to him, but even more unfair to me. I want to help Walter. I want to be here for him, but I also want my own life. I want a life with Carl Morgan. And in less than eight months I will be out of this agreement with Walter and into a life with Carl. That's what I want, I think.

"Walter, do you have a second? I need to talk..." I frightened him and the papers he is holding go everywhere. Walter shifts sharply in the chair and I think he is falling to the ground. I reach for him, but he catches himself and sits up straight.

"Yes, Naturallee, what is it you need? What do you want to talk about?" he asks in a nervous, caught off guard voice.

I notice he missed three of the papers he dropped; they are still on the ground so I pick them up to give to him. It's something to do with me and my brother named Kane. I stand motionless reading the name and thinking that Kane was my dog not my brother. I was going to tell Walter that he had that part of my life wrong until I saw the next sentence.

Kane died three years ago, after a long, struggling battle with alcohol, he was thirty two. The paper goes on to say that he had spent time in prison for arson and robbery. He was somehow married for ten years and left three children to mourn over him. His brothers Havesome Mercy and Righteous Child were with him.

The look on my face must have said it all to Walter. Looking up slowly and with a look on my face that said that I could fall apart, Walter stands up and reaches for me. I can't move. Walter walks slowly over to me and puts his arms around me. I hear him talking but I don't understand what he is saying. I can hear him just fine, but the words are a language I've never heard before as far as my mind is concerned. Where did this information come from?

Chapter Twenty-One

And how long has Walter had it? Was he ever going to share it with me or forever keep it to himself? I don't know whether I should be angry or happy about what I have just read. I feel Walter pull me closer to him and hold me tight. He has stopped talking and is just holding me.

After what feels like hours, I step back out of his arms and look up into his face. Walter looks tired and worn. His eyes don't have the usual dance to them, but I remember that I haven't seen that look in several weeks. But there is something different in his face. Walter had aged greatly since I last saw him a few hours ago. It's like he has been in prison for the last ten years, like my brother. He's finally looking like a man in his mid to late sixties should look. Again, his hair is a mess and he has a coffee stain on his shirt.

Before I can ask my first question, Walter smiled and kisses my forehead; then, he simply walks away. I sit down and read the paper again. The name and the words on the page are all speaking out loud to me. They're telling me what I have never allowed myself to seriously hope for. To start imagining that a real family exists for me is just too much for my heart, my mind, my soul, "Lord," I hear myself say, "Can this be real? Was Kane a part of my family? Tell me if Walter has been hiding this from me or if he, too, has just found out." And I have to ask myself who I am talking to. I seem to do this when I don't know what else to do. I talk as if there is someone here listening to me, as if they have some answers for me. Whenever I can remember to talk to him, them, whoever, I've noticed that I don't drift up when things like this happen. And this is one of those, catch me off guard, times that can really suspend me and keep me suspended for a long time.

Walter returns to me with the other papers in his hand. He gives them to me and sits down in his chair again. "I received these reports a week ago at my office. Ms. Blair gave them to me yesterday when she was here. She has tried to contact Havesome Mercy for you, but there seems to be no response to the calls she has made to him. We don't have any means of contact for any of the other siblings. Truely is married, or at least he was, and he's moved several times over the years. Righteous Child has changed his name and had that name change sealed so we can't find that out just yet. I have even tried to get information from Kane's family, but they didn't know that he had family, plus Kane and his wife hadn't seen each other for more than five years." Words finally stop coming out of Walter's mouth and he takes a deep breath and holds it. I don't know what to say and Walter releases the air he's holding.

"Naturallee, I want you to know that I have not been trying to keep any of this from you. I wanted to have something more substantial to give to you. I wanted you to be able to actually meet one or all of your siblings." Again, he stops talking and waits for my response; I just don't have a response to give. Not yet, anyway.

"I've found your Aunt Joyce, your uncle Stew's wife. She told me that most of the family has either moved away or they've died. I know that Kane died and I have a report that your sister Lovely Girl died when she was three years old, but I believe the rest of your brothers and sisters are still alive somewhere. I just need more time to find them." Walter grabs my hand and intertwines my fingers into his. His hands are very large and powerful. Walter has always made me feel like he should have worked in construction or furniture moving because he is so muscular and his hands are so thick. I think he looks a little strange holding a pencil when he is working. With my hand in his, I feel very small and submissive to him but I always feel safe with him. While I don't like the feeling of submission, I do like the feeling of security he gives. He stands up and pulls me up from my chair, he holds me in his arms again and this time I really like it. We stand like this enjoying the moment until Walter starts to pull away. Then without thinking about it, I tighten my hold on him. Fortunately he doesn't object. He pulls me back into him, and I snuggle into his chest as close as I can get to him and lay my head under his chin. I can hear his heart beating and feel

Chapter Twenty-One

his breath across my face. I feel safe and protected. This is a feeling I have never experienced before. I want to thank Walter for being here for me so I look up into the most beautiful blue eyes I have ever seen. It's like I'm seeing into Walter's eyes for the first time now. Snuggling back into his chest of safety I have to tell Walter some of the things I am feeling.

"Thank you, Walter. This means everything to me. I didn't think I would ever really find any of them. All I have ever known is that I had a brother named Honestly Sweet and one named Truely Grateful but I never knew their real names. I know that my mother left me with my grandmother and Aunt Birdie so she could go and pick up another brother, but that is all I have ever really known. Cousin Ruth told me as much as she knew which wasn't much. She said that she thought my grandmother was ashamed of my mother for having so many children and that was the reason why my Grandma Lucy never really talked about any of the children my mother had," I tell these things to Walter as tears run down my face on onto his shirt. He must have noticed his shirt getting wet and he lifts my chin to look into my face. I'm a little embarrassed for crying and I try to look away, but Walter holds my chin on his index finger. He kisses my forehead and before I know what I am doing, I kiss him. It isn't a short thank you kiss, but rather, it's a kiss with all the passion I have inside of me. It feels so natural to have my arms around his neck and my lips on his. Walter returns my affection and I'm happy. Once I put my heels back on the ground, and catch my breath, I look into Walter's face and see something there I haven't seen before in the eyes of anyone I have ever known. I see what love looks like. I feel it move inside of me and I now know what love feels like. I want to kiss him again, but as he lays his head back, he holds me tight and I am satisfied. We spend several moments holding each other; not saying anything.

CHAPTER 22

"Carl, she hasn't called you in over three weeks. She may never call you again if you don't pick up that phone and call her back."

"Mom, let me handle my own business. I'll call her when I get the time. I'm busy these days and she has Walter to take care of."

"Walter will come to his senses before it goes any farther, I'm sure he will end this thing. I talked to him the day he had his heart attack and I think...no, I believe, he is going to have Naturallee move out as soon as he is well enough to take care of himself.

"Mother the man went back to work weeks ago. I don't think... no, I don't believe he is going to have Naturallee move out as soon as he is well enough to take care of himself. What's that mother, you think that your ex-husband, John Morgan, whose dead brother, Martin Morgan, whose good friend Walter Mayfield, will just put my girlfriend out of the house they share because Uncle Martin was a friend. Didn't Walter tell you he wasn't about to let my girlfriend go the day he had the heart attack? That's right. My dead Uncle

Martin's good friend Walter Mayfield will do anything to fulfill the request of his dead BEST friend Nathan Grey. You see mother, best friends trump good friends every time, besides Walter wants her for himself." Carl looks straight into his mother and reminds her, "They have an arrangement that was put together by Nathan that states that if they live together for one full year they both get the majority of Nathan's estate. Naturallee will either walk away from the situation with more money than she even knew existed or she will gladly marry my Uncle Martin's good, but not best friend, Walter Mayfield and there is absolutely nothing I can do to stop this. Not if I want to get my portion of the money Uncle Nathan left me. Even though Nathan and dad were close friends for thirty five years and Walter and Uncle Martin were close friends, neither of those relationships could undercut the Grey/Mayfield union. I suppose I should be glad that Nathan even considered me as a nephew and left me anything in his will."

"You could have a bigger portion of the money if you would get over there and fight for Naturallee instead of giving her to Walter.'

"I don't understand you, mother, I thought you loved Walter like a brother. What has changed that?"

"Your father changed it when he divorced me after hiding most of the money we had, along with the business we built together all of those years. Nathan changed when he made that stupid arrangement for Walter and Naturallee. Walter changed when I asked him to do this for me and he led me to believe that he would, twice, only I find out that he is lying to me. And you've changed because you won't fight for her. All of you have changed and left me out of the plans.

"What do you mean Walter has lied to you twice? What are you talking about?

"I called Walter the night they started this...this arrangement and I begged him then to stop what he was doing. I asked him to just take that five million that Nathan had already left him and let her alone. I told him Naturallee was too young for him, that he was only making a fool of himself. He wouldn't have even found her as quickly as he did if I hadn't told him about the very beautiful girl you met at school finally and how I was hoping that you would actually call her and stop walking around here saying her name all day long. I even told him you brought her to Michael's birthday party. I liked her name a lot and I remembered it when I was talking to Walter. I should have known that something was up because he started making phone calls almost instantly when he was last here for a visit six months ago. We couldn't enjoy his company because he was on the phone for several hours. Walter hadn't been over to a football game party since Nathan died."

"What do you mean, you told Walter her name. You are the one who is causing me to lose my girlfriend. I'll bet if it were Michael you wouldn't have made such a mistake. You would never have told Walter or anyone else about who Michael was dating until you knew what Michael really wanted out of the relationship to make sure that nothing interfered with his happiness. But for my happiness you could tell the world and take the chance of me losing out." Words fell from Carl's lips like a car going ninety miles an hour over a cliff.

CHAPTER 23

Walter has told me a lot about Nathan Grey and my mother, but there always seems to be something that is said that keeps my attention to Walter's words. I find myself always waiting for that something else to be said when Walter stops talking. I would ask questions but I don't know what questions to ask, so I have to just listen and not really talk. If there is something more about my mother I have to trust that Walter will eventually tell me, if not I have to trust that Walter has a good reason why he hasn't told me.

"I'm sorry, Walter. What did you say?" I have drifted into my own thoughts again for the third time over dinner and Walter seems a little upset that I am not paying attention.

"Tonight may not be the best time to talk about this. Let's save that part of the conversation for next week, alright." Walter gives me an unhappy smile and then goes back to his dinner plate. After a few silent mouthfuls of dinner, Walter clears his throat and then says, "I'll need you to give me an answer by morning about the cards though," he never looks up from his plate of steak and potatoes. I made the dinner with all of the things that Walter likes. When I was cooking earlier, I had Walter on my mind, now; while I still have Walter on my mind I have other thoughts about him that keep my attention. These thoughts are coming between a perfectly good moment between Walter and me. I need to get my thoughts back to whatever Walter is saying especially if he wants an answer in the morning.

"I'm sorry. What did you say, Walter? I have some things on my mind and I guess I'm not really here for dinner. I apologize. Please forgive me," and I give a shy smile, but Walter has become impatient with me. He wants to finish the meal in quiet so that I can give my thoughts my full attention. I guess he figures that once I finish whatever thoughts I am having, then I can give him my full attention.

After all these months, Walter, I find, does have flaws. Walter doesn't like to be ignored, and Walter is a jealous man. He let me know that he doesn't like for me to give my attention to anyone or anything else when he's wants me to pay attention to him. I try to get him to tell me again what he has said, but he changes the topic and says we can try talking again before we close out the night. Dinner ends with lite conversation and no dessert. For the next couple of hours, Walter spends time in his room and I have the house to myself.

Since Walter has gone back to work full-time, I usually have this time of night to myself; although, tonight I feel lonely or at least I think I feel lonely. It might be that I am feeling alone because Carl is out of town. Maybe I will ask Walter if he knows anything about Carl when he comes back downstairs for the rest of our evening together. For now, all I can do is walk the pathway that runs through the doors and into the yard just like the path Nathan had put into the house that he shared with my mother. I can understand why Syvon liked having the path. It probably made her feel comforted at

Chapter Twenty-Three

times. It could have offered a kind of getaway from the things that haunted her. As I walk the path, I have time to think about what Syvon might really have been like. It's funny for as much as Walter has told me about her, I feel like there is so much more about her that I still don't know and usually I don't want to know until Walter starts talking. And then it hits me, that's what I need to ask Walter. It's what has been on my mind throughout dinner. I need to know who Syvon really was. I need to know my mother. And I want to know Walter Mayfield, too.

The path leads me to the grass at its end. Not far from where I stand, is the lake. I want to go to it, but I have a fear of the water and always have so I stay at the end of the path looking out and wanting more. I wonder if Syvon looked out and wanted more, too. When she voiced her wants, Nathan did what he could to get it. Walter hasn't done anything extra for me but I haven't asked for anything extra either though. I wonder what he would do if I did.

My mind goes back to the path which has beautiful flowers along its long straight bricks. Many of the flowers outside are the same ones inside the house. There is a bench and table at the end of the path shaded by two large trees but tonight there's no need for the trees but I sit on the bench anyway to enjoy the water from a distance. While the grass is green and lush it is also soft and cool under my feet. I want this path to stay in my life as much as I want my bedroom to always be mine. At this point of the agreement, unless something unforeseen happens, I guess the house is mine. I want the house but I also want my siblings to share it with. And the money is enticing as well. But that's more money than I have ever thought about so it still doesn't mean that much to me.

Syvon means more to me than she used to. I wish now that I had met her again before she passed away. The first letter from her that Walter gave me last week still stirs my heart. It makes me feel warm and comforted just knowing that she was sorry for the way she treated me.

Suspended

It also hurts to know that she was so messed up it made her treat all of us as badly as she did. I think about when Syvon used to burn me with cigarettes and more than once she slapped me so hard across my face that sometimes it gave me a black eye. I remember the time her gas had been turned off and there had been no water in the house and that, she said, was my fault. We were also stealing the electricity and cable television from one of the neighbors. The food that was being cooked the day the house burned down was from a store, but I am sure that she had stolen that like everything else. I also remember the food was just for Syvon, I was also sure that she had no intentions of sharing any of it with me. She told me that if I wanted to eat I would have to learn how to steal a meal for myself. At five years old, I didn't know where to steal food from so I stole it from her. I only made that mistake once. When my grandmother took me to the hospital I had to lie and say that I fell off my bike while riding down a hill. After that I didn't steal from Syvon again. I just went to bed hungry. She punched me in my stomach for waking her up when the house caught on fire for the second time from her passing out with food cooking on the hot plate. After punching me and leaving me on the floor while the house filled up with smoke, she refused to ride with me in the ambulance to the hospital. The hospital had to finally call my grandmother to pick me up when I was released the next day. Syvon never came to see about me and when I left the hospital, it was three weeks before I saw her again. Syvon came over to Grandma Lucy's to see if she could borrow some money. Grandma Lucy refused to give her money. When asked if she noticed that I was there, Syvon got angry and pushed me out of the way as she stormed out the door. After that I didn't see Syvon for months. I only saw her again because she and her boyfriend had moved into a condemned house a few houses down from my grade school. There were many days that I would see the two of them at the house smoking crack and drinking. One day, Syvon had passed out on the walkway leading up to the door of the abandoned

148

house. Remembering the time I woke her up when the house was on fire, I decided it would be best to let her sleep so I left her there. Fortunately, none of my schoolmates knew she was my mother and I never told them.

Aunt Birdie wanted to take me away from Syvon, but Grandma Lucy wouldn't let her. It turned out to be a good thing because Aunt Birdie wasn't much better to me than my mother was. I miss Uncle Stew. He was the only one other than Grandma Lucy that treated me like I was a living person. He used to tell me stories about God and angels and this place called heaven where everyone should want to go when they died. I never really understood what he was talking about. He would tell me things like *how good life would be when we all got there.* He'd say things like *we could live forever there and that there would never be anything like sickness or unhappiness,* and for a long time I wanted to go there. I looked for this place in the history book that I had in the fourth grade but I couldn't find it. I looked for it in magazines and especially at church because Uncle Stew told me that he'd learned about this stuff when he was in church one time. I wanted to go to church to see if I could find God and heaven or at the very least an angel or two, but I never saw God or any angels when I went to church with Uncle Stew. I asked him one Sunday where the angels were but he just laughed and said they were all around us. Then I heard a man say that Uncle Stew was a phony Christian because he always had a smile on his face and tried to help everybody. The man said he was sure that Uncle Stew had some skeletons in his closet and that it would just be a matter of time before they came out. I was afraid for a long time to go into any closet at Uncle Stew's house; I didn't want to be an angel anymore because if that man was an angel I didn't want to be that way. I also didn't want anything to do with God or heaven. I didn't want God to say anything bad about Uncle Stew and I didn't want to spend time with angels in heaven if they were like that man. I figured that God wasn't as great a God as Uncle Stew thought.

Suspended

Sitting here at the end of the path, I start to think about Walter again and how he thinks about things. I found out that Walter believes in God and he goes to church. Walter has some of the same ways as Uncle Stew had. Walter is kind and willing to help anyone. One evening, when we were returning home after our weekly dinner together, a man came up to the car and asked Walter for something to eat. The man said that he was diabetic and needed to eat and take his medicine. Walter looked up and saw a fast food restaurant a block away and told the man he would take him there and pay for him to get a meal. The man was very grateful and said he would walk to the restaurant because he was dirty and smelled and didn't want to mess up Walter's car. Walter wouldn't hear of it and made the man get in the car. Walter said the car could be cleaned if it needed it. When we got to the restaurant Walter actually paid for the man to eat three times a day for a month. Then Walter gave the man his card and told him to come and see him that next week. Walter did things like that all of the time. It made me think of Uncle Stew at those times because Uncle Stew would feed anyone who said they were hungry. I wonder if Walter believes in God and heaven and angels like Uncle Stew did. He probably does. After all, Walter goes to church at least twice a week, but he hasn't invited me and now I wonder why.

The evening has gotten away from me; it's late and I probably should return to the house and see if Walter is willing to talk. Then the cell phone rings; I forgot I had it with me. I pull it from my pocket and check to see who is calling me, it's Walter.

"Hello, Walter. Is everything alright," I ask then wait for his answer.

"Yes, everything is fine, but where are you? I've checked every room in this house and I can't find you. Are you still here at home?"

I don't know why that sounds so good to me when Walter ask if I'm at home. "Yes, I'm still home, but I'm not in the house. I am on the path, at the end of it actually." Then I wait for him to speak. For a moment there's silence then Walter finds his words as any good attorney does.

"What are you doing on the path? Are you alright? Do you need me to come out and help you?" I wonder what he would help me with. I didn't say I was hurt or sick. Why would I need help? Before I can respond to his questions Walter breaks into my thoughts and says the question was a little foolish. Then the phone falls quiet. Walter is waiting for me to say something but I'm not sure what so I break the odd silence and ask if he would come out and join me. It must have been what he wanted to hear because Walter was on the path before we ended the call.

As he marches his way toward me, I notice the way Walter walks with his back straight and his head up, not in a cocky, arrogant way, but in a confident manner that says he is well aware of all that goes on around him. He is sure that he can handle any situation that comes before him. The slacks that hang just slightly below his waist are black and double pleated adding to the desiring look of Walter Mayfield. His shirt always tucked into his slacks and opened at the collar unless he is going in to the office. As he gets closer to me, I can see the distinguished framework of this well kept man. He has run his fingers through his hair and it is a bit out of place. In one hand, Walter has two glasses and in the other he has a bottle of wine and something else, probably sparkling water for me, and I wonder what the occasion for celebrating is. When Walter stops in front of me I see he has a huge smile on his face and he hands me the sparkling water and a glass.

"What's this all about," I can't help but ask.

"I have good news," is all he says and my curiosity is peaked. Walter takes in a deep breath and releases it. He puts his arms out from his sides and his head back. He starts thanking God for everything and I'm amazed at his words. Why was Walter so thankful to God? He seems genuinely happy so I let him have his moment.

Suspended

He finally goes quiet and sits down on the beautiful, white painted iron bench that sits on the side of the path here at the end of it. The trees, the bench, the water, all of it is so soothing, so relaxing, and so inviting. Maybe that's what Walter is so excited about, after all, I don't think Walter has ever been this far out away from the house, he usually stays closer to the house. I stand over him waiting for an explanation. While I wait, I notice how thick and beautifully black and gray speckled his hair is in the moon light. I want to touch his hair. I guess it's just another one of those things about Walter that makes me have unusual thoughts about him. I have thoughts about Walter that I haven't had about Carl. I really like Carl, and I still want Carl to call me, but I don't feel the same way about him anymore like I do about Walter. I think too much time has passed and Carl still hasn't called. There it is. I've admitted it and I am a bit surprised at myself. Yes, I think about holding Walter's hand and walking this path with him for hours. I think about watching a tear jerking movie with him and crying on his shoulder until his shirt is drenched with my tears. I want to talk with Walter and tell him everything I think, everything I feel, and everything I have ever wanted. I want him to know my dreams, my hopes, and my fears. Until this very moment, I didn't realize that I had fears deep enough to want to share. While I have concerns about me and the direction my life is going, I've never accepted the idea that I have real fears, but right now I know that I do. I realize that I don't want to be alone anymore, and when all of this is over I could be, and this is something I do fear. I fear that my first relationship with a man is over before it got started. I fear that Walter could die and I would not have taken the opportunity to tell him all the things I love about him and all the things I feel. Then I start to drift up and fear grips me with strength stronger than me. I have fear swelling up inside of me so powerful that it has my back pressed against the tree and my chest has a strong hand pressing in on me so hard I can't breathe. The air is so thin that my head spins and I close my eyes to die.

Chapter Twenty-Three

But then Walter's very heavy voice splits the air and crashes me back down beside him, and quickly I hide what has just happened with an inquiry to Walter, Walter, what's all this excitement about? I don't think I've ever seen you quite so happy," even though I am trying to pull myself together, I still want to know. Walter doesn't look up; he just sits on the bench with that little boy in the candy store smile on his face.

"How would you like to take a little trip with me?" Walter is very excited. I can see it in his eyes. He is so giddy he can hardly contain himself. Finally, he jumps up and grabs my hands and squeezes them tightly. I'm excited for him.

"What is it? Tell me before you burst, Walter." While I am excited for him, I'm becoming impatient. I need to know now.

"Well, where do I start? "

"The beginning is always a good place to start." I just need him to tell me something to feed my curiosity.

"About nine years ago, Nathan and I were vacationing in Jamaica. We got lost in the city and ended up on the wrong side of town. We found ourselves face to face with some men who wanted to rob us and probably kill us. They had just started to beat up on us when this older guy and woman with two younger guys came out of nowhere with guns and put a stop to it. They took me and Nathan into their home, which wasn't very much at all, just a couple of rooms that included a kitchen and one bedroom. It had this really tiny sitting room that had a couple of stools to sit on and a small table close to the floor. They didn't have very much to eat but they shared it with us. They patched us up as best they could and had us stay the night to make sure we didn't get into anymore situations before they could get us back to our hotel that next day. We of course, were extremely grateful. Nathan asked what could we do to thank them for their help and hospitality, but they wouldn't take anything for their Good Samaritanship. Nathan wouldn't let it go. After we got back to our hotel, Nathan had the people looked into and found out that they were a family that was known for doing what they did for us. They also were big supporters of an orphanage there that was struggling badly. Of course, Nathan had to go and see the place before we left. The place was in shambles. No running water, the roof had parts of it missing, the kitchen was overrun with flies and the smell was unbearable, but the kids, all thirty-six of them had a place to be. They weren't living on the street which would have been worse than living at the orphanage. This family that had helped us gave all of their time and most of their money to help these children. If you knew anything about Nathan, you knew he couldn't leave that place without doing something to help them. We found the family that had helped us and asked what we could do to help the children. They gave us a list of things they thought would help. Nathan quickly had someone from his organization there within a couple of days to oversee building a new orphanage and getting the right people in there to run it.

The more I hear about Nathan Grey, the more I like him, which means the more I like about Walter. There is very little Nathan did that didn't include Walter's help or inspiration. Walter always tells the stories as if it was always just Nathan, but I have come to know that many times Walter had spearheaded the help effort. "You two were something else; you did all of these things without any recognition, and without expecting anything in return. I find that so amazing," is all I can say to Walter. *Your efforts are so exciting and attractive is what I think to myself.* Carl has never done anything so selfless for another person and neither have I, but being more like Walter is the way I want to be. It's the way I want to live. Being with Walter is making me see who it is I want to be. I can see that my life could really have purpose and I like the idea of that, "...and why are you so happy?" I ask Walter, feeling like there is more to the story.

"OK, Nathan and I have always kept in touch with the people there. A few years ago things over there started to get ugly. Killings

Chapter Twenty-Three

and rapes were happening all of the time. Kids were being taken from their families as well as from the orphanages to be sold on the black market. Boys were extremely valuable for working, but the little girls were sold as sex slaves, girls as young as seven. When we found out what was happening, we wanted to get everyone out. Nathan died before we could even get it started. I had to take care of those things concerning Nathan's death and that caused me to put things on hold for a little while, but I never forgot about any of them. Then a couple of months ago I got a letter from Mrs. Billy, the woman of the family that had helped Nathan and I that night, she said that things were even worse than before, and that the people that had been running the orphanage had been killed. She and her family had taken as many of the children as they could and ran away. The Billys were living with relatives in a nearby town but they would have to find someplace else to go. She said they needed help and wanted to know if Nathan and I could help in any way.

"Where are they now, and is there anything you can do?" But before the words get out of my mouth I know this is the reason Walter is so happy. He has done something to help; I just need to hear what that something is.

"Well, thank God; tonight they are all safe because they are all on American soil. Nathan and I have been able to work with their government to get the Billy family and all of the twenty-seven kids that were still with the Billys out of their country legally. They are on their way to a home in Miami that Nathan and I had bought a couple of years ago when we first wanted to bring them all here. I want to go and meet them. That's the way Nathan would have wanted it done. I hope that you will come with me."

I am so overwhelmed with admiration for this man. "Walter I don't know anyone who has ever done something so selfless like this before." I look into Walter's face and see the stressful lines that had become usual across his forehead are less noticeable now. With the soft breeze blowing, his hair lifts and falls with the rhythm of my heart beat, and even though the sun set hours ago and the light of the moon peeks through with the movement of the leaves of the tree, I can still see the deep blue of his eyes. Walter looks so happy, but not for what he has done, he looks genuinely happy for the people he has just helped.

"Nathan and I have done no more than what any of us are suppose to do for our fellow man," Walter says in a very matter-of-fact way. "Someone once did something even greater than this for me and all he asks is that we pay it forward."

"Who," I ask puzzled over who it could be.

"Jesus gave his life for me, for all of us, the least I can do is try to help someone else." Walter smiles really big again, and before I know it, I want what he has. I feel a little ashamed for desiring what another person has. I have never wanted what someone else had before and the feeling made me feel a little uncomfortable.

"Will you come with me," Walter asks again and I can't imagine how I can say no to him right now. He wants me with him and I want to be there to support him in all of his joy. Yes, I want to support him in his joy this time, but the next time Walter is this happy, I will be sharing his joy. This I promise myself.

"Of course, I will go with you. I wouldn't miss it for anything." I give Walter a hug and for some strange but natural reason, I entwine my fingers into his and walk off the path and onto the grass leading him and taking myself to the water's edge. Walter doesn't take his hand away nor does he refuse the short journey. We walk together in silence but we are both happy.

We spend the better part of an hour at the lake walking around it and talking about other things that Nathan and Walter have done with their lives, things that always seem to involve helping others. I can tell that Walter has lived a very rewarding life and that Walter is a very humble man. He always remembers to say that it isn't him who does all of these things, he just follows orders and gets them done.

Chapter Twenty-Three

As we start to walk back to the path, I'm aware that we are still holding hands, and I think to myself that we must have let go of each other at some point, but I can't promise myself that we did. When we get to the edge of the path, Walter stops and turns me to him. He wants to say something, but then changes his mind and gives me a big hug. It's late and Walter doesn't think he can sleep so we spend a little more time talking about different things that he and Nathan did over their lifetime, funny things they did in college and how they were always there for each other. Sitting in the yard on the swing he tells me how they both used to spend Thanksgiving at different soup kitchens throughout the city, and always left anonymous financial gifts at that soup kitchen for Christmas. They couldn't spend Christmas feeding the homeless because they were at the hospital playing Santa Claus to the sick and dying. They started a jobs program for the inner city youth, but they closed it down when they found out that the ones running it only gave the jobs to their kids and kids of their friends. Walter and Nathan pressed criminal charges against them and they made sure that the community knew what those responsible had done making it almost impossible for them to get a job anywhere for years.

Then Walter tells me something I didn't know even though we have lived together all these months. Walter goes to church every Sunday morning and he attends a bible study class every Tuesday evening. It's something that he and Nathan both did for twenty-nine years. They attended the same church and Walter still goes there. He is a moderator now and he has been on every board the church has ever had. Walter even sang in the morning choir, taught Sunday school, and was a youth group leader. He and Nathan used to take the young men of the church to the annual church conventions across the country as well as camping trips in the fall. This man amazes me more and more with everything he says.

He tells me how glad he is that I'll be going with him to Florida. We leave the yard and walk to the house in silence. At the door of the house, Walter kisses my forehead and says good night. He's still not ready to go in. I'm tired so I go into the house with some of the words Walter has said to me as my company. I feel proud to know this man. Walking up the stairs, I think about my first time coming up to my room. I ran so fast up the stairs I missed the beauty of the stairway. I also missed the fascinating pictures that line the wall all the way up to the top nor did I notice the word forgiveness at the bottom right corner of each painting. The elegance of the crystal and gold chandelier that hangs at the bottom of the stairs is something else I missed that night as well.

Tonight the house is like new; like I am seeing it for the first time. I see things so differently after talking to Walter. As I enter into my bedroom, I know that I want to do things differently in my life. I want my life to count for something; I just don't know how to do that. Tomorrow I'll have to talk to Walter and ask him what I can do to make that happen.

Going from my bedroom to my closet off the bathroom and turning on the light, I notice something else that I hadn't noticed before. Right behind the coats that hang at the far end of the closet just about eye level to me is a small brass box with a glass knob that fades into the wallpaper. The box is about the size of a mason brick, maybe that's why I haven't noticed it before. Walking closer to this newfound surprise I see that there is something written on it. I stand directly in front of this odd discovery wondering if I should open it or go and ask Walter about it. I decide that I can open it by myself, and so I reach for this bit of unknown curiosity.

When I pull at the knob, it feels strange in my hand and I pull my hand away. I think to myself that maybe I should go and get Walter. It takes me a minute to get my nerve up, but I do, and I reach for the small glass knob again. This time when I pull it, it opens and slowly I open the little door and look in. Inside the tiny mason brick-like, brass box is a key that is in a keyhole in the wall. It's an odd thing to see, but then my life has been odd since I met Walter Mayfield.

Chapter Twenty-Three

Should I turn the key? I'm not sure, again, so I wait. I'm not sure of what I'm waiting on, but I think it is best to wait just the same. While I wait I ask myself, how is it that I've missed this brass brick for so long. I have lived in this house for more than seven months and I've entered this closet at least once each morning and once each night and this is the first time I've noticed it. The wallpaper is a royal purple and rich gold print. The border is white and purple with specks of gold in it. Maybe the beauty of the room has kept my attention all this time. But the box is here behind my collection of coats and jackets, perhaps that could be the reason why I haven't seen it.

When I come back from the thought of trying to figure out why I haven't seen this before, I see that my hand is on the key ready to turn it. Surprised and a bit scared of my decision to move forward with the turning of the key, I see both the key and the box are far off now. The coats are out of reach and I am at the top of the closet with beads of sweat on my top lip. I can't feel my feet on the floor or hand on the key any longer. I am going up farther and farther. But this time it's different because I can't see a thing and I hear the roar of a train all around me. I black out.

CHAPTER 24

When I awaken, I am on the closet floor. My blouse is still wet with sweat and I feel exhausted as if I had just finished one of Walter's morning runs. Pulling myself up off the floor I remember what I was doing before I blacked- out. I look up to my right where the brass box was and I see that it is still where I remember it. The small door is open and the key is still inside in the keyhole. With a made-up mind and little regard for what might happen, I quickly get up, reach for the key and turn it. I hear a click and then a pop. Looking down in the direction of the click, I see another door swing open but this one is at the bottom of the closet near the floor. It's a safe about two...two and a half feet tall, with the name Syvon Grey inscribed on the top ledge of it. I'm surprised and step back as if spiders are about to jump out and eat me. Once I clear my head, and assure myself that nothing like that will happen, I step back up, reach down and open the safe door. Bending down and peeking in, I see money, papers, and jewelry on the top shelf. There must be ten to fifteen thousand dollars just laying in the safe and several of those brown legal size sealed envelopes as well, three with no names on them, and five with names that had been mailed and returned to Syvon. There are five additional envelopes with only a return address on them; no mailing address had been added. Some of the envelopes seem to have only one sheet of paper in them while other envelopes may have ten or more. There are envelopes to some of my brothers and sisters, at least I think they are for my brothers and sisters, and there is an envelope that's addressed to Birdie Sessions, and one to Uncle Stew's wife, Joyce. There are several that are addressed to names I don't know. There is an envelope for me.

On the bottom of the safe is a hand crafted jewelry box from China. Syvon's name is on this as well. The writing is very elegant. I run my finger over the writing and feel the smooth texture of the material used to write out her name. This jewelry box looks a lot different from the jewelry boxes that I'm used to seeing. This one is about twelve inches long and eight inches wide and about three inches deep. The carving on the top around Syvon's name and on the sides of it is done in great detail. The latch that keeps it together is of soft gold and it, too, is smooth with a fancy design on it.

I open the jewelry box slowly to make sure that I don't disturb what's inside. Whatever is in it, lies on an expensive red silk cloth with bits of gold embedded into it which I see as I crack the lid. Then like the sunrise coming up over the Grand Canyon, the incredible beauty of what's inside explodes before me. I've never seen anything as captivating as this before in my life, not even on television. The inside of the box is lined with miniature white lights that add to the brilliance of the powerful, flawless, custom cut, eight karat diamond that is surrounded by a dozen smaller pear shaped diamonds all mounted in the center of the box. The gold-speckled red silk cloth causes the stone to shimmer against the light in a way that keeps my eyes paralyzed on it.

Chapter Twenty-Four

I feel my right hand go to my neck as though I can feel the strength of this jewel against me. The allure of its dazzling brilliance has me so captivated that I missed the moment when Walter touched my shoulder. When I realize I'm not alone, I can only ask him how long he's been here. I can't look away to see his face. I take my middle finger of my right hand and traced the stone. Walter has the same desire pulling at him because he too, traces the diamond with his finger on top of mine.

"Where did you get this exquisite stone from?" Walter's voice sounds strange and distant, even though he is standing so close to me that his chest touches my shoulder as he reaches around me to feel the magnificent stone in my hand. Walter isn't wearing his shoes but I am wearing mine, so he doesn't seem to be so much taller than I am now and this put his mouth closer to my ears; I lean back into him a bit before I catch myself.

"Where did you get this Naturallee? Where did this come from? Is it yours? Did you buy it today?" Walter's questions come like debris flying around in a tornado. The lawyer side of him is showing up. I am finally able to take my eyes off of the exceptional find I just made. I look into Walter's deep blue eyes and the smell of his cologne seeps into my nose and causes me to remember our first and only kiss. The memory of it makes me forget about the stone. All I see now is what I want. It isn't Carl's young, inviting face with his soft brown eyes that I want any longer. I'm frozen in amazement that I'm fixated on the face of a much older man that has me locked in his gaze and the stone no longer has the power it had a moment ago. A feeling starts to rise up in me that I have not felt before. From the lower part of my insides I feel like I want to hold onto this man and never let him go. His eyes are more precious to me than the stone I'm holding.

Looking into Walter's eyes I can't speak until I hear him speak my name again and I feel his hand on my arm. The stone, the thoughts of what my mother must have meant to Nathan and how much he loved her all of it has my mind jumping across fences and chasing butterflies, so to speak. But all of this is a distant second to what I am feeling toward Walter right now.

"Naturallee, where did it come from?" Walter asks again with a bit of force in each word, and it makes me snap out of my trance.

"The safe," I hear the words falling from my lips as if they were cascading down a waterfall, but I still can't make myself pull my attention away from Walter's probing stare.

"What safe?" Walter asks as he surveys my closet first scanning the row of blouses lined just above my head. Then he lowers his eyes to the pants I have acquired since I first moved into the house. I haven't realized how much spending I have done until now. As I follow Walter's search around my closet to the wall of mirrors, pictures, and shelves I suddenly remember my closet at my apartment and realize that it wasn't even as big as my bathroom here at the house and I know that I don't want to go back to the apartment. I want to keep what I have, or at least what I could have here. It's not just the things that I have here but I also want to keep Walter. I want to keep things the way they are for the rest of my life.

Walter sees the safe. "Where did this come from?" I hear him ask as he kneels down to look inside. At first he only looks inside, surprised at all that is inside of it. The safe has depth to it and there is more inside than what I first saw. Walter starts to pull more things out of it. There is more jewelry, papers and envelopes. Walter pauses, then draws his hand back and sits on the floor as if he has lost all the breath he had inside of him. He puts his hand over his eyes and slides it down his face as if he could pull away that which he has just found in the safe. Then he lets out a deep sigh and shakes his head. I'm frightened there could be a big problem he is about to reveal to me and I start to brace myself for the words when his shoulders start to shake and I hear small sounds coming from Walter. I reach for his shoulder, but before I touch him, he lets out a roar of laughter and claps his hands together vigorously.

Chapter Twenty-Four

"Can you believe Nathan kept this," and he reaches for something in the safe as his entire body vibrates with laughter. Shaking his head while reaching for it, Walter pulls out a small, Hawaiian grass skirted, lay wearing plastic male doll. The doll has a missing foot and one arm has black marker all over it. Walter continues to laugh as he holds it up to look at.

"It's Macho Man, and since Nathan isn't here to challenge me his name is Macho Man Nathan Grey. He was Nathan's hero, Nathan wanted to be just like him," Walter says and continues to laugh for just a few more moments, then the laughter starts to fade followed by the melting away of the wide smile and the twinkle in his eyes until nothing is left but a tear in the inside corners of Walter's eyes. Now the closet is filled with sadness and the surprising laughter that was once all Walter had to offer is gone. Walter just sits on the floor now staring at the little plastic man he calls Macho Man. I wonder why Walter has changed to this pile of hurt and pain here at my feet.

Walter's sexy disheveled look just hours ago has become a vision of an older, confused and lost man, a man I don't recognize. I want to wrap my arms around him and tell him everything is going to be alright. I want him to know that the little plastic man can't hurt him, but I don't move. I can't say a word. I just stand there just over Walter's shoulder peering into his hair and thinking how much grayer it is right now as compared to the slightly gray look this morning. What is it Macho Man? Has his coming out of the safe somehow aged Walter? I have questions rushing around inside my head faster than I can answer any of them. I can't even complete a thought before the next one enters my head. I want to say something to Walter, but what, what could make a difference to him right now. There is nothing to say I finally decide so I sit on the floor beside Walter and wait for him to speak again.

Somewhere in the wee hours of the morning we both fell asleep because when we wake we have slept together on the closet floor. I have never felt like this before. The emotions inside me are new and frighteningly wonderful. I have always kept my mind away from moments like this but this morning has caught me off guard. How will Walter feel about me if he knew my desires right now? I don't stir not wanting to wake Walter. Also, I find myself pinned to the floor at least until Walter moves in the other direction, and I hope that doesn't happen. For someone whom I never met, Nathan Grey knew this much about me. Then Walter shifts his position away from me and my heart drops a little. But it does help to clear my head and I slide away from him. Although I am still lying on the closet floor, I watch him sleep and wonder what his dreams are. I suppose he is dreaming about the kids from the orphanage and the Billys all in Florida. All safe and on American soil. I think I love this man. I don't want to admit but I think I love this man and I want him to know it.

"Are you going to watch me sleep all morning or what," Walter whispers.

I blink hard at the realization that he's awake and aware that I am watching him. I wonder if he has been able to read my thoughts as well. I feel embarrassed but I can't move and I can't speak. I listen to Walter speaking but I'm not sure what he is saying, my mind is only able to think about how much I love him and how much I want him to know how I feel.

Then, without warning, as Walter is speaking, he reaches for me and finds my left thigh and now I find myself four years old again and frightened. My mother's drug dealer's nephew is in the room touching my thigh. The scars on his face and hands frighten me so much that I can't move; I don't think I can blink my eyes. He just sits there with his hand on my thigh looking at me with one regular eye and one big eye that has no eye lid; that eye never blinks, I'm sure of that. His hair is short and missing is some spots and he is still touching my thigh. This man with the one big eye doesn't say a word to me whenever his is there and that's whenever my mother

Chapter Twenty-Four

needed her drugs. His drug dealing uncle brings him along every time he comes to bring Syvon her drugs. I hear Syvon in the next room telling the drug dealer how much she likes her drugs and that I will like it too, once I get used to the feeling. But I think I will never get used to the feeling of his crumpled hand on my thigh; his hand is hard and rough and scaly, it reminds me of dead dry fish Grandma Lucy would spend the day catching on the river bank. I don't want to get used to this man with the one big eye, I want to leave this room but he won't take his hand from my thigh. Syvon told me that if I cried she would beat me to death and I would never cry again. I had been beaten by Syvon before so I didn't want that to happen either so I don't cry but I have to get away. The only way I can get away from this man with the one big eye is to go up to the ceiling. The man with the one big eye is short and won't be able to reach me there so I tell myself to go up so I can get away, and I do. Here at the top of the room I can't feel his hand on my thigh anymore and I can't see his one big eye; I feel safe up here. The last time I felt him touch me with his scaly hand moving over my skin and him looking so deep into me that I couldn't breathe and I thought I would die. But he must have seen the fear inside of me because he jumped up and left the room quickly slamming the door against the wall running past my mother and the drug dealer. Fortunately Syvon already had her drugs so she didn't notice how upset he was when he left and that was the first time I was ever suspended.

I want Walter to love me but I can't have his hand on my thigh, he has to stop. I want his love but he has to keep his hands to himself. Maybe he can put his hand on my arm but ....but he has to stop touching my thigh. NOW. I feel the pressure rising up inside me; I need him to take his hand off my leg. Walter is saying something to me but I can't listen. Fear has me and I can't get away from it and I see the one- eyed man again. I can't open my eyes; he might be standing there looking at me. He may want to kill Walter, after all, I always believed that he wanted to kill me when he looked at me. I try to move away from Walter; tears sting my eyes before running down my cheeks and I've stopped breathing; I am dying! I love this man Walter, I want him to love me but this won't work. I hear myself say his name and then everything stops. Then finally, Walter's hand is no longer on my thigh.

"I shouldn't have told you all of that. This isn't right, not for you. That isn't who I am. It's certainly not who I think you are. You have to have the time you need to make up your own mind. I respect you too much to pressure you in this way." Walter sits up and pulls his knees to his chest before crossing his arms over his knees and resting his chin on his forearms. His eyes are closed and he says nothing.

My relief is so great I can't say a word either. But, out of nowhere, I see my hand on Walter's back and I feel myself rubbing his shoulders. What's worse; this feels right for me to do, but I can't say anything to Walter; my lips are stuck together, my hands work but my lips won't. Walter must be enjoying the moment because he doesn't move as a matter of fact I feel him relax a little as his back goes from a firm angle to a bit of a bowed back position. Finally, I find the rest of my body and sit up next to him. We don't talk; we simply get up together and walk out of the closet that was our bedroom for the night as we hold on to each other.

CHAPTER 25

MaLyce Peoples loves her husband, but he isn't takeout material. Truely Grateful Peoples doesn't like movies or shirts with ties or combing his hair, or restaurants that only serve him one meal; he likes smorgasbords. Truely doesn't like crowds, either so MaLyce spends much of her time single as a married woman. She has only four girlfriends that she trusts and all four are in Vegas while she sits in the doctor's office with her third youngest child for the second time in as many weeks. Seventeen and clumsy; the thought takes her back to the day she met his father, Truely. They were both waiting for a bus to take them to a new city. Neither of them knew where they wanted to go, they just knew they each needed to leave town before the town ate them alive.

Truely wanted out for many, many good reasons. He hated knowing the truth about his mother and the fact that he didn't know who his father was. The fact that his mother named him Truely Grateful because she was truely grateful that he didn't look as black and ugly as his father did chipped away at him constantly. The fact that he never knew his father and his mother walked away from him when he was nine years old after biting him close to death left a deep hole inside of him that nothing was able to fill until that day at the bus station seven chairs away from the women's bathroom.

Malyce Miller was nineteen, beautiful and sexy and she well knew it. Even today as she sits waiting for the nurse to call her son's name. She remembers how she could turn heads back then. The memory makes her smile and helps her to settle in the uncomfortable doctor's office chairs as she and Truely's son, Winston sits in waiting as the second set of fifteen minutes creep to an end. Malyce returns to her memories to avoid going back up to the receptionist's window. She lets her memories take her back to the first time she saw Truely Grateful Peoples. He was sitting in a chair at the bus station with a can of red pop in one hand and a hot dog with mustard, relish and onions on it in the other. Both the hotdog and the pop dropped at the same time when he reached for his newspaper while trying to keep his eyes on the message board as the next bus cancellation was being posted. Truely grabbed for the pop on its way to the floor but he was obviously not athletic because he didn't catch it. Instead, he knocked the can into the air forcing the can of red liquid fizz to splash out in midair then onto Malyce's shirt and pants, and into her face.

After apologizing continuously, Truely tried to clean the pop from Malyce's face only to realize too late that he was also removing her make-up, as well. While apologizing for that mistake, he starts to brush the pop from her white shirt with the paper towel that had the make-up on it. He had brushed across the shirt several times before he noticed his third mistake; at that point he finally stopped and sat down. Malyce fell in love with Truely Grateful at that very moment.

They sat in the Greyhound Bus station for fourteen hours talking, and every few hours Truely apologized, until they realized they wouldn't be able to leave town until the afternoon of the next day at the earliest. They would have to spend the night on the floor with the rest of the stranded travelers the late season winter storm had displaced. Hungry and tired, Truely offered Malyce the opportunity to go back to his house with him and stay there until the busses were running again.

"Winston Peoples," the nurse said waiting at the open door with Winston's chart in hand, but MaLyce is too far away in thought to hear her.

"Mom, mom it's my turn. I need you to help me up, please," Winston snaps his fingers in her face and calls his mother once more before she is able to return to the doctor's waiting room. The pain in Winston's stomach had increased while MaLyce was in her daydream.

"Oh, I'm so sorry sweetheart, here lean on me." She helps her son to the door and hands him off to the nurse. Winston had stopped MaLyce from going back to the patient's room with him when he was twelve. As Winston's mother passes him off to the shoulder of the nurse, a wave of concern takes the place of reminiscing in her thoughts and Malyce wonders if the doctor will find out what is really making her son sick. Just last week she had spent two afternoons in this very office. Over the past several weeks their oldest twin Mark had become sluggish to the point of not being able to get out of bed until late afternoon. For a kid who made all-city three years in a row for his football skills, getting up after noon and unable to eat didn't fit.

"That's reminds me, they never called with the results," MaLyce says just under her breath then heads up to the window only to have the receptionist tell her that the nurse will have to come out to speak with her when the she gets the chance.

Sitting back in her chair Malyce closes her eyes and whispers a short prayer to God. As she thanks God in advance for His help, she is startled by the quick kiss that's placed on her forehead. Truely sits quickly in the chair next to his wife and squeezes her hand.

Suspended

"How long has he been in there," Truely asks, a little out of breath. Looking at his watch and realizing he only has twenty nine minutes left for his lunch break, Truely drags his hands down across his face pulling at his graying well trimmed-beard. At forty-two Truely is still the best-looking man in a room, MaLyce thinks, as she looks into the face of her tired husband. If she didn't know Truely and saw him in a line up with other well- distinguished men in three piece suits and he was in his work "Tee's" and a pair of jeans that fit snug around his hips, MaLyce always said she would still have to say Truely was the best-looking, most sexy man in the entire line. After twenty years of marriage, her husband still caused a deep stirring within her. And where did he get those beautiful green eyes? MaLyce wanted to thank whichever relative it was that gave him that gift. She also wanted to thank whoever it was because if it had not been for them, her twin sons Mark and Mitchell would not have received the gift either. MaLyce felt sorry, sometimes, for Winston. After all, Winston is just a typical looking seventeen-year old boy, but her twins are desired by all the girls and admired by their male friends. The twins are like their father in so many ways; athletic, intelligent, sexy and have an aura of success that commands attention. A mother couldn't be prouder of her children, all of her children. Even though Winston doesn't possess the qualities of his father, Truly, like Mark and Mitchell do, MaLyce is still very proud of her youngest son especially for not letting the success of the twins overshadow his life. Winston is very secure in who he is, and this puts a smile on Malyce's face.

"Sweetheart," Truely nudges his wife's arm like a little boy after the candy in his mother's pocket, "How long has Winston been in there?"

"He just went back about three minutes ago. Why don't you see if he will let you go in with him, you know I can't. He thinks he is too old for his mother to be in the room with him." MaLyce hopes Truely will say he will, and he does.

Chapter Twenty-Five

Alone again with only her thoughts to sit with her, MaLyce drifts back to her early days with Truely. Truely has only ever asked one thing of his wife and she has only had to keep that request to keep her husband happy. MaLyce loves her husband and she knows how much he loves her. And, if she doesn't ask anything about his past he will give her all she asks for; all that is within reason that is. She could have even been in Vegas at this very moment if it had not been for Winston getting sick.

Her thoughts take her back to that night at the bus station when they left and went to his house. She can still see the plain little home Truely had made for himself. There were no pictures on the wall, no color in the rooms. It was simply a place to lay his head. Truely didn't even have a set of matching sheets. The refrigerator was still stocked with food and there was enough food in the cabinets that lasted them several days. Even though the bathroom was clean like the rest of the house it, too, was plain making it more sterile than livable. Truely had told MaLyce he had had enough. He said his only choices were leaving town or suicide which he had seriously considered the night before. Truely told MaLyce all she has ever been told about his past that night; they never spoke of it again.

Once more, her walk down memory lane is interrupted by Truely, and Winston who is with him walking better, relieved of some of the pain. Truely stops in front of his wife and gives her a big smile. He reaches for her hand to help her up and says, "Let's go, I'll tell you about it when I get home tonight."

CHAPTER 26

The passing of Kane has had a real effect on Mercy. Mercy has not had a drink in over two years and has held the same job for the past eight months. Wrapping his apron strings around his waist and then tying it over his stomach, Mercy sings his favorite song as he closes the door to his new apartment and heads off to his job at the restaurant. He pats his pockets for his keys again then tucks his chef's hat under his arm. Not wanting to let pride override humility, Mercy fights with himself to keep his happiness at a respectable smile. "Mr. Bailey was right, there is a God and God has been gracious to me," Mercy says to himself while skipping down the steps to the sidewalk. Taking one last glance back at the window to his first floor, 525.00 dollars a month, newly acquired and newly furnished home, Havesome Mercy Peoples shakes his head as if to shake off the disbelief of the blessings he has been given lately. *Macy's is the nicest restaurant in town and it pays well; it also helps to have a manager who understands Alcoholics Anonymous and those who meet behind the very private doors. Man, Bailey knew what he was talking about for sure.* Mercy continues to the bus stop with his words spoken only in his mind. After being an admitted alcoholic, people might just mistake his happiness for drunkenness and his talking to himself as crazy and have him arrested. Any other day that might be alright to put up with, but not today. *Today is my first day as head lunch chef at Macy's Restaurant and I don't want to let anyone down, including myself,* Mercy continues to himself. Humility is something Mercy is trying to integrate into his life because Mr. Bailey once told him the importance of humility. The fact that he no longer participates in drinking with the guys, or drinking alone for that matter, is something else he wants to stay humble and committed to. Mercy saw firsthand what drinking and drugs can do to a person's life and now that he has family, he doesn't want it to happen to him.

The day they found Kane it was almost too late to get to know him. When Hellinher called to say that she had found their brother Kane, Kane was in the last stages of dying. Too much drinking and drugging for far too long took from Kane the opportunity to get to know Mercy, their brother Righteous Child, who legally changed his name to Ronald, and their sisters Hellinher and Surely Fine.

Walking to the bus stop, Mercy's mind slips back to that first wonderful day he met his siblings Ronald Charles Peoples, Surely Fine Peoples Wellesley and Hellinher Peoples Thompson. Surely had called from the Family Services office, where she worked, to say that someone had suggested she give him a call because she was in need of a good chef for an important dinner that she and her husband were hosting. She said that Havesome Mercy Peoples had come highly recommended. Mercy felt obligated to tell her that he was having some personal problems and wasn't sure he could keep the commitment but Surely convinced him to meet with her anyway. When Mercy got to the address he had been given, he was introduced to Surely, Hellinher and Ronald. Whom Surely had already found. Surely told them that day that she believed she had found Kane but that they would have to move fast; if she was right in who she found this brother didn't have much time left. Surely knew Kane was dying. Three days later the four of them were standing at Kane's hospital bed introducing themselves to him. At that time, the doctors had given him up for dead saying he was in his last few days. But after meeting some of his family he seemed to have a reason to live. Kane lived seven months longer than the doctors had thought and when he died all four of them were there.

Before he died, Havesome Mercy, Ronald (Righteous Child named at birth) and Kane spent an afternoon together trying to piece whatever parts of their past together they could. Three green-eyed men with three strange names and all born in the same city over the course of thirteen years born to a woman whose name was unusual but as beautiful as she was. They were born to a woman who left one of her daughters at age three, at a hospital when she said she was visiting a sick friend; Babydoll spent the rest of her childhood years in foster care. Kane was simply left at home until a neighbor finally decided to call the police after listening to him cry for two whole days. Syvon left Havesome Mercy and Hellinher at a gas station when they were four years old. Yes, Mercy thought to himself, *I have more than siblings, there is a whole 'nother half to me.* Mercy couldn't help it; he had to laugh out loud. The other four people waiting at the bus stop looks strangely at Mercy but he continues with his thoughts of his family.

Kane struggled with his past all the days of his life and to a certain point so did Mercy. They both struggled more than Ronald or the girls. Kane could not accept that fact that his mother loved him so little. This complicated with the problems he had to deal with growing up didn't make life any easier. By the time Kane was sixteen, he had been living on his own for three years. Life also ate him up, the loneliness of it, the not knowing about the rest of his family and unable to find any of them took its toll on him. At the young age of eight when Kane took his first drink with his second foster dad, he found that his past didn't bother him as much. Kane continued doing drugs and drinking which eventually killed him. He never amounted to much; unable to stay in school, not willing to trust anyone, and having issues with women especially, kept Kane from living like he should. *Too bad there wasn't a Mr. Bailey in Kane's life,* Mercy thought. Mercy is no longer smiling now but it's time to board the bus so no one notices the change in his mood.

Sitting down next to an old man who reminded him of Mr. Bailey, Mercy remembered how he met Mr. Bailey on the bus one day while he was on his way to another halfway house for men. Mr. Bailey was on his way to work in a high rise just a few blocks from the halfway house. To Mr. Bailey, there was no difference in the two of them; several times a month, they had lunch together and Mercy had gone to a full season of baseball games with Mr. Bailey; sitting in the office sky box each time. Bailey never asked Mercy questions about how he got to where he was in life or if he wanted help in getting his life together. Bailey would sometimes give Mercy information to jobs that he could look into and use his name as a reference but Bailey never asked Mercy if he applied for the job or if he got hired at one of them. Mr. Bailey's main concern was always Mercy's soul and that is what he would inquire about with Mercy. Did you get a visit from the Lord this week? Did you recognize that the Lord did something special for you? Has anything new or exciting happened to you, lately? Have you remembered that the Lord is the one who woke you up this morning and has kept you everyday of your life? Did you remember to say thank you?

At first, it kind of bothered Mercy that Bailey would bring that up to him while a movie was going on or when there was a quiet moment between them over lunch or when they were waiting for the bus on the fifteenth and the last day of the month. The fifteenth and the last day of the month is when Bailey goes out and to see his mother at the nursing home. He rides the bus out because his

Chapter Twenty-Six

sister-in-law works there and she brings Bailey back to his office in her car because it gives them a chance to talk before he gets into his car and goes home.

CHAPTER 27

"Reverend Harris, I have to say these past two months have been far more enlightening than I thought they would be." Lisa Dalton, Grove Road Church secretary always means well but she is always saying the wrong thing at the wrong time. Right now she's done it again. The look on Lisa's face lets her know that she has said one word too many. Right away, she wants to take her words back or at least try to fix them, unfortunately she can't do either. After fumbling over her words in search of the right ones, Reverend Harris gives her a smile and squeezes her hand then returns to his work.

David had to agree things were going better than he ever expected. His prayers have been answered. The church has already started to increase in membership and the finances are starting to balance out. When a church is without a pastor, there is a tendency for that church to fall apart a little but Grove Road Church has held things together quite well. He is feeling better about following God's direction rather than staying in Michigan at a church there. Michigan had sweetened the pot greatly hoping to entice him to come to their church. Great Hope, being one of the biggest churches in Michigan was very interested in getting Reverend Dr. David B. Harris to be their new pastor so much so that they more than doubled the salary offer and vacation time, as well as used a life insurance policy to enhance his retirement plan. The enhanced retirement plan was so appealing to Rev. Harris that he asked Grove Road Church to add it to their offer, they did and the deal was sealed. Grace's encouragement didn't hurt either. Knowing what this town held for her husband Grace wanted him to face whatever it was that caused him emotional hurt here in this town before so he could move past it.

"Reverend Harris," the voice at the door brought David Harris back to the here and now.

"Yes, Lisa; what is it," Rev. Harris looks up from behind the paper he holds in his hand and waits for her response.

"Walter Mayfield and three of the grounds committee are here along with Creative Care Landscaping Company," Lisa spins around quickly and walks away.

Reverend Harris takes a deep breath and pushes away from his desk. At full height David stands six foot two inches tall, a bit slim but with caramel colored skin and hazel green eyes, Rev. Harris is still sexy for a man almost thirty six years old. Reverend Harris seldom allows stress to enter his life which is something he credits his physical, emotional, and mental health, that and the gift that God has given him. He walks out to meet those who are awaiting for him in the outer office.

Extending his hand to everyone, Reverend Harris makes eye contact with each person and greets them with a smile. He notices that only those from the church committee are present but Reverend Harris sees that the representative for Creative Care Landscaping is missing so he asks.

"Sorry, Reverend I forgot my ..." for a moment Big Man Peoples loses his words. Caught off guard by the feeling of self-imagery Bigg Man tries to recover his introduction to Reverend Harris. "Sorry, again Reverend Harris," Big Man extends his hand to Reverend Harris as he introduces himself. "It is good to meet you. I have heard a lot about you and the new work that you have started here at Grove Road. You know this community is in need of the services that the church provides. I also wanted to personally thank you for helping one of my workers last month. John Richardson and his family live right down the road. They were burnt out of their home in the middle of the night and John tells me that this church was there before any of the agencies were to offer them help. John can't stop talking about this church and your members and the help his family received. So I thought you should know some of the good work you are doing is paying off. John's family has started attending here, and for that I'm glad. I believe everyone should be affiliated with a good strong church." Big Man means every word, but he knows he is also talking so much because he can't shake the feeling he has gotten from meeting Reverend Harris.

"Oh yes, you are referring to the man and his wife with the five children, they have one little boy with the artificial leg. Yes, we were more than glad to help. When our church deacon called to say that there was a fire and wanted to know if we should help, I knew it was something we needed to be a part of. Glad we could help him," looking eye to eye and standing shoulder to shoulder to this man, Reverend Harris is feeling like they share the same skin. He also feels the same thing that Big Man does and is engaging in extra chitchat for the same reason Big Man did.

Walter remembers the reports he has about Naturallee's brothers; all of them are described as either caramel or dark-skinned and it was found out that the males in the family usually have green or hazel eyes, it's been like that in Grandma Lucy's family for generations. Walter remembers reading that Naturallee's uncle Stew had hazel green eyes. What's more, Big Man has the same last name, he too, is a Peoples. He was thinking again of the report he received just two days ago that said that many of the children of Syvon Peoples had changed their names probably due to the ridiculous birth names they had been given. Maybe Reverend Harris has changed his name, maybe the B.B. stands for Baby Boy. Could he be Baby Boy Peoples?

The room is uncomfortably quiet as it seems that each man is thinking over the same thing. Before anyone has the presence of mind to ask the question that is looming over them all, the door opens and the trance is broken." Lisa has the worse timing, Reverend Harris thinks to himself, but at this very moment she's right on time.

"Reverend Harris, there are two more committee members here. Can I show them in," she asked.

At the moment, it could be a robber; Reverend Harris doesn't care as long as the air in the room changes, that's all that mattered right now.

"Yes, by all means show them in... Please.

The entire committee along with Reverend Harris and the owner and president of Creative Care Landscaping Company, Big Mann Peoples spend the first part of the evening discussing how the church wants the landscape around the church to look. All parties agree with all parts to the contract and the work to be done without any need for haggling. After a few minutes of small talk Walter, Big Man and Reverend Harris find themselves standing in the middle of the church yard feeling awkward again.

"I need to say something at this point to both of you that I know you are not aware of. It will probably answer the many questions you are both asking yourself and it may give you answers to other questions as well," Walter looks from one man to the other not sure which one to surprise first. Deciding it would be best to shock them together, he proceeds.

"I know a lady whose mother was named Syvon Peoples. Syvon

had a total of thirteen children over the course of about twenty years. She had two sets of twins, I believe only two sets, and she had a set of triplets along with six individual children. Her oldest children, the first set of twins, are named Truely Grateful and ...,

"...Honestly Sweet." Reverend Harris states as if a dream is returning to him. "She then had a daughter and named her Shirley Mine and then the other set of twins whose names I've forgotten," Reverend Harris stops talking in the same foggy way he started. As the fog in Reverend Harris' eyes clear, he looks at his brother Big and asks, "Was Syvon Peoples your mother too?"

Big Man can't answer with words but the smile on his face said more than any words could have at the moment. Then both men laugh and hug each other holding on as if the ground around them would open up and take one of them away.

Walter gives the two a few minutes to remember that he was still there before he asks if he could fill them in over dinner with more of what he already knew about their family. Reverend Harris and Walter have meetings requiring their attention but they agreed to meet for a late dinner.

Knowing how happy the news will make Naturallee, Walter wants to stop at home and tell her what has just happened. As he gets into his car, Walter remembers that tonight is the night that Naturallee is going to see Carl again. While the thought of her spending the evening with Carl bothers Walter more than he likes to admit, he knows he has to let her make up her own mind about who and what she wants. But he has good news for her now before her date and he wants her to have it as soon as possible and he wants to be in front of her when she first hears it.

CHAPTER
28

Carl says he has been out of town for the past two months and meant to call me before he left. The weather was more than he wanted to deal with this past winter and he had to get away; at least that's what he says. I'm happy to hear from him but I wonder if his family knows about cell phones and how to use them. He wants to have dinner and talk with me about something he says is very important to him. I think dinner is a good idea, as well. I never brought up the papers about Carl that I found on the table to Walter, I decided that the one I wanted to ask about it first is Carl. Since I last saw Carl eleven weeks ago, a lot has happened. There are things I want Carl to know about and things I want Carl to tell me about. I have waited a long time to get this call from Carl, but so much has changed between Walter and me and between me and Carl, and the things I wanted to say before have changed, as well.

Dinner is at seven and I'm not sure what I want to happen. I have to ask myself if I have let my feelings for Walter grow and develop into what they are because Carl has been unavailable. I think about the first time I got ready for a date with Carl, I could hardly wait for the knock at the door letting me know he had arrived. But today, I seem to have more patience. It's already four in the afternoon and all I want to do is see Walter before Carl get's here. I told Walter a couple of days ago about Carl's call and my going to dinner with him. Walter said he was glad that Carl finally called, but I got the feeling that he didn't really mean it and for some odd reason that made me a little happy.

Walter and I only have a few months left with the agreement and then we can get our lives back. When I think of this now sadness, comes over me with the possibility of my life changing again. I want to ask Walter about his feelings concerning the date marked on the calendar with the red marker he put there the week the agreement started. I want to rub out the red circle now and add a few more months past the date. I don't know what I want anymore and I don't know what Walter wants to do either. Why did it take Carl so long to call me again? Why didn't he answer me when I called him? Is he still interested in having a relationship with me or has he found someone else and wants to tell me in person instead of over the telephone? These are all questions I need to have answers to. And now, I realize this is the reason I want to have dinner with Carl, I need answers more than I want the relationship to continue. If this is how Carl handles life's little problems I know it is not the way I want to handle the little situations that come up in my life. I want things handled differently. I want to be more mature with my life. I want someone like Walter Mayfield. And now I'm not being honest with myself, I'm acting like Carl, I don't want a man like Walter Mayfield; I want the original Walter Mayfield. I want the man I have lived with for the past eight or nine months. There. Now I've said it out loud and I almost hope Walter is in earshot to hear it. I thought I was falling in love with Carl but he was just a silly first date crush. Carl seems so young and immature compared to Walter or maybe

Chapter Twenty-Eight

it's because I've spent more time with Walter than I have with Carl. But that really is Carl's fault and I don't mind saying this out loud either. I want to tell Carl about Walter and the kind of man he is, the things he's done and how much people respect him because Walter has earned their respect.

My cell phone is ringing and I feel a smile coming over me, it's Walter calling and I let myself be happy about the call. Walter wants to talk with me before I go to dinner, he says it's important. I hope he has found out more about my family.

CHAPTER 29

Walter got home about fifteen minutes ago but he hasn't come in to talk with me yet. Something doesn't feel right; Walter seemed different on the phone, he was more serious than I have heard him in a long time. He needs to tell me what he's come home early to say so that we will have time to discuss it if necessary before I go out with Carl.

Finally, I see Walter coming through the kitchen out here to the swing to sit with me. He has his lawyer face on so I know that what he has to say is serious.

He is a sexy, good-looking man for being sixty-four years old in a few days when we go to Florida. I have planned a surprise dinner for him there and we will take a short trip over to the Bahamas. I called Ms. Blair who actually made all of the arrangements for me. She and I have become friends over these past months and although she hasn't said it, I know she is hoping secretly that Nathan Grey's hopes come true as well. But right now watching Walter's approach stirs that something inside of me again and I want to run to the phone and call Carl to tell him I can't make it tonight.

The smell of his cologne on his dark suit and white shirt along with the way his pants hang just below his sculpted waistline, the way his shoulders move when he takes each step and even the blue of his eyes have me spellbound as he takes his place beside me. Taking a moment to gather his words reminds me of the day we first came to this house and Walter had to try to explain what Nathan Grey wanted of us. That was a serious day for Walter and so is right now. My concern starts to rise.

"Walter, what is it?" Now he must tell me something before he frightens me but he can't seem to find the words, he just sits there staring into me. Then Walter catches me off guard and puts his hand on my thigh. Without thinking about who it is, the man with the one big-eye flashes before me and I push Walter's hand away and jump up.

Walter is surprised by my reaction. The hurt in his eyes is so profound that I can't escape it. Walter just looks at me for a long moment. I reach for him to apologize and try to explain my actions but Walter puts his hand up for me to stop talking and walks back to the house. I'm left with the worst feeling I have ever had in my life. I feel worse than I ever did when the man with the one big-eye touched me. Walter must hate me now; I know I hate myself for reacting that way. I have to explain things to Walter so I run to the house just in time to look though the window and see Walter's car pulling away. I try to reach him on his cell phone but he doesn't answer it. I decide to follow him to his office and talk with him there. If I hurry, I may still make dinner with Carl. Then I remember the last time I went to Walter's office with a mission, he had a heart attack. I don't want that to happen again so I walk back into the house and decide to wait until Walter gets home. I probably won't get to talk with him until after my dinner with Carl.

CHAPTER 30

If Carl is nothing else he is punctual and I'm glad I just want this evening over so I can get back home and talk with Walter. Macy's Restaurant is the nicest place in town. Each day, there are six dinner entrees from which to choose and each day has six different choices. The restaurant use to be closed on Mondays and they still don't serve lunch on Fridays.

Walter and I have dined here several times over the past several months; we have been here so much several of the waiters and the waitresses know us. But tonight Phillip shows Carl and me to our table and gives us a list of the day's menu then he gives me a wink and a nod and excuses himself from the table. Before the spot Phillip was standing has a chance to get cold, our waitress shows up at the table with a pitcher of water. Andrea introduces herself to me then turns to Carl and reminds him who she is and why he should know her.

Suspended

"Oh, oh yes, Andrea, how have you been. It's been a while since we last saw each other, I heard from your roommate Sandy that you were still in Canada with your friend oh, what is his name," Carl snaps his fingers as if trying to remember then gives her a half smile and tells her we will need a few minutes. Carl says nothing about what just happened and I don't care enough to ask for fear that it could prolong the evening and I want to get back to the house and explain things to Walter.

"I suppose you're wondering why I didn't call before I left town," Carl inquires as if I were on the witness stand; then softens his look.

"I did at first but then I realized you don't owe me an explanation or a next call for that matter. Besides, I've been pretty busy with Walter and helping him to get back to being himself. He went back to work weeks ago and he is even back to his workout routine. You know I did try calling you a couple of times but I figured out that you were busy and didn't have the time then to spend on a relationship just ," before I can finish my statement Andrea returns to see if we are ready to give her our dinner choices. I'm not too hungry so I order Macy's Chicken and Cashew salad and Carl orders Walter's favorite meal; Chicken Romance. No kidding, that's the name of the meal Chicken Romance and every time Walter eats it it's like he's having a romantic eating relationship with it and when Walter finishes his meal, he's always in a more loving, tender mood. I certainly hope it doesn't affect Carl this way. When Andrea leaves the table Carl doesn't let me finish my conversation instead he starts in with his own small talk. We discussed his mother and grandmother among other unimportant topics then from out of nowhere Carl's tone, words and complete conversation changes.

"You know, Naturallee, I need to tell you that I was quite disappointed when you decided to stay with Walter in the hospital. I thought we had something special building up but you didn't even ask me what I thought you should do, you simply agreed with every-

194

thing that was going on even playing the role of the worried wife." Carl's words take me by surprise and I find myself unable to say anything so Carl continues with something that sounds very foolish to me but I don't say anything. I want to see where this is going.

"He's my uncle. Did he tell you that while the two of you have been playing house? And did he tell you that he and Nathan Grey and my father were best friends until the two of them cut my dad out of everything because my mother loved my dad and not him." Carl spit the words across the table as though I were Walter. Then as if the first Carl returns to the table he asks if I'm interested in dessert. I say no to dessert and to not knowing about the things he has just said. Carl goes back to his meal and a more pleasant conversation but I have lost my appetite for both the dinner and the conversation, and I've lost my respect for this man. Carl is nothing like Walter but I do have to ask myself why Walter didn't tell me this himself. I was going to try and finish the dinner before leaving early but after the information Carl has just given me I need to see Walter again. I tell Carl that our relationship wouldn't have worked out, that he has allowed too much time to get between us, which is the truth but it's not all there is to the end of us. I tell him I want to go home and Carl gives me a look of total devastation, if I didn't know better I would have thought that I just dropped some unsettling information on him. But he does agree to take me home. The ride home is very quiet, very uncomfortably quiet and I don't care. Carl wants me to have pity on him but I have just realized that I find that pathetic in a man. I wish he would drive faster.

After what feels like a lifetime of driving Carl pulls up to the house and shifts the car into park then turns off the engine. I feel for the door handle but the doors are still locked and Carl makes no effort to unlock them.

"You're home so what's the big rush to get out of the car, can't I have a few last moments with you, I mean I'm sure that this will be the last date we will ever have. Can't I even have a goodbye kiss?" I can't believe this guy is asking for a goodbye kiss after the evening he just gave me but if it gets the car door open I'll give him two.

"Naturallee, why did you choose Walter over me? I thought we had something special building up between us. And that day when Walter had his heart attack and you passed me on the way in town why were you in such a hurry and why did you hang up on me? And for the life of me, why didn't you tell the hospital that you and Walter weren't married. Do you know how that made me feel, standing there beside you, I was there for support for you and then you do that without even talking to me about it first. Why did..."

I can't sit patiently waiting for Carl to finish his list of complaints; I have to cut him off right here. "First of all Carl, I would like to know how you found out that Walter had a heart attack and was at that hospital. And since you brought it up, what makes you think that I'm not Walter's wife already and if that was a problem for you with me agreeing that I was Walter's wife why couldn't you come to me and discuss it sooner than today. And I have a few other questions for you since you seem to want to clear the air. Can you tell me when were you in jail and why were you there and tell me how many children do you have and how many marriages or almost marriages have you had. Was our waitress Andrea the last lady you left at the altar?" I have to stop and catch my breath. I have a lot more to ask Carl but from the shocked look on his face I think I have evened the score from dinner. Carl isn't even breathing and I don't care, I find the unlock button myself and get out of the car without looking back and for a split second I think about my dog Kane and how the squirrel he was chasing never looked back and I knew Carl was as dead to me as the Kane was to that squirrel.

CHAPTER 31

Our house is usually quiet, but tonight it, is eerily quiet. There's no life in it and I frightened. There is no lingering scent of Walter's cologne when I open the door, no briefcase at the stairs with his shoes by the table that holds his glass of wine. Perhaps, he's not home yet, but the atmosphere doesn't feel like the yet part is coming. It's just that Walter isn't home and I don't feel like he's coming home tonight or maybe any other night.

I'm more worried than I have ever been; I can't move. I think I'm more frightened now than I was of the man with the one big eye. Where is Walter spending the night? Who is he going to be with? He will be with someone who won't knock his hand off her leg and move away from his as if he were some kind of monster. "His bedroom, go to his bedroom and see if his clothes are still there," I hear myself saying as I find my feet and race myself up the stairs past my rooms to Walter's door and I push it open. The room is cold and empty feeling; it has no life or love in it. The room, too, feels hurt by someone because it offers no comfort to me. Some of Walter's things are missing and so is some of his luggage.

I can't breathe and I can't cry. I don't have the desire to drift up suspended in the room because I don't want to get away, I want to get closer to Walter. I want to find him and tell him how much I love him, how much I want him and I want him to know why I pushed his hand away; why I was so scared. But Walter isn't here to tell these things to and I don't know what to do now. Slowly, I make my way to my bedroom and curl up on this bed that I have come to love sleeping on. But the bed offers no comfort tonight and I find myself sobbing almost hysterically into my pillow.

I must have eventually cried myself to sleep because I'm waking up and its six thirty in the morning. At first, I only think of the bed and how much I usually enjoy waking up in it. Then, I remember last night so this morning I feel terribly sad and unhappy. Then tears swell up in my eyes again. I want to cry but that won't help me. I want to scream but that won't change a thing either. Then I have a thought or more like a hope; what if Walter returned last night and is sound asleep in his bed. I jump up and feel the carpet under my feet, usually I spend a few minutes just enjoying the feel of the floor but I can feel it on the way to Walter's room just as well. By the time my thoughts of the floor are finished, I am at Walter's door. The door is closed and I can't remember if I closed it last night before I stumbled to my bedroom. Could it be that Walter is home and sleeping? After all, Walter only started sleeping with his bedroom door open when we moved in together. I hope for the sake of love that he has reverted back to his old way of sleeping.

I take a moment to gather myself before I open the door. What if he's not inside? What if he never returns to this house? I have to shake away such thoughts; Walter is bigger than that. If things between us are over, he would tell me himself. He wouldn't do it this way. Maybe he just needs a little time to figure out why I did what I did, but if he would just come home, he wouldn't have to figure it out, I would tell him.

Chapter Thirty-One

Before I can bring an end to all the desperate thoughts racing through my head, I'm brought back to the door by the ringing of Walter's cell phone. I freeze and start praying that he will answer it. After the fifth ring, I lose hope of him being in his bedroom and I push the door open slowly while calling out his name. But there is no answer for me or the cell phone, finally it stops ringing and the hope of both me and the phone are silent. I look around for his phone and I see he has left it on his dresser. Right next to it is Macho Man and some papers. I pick up Macho Man and cradle him in my hands. I never learned all there was to the story of Macho Man. I know what it meant to Nathan Grey but Walter never said what it meant to him, I only know that it holds some strong memories for him. Then I see that the papers next to Macho Man are addressed to Walter and me. It's handwritten, addressed to Walter first and then to me—but to me as Naturallee Mayfield:

Dear Friends,

I am so happy that you have worked through this past year and have arrived here in Paris safely, the next three weeks will be the most fun you two will have up to this point. Let me say how glad I am that you are here, Naturallee. This is where I brought your mother for our honeymoon. She loved it so much we spent the first three weeks of our honeymoon at this very hotel. I left instructions with the staff that you are to be treated like royalty. Naturallee, I want to thank you for loving my best friend, no, my brother. I want to thank you for loving my brother, Walter so deeply that you could trust the love he has for you and give him the chance to finally open his heart up to someone who would love him back. I know that you are very young and you have your whole life in front of you still and Walter like me may not have as many years left to him (sorry old friend but it's the truth) but when Walter loves someone he does it with his whole heart so I think it is safe to say that you will never be loved again the way this man loves you.

Please take great care of each other. Always put God first, each other second and yourself third and you will be fine. You two can thank me later when you get here, but I want to thank you for allowing me and your mother to let us live just a little while longer by living on with you two this past year. Now get on with your happiness and forget about me and Syvon for the next six weeks at least.

Love always because of Jesus Christ,
Goodbye my family,
Nathan and Syvon Grey

"No, thank you, Nathan. Thank you, Syvon," is all I can say. But I know that I must find Walter now. I don't even want to read what Nathan has said to his best friend after reading what he said to me. I close up my letter and take it back to my bedroom with me. Forgetting everything else, I stand staring out my bedroom window and wondering how I messed things up so badly. Finally, I remember Ms. Blair and I run to the telephone. I listen to the office phone ring and then wait while the voice mail system plays its message before I remember that it is Saturday and the office is closed. Ms. Blair isn't there and what's worse it's a holiday weekend, the first barbecue of the season and the office is closed for the next three days. My heart sinks just knowing that I have to wait until Tuesday to talk with Ms. Blair. I have fought off the tears all morning but I can't fight anymore. I release all the hurt and anger I have in me. I have never loved anyone before and that never bothered me until now. I don't want to ever feel this kind of pain again and I'm afraid it won't go away until I have Walter back in my life again.

CHAPTER
32

"I can't wait for this weekend to be over with; what was I thinking throwing a pool party for a bunch of high school graduates tonight, a backyard party tomorrow afternoon for eighth graders and a formal sit-down dinner for your partner's retirement at eight...and I have a trip to Paris in a few weeks." Surely slaps her husband's chest and gives him a mischievous smile as she hangs up the phone after confirming all the weekend's food arrangements with her brother, Mercy. Surely Fine always thought she had put the ugly part of her life behind her and was now happy until she found some of her siblings. She realized that with beauty comes ashes, but the beauty is enough to make the ashes worth it. Once she found Mercy, another part of her life had come together, putting together another part of the puzzle, completing who she really is. Surely likes the feeling of completeness and her husband James has been noticing the change in her and liking it.

James, a psychologist in Surely's building, knew when he met her the first time, almost nineteen years ago, that he would need to refer her to a different doctor and after three sessions with her, Surely was wondering if it was legal to date her therapist. Once things were straightened around, James and Surely married a year later. James was more than happy when this woman married him. For the past eighteen years, Surely, too, thought she was happy until that day a year and a half years ago when Surely told James she thought she had found one of her sisters.

When Surely Fine Peoples called Hellinher Peoples Thompson who lived only a few miles away Surely instantly knew Hellinher was her sister. Surely and Hellinher meet two days later and are almost inseparable, these days. Together, they've continued their search for the rest of their brothers and sisters, accidentally finding Ronald while they were looking for Baby Boy.

At the age of twenty-five, Righteous Child was in the process of changing his name legally, when Surely and Hellinher ran a search for Baby Boy. They noticed that there had been another search for the same name not more than a month earlier. With a little detective know how and a few clicks of the mouse, the ladies had the name of their brother, Righteous Child now known as Ronald R. C. Peoples. Ronald was living twenty-three miles away from the girls. That following Saturday morning, the girls took a road trip to the next county, pulled up in front of the address they had found, walked right up to the door of his home and knocked. When a young man with hazel-green eyes answered the door, the girls could hardly contain their happiness. Through tears of joy and happy weeping, they stood there in the doorway and introduced themselves to their brother. Within minutes, there were three weeping Peoples at the door.

After finding Ronald, he and the girls wouldn't let anything stop them from finding as many of their siblings as they could. The three met every week to give updates on the progress any of them made from the searches they were all conducting. Ronald, Hellinher and

Chapter Thirty-Two

Surely Fine also told each other as much as they could remember about their part of their childhood with Syvon, Grandma Lucy, and Aunt Birdie. Surely Fine being the oldest of the three, remembered the day Syvon came home without the twins, Hellinher and Havesome Mercy. Then a few weeks later, Syvon came home without Kane. Surely asked Syvon once where they were but the look on Syvon's face told Surely Fine that she shouldn't ask again, and Surely didn't. Surely remembered an argument between Grandma Lucy and Syvon about Grandma Lucy not being able to see the kids but Syvon said they were her kids and she didn't have to let Grandma Lucy see them if she didn't want her to. It was about three days later, Surely watched Syvon give a woman some papers and the woman gave Syvon some money then, never looking back, Syvon, walked away and left Surely standing there. The woman Syvon left Surely with took her to another woman who lived in a very big house a long car ride away, it took two nights to get there. This second woman told Surely to call her "mom" from then on because she was going to be her new mother. At eight years old Surely's life changed for the good. Shelia and Charles Anthony were very good to Surely Fine; they sent her to private school and college and gave her everything a young girl could want. The only thing they asked of her was that she not tell anyone she was adopted. After eating everyday whenever and whatever she wanted, Surely silently agreed and her new life was born. But Surely could not forget her real family and promised herself she would find them all when she got older. She was happy that she kept that promise she made to herself.

Surely was telling Hellinher and Ronald about Syvon leaving the twins someplace and coming home without them when Hellinher's mind released a memory that she had tucked away the night the memory happened. Hellinher had a twin, a brother, who always tried to keep her safe from Syvon. Her brother had taken several hard beatings from Syvon for her, once having his jaw broken because Syvon was trying to hit Hellinher with an iron and her brother got between her and the iron. Syvon got so angry with them both she punched her brother right in the face and kicked Hellinher down the stairs all the while yelling at Hellinher about how much she hated her. Hellinher never knew what happened to him but she did all she could to forget that part of her life and forgetting included him as well. Hellinher couldn't even remember her twin brother's name.

"Mercy. It was Mercy or Merciful or some kind of Mercy," the words slip from Surely Fine's lips like water in a shallow stream rippling over the rocks on the water bed. It was a memory Surely, too, had put away from her mind for years but now as the flashes of blood shooting from Mercy's face raced to the forefront of Surely's mind, she had to remember. Now she could see Mercy as he spun around and fell to his knees, grabbing the left side of his face as he went down. A clear vision of Syvon as she loomed over him materialized as Syvon backhanded Mercy across the other cheek and he hit the floor like dried cement hitting a sidewalk. Then turning her rage to Hellinher, Surely witnessed Hellinher tumble and bounce down the stairs from the hit Syvon gave her. Hellinher finally stopped at the bottom of the stairs where Syvon kicked her in her side and she stepped over Hellinher. Surely remembered how scared she was as she ran to hide under the table in the kitchen in the dark, hoping Syvon would not remember that she, too, was in the house.

Ronald wasn't born when that happened, Surely only knew about him and some of the other siblings because Cousin Ruth's boyfriend, Rayford was in prison with Surely's husband, James' youngest brother, Johnny; cell mates as a matter of fact. Once, when Surely and James went to visit Johnny, Surely saw Ruth in the visitors home. When Ruth left, Surely followed her out and talked with her.

Ruth told Surely as much as she knew about the what happened to the kids and how many kids there probably were. Ruth didn't know what happened to Syvon after she left town because Syvon never came back even when Grandma Lucy died. But Ruth

Chapter Thirty-Two

was able to tell Surely that she had a sister named Naturallee Joy and that Uncle Stew and Aunt Joyce had taken her in when Aunt Birdie lost custody of her. Syvon had left Naturallee at the church with Grandma Lucy when she said that she was going to pick up the other two boys from their fathers, but of course she never returned. Ruth also said that Syvon never picked them up from their fathers either, kids that were probably in their twenties by now. The one boy, Ruth knew for a fact, stayed with his father. The other boy stayed, Ruth thought, with the wife of his father after they got a divorce. She said she thought his name was Big Man or Big Manny or something like that, "You know, it was something that was like the rest of our names," Surely said before she continued with the information. "Anyway," Surely went on with the story, "the baby, Lovely Girl, died around three of four years old. Lets see, there were a couple sets of twins, one set of boy twins and one girl and boy twin, she said, but she didn't know what happened to any of them. She only knew that Syvon somehow got rid of all of the kids except three or four of them before she left town. Anyway, that was all cousin Ruth knew.

Ruth gave Surely her phone number so they could keep in touch but the number was disconnected, and Surely never saw Ruth again in the visitors room when they went to visit James' brother at the prison again. "But cousin Ruth had remembered one more very important thing, another child's name," Surely smiled while saying, "It's how I was able to eventually find Hellinher," Surely said still smiling, " and we were able find you," she said pointing at Ronald.

CHAPTER 33

Today the doctor's office chairs are more uncomfortable than ever. No matter which way they twist and turn in their seats Truely and MaLyce aren't able to relax or sit still. Squeezing his wife's hand, Truely gives MaLyce a nervous smile trying to reassure her. When Dr. Morehead opens the door to his office Truely and MaLyce see the same look on the doctor's face they feel is on their own.

The Peoples chose Dr. Morehead to be their children's pediatrician because of his honesty and frankness but today they aren't sure if that's what they want.

"Truely, MaLyce, thanks for coming in today. As I said on the phone, I have the results of Mark's test back and I had them run twice to be sure. I won't lie to you, the news isn't good. I promised you some years ago that I would always be honest with you about your children. The truth is Mark has kidney failure due to that virus he picked up last summer in Cancun. I thought—I hoped that the treatments we gave him would have taken care of it but you know we've been fighting this for months now. I hate to say it but nothing has worked. As a matter of fact things are worse—a lot worse. The results of his test tell me that something has to be done soon. Very soon. We have to make some hard decisions and we have to make them now. Truely, MaLyce, you need to know this is extremely serious." Dr. Morehead stops talking to give Truely and MaLyce a chance to digest the words he's just given them.

MaLyce grabs Truely's hand with both her hands as the blood drains from her smooth, dark brown, blemish-free face. Not that anyone ever knew it, but MaLyce blushed easily and she frightened even easier. The information she has just received is more than just frightening, it scares her to death. She can't speak. What can she say? What will she and Truely say to their son Mark and their other boys when they get home. She isn't able to accept what she has just been told. What is going to happen to her son?

Truely finds his voice first and whispers out a few small, quiet words that don't make much sense to anyone in the room. He stands up and walks around the office before he speaks again but this time he has a more constructed question, "What do we do for Mark now," Truely asks with a firm, but loving voice. "I need something to give him hope once we tell him this. Mark is already too tired and sick to get out of the bed and he isn't eating. The pain in his back is increasing and I can't do anything to help him. What am I supposed to say to this kid who thinks he's going to college in a few weeks?" Truely returns to his seat with a heavy flop while looking to Dr. Morehead for answers.

"A kidney replacement is the most reasonable choice we have and it is the best one for Mark, his condition has slipped a lot over this past month. We need to get all of you tested as soon as possible to see if there is a possible donor match in the immediate family." Dr. Morehead put the statement on the table without hesitation, he doesn't even blink. He wants them to know how dire the situation is.

Truely and Dr. Morehead continue to discuss what needs to

Chapter Thirty-Three

happen but MaLyce isn't able to participate. She sits quietly and motionless as the decisions for her oldest child are being made without her. As the voices in the room became more like white noise than anything else, it also becomes irritating to her ears as she hears another voice in the room screaming. MaLyce knows it is her but she can't stop. Not until she comes to herself in Truely's arms being held so tight she can hardly catch her breath for the next scream. Finally, giving up and clasping his arms, MaLyce passes out.

CHAPTER 34

"These past four months have been far more than Honestly Sweet could have hoped for. On his own and without the help of any other person, Honestly has developed a successful relationship with the woman of his dreams. "You, my man are one lucky dog." Honestly gives himself a playful slap in the face as he talks to the man in the mirror who is preparing for another date with Beverly. He takes another minute to think about where his life is now and where it was only one short year ago. A year ago, he lived by a very rigid schedule, one that he had even molded (or so he thought he had molded) his ex-wife Gail into. But today, he is living free of schedules and rules for the first time in his life. That's the way Beverly enjoys living and Honestly wants his life to live with hers.

In just the last month, Professor Peoples has missed a class, forgotten to post student grades, and blown off the every other Tuesday morning meeting. After sixteen years of never missing a day of teaching, he has skipped his first class and went on an impromptu weekend getaway to Mt. Rainier. Honestly Sweet did things he had only read about. But the big thing was finally taking the once white, stain-free schedule he kept on the refrigerator down and throwing it away. He had read the schedule ever day as though there was going to be a change to it. Everyday, Honestly read it and made a mental note of the day's activities as if he could forget some of it. But for the past sixteen weeks, he has been living by the direction of the wind; wherever it blew Beverly that is where Honestly was willing to go.

His students had noticed the change in him and had remarked several times how much different he was from the beginning of the semester. Honestly even changed his final exam for the spring semester and had the students to simply give an oral presentation of life as they saw it. This summer is the first summer he didn't teach at least one summer session at the college.

Tonight he wants, to take Beverly someplace special for a romantic dinner and dancing. Dennis' Lounge is the place. The food is second only to Macy's Restaurant and Dennis's Lounge has dancing. "I believe Beverly will be good with that," Honestly says to the only person now in the kitchen. Glancing at his watch, he realizes that he needs to leave now if he is to pick up Beverly on time. He grabs his keys from the key rack at the door and whistles as the door closes behind him. Sliding into his new sports car, Honestly takes in the smell of Italian leather and sinks into the soft tan seats before starting the engine. Driving away, he eyes the For Sale sign in his yard and accepts the fact that selling the house is long overdue.

◆

Dennis' Lounge doesn't serve seafood and in the car, Beverly mentions tilapia would taste good for dinner. Besides after a second day of the big annual sale at the sporting goods store Beverly and her husband opened seven years ago, she isn't in the mood for being light on her feet tonight.

Chapter Thirty-Four

Beverly and her husband Randal saved for ten years so that they could start their dream of opening the store, but in the first year, Randal was diagnosed with cancer and died the next year. Beverly has kept the store going and done well but it's a lot of work even with a full office staff and fifteen part-time floor employees.

Beverly says she is tired but not exhausted. She loves spending time with Honestly as much as he loves being with her. They settle on dinner at Macy's then home to her place by ten o'clock.

CHAPTER
35

"How about I let you go home now, get some rest and you be back here by five. I'll pay you for the whole day and you don't have to finish the lunch hour." Stan Whalen is a hard man to say no to. He knows where a person is weak at and uses it to his advantage whenever it's necessary. "...and I'll pay you time and a half for the whole day with tomorrow off so you can rest up." He has just sweetened the pot to the point of irresistible for Mercy and he knows it. "I'll tell you what, Mercy. I want you to come out and speak with the customers tonight whenever there's an order for tilapia or a princess dessert, and every time that happens, I'll pay you an extra hour of work, how does that sound?" Stan doesn't wait for an answer; he knows this is something Mercy has wanted secretly since the day he started as the afternoon chef. Stan slaps Mercy's shoulder and walks away feeling successful about solving another restaurant problem.

Mercy can't believe how things are happening for him again. He slips away out the back door to celebrate. After he regains his composure, Mercy returns to the kitchen to take a look around. He will be head chef for the dinner hour tonight, and if it goes well, he could be asked to run the kitchen for the next several months or at least until head chef Preston Long returns from his medical leave. Mercy doesn't want to get bigheaded but he owes himself a smile and an extra deep breath to raise his chest a bit higher than usual. He has worked hard for what he has and as Mr. Bailey says, God doesn't forget his children. Mercy finds that he can speak about God more than he used to because he feels God more than he used to. Not because of the things that have been happening for him but because of the peace he has when the things he wants to happen, don't happen. Mr. Bailey is right, you always feel good and at peace when the good happens. It's at the harder, darker times that peace becomes illusive but you feel better about yourself for holding on to God once the hard times are over. But peace isn't illusive today, no today, peace is walking with Mercy.

Living on adrenaline, Mercy spends the afternoon at the park sampling some of the park vendor's cuisine. "There is nothing like a Billy's Burger and fries with a strawberry shake on an afternoon such as this," sitting on a park bench, Mercy closes his eyes to take in the moment.

"I thought I might find you here. I went by the restaurant and they told me you would be working the dinner hour. Stan told me your bit of good fortune. Congratulations, my friend," Bailey had the usual big smile from ear to ear that he gives when someone other than himself has a good thing happen for them.

"When did you get back in town? I thought you were due back for another couple of weeks," Mercy says as he loses his burger in all the excitement of seeing his friend. He gets ups and hugs Bailey then motions him to sit on the bench with him.

"I'll tell you about me if you tell me about you, first. What is this I hear? My good friend is head chef at the city's most prestigious restaurant, Macy's on the River," Bailey asks his friend of only a few years.

Chapter Thirty-Five

Mercy tells the story, as much as there is to the story, to Mr. Bailey and then Bailey tells Mercy why he is back home so soon. It turns out, Mr. Bailey's mother passed away a couple of days ago so he had to return and take a personal leave for a few weeks to get things settled. Mercy and Mr. Bailey spend the afternoon catching up on each other, after being away for two months, there seemed to be so much that had happened in Mercy's life that even he hadn't realized until he started telling Bailey.

The afternoon rushes to a close and Mercy knows he has to get back to the restaurant but has Bailey promise him that he will bring his wife, Rachel, in for dinner one evening soon.

The dinner hour is more stressful than the lunchtime and Mercy feels the pressure. There has already been one complaint about a dinner and one of the ovens has quit working. Two waiters have called off work for the night and the prep chef has been taken to the hospital after almost cutting off two of his fingers and all of this happened before eight o'clock. Even though there have been a lot of problems, Mercy isn't ready to throw in the towel yet. There have been some good things that have happened tonight as well. As promised, Bailey and his wife came to dinner and asked to speak to the chef. Because of their compliments to Mercy when he came to their table, another table ordered the tilapia, causing what Mercy thought to be a chain reaction in the restaurant. There are also more than usual the amount of princess desserts being sold, as well and Mercy and his manager, Stan, couldn't be happier about it.

Tonight, as it is every Friday night for dinner the restaurant closes late and because of the extra orders of tilapia, there isn't any left by nine thirty. Mercy feels bad about not being able to please the last of his customers and goes to the table to apologize and to suggest another of his special dinners.

"Sir, my name is Mercy Peoples and I'm the head chef here. I must apologize to you tonight but we have just sold our last tilapia dinner a few minutes ago. We are all out but I would like to suggest, if I may, to try either of the other two seafood choices or the grilled chicken and I will give even greater attention to your meals tonight making sure that everything will be pleasing to your palate right down to the last tantalizing bite." Mercy keeps his eyes on Beverly Young mostly as he speaks giving her a pleading smile in hopes that she will agree to one of the other meals.

But Honestly Sweet sits stoned in his seat. The green eyes, the name, even the smile reminds Honestly of someone he once knew. Thirty years ago, she smiled at him when a man Honestly called *Uncle Stew,* told him he loved him and that he would see him later. Honestly never saw the man again but he remembers the smile his mother gave him and the green eyes his Uncle Stew had. It's the same smile and green eyes this man has. It's the same smile and green eyes that he believes he, too, has. The fact that this man says his name is Peoples keeps Honestly trapped in memory freeze.

"Sir, the lady has ordered the grilled chicken can I cook an order for you?" Mercy asks the second time but still no response to Mercy's question. But Mercy is also giving Honestly a closer look, staring straight into Honestly's eyes. Mercy knows why this man can't answer. This man is his brother, Mercy is sure of it. Now both men are silent, unable to take their eyes from the other.

Finally, Honestly is able to speak first, "What was your mother's name, her first name, sir, if you don't mind my asking."

"It was Syvon, her name was Syvon Peoples. Her father, I'm told had the same green eyes that you have."

"...and you have."

"...your mother's name...sir."

"I'm Syvon's second oldest child. I believe. I am three minutes younger than our brother Truely Grateful. My name is Honestly Sweet." Honestly stands up to hugs his brother Mercy. The two men embrace. Joy mixed with tears holds them together for a long minute. Three other tables in close proximity to the men clap and cheer. Someone even takes their picture for the newspaper.

Chapter Thirty-Five

Mercy somehow finished his work for the evening, at least until the doors closed at eleven. Stan understands the preciousness of the moment and sends Mercy home the minute the doors are locked. Mercy calls Surely Fine, Hellinher, and Ronald and lets Honestly speak with them all. Then the two men and Beverly drive to Surely Fine's house, arriving just before midnight.

Mercy and Hellinher suggest they remember who made this moment possible and so they take a moment of the morning thanking and praising God for the chance meeting of yet another sibling. Like little kids on Christmas, it's five thirty in the morning before they are able to close their eyes and drift off to sleep.

CHAPTER
36

It takes me most of the morning to find Ms. Blair's number but I find her home phone number in some of Walter's papers in his desk. I take in a deep breath as I punch in the numbers and wait for the phone to ring.

"Hello, Naturallee. What can I do for you," Ms. Blair sounds different; she has a cold, hard tone to each word she says. But I can't be concerned with that now, I need to find Walter and talk with him.

"Hello, Ms. Blair. I need to speak with Walter. Could you please tell me where he is and how to contact him, please." I know she is very loyal to Walter and I can appreciate that but today I need her to let go of the gatekeeper role and become a woman who knows something about love.

"Mr. Mayfield doesn't want to speak with you at this time. He has asked that you respect his wishes and he will speak with you once he returns in ten days. Naturallee, I hope you will be considerate enough to do this for him. Let him have some time and space to sort things out. I don't know what happened between the two of you but he is very hurt by it all and..."

I can't wait for Ms. Blair to stop talking so I cut across her with another desperate plea. But she acts as if my words haven't even been spoken; she continues to speak her piece.

Then I hear myself yell into the phone, "Stop it, stop talking as if I don't exist on this line. I need to explain something to Walter. If you are so concerned about how hurt he is then let me know where he is so I can clear this up. I love Walter and I don't want to lose him. I want him to know why I did what I did. It has nothing to do with him, it's from my past and I should have told him months ago but I didn't because I couldn't explain things then. I had forced those memories down and out of my mind for years and then something happened and it all rushed in on me at the wrong time. But it didn't have anything to do with Walter." I can't say anymore. My voice is cracking through all of the crying that I can't stop myself from doing. Then I hear myself telling her how much I love Walter and how much I need him in my life and how sorry I am that I didn't tell him how I felt sooner. I ask Ms. Blair if she's ever loved anyone before. I mean really loved anyone before, and if so, had she forgotten how that made her feel. I tell her how I know that I have a lot to learn about loving a man; I've never been in love before so it's new to me. I will make mistakes in our relationship but I have to have a chance to make it right or to at the very least, explain things to Walter and perhaps take away some of the hurt and pain he must be feeling.

"He went to Florida already; he left last night on the red-eye. He wants to have time to get himself together before the dedication. He's staying at the Hilton but he is using Nathan's name." Ms. Blair pauses, and then with iron strength in her voice again she warns me not to hurt Walter anymore than I've hurt him already.

She makes no threat but I understand her warning clearly. I thank her and ask how to get to where he is. I've never made a plane reservation before; I've never been outside this city before, now that

Chapter Thirty-Six

I think about it. Ms. Blair does love Walter and thought it may have been a big misunderstanding between us. She knows that Walter has been hurt before and he is cautious, not wanting to be hurt again. Ms. Blair said she is on her way to the house with my ticket and that I should pack quickly, my plane leaves in three hours. She hoped I would call with an explanation that would warrant her giving me the ticket to go to Florida today.

◆

When the Lincoln Towne car pulls into the driveway, I skip over the newspaper and hop in before Ms. Blair has a chance to put the car into park.

"Thank you, Ms. Blair," I choke the words out as tears stream down my face. "I don't know what's wrong with me but I can't seem to stop crying." I tell her as I wipe away more tears. I cried when I didn't know where Walter was or if I would see him again and now I'm crying because I know where he is and I am going to see him. This is crazy. Love is crazy and it's making me crazy.

"It's a crazy little thing called love that keeps the tears flowing, sweetheart. And it sounds like you got a bad case of love for this man. You're in so deep it won't do any good to tell you to guard your heart; it's already captured."

Ms. Blair is right, it's too late. I'm totally and completely in love with Walter. I can't hide it and I don't even want to fight it. I just want to be with him as fast as that airplane can get me to him. Ms. Blair gives me my ticket and information about where Walter is. She even tells me it would be best not to let him know I'm coming but rather to just show up at his hotel door. She said he wouldn't leave me standing there and I would be able to catch him off guard a bit making it possible to explain things to him and he would listen. She told me about how hurt Walter was when he found out that his wife had only married him for his name and money, and when she left him for another man. She told me that he had other relationships that just didn't work out for one reason or another. Then Ms. Blair told me that she knew that Walter had prayed that I would love him because he was in love with me but he didn't want me to be with him if I didn't really want to be there. She said he'd rather live alone the rest of his life than to be in another relationship like the one he had with his wife. Ms. Blair helped me through check-in and walked with me to the gate. As I was about to board the plane, she warned me again not to hurt Walter anymore than he already was, then she gave me a hug, pushed an envelope into my hand. She said it was reading material for the flight. She asked that I call her first chance I got. I promised I would and made my way onto the plane and to my seat.

◆

I can't think of anything but talking to Walter, it was forty minutes into the flight before I remembered that I was even on an airplane. My first airplane ride and I missed the rush of takeoff. The envelope Ms. Blair gave me is sticking out of my purse but I think I will look at it later. I don't think I will be able to concentrate right now. Just then the plane runs into what the captain calls "a little turbulence," so I now want a little more to keep my mind occupied. Maybe the envelope can keep me distracted. I turn it over and see that it is already addressed to be mailed to me and it's from Walter or at least the return address is his office. It's sealed and postmarked by his office; it makes me wonder why Walter didn't just bring it home to me but then I notice that the office postage stamp is for yesterday's date. Walter must have decided to mail it to me knowing that he wasn't coming back home, not for a while anyway, and he wanted me to have it. Then the plane hits a little more turbulence and I rip the envelope open.

Chapter Thirty-Six

Naturallee,

I had hoped that things would have worked out better between us; honestly, I thought things were going very well between us until today. I understand that Carl is more your age and can offer a younger, longer life to enjoy than I could. In a few days, I will be sixty four years old and looking toward retirement in the next year. I also know that Carl offers more than youth to you and I want you to know that I don't blame you for your choice. I only wish you could have turned me away without the fear in your eyes that I saw today. I thought you knew that I would never hurt you in any way; I'm sorry I didn't make that clear to you. I'm sorry I didn't make you feel safe with me. I know you've had a rough life and I certainly didn't want to add to that, and for doing so, I'm sorry. But I hope in some small way the information in this envelope will help you to forget the fear I've caused you.

This week has been very successful in finding some of your family. I found two of your brothers, David Baby Boy Harris and Big Man Peoples. "Baby Boy" is married with a beautiful family and Big Man owns a landscaping company here in town.

I was able to find a friend of your Grandmother Lucy Peoples. Do you remember a neighbor, Gurtie Brown? She was able to give me the name of several of your siblings, the older ones at least. Gurtie remembers that Syvon had two or three sets of twins; she couldn't remember but she was sure that a set of twin boys were Syvon's first children. The next year, Syvon had a single child then twins again or twins then the single child, she's not sure. Syvon had another child, but she couldn't remember if that child was a boy or girl, but that child died. She verified that Syvon left her prettiest child, a little girl named Joy, at a church with Lucy. Gurtie heard that over the next couple of years, Syvon had other children but Gurtie and no one else ever saw Syvon again. Gurtie remembers Hellinher (just the way it sounds, she said) and some kind of Mercy are the names of the other set of twins, I believe the investigator has a strong lead on Mercy but he is still working on Hellinher. This Gurtie does remember that Syvon hated Hellinher. She thinks Syvon hated all of children but Hellinher, Joy and the oldest twin were despised by Syvon.

But this news may be the very best news of all. My church has just hired a new pastor from Arizona; his name is David B. B. Harris, (the B. B. stands for Baby Boy). He had his name changed but kept the Baby Boy hoping it could lead him to his family some day. Pastor Harris and I along with a couple other building and grounds committee members met with the new landscaping company the first part of this week. It was a strange meeting because the men, Pastor Harris and the owner of the landscaping company could have been twins they looked so much alike. After we finished the meeting, and the other committee members left, I asked both men if they would mind meeting with me yesterday morning here at my office. I asked them if they would tell me the name of their mothers. They both said in unison, Syvon Peoples. Then I told them your story. They are anxious to meet you. I have arranged a meeting for the three of you Sunday afternoon at Macy's on the River at three o'clock. I won't be able to make the meeting, but you will be fine. You will know them because they both have green eyes and they look just alike but they are not either set of twins. They also have that big beautiful smile like you.

I know I have never said this to you, Naturallee, but I would like to say it now. I never considered guarding my heart when we started this. I was sure that we would only be doing the arrangement as a means to an end, but I fell in love you. I love you more than I should have allowed myself to. I think I just took it for granted that you knew that. Maybe it is better that I never said it to you. But I do want you to know that Nathan left us an out for this arrangement; one that I was forbidden to say until last week. Nathan only held you to the arrangement first for three months and if we were doing alright and not ready to kill each other, I was to let it go for ten months; the year was only if things were going extremely well between us. You are free to go. I have left instructions for Ms. Blair to open and follow once you call her. She will release the house, the money, and everything else that comes with the completion *of the arrangement. The only stipulation is that you keep looking for your brothers and sisters. My office will continue to assist you with that. Also, the letters you found in the safe in your closet are to be given to each sibling from Syvon when they are found.*

I hope you will be happy, Naturallee Joy, you deserve at least that. Again, I apologize for yesterday; it was never my intent to hurt you.

Good-bye
Walter

The letter takes me away from the plane and the turbulence. I even find the information about my brothers secondary to Walter's words and how hurt he is. I know now how very much Walter must love me and how much it must have dug into his heart to write these parting words. And to have come home in the middle of the afternoon to give me this exciting news only to have me pull away with a look of fear or even worse in my eyes. I have to remind myself that tears won't help. I need to explain everything to Walter. This plane needs to land soon. I need the chauffeur Ms. Blair said will be waiting for me when I land to get me to Walter's hotel right away. But the thought of meeting two of my brothers tomorrow is becoming exciting, too...oh no, I won't be there. What am I suppose to do now?

CHAPTER
37

The last few weeks have been the hardest the Peoples family has ever had to face. Mark had to be admitted to the hospital and is in great need of a kidney transplant but none of his immediate family is a match. MaLyce hasn't seen or spoken to her family since the day she met Truely at the bus station over twenty years ago. Truely knows he once had a brother but after being separated before they were ten years old, he doesn't even know if his brother is still alive. When Truely was younger, he did what he could to try to find his brother but he never had any luck. He wasn't sure if Honestly Sweet had changed his name or if his brother was still living. But now would be a good time to try again to see if he could find him or maybe even his grandmother Lucy or some of his other four siblings. He didn't want to think about finding Syvon but he would if there was a possibility to save Mark's life. Truely and MaLyce spend every evening and most of their emergency savings trying to find their families.

Suspended

Winston is feeling better after his bout with pneumonia complicated with severe dehydration and a bad reaction to his girlfriend's cooking of spoiled meat. It took him several weeks to recover but it was nothing life threading just painful and a little embarrassing. Mitchell stays at the hospital with his brother, Mark. The twins have always been close and with the open fear of the possible loss of his brother, Mitchell is compelled to stay and see Mark through this rough time. Mitchell was angry with himself for not being a better steward of his own health. Just two years ago, while he was pushing himself physically to try out for the Olympic swim team, Mitchell took some vitamins that a teammate offered him. Believing that the vitamins would naturally enhance his strength, Mitchell used them without question. The pills caused him severe internal problems with several internal organs, his kidneys were affected. He still takes medication for his left kidney today making it impossible to even be considered as a donor for Mark. Winston isn't a very good match and MaLyce and Truely are both poor choices. MaLyce and Truely now know they need more than just each other, they need the rest of their families and they need them now.

Tonight, when MaLyce goes to bed, she has her husband hold her hand and they pray together for their son. She tells God some of the things she and her family has done for others and how committed their family is to the church and the community. MaLyce reminds God that her family, like all others, is only human trying to be more of the Spirit He would want them to be. Then MaLyce reminds God of His promise to her some years ago and she asks if the promise could be filled at this time. She wants her son's health restored. She and Truely cry together in each other's arms until they fall asleep.

Unable to sleep for long, MaLyce finds herself in front of the computer at four in the morning but not sure what she's doing there. She sees her fingers moving across the keyboard and her hand moving the mouse but her mind doesn't let on as to why she is doing any of it; she just knows she should go with it. She types Honestly's name into the search engine and sits wide-eyed waiting to see what kind of response she'll get. After several seconds, she realizes the computer is still on the blink because it freezes without giving any response. Disappointed, MaLyce whispers to God once more and returns to bed. Finally, after much tossing and turning, she drifts off to sleep again.

◆

After another long, hard day of watching her son dying in a hospital bed with no good news to be had, MaLyce and her girlfriends meet in the hospital cafeteria for dinner. MaLyce loves all of her friends and they each bring good things to the relationship. Rhonda and June are always first to arrive for anything, they are the anchors of the group. If the ladies go out to dinner, Rhonda and June are always the first to arrive and hold down the table until the others arrive. Though they are not sisters, they certainly act as if they could be and they have similar thoughts even when they are apart. Once, when Rhonda was out of town for training with her job for the government, she had little access to the outside world. She decided one morning, that she was tired of her hair and had it all cut off right down to it being shaved in the back and she changed the color. She looked great with the new look. Rhonda's long, thin caramel-colored frame and hazel eyes made the very short, now bronze color hair look great. But back home, that same week while Rhonda was gone, MaLyce, Barbara, and June met for lunch one afternoon and right in the middle of lunch June announced that she had made an appointment for later that afternoon with a hair dresser. When the ladies saw June again she had cut her hair to the point of having it shaved in the back and even though June is a couple of shades lighter than Rhonda she too carried the new look fantastically. If one of them is having something at their house, Rhonda and June are there to help set up and they are the two who will stay and help clean up. In a situation like this they are the two who are work-ing the phones or computers or pounding the payment trying to get something positive done.

Lynn is almost a must-have at any of their get-togethers. Lynn always lightens a load. She has that quick wit and dry humor that catches the ladies off guard causing laughter even when they don't think they want to laugh. Barbara is the processor of the group. She's the one with the smarts and know how, and she's the one who will tell you the truth when you don't want to hear it.

Barbara wants you to face whatever it is with your eyes wide open to help keep down unwanted surprises. Barbara is the realist with patience. She wants everyone to eventually get there with whatever it is they need to deal with.

MaLyce is grateful for each one of her good friends. At this time in her life, she needs every shoulder she can find to lean on. The girls have come to have dinner with MaLyce and to try to help her relax, if only for a few hours. Truely comes to the hospital after work each day but today he has to meet the electrician at their home. The old adage that "when it rains, it pours" and "if it ain't one thing, it's another," are both true. In the past month, Truely and MaLyce have had the plumber, and the waterproofing company out to the house, as well as having the garage door replaced. They were just teasing each other over breakfast asking if they may have been bad in an-other life and this was payment for those sins. They both laughed about it but they both also wondered why all these things were hap-pening to their family at once.

"MaLyce, are you still with us or have you left the building," Lynn nudges MaLyce and gives her a smile. Before Rhonda and June cut their hair, Lynn had cut hers. Now Lynn's hair is almost as long as it was a couple of years ago before she cut it all off but long hair or short, Lynn is still the sexiest woman MaLyce knows.

"Sorry, girl. I can't be very much fun these days and I want you guys to know how much I love you for being here for me and

Chapter Thirty-Seven

Truely and the boys. What would we do without you?" MaLyce means those words. Each day, one of her friends goes over to her house and cleans, cooks, and washes their clothes making it possible for her and Truely to stay at the hospital as much as possible. Her friends are even taking Winston to his practices and games. MaLyce and Truely want him to keep his schedule as much as possible trying to have some normalcy in his life. Truely and MaLyce suggest to Mitchell to do the same but their words were met with a glare that said his parents didn't really know him if they thought he could live without his brother at his side.

"Well," Barbara leans back away from the table and says, "If you don't start lightening up a little I might have to skip my day of cleaning your already clean house. Besides, you have stood in church and told some pretty powerful testimonies, now you act as if all you've been saying has been a lie. Girl, need I remind you that if it hadn't been for your testimony about how you and Truely overcame the troubles you've faced over the years as recent as two years ago when Mitchell had his bout with sickness himself, I probably won't have a relationship with God right now? MaLyce put some faith with your heart and start trusting God to step in and do what only HE can do."

Everyone at the table turns to look at Barbara. For a woman who has just confessed her faith and love for God only two years ago, the women are taken by surprise by her words.

"Well, am I wrong? You've convinced me that God is real and able to do anything including heal those who need it in accordance with His will. Well, I say believe Mark's healing is in accordance with God's will and Mark is going to be healed. Believe something that your family needs will happen."

Still shocked with the words that are coming from the one they least expected to say those things, the ladies don't say anything as Barbara continues talking to her captive audience.

"I have already sent e-mails to my family and friends telling them about your-- our situation here and I've asked for help and for their prayers. And if anyone feels like the Lord moves them in such a way as to consider donating we would greatly appreciate it."

"I have to say something, MaLyce." June finds her voice, "I've noticed," then June looks around the table as if to get the approval of the others to speak on their behalf before she continues, "We've noticed that your prayers have changed a lot in these last few weeks. Don't get us wrong. We understand how it has happened; if we were in your shoes, our prayers would change, too. We're sure of it. But perhaps, now is not the time to change the way you pray." June stops talking for a minute to give MaLyce a chance to reflect on her recent prayer life.

"I don't know what you mean June. I still pray every day, I pray now more than ever. Truely and I both do," MaLyce answers June with a bit of insecurity in her voice.

"Yes, I know what you mean," Rhonda adds. "I just didn't know how to put it, but there is a change in your praying style or in the kind of prayer you're praying, not so much in your frequency of prayer." The words seem to linger a bit on Rhonda's tongue as if it's a revelation.

"What do you mean the style or kind of prayer I pray?" Feeling as if she is being ganged up on, MaLyce is becoming defensive. But Lynn grabs her hand and catches Malyce's attention.

"Hey, girl, we have been sisters from the moment each of us met, we would never do or say anything to hurt you. After all these years, you have to know that. I think what the twins," she teasingly calls Rhonda and June before continuing, "What they are trying to say and what I think I agree with them on is this: You have always started your prayers with how much you love God. You spend a lot of your prayer time telling God how much you love Him. There are times when the four of us tease about how you need to write a psalm and have it put into the Bible. Girl, you sing to God so much in a prayer about how much you love Him, we get tired of hearing it,"

Chapter Thirty-Seven

Lynn continues to tease.

"I do but I didn't know it bothered you guys," MaLyce cut in.

"It doesn't, as a matter of fact, we have changed our prayer style to making that the first thing out of our mouth when we pray now," Lynn gives MaLyce a reassuring smile then she goes on. "But we have noticed that over these last really rough couple of weeks, you have changed your prayer to start right away with what you need...,"

"But I ..." MaLyce starts to speak but June stops her.

"We understand your need. Believe, me if it were any of our children, we would be the same way honey, but have," June stops and gives MaLyce a tissue to wipe away her tears.

"Have you stopped to think that this could be a test you and Truely are facing. You have always started your prayers with your love for God but these days that is all but forgotten. Maybe God is feeling forgotten by you, the one who used to sing to him daily and would give him praise just because he is God. You would tell Him how great He is and how truly grateful, no pun intended, "you are for Him choosing you to belong to Him. Remember?" All the ladies agree at once.

MaLyce continues to cry only harder as she struggles to get the words of her defense out of her mouth. She can't really justify her change in prayer and MaLyce knows it but she is fully aware that God is a forgiving God and now that she knows the mistake she's been making, she can change it. She can ask for forgiveness and trust she'll have it.

"I feel like we should pray right now," Rhonda urges them to put down their drinks and forks and grab each other's hands. They do and spend the next few minutes each taking time, to say a prayer for Mark and Malyce's entire family. The ladies share so much together and tonight they share even more. As usual they get through it together and find that they are knitted together even tighter.

After a few minutes, more the women start to relax and the table finally finds laughter. But it's getting late and all of the women have families to get home to so they leave one at a time, hoping Truely will get there before the last one has to leave. June picks up her purse to leave when Malyce's cell phone rings. It's Truly; he's so excited, he can hardly get his words together.

"What? What? Truely what's wrong? What's happened? Honey, you have to slow down and..." MaLyce is cut off by Truely's words.

CHAPTER
38

Regina "Babydoll" Peoples Whitham has found her brother, Honestly, or she believes it's her brother Honestly, almost four months ago. She's wanted to contact him almost every day since his birth certificate came up in the search that the investigator did on Regina's last birthday. She has found her older brother, Honestly Sweet, as well as her sister Hellinher, Regina's older sister or maybe her oldest sister along with Hellinher's twin brother, Havesome Mercy. Since finding out their names, Regina has found out where Mercy is employed and has recently acquired the lunch chef position at Macy's a well established restaurant in town and Honestly is a highly-respected professor at the college where he works. Regina knows about the investigator Walter Mayfield hired on behalf of her sister Naturallee Joy, and Regina knows about the death of her brother, Kane. Regina Babydoll also knows that if she opens herself up to her siblings, everything from the past could come out and her brothers and sisters would know that Syvon left them all that day because of her. Afraid that they would hate her for driving away their mother and robbing them of the life they could have had with her, Babydoll wouldn't let herself call any of them or interact with them in any way. She's made herself content with following their lives through others'.

But Regina "Babydoll" knows she can't continue to live this way any longer, her desire to have contact with her family has become too great and after all this time, the need demands to be fed.

Regina and Markus still want to keep their real identities a secret, neither are ready to face the possibility that someone else knows their past, but Regina knows that isn't possible to do any longer. Her need to know her brothers and sisters is all that she thinks about these days. Markus does understand, he's just having a hard time with the possibility of exposure. But tonight, Regina has to tell Markus that she sent an e-mail. After all, this time they may still have to face their demons. As Regina signs off her laptop and closes the lid, she hopes her husband will understand. In an effort to heighten the possibility that he will, she says a short prayer.

◆

Trusting that Markus is still the same man he was this morning before he left for his office, Regina makes him his favorite meal for dinner. Her famous fried chicken, pinto beans and rice with home-made biscuits is something Markus could never turn down and has never turned her down for whatever she's asked for when he's eating it. Regina is hoping tonight is no different. She knows Markus likes to talk about work and he loves it when she listens attentively. So tonight, Regina has sent the kids to her best friend, Olivia's house. It will be just her and Markus to discuss her decision alone, right after she hears about his workday. They may not have the traditional marriage but they do have a great working relationship and Regina doesn't want that to change, at least not too much.

Chapter Thirty-Eight

Regina remembers the agreement they made years ago when they married, but Regina has been noticing the many different relationships that are a part of her and Markus' lives. And as of late, she has been watching, from a distance, her sisters Surely's and Hellinher's relationships with their husbands as well as Honestly and Beverley. Regina has noticed the way that couples laugh together and the way they touch the arm of their partners. Regina has found herself reminiscing over the dinner Naturallee and Walter had several weeks ago. They seemed so in loved with each other. The way Naturallee looked intensely into Walter's eyes, the way Walter held the ends of Naturallee's fingers as he explained something to her. The whole delicate scene made Regina smile and her husband, Markus question where her mind was that night. The two of them were there to celebrate their fourteenth wedding anniversary.

For Regina the things that brought she and Markus together and has been the heavy rope that has kept them together is becoming less and less important to her. Regina has been able to see Markus as other women see him. He is handsome enough but he is so much more than physical. Markus has that, everyone-wants-him-at-the-party personality. He also finds the good in everyone no matter how others feel about the worst person in the world. Markus loves everyone and everyone who meets him, loves him instantly. Regina and Markus have a good life. Regina thought it best to try to keep her changing feelings to herself.

Right now, she's not sure he will accept her new feelings for him and she doesn't know how to convey them to him at this point, anyway. Yes, right now it's best to keep her feelings quiet.

CHAPTER 39

After circling the airport an additional forty minutes, the plane finally sets down with a thump. As it taxies its way to the terminal for departure, I wonder how much longer it will be before I'm standing in front of Walter Mayfield. This isn't going to be easy. I can't find my luggage. The airline says they will find it and send it to my hotel. The car that picks me up has a driver that doesn't speak very good English and it takes an extra half an hour to get to the hotel. Fortunately, Ms. Blair booked my room and made sure it would still be available even though I'm arriving late.

Once I get settled in my room, I go to find Walter. I know it's late but enough time has been wasted. I need to see him tonight. I ask the desk but they say Walter has left for the evening. Hungry and tired, I don't want to wait for breakfast and I don't want to pay for room service so I'll have to eat in the restaurant tonight. The hotel is beautiful. I've never been in a place this large and spacious. I thought my rooms were nice but the restaurant and lobby, as well as the bar, makes my room seem like a doghouse, almost.

Suspended

It's too late to have dinner in the restaurant and I doubt eating in the lobby is acceptable but I understand I can get great appetizers large enough for four people in the bar. I head in and find myself a table and order myself a glass of wine. After living with Walter for the last ten months, and seeing him enjoy a glass of wine each night, I have allowed myself the same pleasure. But Walter would always bring me a glass; I don't even know what brand name of wine it is, I only know he says I like the ports better. Not wanting to sound too young to drink I just ask for a good port wine and the appetizer. The guy at the desk was right. The appetizer is so large, I can't eat all of it. As a matter of fact I can't even eat *half* of it.

If it weren't for having something so important to do that keeps my thoughts occupied, I could really enjoy the soft lights and soothing sounds of the night here in the bar. But even this atmosphere, as intoxicating as it is, gives way to the drain of adrenaline and I tire to the point of exhaustion. I return to my room without any success of seeing Walter. Well, I do have the room right across from his room so I should be able to catch him in the morning before he gets going.

◆

Eight-thirty! Walter is always up and out by seven-thirty. I rush to the door but that won't tell me anything. I freeze for a minute to think. I'll call his room—no I will call the front desk to see if he is in his room. I reach for the phone but change my mind. I have to grow up if I want to have an adult relationship with this man. I take a deep breath and go to the bathroom to get ready to actually face Walter. In the shower, I go over what I want to say to him a dozen or more times and I'm still not satisfied with my choice of words. As I brush my teeth with the toothbrush I threw in my purse from home, I still can't find the right words. I can't mess this up anymore than I already have so I keep playing things over in my mind as I move forward with my plan to knock on his door and tell Walter everything I need to say.

Chapter Thirty-Nine

I check my purse to make sure that I have brought our plane ticket to Paris. Walter and I are to leave from Florida to go to Paris in a week and I don't want something as small as a ticket at this point to get in my way of making things right with Walter. I hold the ticket for encouragement and then I put it away. Still trying to figure out what I want to say to him, I have to pause and catch my breath because I am actually in front of Walter's door. I can't stop the momentum I have built up and before I can stop myself or talk myself out of it my hand is knocking on the door. But I hear two voices and I lose my courage. Then just before I can turn around, the door opens and I have what I have come for. Walter is standing in front of me and now there are no words that come to mind. I stare at him and see things I hadn't seen in Walter in a long time. Walter's eyes still look young and full of life. His lips are still strong and inviting and the brown mole on his throat is more centered than I realized; it moves when he swallows. His hair is messy and that's the way I like it, I think he looks sexy when it's messy. The smile that he has when he opens the door is starting to fade and I know right away, I've made a mistake in coming. I should have told Walter I was coming. Ms. Blair was wrong; I should have called and asked him if I could come out and talk with him. Now, as if a cat really does have my tongue, I can't find my words, as much as I have practiced. As much as I have wanted this moment, I can't open my mouth.

"Walter," is all I can finally get out of my throat. I've been standing here it feels like for hours and all I can say is 'Walter'. Then before anything more can happen or I can say the next word, even before Walter can say my name, that woman from his office appears in the background. I've seen her somewhere else other than at his office. I know I've seen her before and, now that I see her closer, I realize I do know who she is. But what is she doing here with Walter and what is Walter doing with her. What is Carl's mother doing here with Walter? How do they know each other? I'm shocked, I can't move. I can't think. I can't say anything and at this point I don't know what it is I should say. I feel myself drifting up then as if an invisible hand grabs the back of my shirt I feel myself stepping back away from his door, away from Walter. I can feel my eyes filling up with hot, steamy tears. I know my ears are on fire because I feel the heat around them under my hair. I must be stepping back into a tunnel because I see Walter's mouth moving and I hear a grueling noise but I can't make out his words. Now I am pressed against the door of my room but I can't remember how to open the door so I turn to walk away. Then I feel Walter's hand on my arm but I can't stop walking and I know now that I'm crying. I can't see anything anymore but it doesn't matter. All I can think of is how badly I have messed up my life and Walter's. Then I think about the hurt Walter must have felt when I rejected him. This is more pain than I have ever felt in my entire life including when Syvon made me stay in the room with the man with the one big eye.

I want to run away but I can't move. There is something holding me so tight I can't breathe. Something has wrapped around me but it's something I remember, something familiar that I have always enjoyed and feel safe when I'm here. Now I must be dreaming because this safe place is in Walter's arms. I feel his arms around me so tight it feels like we're one again.

I hear him say, "Shhh, Naturallee don't cry. I'm sorry for all I've put you through. It was selfish of me. Can you ever forgive me? I'm very sorry." Then Walter takes a breath so deep I feel I'm sucked inside of him I feel I am inside of his heartbeat. It pounds in my ears clearly, so clearly I can't hear his words anymore only the beating of his heart. I do feel safe and loved again. I know whatever has happened between us can be fixed. I know because I love him. And I'm never letting go. Ever.

I find myself crying harder now but I'm happy. But again, Walter must be getting the wrong idea about my tears because he starts to let me go. But I can't let the wrong impression happen this time. I grab onto Walter so tight, I pinch him and he flinches. He starts

Chapter Thirty-Nine

to talk but this time I reach up and grab the back of his head and pull his mouth down to mine and kiss him until I can't breathe. I feel Walter's response to my kiss as he slides his arms around me and pulls me into him again. I don't want this kiss to ever end and apparently, neither does Walter. I feel him take in more air and release it against my cheek while kissing me feverishly. We breathe as one in this way until we have to stop but we don't have to let go of each other, and we don't.

"I need to tell you something," I tell Walter as I cover every inch of his face with my kisses. "I wasn't rejecting you when I pulled away at the house the other day. I could never reject you or turn away from your advances Walter; I love you too much for something like that. I should have told you how I feel months ago but I've never loved anyone before and I didn't," but Walter's lips find mine again and my words are lost with the probing of his tongue. One thing is for sure I do know what love is now. It's Walter.

CHAPTER 40

Honestly Sweet has joined in with the once a week afternoon meetings of Mercy, Ronald, Hellinher, and Surely Fine. Together, they've found out that there is someone else looking for the family. Hellinher remembered the name of one of the neighbors that lived across the street from Grandma Lucy's for a few years. Mrs. Hadley and her daughter Robin stayed in the house that was said to be haunted. Mrs. Hadley was kind to Syvon's children feeding them every time one of them said that they were hungry. She would bring food and clothes over to Grandma Lucy's for the grand kids, she'd say. But that was more than twenty-five, thirty years ago. It wasn't easy to find Mrs. Hadley since her daughter had taken her to live with her. Robin had moved to Nebraska and then Maine before moving back to Oregon and then she had moved several times around the state before finally settling about four hours away.

When the small band of siblings got to Robin and Mrs. Hadley's house that afternoon, they were anxious and nervous about what she would be able to tell them. Robin had warned Honestly when he called that her mother had a stroke several months ago and that some of her memory was gone. The siblings still want to speak with her just the same as long as Robin is there in the meeting.

The meeting went well. Much of what Mrs. Hadley couldn't remember, Robin did. The two women together were able to fill in a lot of the blanks in the lives of the Peoples children. They told them that there had to be a lot more of them than the six or seven they knew about. Robin remembered the names of the youngest children as well as the most of the older ones. She remembered that Syvon hated all of her children, hating some of them more than others. Syvon hated Naturallee Joy and Truely Grateful the most. She had been arrested for what she did to Truely. Robin didn't know what it was that Syvon did to him but when the ambulance got to the school, the police came with them. Mrs. Hadley had told Robin when she got home from school, back when it happened, that the police had been to Grandma Lucy's that afternoon looking for Syvon. Robin remembers the night they found Syvon behind Grandma Lucy's house, hiding in the garage. Grandma Lucy never came out of the house to see what was going on; she never even cracked a curtain at a window to look out. But Mrs. Hadley spoke up then to tell them that Syvon had tied Truely to a chair and poured boiling water into his lap and made him sit in it that night for punishment. Rumor was that Truely had called the man visiting his mother by the wrong name causing the man to get really angry. The man slapped Syvon around and left her there with Truely. Syvon said Truely needed to be punished, she said that Truely got what he deserved.

The police were never able to actually charge her because Syvon said she didn't do it, the man was never found and Truely was so afraid of her, he would not say who did it. The crime was so ugly to every police officer, doctor, and medic that was connected to the case, they were intent on finding out what happened so that Syvon could be arrested. But one of the police officers lost control and shot

Chapter Forty

her, he said, accidently. To avoid the lawsuit, Syvon and Grandma Lucy brought against the city, they gave Syvon probation and custody of Truely to Grandma Lucy who already had custody of two of the other kids. Syvon was forbidden to see Truely ever again and she could only have supervised visitation of the others.

Then one day, when the social worker was at the house checking on the kids, Syvon had slipped in and took the kids. Months later, when Syvon called Grandma Lucy, she told Lucy the kids were fine but she was not going to let strangers take her kids from her. A year later, Syvon gave birth to the last child that Robin and Mrs. Hadley knew about. After that, Syvon left Grandma Lucy and the little girl Joy at a church. Syvon never returned to the church or the family for that matter.

The small band of siblings spent the entire afternoon with Rachel and her mother before returning home filled with information about other siblings but also angry, hurt, disappointed, and sick with the thought of who their mother really was.

CHAPTER 41

"Don't try to back out now, Hellin; you already told James you would use the ticket. You know Ronald is in the middle of his classes and Mercy just got his position at the restaurant and Honestly and Beverly are going south for the week. That leaves you, besides, what else are you going to do Hellin," Surely is surprised over Hellin's lack of desire to go; most people can't wait to go to Paris for free. Surely knows Hellin enjoys travel but this trip she has no interest in at all.

"Surely, I have a confession to make."

"What's that Hellin," Surely wants to know.

"I've never been on an airplane before. I'm afraid to fly." Hellin feels a bit embarrassed to make the confession especially to Surely. Surely's life seems so upscale compared to Hellinher's. Hellin has traveled the country a lot. She's been to twenty-two of the fifty states on different vacations and weekend excursions but she has always driven or taken a train. She has also been to Canada on the train.

Twice she and her husband drove to Vancouver for long vacations there. But Hellinher has never flown anywhere. Now Hellinher waits for Surely to say something but the line is quiet.

"Surely, are you there?" Hellinher asks her sister just to confirm that Surely hadn't hung up.

"I thought you said that you have traveled from one of the countries to the other. You said you liked traveling and you've always wanted to travel abroad. How were you going to get there," Surely had to ask since they were due to leave in less than a week.

"I'm still going, you may need to fill me with some Dramamine or something, but my plan is to go. I don't know when this kind of opportunity will come around again. Hellinher means every word she's saying. She just doesn't know how she is going to get on the plane but she does plan to go.

A few more minutes of sisterly conversation and encouragement on Surely's part to Hellinher and the girls hang up the phones. Hellinher's husband chuckles at her reluctance and continues to read his newspaper. George knows Hellin's reluctance and understands it. George would never have put himself in the position Hellin is now in. He would have said from the start he doesn't like flying, he likes to keep both feet on the ground and play it safe. But he knows Hellin won't do safe, she can't. There's that something inside of her which makes her move forward and face her fears. George admires his wife for that, but he has never been able to embrace that way of living. He has already taken money form his own personal savings account to give Hellin for her trip. He has told her boss and his best friend Roger Lane that Hellin will be away on vacation for three weeks even though she will only be away for ten days. George told Hellin he wants her to take a few days off before she leaves and he wants her to take the week off when she gets back home.

Knowing Hellinher's past, George wants to help make her life as well as he can in part because of her past, but George mainly wants to make her life good because he loves her. Hellinher doesn't

Chapter Forty-One

have her mother's beauty or gorgeous figure and most times she prefers to stay at home rather than going out but George knows that there is so much more to this woman with the full lips and wide hips that her dark-brown skin and eyes just don't tell. He knows that Hellinher has secretly searched for her family for years and that she hold's no grudge against her mother for the way she treated all of them. And even though Hellinher had buried her scars deep inside of her she always wants to help someone in need of being rescued. George loves her resilience; it's what kept him going when the world became too much for him to handle alone. Hellinher is always able to bounce back and find the good in any situation and George loves her for that.

"George, are you sure you don't want to come tonight. You know Mercy loves it when you show up." Hellinher and Ronald are meeting Mercy, Honestly and Beverly at the restaurant for dinner. Honestly wants his family there when he surprises Beverly with her engagement ring. He knows she could say no but he feels the rejection could hurt less if he has family there to see him through it. Hellinher laughs as she thinks about how much the five of them do together. They love each other without reservation, without judgment, and with everything inside of them. They sometimes tell each other it might have been a good thing that life happened as it did because they don't know if they could be any closer to each other if they had known each other all of their lives.

"No, woman, you guys don't need me there every time you get together, at least not right now. Go on, get to know each other then when you're sick of each other, me and the other spouses can become regulars," George kisses his wife as he pushes her out the door. Waving good-bye, Hellinher gets into her birthday present from two years ago and puts her Jeep into reverse then drives away.

◆

Suspended

Macy's on the River is always quiet, elegant, and romantic except for Monday and Tuesday nights. The restaurant has only recently started opening on Monday nights since Mercy took over as night chef. The manager gave him the opportunity to show what he could do to improve business by twenty percent, and Mercy accepted the challenge. Within two months, Mercy showed a twenty-three percent increase in business. Stan, the manager, was so happy that he told Mercy he could try almost anything he wanted after that. Mercy wanted to offer the rest of the world the chance to enjoy the restaurant so he asked for Monday and Tuesday nights as a more relaxed atmosphere and attire. Mercy created a menu for the new crowd and an almost second restaurant was born along with what customers called the "new-week weekend." Stan loves things so much that Mercy has become irreplaceable to Stan.

Stan has designated a table for Mercy's family and the meals are always free. For everyone else who enters the doors of Macy's on the River on Mondays and Tuesdays, the atmosphere is relaxed, fun and less expensive than the rest of the week. Many of the patrons have told Stan that Macy's on Mondays and Tuesdays is like turning the weekend into four days instead of just the two. The restaurant is always full to capacity and there is never a dull moment with the games in the back room and out on the patio. Buffet-style eating instead of the very lavish waiters and waitresses, standing high tops take the place of triple padded over-sized seats, and a DJ instead of the piano player or jazz band has given the place lively appeal to the younger, more laid-back crowd. Even though Honestly, Surely, and Hellinher feel a bit out of place some evenings, they can't imagine being anywhere else when their brothers Ronald and Mercy are there waiting for them. The four of them, Hellinher, Surely, Honestly, and Ronald are so pleased for Mercy and hearing his life's story. Knowing what he has had to overcome, gives his siblings a sense of pride for him. Bailey sometimes meets with the family to share what part of Mercy's life he has been allowed to be a part of.

◆

Chapter Forty-One

Tonight, Bailey is meeting with Mercy and the other siblings for a relaxing evening and to continue to do what he is hired to do. Bailey has known Mercy for a couple of years but he has only known Honestly, Surely, and Hellinher for a few months. Bailey loves what he does but he doesn't understand most of his clients. Why Regina Babydoll didn't want to meet her siblings, he couldn't figure out. But he's not paid to find that out. He's first paid to find the rest of Regina's family and now he has the responsibility of keeping an eye on them. He is paid to know from time to time where they are and what they are doing. The night Honestly met Mercy, Regina was there to witness their meeting. Regina spent several nights that month at the restaurant hoping Bailey had guessed the right night that Mercy and Honestly would meet.

After almost twenty five-years of looking into the lives of others and being invisible while working for people, families, and corporations, Bailey seldom got personally involved with a case. But there is just something, he told himself and his wife, that's different about each of the brothers and sisters he finds obsessive as well as the woman who hired him. Bailey listened to some of the story Regina had to tell him about her family but the information wasn't much. Bailey usually wants to know something about each case he works; he believes it helps him to understand the way those he's trying to find could possibly think and act. The back-story could help him to know what they might be willing to do to make sure they're not found. It could help him to know if they want to be found.

Once Bailey started finding people who knew Regina's family, it became clear just how much each one of the children would need the others, even if they hadn't realized it yet. After reading all of the police reports about Syvon Peoples, Bailey couldn't understand how it was possible for her to keep custody of her children as long as she did. He also couldn't understand how any person could do the things she did to another human being, especially her own children. When he read the reports about Truely and Regina, Bailey thought long and hard about continuing his search for the family. It wasn't until his wife reminded him that Syvon, herself, was already dead and unable to hurt any of the children any longer, that Bailey was able to continue looking for Regina's siblings.

Regina's mother, in Bailey's mind, was someone who deserved to have hot water thrown on her, she should have been beaten so badly that she too would have spent two weeks in a hospital's intensive care unit and she should have been left in another country at the mercy of others. Syvon Peoples is someone he wondered why she hadn't been killed earlier on in life. When Bailey asked an old boyfriend of Syvon's what kind of woman she was, he spat on the ground, stepped on it, then kicked dust over it, and with hatred in his eyes and grinding his teeth the man said, "I never hated anyone until I got involved with that woman." He went on to tell how even after many years of not even seeing Syvon, his life was still suffering from the very mention of her name. Syvon caused him to spend nine years of a twenty year sentence in a state prison for the illegal things he did in the name of love for Syvon. The man had robbed and beaten another man almost to death because the man had tried to date Syvon. The man who told Bailey this added that he wished he had let that man have her. It wasn't until the boyfriend was arrested and sitting in jail awaiting trial that he found out that Syvon had been dating the cop for several months. The cop knew that she had been cheating on him with her drug dealer.

Bailey had only seen pictures of Syvon and hated himself for understanding how easily men could get into trouble for this woman. Bailey was also extremely glad he never met her. Someone had told Bailey that Syvon had one daughter that looked exactly like Syvon as a child and would probably be as beautiful as Syvon when she grew up. Bailey hoped that wasn't true or at least he hoped he would never meet that sibling.

But Bailey had to smile when he thought about the way he and Mercy met at a bus stop that Mercy waited at when he went to his meetings. Mercy was new to the rooms and was more afraid than just nervous to go alone; that's what he told Bailey who was a complete stranger at the time. Bailey offered to go with him and the friendship was born.

◆

Regina has asked Bailey to give her a call the next time the gang gets together here at Macy's. Of course, Bailey has done his job again, but tonight so far, Regina hasn't shown up.

Bailey continues to remember different moments about each of the family members including what he found out about Regina and Markus Whitham or should he call them Babydoll Peoples and Daniel Howell. Bailey has a file on Regina that's larger than the file he has on Honestly. When Bailey takes a case that has what he deems strange elements to it, he always looks into the life of the one that hires him, as well. Babydoll has a lot of baggage to deal with but Bailey is sure that once Regina Babydoll met her brothers and sisters she will be able to let go of most, if not all, of that baggage. After all that she and Marcus have been through, they deserve more money then what they and three others received from the state for the lawsuit they won six years ago. The Withams and three others who suffered at not only the Graybar Foster Home but the Sullivan's and the Longs, as well, before those three foster homes and two others were closed. The foster care parents as well as some of those from the state foster care agency who closed their eyes to what was happening to the children in their care were arrested and put into prison. Because Regina, Markus and the other three foster children had tried for years to tell someone about the abuse that was going on but no one would listen especially their case workers. Markus, Regina and the others were able to win what was deemed an unwinnable case by the legal system until a civil rights attorney from a prestigious law firm in town took their case. Regina and Markus waited until they were oldest enough and then sued the city, the state, and the agency as well as nine people individually. They won their case and received just short of three million dollars each. The Withams still live very modestly, not wanting to waste what they have. If Bailey hadn't done research on the Withams he would have given Regina a huge discount on his fee. But with a combined net worth of better than six million, he realized he could charge his standard rate plus expenses.

"Hello, Bailey. Are they all here?" Bailey chokes on his drink, caught off guard by the woman standing before him.

"You came, Regina I'm so glad." Bailey hugs Babydoll before he realizes what he's doing. After expressing her concerns to Bailey again, Regina admits she can't wait to hug them all. Without giving her a chance to change her mind, Bailey asks for everyone's attention.

"Hey, guys, what have I missed? Sorry, I'm late but James Jr. needed a ride and of course, I was the only one who could drop him off. You will not believe what I found out today." Surely Fine is so excited about her news that she doesn't notice Bailey who is just about to introduce Babydoll to the family. Surely continues with her news. "I think I've found Baby Boy and Big Man. Look at this," she says as she begins to pull out papers from her purse. Bailey is about to speak up but Regina pulls on his arm to stop him.

The table gathers around to see what Surely has found. While spreading out the papers, Surely tells them that both brothers are still in town and Baby Boy is the head pastor at Grove Road Church on the other side of town. Big Man owns a landscaping company just over the line in the next county. Surely has pictures of both brothers and spreads the pictures on the table.

The table is silent as they examine the pictures. "The men look like two thirds of a set," Regina speaks without intending to. All eyes turn to her and every mouth drops open.

"You're a Peoples, aren't you?" Honestly asks slowly.

Chapter Forty-One

"I'm Regina—Babydoll Peoples," is all she can say as the siblings sit locked into their seats. Then Mercy lets out a loud roar of laughter and grabs Regina up, lifting her feet from the floor. The rest of her brothers and sisters regain their senses and all the siblings are crying and laughing together, overwhelmed with the joy of finding another of Syvon Peoples' children.

CHAPTER
42

The ceremony is wonderful. Walter refuses to accept any credit for all the work he has put into trying to get the children and the Billy's family here to Florida and the new orphanage. He gives all the credit to Nathan Grey who had the foresight to know that the orphanage needed to be moved to the states and he gives credit to Carl's father, John Morgan who knew how to get things done. Walter has to accept the name on the building as the Mayfield-Grey Children's Home. Walter can't change it; Nathan Grey had put it in the legal papers that way.

After a full day of meeting the staff, the children, the media, and financial supporters and well-wishers of the Home, Walter and I are both exhausted. We return to our rooms at the hotel bone weary and starved. Walter suggests we meet in an hour for a quiet dinner in the hotel so we can retire early for the evening. It sounds like a great idea and until I turn left to enter my room and Walter turns to the right to go into his room, it doesn't really hit me until this moment that Walter and I are not sharing the same house as we do back in Oregon. At home, we don't share the same bedroom but we usually retire at the same time. We walk up the stairs together having some light conversation, sometimes laughing about something totally unimportant to either of us but it helped to bring us closer together and more loving each night. It's something I hadn't noticed how much I enjoyed until now.

◆

We must have been more tired than we were hungry because I wake at five-thirty the next morning still in my bath robe and slippers so I know I didn't meet Walter for dinner. That's right. I was supposed to meet Walter for dinner. I spring up and run to the door and open it. I'm not sure if I thought I would find Walter standing there waiting for me or what it is I expected but the hallway is empty. Walter's door is closed and I get the feeling he slept through dinner, too. I step back into my room and close the door.

There's nothing to do on a Monday morning in Florida. Since I've never been here before, I have no idea what there is to do or where to find it so I turn on the television and stare at it. I think about how much my life has changed this past year. Today, television seems foreign to me but last year this time television brought all my friends to me—one week to the next—one episode after the other my TV friends would visit me. Today I don't know any of them; I've even forgotten most of their names.

Walter and I haven't had much time to ourselves since I got here. There have been so many things to do in late preparation for the ceremony and the opening of the Mayfield-Grey Home so the chance to talk has not presented itself, and as happy as I am and as happy as Walter seems to be that I am here, there are things that we need to discuss. I don't want any more misunderstanding between us. I love this man. I want to marry Walter. I want him to love me and marry me right here in Florida – today! I want to march right over to his room and ask him to marry me right now.

I bounce up and start dressing for the day. I want to look my best when I ask Walter for his hand in marriage but in my haste to pack, I see that I have left some of my best things at home. My yellow sundress or even my white Capri pants with my bright green crew neck top would be perfect but neither choice is available. I finally settle for my khaki shorts with my red tank top. Red is said to be a powerful color and I want Walter to see just how serious I am about getting married. And, I think I will have to ask him if I want to marry here in Florida, I just don't see Walter wanting to rush me into marriage. I can hear him saying it now. I will wear my hair down across my shoulders, it's the way Walter likes to see it and this morning I don't want to disappoint him. I'm almost ready to go to Walter's room when there's a knock at my door. Thinking it's Walter, I run to the door and open it. Tearing open the heavy hotel door as though it were a bird's feather falling to the ground, I see it's Beth, Carl's mother. I'm surprised. I'm not sure what to do or say so I squeak out, "Hello," and wait for her response.

"Hello, Naturallee, it's me Beth Morgan, Carl's mother. I hope you remember me," Beth says. "I realize it is quite early but I wanted to see you before I return home this morning but it looks like you're on your way out. I do need to speak with you. Will you be gone long? Could I come back in a bit?"

I recover from the surprise of finding her at my door and explain that I'm not leaving. I was just going over to see if Walter was awake yet, but that can wait. I need to know what brings Beth Morgan to my door.

"Naturallee, there are some things I feel I need to tell you. I know Walter never will. Walter is too kind a person to say anything less than positive or encouraging about anyone and he would never pass on something negative about anyone he loves." Beth announces this affirmation to me as I show her to the one of three chairs or the couch in the far side of my room. Sitting down in the beige chair next to the window, Beth continues with what she has to say.

"Naturallee, I know you and Carl have broken it off and I am sorry to know this. I was so hoping things would have worked out for the both of you together. I have known from the beginning, well almost from the beginning that you are the woman my son was interested in and the woman Walter was living with." When Beth said *living with Walter* I felt uncomfortable almost dirty. She must have seen my discomfort over those words because she tried to change up her words to make it sound better. But the words are already out there and she can't fix it so she moves on with what she is saying. "I didn't mean to make you uncomfortable. Forgive me. It was a poor choice of words." Beth has something she needs to say and maybe I need to hear but I've never been in a situation like this and I don't think I really like it. But I see that it's important to her so I ask her to continue.

"I want you to know that I love my son very much and his happiness is paramount to me. I know how taken he was by you and how proud he was the night of his brother Michael's birthday party. Carl felt so successful showing up with you on his arm—he was with the most beautiful woman in the room—in the town probably. Then knowing that you were interested in him really gave him a big boost. Carl has low self-esteem issues so that night changed him a lot, at least temporarily. Anyway, it was a few weeks later that we found out that you are the woman Nathan Grey had left instruction for Walter to find and then live with for a year. And knowing that you had taken up the challenge Nathan Grey had set before you, disturbed Carl more than he was willing to admit. He tried to look past it but after Walter had the heart attack and you decided to stay with him, Carl couldn't handle it. And needless to say, he didn't handle it very well." Beth stops talking to see if I am still following what she is saying. And while I am following her words, I'm still not sure what it is she wants or just feels she needs to say.

Chapter Forty-Two

"Naturallee, I love my son as I have said, but my son has too many ways that are like his father, John Morgan. Do you know why I'm here with Walter and you for this opening?" Beth asks as if she is sure I don't know and of course, she is right. I don't.

"Well, no. I don't know why you're here. I thought you came to be with Walter." Once I said it out loud the words made me a bit angry.

"Yes, I came to be with Walter but not the way you mean. Walter made it very clear how much he loves you."

I'm more than happy to hear that but it doesn't explain why Beth is here, so I just need to ask her. But before I can ask anything Beth continues with her story.

"Years ago, Walter, Nathan Grey, and John were all good friends they did almost everything together. And while they were all good friends only Nathan and Walter were best friends, meaning they were closer to each other than they were to John. After all, Walter and Nathan had been friends for all but three years of their lives; John didn't meet them until the three of them were in their second year of college. They became fast friends, each traveling their own road so to speak, Nathan was in medicine, Walter in law, and John in business. Nathan and Walter were both driven, taking their studies seriously. They played a lot but they also knew when to stop and get back to the books but John didn't. Too many times, John found himself on probation at school and then to graduate, he had to transfer to another college. One that didn't require as much as University of Michigan and one that didn't cost as much. Don't get me wrong, John was very bright. He just didn't have the discipline like Nathan and Walter. Finally, the three ended up business partners. John decided that being an entrepreneur wasn't exactly what he wanted so he sold his part of the partnership and worked for the company instead. John was good at what he did. He just wasn't a leader. He was a great worker. Anyway, one year Nathan and Walter went to Jamaica for a vacation and that is when they met the children at the orphanage and the Billy family. That is also when Nathan had someone to go down to Jamaica and get things straightened out for the orphanage. That someone he sent was John. When Walter and Nathan decided to build the home here and get everyone out of Jamaica, John, to everyone's surprise, asked to take the lead on the project. But a year into the planning, John was diagnosed with cancer. Two years later, he killed himself. He said he couldn't take it anymore." Beth seems to be remembering a particular moment with her husband so I wait quietly for her to come back to the room and finish the story.

"Oh yeah," Beth remembers she is still telling me her story. "Even though Nathan and Walter always included John in the business affairs and most of the time in their fun and travels, they recognized, even more than John did that John was married and couldn't zigzag across the country and across the world at a moment's notice. I mean John and I had a family to raise. Both Walter and Nathan were single and free at the time; they could do as they pleased. Anyway, John couldn't handle both family and friends. He didn't know how to separate the two, and neither does my son. Carl is married. Did you know that? He is in the middle of getting a divorce but he is still married and his wife or soon to be ex-wife has two children from a prior relationship. This is something Carl should have told you instead of trying to make the two of you work out in spite of his baggage. He ended up hitting Staci one night and she called the police. Carl spent six months in jail behind that because after Staci bailed him out the next day, he hit her again the next week. But when he hit her this time she fell down some stairs and split her cheek open. Carl did that in front of Staci's oldest child, a little girl named Bethany. Staci felt she had no choice. She didn't want Bethany to feel it was right to take that kind of abuse. Staci had to press charges and Carl got the six months. I couldn't blame the woman. I think I would have done the same thing. But these are some of the things I believe Carl should have told you himself." Beth stops talking again and looks at me as if she's surprised I didn't run out of the room screaming. Then she goes on.

"But none of this explains why I am here with Walter," Beth makes the million dollar statement. "First, let me say that I am here with Walter but we are not here together. After he got the call, Walter asked me to join the two of you to represent John's part in making this all happen. I know the two of you are staying another day or two and then going on to Paris. If there is someplace I would love to be with Walter, it would be Paris not Florida," she smiles openly and stands up to leave.

"Naturallee, please if you love Walter, hold on to him. Treat him good; I mean really good. Walter's a good person and deserves to be loved by someone who loves him and no other man, including my son," she gives me a hug and walks to the door.

"I hope you and Walter have a great life together. Forget about Carl so that he can get his life together and be a good husband for someone else, one of these days." And with that, Beth opens the door and leaves.

I just stand there and watch as the door closes.

CHAPTER 43

It's nine thirty and Walter is still sleeping. I wonder if he's really that tired or if he's just relaxing in his room this morning. He's been moving continuously for the past week so taking a little extra time this morning is probably good for him. After Beth's visit I decide I can wait until after breakfast before asking Walter to marry me so I go down to the restaurant to have breakfast alone. I get to the elevator before panic grabs me. Is Walter alright? After all he's had one heart attack. Before I know what I'm doing, I'm at Walter's door and pounding on it quite vigorously. I find that I am also calling his name loudly. There's no answer and I hit the door with both hands. I feel tears build up and now I'm getting angry and scared. I need to get in this room. Then I have a thought, I'll call the front desk and tell them I have an emergency; they'll have to come and open the door. I fumble in my pockets for my cell phone. I find it but remember that I don't know how to call from my cell phone. I need to go back to my room. Turning to open my hotel room door I hear Walter's door click and I spin back to see who opened the door. Walter is standing before me with only a towel at his waist, his hair dripping with water and he's breathing heavy with a frightened look on his face.

"What, what is it? What's wrong? Is the hotel on fire? Naturallee." Thank God. Walter's alright but now I feel foolish for letting my imagination get the best of me. I don't know what to say so I say nothing. All I can do is look at Walter. Then I notice some of the other guests have opened their doors and are now wondering what is going on. I want to melt into the carpet. As if things aren't bad enough now a security guard steps around the corner.

Moving quickly toward me, he asks if everything's alright as he flashes his eyes between me and Walter. He has a serious look about him and he's grabbing for something in his pocket and I pray it's not a gun. He pulls a phone from the right pocket of his ocean blue jacket and starts giving information to someone on the other end of the line.

I spend the next few minutes trying to explain to the security guard what I thought was going on and why as Walter dresses quickly and returns to the hallway. Finally, the whole thing is over and Walter brings me into his room while he finishes dressing and to let me pull myself together.

"What were you thinking, sweetheart? What made you think I was having a heart attack?" Walter asks.

This is the first time in a very long time he's called me sweetheart and I like the way it sounds. But I can tell he wants an answer so I can't spend time enjoying the sound of it. I can tell Walter wants an answer.

"Walter, I'm sorry. I thought it was strange that you were still sleeping but I had decided to go down to have a late breakfast after Beth left and I thought at the elevator that maybe there was something...," I can't finish my babbling because Walter stops me with a question.

Chapter Forty-Three

"What did you say about Beth?" He looks serious now. After repeating what I've already said, Walter wants to know what all Beth told me. I'm feeling like this morning can't end fast enough; hopefully the afternoon will be better. After spending more time telling Walter what Beth told me I finally had to let Walter know he's making me feel like I'm on the witness stand being cross-examined by prosecutors before he finally lets it go.

We leave the hotel after all the excitement ends and Walter shows me the town. It turns out Walter has a house here in Florida that has a part time staff. It's occupied by a couple who will be leaving to go back home to Australia in four months. He's not sure what he will do with the house then. He and Nathan Grey have their names on a couple of buildings and on a children's hospital here in Florida and now on the new Mayfield-Grey Home for Children. I can't help but love this man.

After an afternoon of sightseeing and fun, Walter and I have dinner at a small family restaurant a few blocks from the hotel. The new Staffing Director for the Mayfield-Grey Home is having dinner here, as well. Gary Joseph and his wife are in their late fifties, maybe early sixties but they are both older acting people than Walter. Madeline Joseph walks with a cane and Gary shuffles along with her but they are both charming people. They are foster parents, as well as they each hold down full-time jobs; Madeline is a teacher. Over a dinner of shrimp and crab legs, the Joseph's tell Walter and I how they met and fell in love. They married thirty-three years ago and have been happy together since their wedding day. Madeline congratulates Walter and I on our engagement and we both caught by surprise. Walter drops his fork full of shrimp and I stop chewing and let my mouth hang open. Neither Walter nor I know what to say but Madeline does. She apologizes for "letting the cat out of the bag," she says. But she wants to confirm to us that we are in love with each other deeply and that we will marry soon. Gary seems quite agreeable with his wife's assessment of Walter and me as he

271

continues with his dinner. We finally get Gary and Madeline to talk about something other than us so the dinner finishes nicely. The Joseph's have to leave to pick up one of their children; they have seven. After the Joseph's leave the restaurant, Walter chuckles lightly remembering the night's conversation. I want to chuckle with him but I can't, Madeline was right, there is going to be a marriage. Walter just doesn't know it yet.

Walter and I discuss Beth and John Morgan. Beth loved John. Even with his lack of leadership desire and drive; she loved him. Just before the caramel cheesecake is served, Walter and I finally get around to discussing Carl.

I want Walter to know how I feel about Carl, but more importantly, I want Walter to know how I feel about him. I can't tell Walter when it happened or how it happened but it has happened and I couldn't be happier. I want Walter to know that I am happy because of the love I have for him, I've never loved anyone like this before.

I need Walter to know about the man with the one big eye and why I pulled away the other day. I want him to know the things I have kept to myself all these years. I need Walter to know about my being suspended when certain things happen in my life.

Walter needs to know I appreciate all that he has done for me in finding my family. Just knowing he had Ms. Blair contact my brothers to let them know that I had to miss the surprise lunch Walter had planned for us, makes me feel even closer to Walter. I want Walter to be with me when I meet my family. Walter should be with me after all he's done to find them.

Walter says that I will be able to talk with Baby Boy and Big Man both; I can hardly wait to hear their voices. Walter has things set up so I will also be able to see them while we talk. My statement bears repeating, I really do love this man.

CHAPTER
44

I can hardly wait for eight o'clock tonight to see my brothers' faces show up on the computer. And as if meeting my brothers for the first time isn't enough, Walter says he has one more surprise for me tonight. I did see a gift box in his closet earlier today but he didn't try to hide it so the box must not be for me. But I can't really think about the box right now it's almost time to meet my brothers. Walter is so calm about this whole thing and as hard as I'm trying, calm is not something I can get to now.

Then the computer pings and I hear conversation and see a white wall with a painting on it but there are no faces just voices. Walter speaks up and asks Ms. Blair if things are working on her end. The computer goes quiet and then as if the curtain is lifted I see both my brothers and another man come into view. I know right away who my brothers are they look just alike. I can't help it. The tears are already flowing and I don't care. I thought I was as happy as I would ever be being here with Walter, just loving him, but I was wrong. I love both these men and I can't even hug them yet. I love the other guy, too, and I don't even know who he is.

My brothers and I talk for several minutes before I think to even ask who the other man is. Baby Boy or David as he is now known as, reminds me that Walter should have already told me about another surprise he has for me. This man is your surprise. Then David introduces me to another brother Walter found just yesterday. It's our youngest brother Monkee. I hear myself scream before I cover my mouth with my hands. Walter reminds me of this morning and the security guard so I continue to scream quietly. Walter even tells my three brothers about the situation with the security guard. We all laugh about that and other things. They tell me how they all met and what Walter has done to make this moment special for me. We talk and laugh for nearly an hour before we have to start saying our good-byes. I start to tear up again and find that Walter is standing next to me and he holds my hand. Big Man says he believes there is one more thing that needs to be said before they can let me go so he needs me to stand up so that he David and Monkee can be witnesses. Before I can ask what they will need to witness Walter is speaking and pulls my hand to his chest.

"Naturallee," I hear him saying my name but he is in the way of my brothers trying to say good-bye to me and I get a little flustered. I ask him to wait a minute. The boys laugh loudly and ask me to turn my attention to Walter just for a second they want to hear what Walter has to say, as well. So I turn to Walter and smile hoping he will say whatever it is quickly so my brothers and I can say whatever we can before our time runs out. Walter starts again.

"Naturallee, I hope you know by now that I am in love with you. Nathan was right when he put this arrangement together for us. I never thought I could feel this way about a woman and now here I am so deeply in love with you that I've had to take a month away from the office hoping that I can spend it with you. Naturallee, this one month won't be enough for me though. I need to know if you

Chapter Forty-Four

would consider spending the rest of my life with me," then dropping to one knee Walter asks, "Would you marry me Naturallee, please." Walter goes on to say, "You'll make me the happiest man in this state if you will say yes."

I'm not sure I've heard Walter correctly but when he gets on his knee I feel my mind spin all of a sudden. I wanted to ask him to marry me this morning but here he is on bended knee before me and my three newly found brothers asking me instead. I am happier than I can put into words. I look into Walter loving, blue eyes unable to answer with words, I shake my head yes. And from nowhere I see the diamond I found in Syvon's safe that day inside my closet. That very same exquisite diamond is now surrounded by brilliant blue stones mounted on a platinum band. The ring is so alluring it holds me captive again as it did the first time I saw it. I still can't take my eyes away from it. Walter takes the ring from the box and slides in onto my finger. I hear my brothers and Ms. Blair cheering in the background. This is the best day of my life and I don't want it to ever end.

CHAPTER 45

I haven't slept in three days. First believing that I am only meeting two of my brothers and being surprised with three of them, then Walter's proposal, my ring, two nights in New York and now here we are in Paris. Walter hopes the investigator will have found most if not all of the rest of my family by the time we return home. My brother David, that sounds so good to say, my brother David. Anyway, David said a prayer to God that by the time we return, Walter's hopes will be reality.

There is only one thing that could make this part of my life perfect and that would be if all of my brothers and sisters were here to share this time with me and Walter. Walter and I haven't set a date for the wedding but I hope he will agree to it being soon. I've only just met three of my brothers and none of my sisters and I don't have any friends back home that it would matter to if they missed our ceremony. With that thought in mind, Walter and I could get married today, right here in Paris if he would agree to it. I think about asking him but I don't want to push him so I spend the rest of the afternoon with my thoughts going in and out about our wedding.

Walter has gone to his room for a nap but still I can't sleep so I sit in the café in front of the hotel and simply watch the people for a few hours and I try some of their wine. The afternoon turns out to be very pleasant --me with only my glass of wine and my thoughts to keep me company. But the afternoon is getting short and the change in the street activity tells me I should change, too. I go back inside the hotel and up to Walter's room, this time he has given me a key to his room so I don't get hysterical in the hallway again. I slide the key into the keyhole and turn the doorknob slowly trying to be as quiet as possible. If Walter is still sleeping, I don't want to wake him. I wish I could sleep but I am still wound too tight for it. But Walter evidently isn't, he's still sleeping. So I sit and watch him. He likes to sleep on his side I've noticed. Every time I have seen him asleep he has been on his side with his hand under the side of his face. Every so many regular breaths Walter takes, he then takes a deep breath and lets it out slowly as if he is going into a deeper and deeper more restful sleep.

I sit thinking about the fact that I will get to spend the rest of my life watching this man sleep and the very thought brings tears to my eyes. I want to start our lives together today. I want to wake him up and tell him. I move over to the bed and sit next to Walter on the edge of the bed. I tell myself he left the space on the bed hoping I would sit here but I know that's really not true. Walter always sleeps in the bed not on the edge of it and I wonder if he will be able to sleep with me in the bed with him and I have to catch my breath. I, we will share a bed. We will be husband and wife. I will enter a part of life I have never been in before. I will be sharing all of me with this man not just dinners across a table or retiring to separate rooms. Walter and I will be married and there are certain things that come alone with the unity of marriage. I don't know that I am ready for all that comes with marriage now that I think about it. Maybe it will be better to set a date for the future so that I can get used to the whole idea. But for right now I sit down on the side of his bed and stroke Walter's hair and the side of his face and I imagine what our lives will be like.

◆

I must have finally fallen asleep watching Walter. I remember Walter turning over and sliding to the middle of the bed and I remember kissing him on his cheek. I thought I got up after that but I couldn't have. Now I am in Walter's bed and Walter is nowhere to be found. It's dark outside so I know it's late. I know I'm in Walter's room because I can still smell his cologne lingering in the room but where is Walter? I look at the clock and see that it's only six o'clock. It's awfully dark for only ten minutes after six, last night at seven thirty is was still light outside. I hope Walter wants a late dinner because I'm starved. I put my head back on the pillow and I can smell Walter on it, his scent makes me smile. After a couple of minutes I decide I am too hungry to stay in the bed so I get up and look for my key. It's not in my pocket. I find it on the night stand. Picking it up I make sure that I still have Walter's key then I make my way out of his room and down the hall to my own room. As I go back to my room I think to myself if I weren't so hungry I would go back to sleep. Maybe I will return to bed right after dinner.

I open my door and go into the room and sit down. The door to my bedroom is closed but the sofa is comfortable enough to spend the night on if I fall asleep so I sit for a while and fondle over in my mind, the events again of this past week and again I feel I'm happier than anyone has a right to be. I think I will go lay down until Walter calls or comes to the door. I stand up and go to my bedroom door and open it only to find that there is someone in my bed. I jump and step back before realizing its Walter. I don't mind that he's in my

Suspended

bed and in my room but I wonder why. I go back to the sofa and sit down. Never mind dinner right now maybe I can get a little more sleep. But then I hear Walter's phone alarm go off. I wonder if Walter has set his alarm for dinner. I guess I won't get that extra sleep so I wait for Walter to get up. After a few minutes, Walter comes out of my bedroom looking well rested.

"Good morning, sleeping beauty. I'm glad you finally got some sleep," Walter says as he gives me a kiss on my forehead.

"I only slept for a few hours but I feel like I've slept for a full day. I could still sleep a few more hours," I tell Walter.

"You almost did," Walter tells me.

"It's only six thirty. I've only been asleep about two hours, Walter," I tell him. But Walter laughs.

"What time do you think it is, Naturallee," he asks.

"It's time to get some dinner and I want to go to that nice little restaurant we passed this morning, you know, the one with the extreme art in the window," I say to Walter.

Walter laughs harder as he tells me, "I'm afraid you've missed dinner, sweetheart. It will be breakfast in about an hour so why don't we get some of *that*."

I don't really believe Walter until he points out that the sun is coming up not going down. I can't believe I slept right through dinner and the entire night, no wonder I'm so hungry.

"When I turned over yesterday afternoon I found you had fallen asleep in my bed and I just didn't have the heart to wake you so I left you in my bed. I even had dinner alone and brought you something back from that nice little restaurant we passed by that morning, the one with the extreme art in the window," Walter teases with my own words.

"Anyway, after you were still asleep and it was getting so late, I decided to switch rooms with you so I came to your room and spent the night here. I would have asked your permission but with all the drool and loud snoring coming from such a thin woman, I decided

280

Chapter Forty-Five

it would be best to play it safe and let you sleep," Walter smiles as he tells his tale about my sleep habits and the events of the evening.

I have lived with Walter for almost a year and I can't remember Walter being this relaxed and happy. It's like he is a different man. He's more carefree and he's funny. I have always thought of him as fun to be with, I never considered him to be funny, at least not until now. I like it.

Walter's cell phone rings at the same time mine does. We give each other a puzzling look and then answer each other's phone by mistake. We don't realize it until we say hello to the person on the other line.

"I'm terribly sorry but I believe I've dialed the wrong...Naturallee, is this you," I was hoping she wouldn't have recognized my voice.

"Yes, Ms. Blair, hi, you didn't dial the wrong number this is Walter's phone I just grabbed the wrong phone. I thought it was mine ringing. Hold on, I'll get Walter." I start to hand the phone over to Walter but he is giving the same explanation to whoever it is on my phone. Then I hear Ms. Blair calling my name on the phone again so I answer her.

"Naturallee, that's alright. This message is for you more than it is for Walter anyway." Ms. Blair catches me off guard with her statement.

"What is it, Ms. Blair? What can I do for you?" I can't possibly imagine what I could do to help her.

"No, Naturallee, it's what I can do for you," just then I hear Walter's level of excitement increases about ten levels when he says in a louder than usual voice,

"That's wonderful. Perfect. I can't believe it. How did it happen? When did it, oh what does that matter? The point is, it's happened."

Then I hear Ms. Blair say, "...And Surely, Hellinher and Babydoll are in Paris as well, right now and just a few blocks away from you. Can you believe it; all of you go halfway around the world to meet each other." Ms. Blair is excited about something that I only heard half.

"What did you say," but as I ask her to repeat it, I begin to realize what she must have said. But that couldn't be what she said. With those names they would have to be my sisters and they couldn't be here in Paris at the same time as we are. But it must be true because Ms. Blair is still talking and saying some of the same things, she's still saying the names Surely Fine, Hellinher, and Babydoll. My sisters are at a hotel a few blocks away. They don't know that Walter and I are here.

While I am talking with Ms. Blair, Walter is talking with David and hearing the same things from him. Walter and I look across the room at each other and watch as the smile on each of our faces grow wider and wider. Once I finish talking with Ms. Blair and David and Walter speaks with each of them, we say our good-byes and map a quick plan to try to meet my sisters. Ms. Blair and David said that the girls don't know about me and the fact that we are here in Paris. Walter and I don't want to mess up their trip but we are sure they would want to meet as soon as possible. We decide to call their hotel first and ask if we can meet with them.

Walter agrees to do the talking; I'm too nervous, I'm sure I'll say the wrong thing. I wait as Walter listens as their hotel's front desk rings their room. After what feels like some years of time passing, a lady with a very French accent answers the phone. Walter speaks to her in fluent French. They discuss things in French for a few minutes. He introduces himself as an American attorney and I think he is saying something about being here in Paris on vacation and his office calling him with important information. Either that or he said he was from the planet Krypton; I really don't know what he's saying. What I do know is that after he says Peoples, he switches to English to say your sister, Naturallee Joy another daughter of your mother Syvon Peoples is here in Paris and would very much like to

Chapter Forty-Five

meet with the three of you. There is an even longer silence on the phone than there was when we were waiting for someone to answer, as Walter's words must have been Spanish to her American/French ears. Then words and mind must have connected. I hear yelling and screaming in the phone and someone yelling what's wrong and then they take the phone away from whoever had answered.

"Hello, this is Surely Wellesley, to whom am I speaking and what is going on," while Surely is sounding very professional, I can hear the stress in her voice. Walter clears his throat before saying everything again but in English this time.

"Is this some kind of cruel joke?" Now she is sounding a bit upset. I hear yet another voice in the phone asking Surely what is going on. I then hear Surely telling her what Walter is saying. Now Babydoll asks for the phone.

"Mr. Mayfield, this is Regina Peoples Witham, yes we want to meet Naturallee as soon as possible. How about in one hour in the hotel lounge of our hotel," Babydoll's voice is calm and controlled almost as if she was waiting for our call. After a few more words, Walter and Babydoll hang up the phones.

Walter and I discuss more of what has transpired and Walter fills me in on the fact that the investigator had closed in on the rest of my family the day we left Florida but he didn't want to say anything until he was sure that a meeting could happen. The investigator found another investigator by the name of Richard Bailey. Bailey it turns out is the investigator for Regina who has been looking for the family for a little while now. Regina knew that we were looking for her for the past six months but Bailey isn't sure why she hasn't contacted anyone until now. Walter gives me so much information I'm not able to retain it all. Walter can account for all but what he thinks is the oldest set of twins named Truely Grateful and Honestly Sweet. It would seem that Walter's office has sent two e-mails to Honestly Sweet and one certified letter to his home yesterday asking if he is a child of Syvon's. Since Ms. Blair didn't mention it on the telephone when she told us about the sisters, it is safe to assume that Honestly is not a child of Syvon Peoples or he has not received or responded to the letter.

Even though Walter spends the next thirty-five minutes telling what he and the investigator have found, we still have more than twenty minutes before I meet three of my sisters. I find myself whispering a word of prayer to God and I wonder who this God is I'm talking to. Then for some unknown reason, I ask Walter who God is. Walter becomes as happy as I am that I found my sisters. He tells me a little bit about who God is but then says God is too big to fully explain in a lifetime and much too much to discuss in a matter of minutes but he does want me to know that God is the one who has brought all of us together, Nathan Grey and Walter, Nathan Grey and Syvon, Syvon as our mother, Walter and me, and me and all of my siblings. God had this planned out as to how it would all come together long before any of us started looking for each other.

I think God is pretty alright with me right now. I am going to have to find out more about Him and see what more there is to Him. The way Walter talks about God makes me think there's a lot I'm missing. I'd like to know God and Walter says he will help to me to do just that.

CHAPTER 46

I can't take it any longer; this waiting is driving me crazy. Walter suggests that we wait the last fifteen minutes in the lounge. I know it won't speed up the time but I will be a step or two closer to my sisters. I'm nervous; I want to see their faces and hear their voices in person. I wonder if I will look like any one of them. I don't know if they are all older than I am or if I'm the oldest. Are any of them married and do any of them know about David, Big Man, and Monkee. Walter told me they know my brothers; Mercy and Ronald. Walter also told me that I had a sister named Lovely Girl but she died when she was three years old. I already know about Lovely Girl and the death of my brother, Kane.

Walter's investigator found an old neighbor of Grandma Lucy's who was able to tell him a lot about the family and how many children she knew Syvon had. Mrs. Hadley and her daughter Robin also told the investigator about what Syvon did to Truely and about how much she hated me. But none of that matters now because we are finding each other and it's only a matter of time before all of us are together for the very first time.

I strain to see everyone who comes into the lounge. Over the course of twelve minutes a total of nine men and seven women come in the lounge but not a set of three women. I start to fear that they have changed their minds but then as if they simply materialize out of thin air they are standing in the door looking around. I stop breathing and feel perspiration on my top lip. Then without warning, I feel myself leaving the table. I don't want to go but my feet have already left the floor and I'm going up to the ceiling faster than I ever have. I hear Walter calling my name but I can't stop. I need him to catch me and pull me back to the table. My sisters are coming and I'm leaving the room.

All at once, there are six arms on me and my feet hit the floor and bring me back into the room. I'm able to hug my sisters and cry with them. Once we are able to release each other from the arms of the others we sit down and try to have a conversation. We talk about our lives when we lived with Syvon and life as it was then. We talk about so much. I tell my sisters, boy that sounds so good to say, but anyway, I tell my sisters about our brothers and the possibility of reaching our oldest twin brother soon. We laugh and cry together. Regina tells me about our brothers and how she found them. Surely says for some reason Regina isn't ready to say why she didn't bring them together sooner, but each sister is more than happy we are together now. I tell them Walter has been true to his word. Before I realize it, we have been talking for over an hour and Walter isn't here. I don't know when he left or where he went to and I feel horrible. Meeting my sisters for the first time is more important to me than I can say but so is Walter. I need him to know that. I want him to meet my sisters. I find my cell phone and call him. He never left the hotel but went over to the bar to give us some time together. I tell him I want him with me. Before we disconnect the phones, Walter is coming over to the table. I feel my world is complete again.

Chapter Forty-Six

I stand up, hug Walter, and give him a kiss. I thank him again for making this meeting possible then I introduce him to my sisters. Each one gives Walter a hug and they thank him for his part in finding us. Walter sits down and joins us for the rest of the evening. I tell my sisters about the engagement and as easily as that part of my announcement comes out of my mouth so do the words, "I wish we could get married here before we leave," if I were a little bit lighter I would turn red. I didn't mean to say it out loud. Or maybe subconsciously I do want Walter to know. I'm not sure but it's out now and I could just melt into the floor. The table goes quiet as their eyes fall on Walter. Now I've put him on the spot without meaning to.

"Well, Naturallee that's putting all your cards on the table. Maybe you should let Walter answer that in private." The table of sisters switch the topic as Walter and I fade out from the conversation as if there's a glass wall separating us from Hellinher, Surely, and Regina.

I turn to Walter to apologize. I feel foolish and I can't look at him. I can feel his eyes on me and I start to say how sorry I am for putting him on the spot but he puts his arm around me and squeezes my shoulder. I decide to let it go if that's what he wants to do.

We spend the rest of the evening having dinner together. After dinner and conversation all of us go up to my room for a while so as not to have to let go of each other again. Finally, Hellinher brings us back to earth and reality. After all, that has transpired today and having such an adrenaline rush, she is beginning to come down from her high and is feeling wiped out. She wants to go back to their hotel and rest. It takes us another fifteen minutes to say good night. I ride back down the elevator with them to have every minute possible together. We hold on to each other a few minutes more then, holding hands, we let our fingers slip away from each other's until our arms become too short to reach.

◆

Suspended

I promised Walter I would stop by his room after Hellinher, Surely, and Regina leave and I can't wait to tell him everything. I love my sisters already. I hope he likes them all. Knocking on Walter's door, I say to myself how lucky I am. I'm still hyped from meeting my sisters and talking with my brothers so I tell Walter we could be up all night, he smiles and says that will be fine with him.

Walter lets me talk for an hour straight then we order one of two American movies on television and curl up on the sofa together. I have no idea what movie is on; my mind is on my life and how much it has changed over this past year. I smile to myself and snuggle into Walter's arms. From time to time I tell him something more about one of the girls and each time, he breaks away from the movie and gives me his complete attention. Finally, I run out of things to say and try to get into the movie.

"Would you really like to get married here? I mean in Paris before we leave," Walter asks without looking away from the movie.

"Walter I am sooo sorry for putting you on the spot like that earlier. I shouldn't have blurted it out like that. It just came out before I could..." but Walter stops me.

"Miss Peoples, could you simply answer the question please, a yes or no will do. And Miss Peoples, please answer the question honestly, thank you."

I know Walter is playing around but he also wants an honest answer from me. I feel I have no choice but to answer truthfully. But thinking about it I do want him to know the truth. I do want to marry him here before we leave and now that I have some of the only people I care about already here with me it makes it easier so I tell him very matter of factly, "Yes. Yes, I would love to marry you tonight, if we could."

Walter doesn't say anything for a long minute and I think I've scared him off. But then a smile starts to spread across his lips and he says, "Good because your brother David and Ms. Blair will be here day after tomorrow and your sisters are here till the end of the week so we could marry in the next two days. That is if you really do want to.

"If I want to. If I want to," I hear myself getting louder with each word. "If I want to. Walter, I want to but I'm afraid I'm pushing you without thinking before I let those words out of my mouth. You need to take time to think this over. Walter, it would destroy me if you did this now being caught up in the moment and regret it later. I couldn't take that. I haven't loved anyone since my Uncle Stew died and I have never loved anyone the way I love you."

"That's my concern for you, Naturallee. I know how young you are and you haven't experienced a lot of life yet but I have and I feel the same way for you. I would never forgive myself taking your love at this time only to have you feel you've missed out on a younger, more vibrant love with a younger man. That would destroy *me*." There is such a seriousness and pain in Walter's eyes. I would look away if I could to save my heart from being hurt from the pain in his eyes but I can't. I don't want Walter to get the wrong impression of how I feel again.

I hold Walter's face in my hands and look straight into his eyes because I want him to know the deepest part of my heart when I tell him how much I love him. I tell him I don't need to know another love or loves to know that I love him now and I always will. No other man could ever mean as much to me as he does. No one could ever take his place. I need him to know that so I tell him to ask God about my love. That's enough for Walter. He kisses me and tells me again how much he loves me. Then I remember what he said and I have to ask him, "Are Ms. Blair and David *really* on their way," I have to ask.

"Yes, and David is bringing your sister-in-law, Grace."

I have one sister-in-law, three brother-in-laws, a brother who's engaged to a wonderful lady I'm told, and several nieces and nephews. This life is great. I'm so glad I decided not to give up on it when I was seventeen. I'm so glad I'm here for this part of my life.

Suspended

Walter is starting to nod off so I wake him with a kiss and say good night. He wants to walk me to my room but I tell him I want to get something I left in his bedroom last night or rather this morning and that I will be right back. When I return to the sofa Walter is already asleep as I suspected he would be so I slip out of his room without waking him and return to my own. I'm so glad I didn't end my life when times were so rough for me ten years ago.

THE VOW

CHAPTER 47

Walter and I spend the early morning making a few plans for our wedding tomorrow. Our wedding I can't believe it. I'm making plans for mine and Walter's wedding; I'm so happy I can hardly contain my excitement. Walter says Ms. Blair has sent some important papers to him that should be at the front desk this morning. Walter also remembers that the hotel has a dress shop which means, he says, that one of the ladies there will be able to help me in finding a wedding dress and whatever else would go with the day. I hope he's right. Even though I want to marry him tomorrow I want to have as nice a wedding a possible. I know I'm asking a lot but I'm going to try to make it happen. Maybe I will see what Hellinher, Surely, and Regina are doing today, if they have the time I'd love for them to help me. But I have to see what plans they already have. After all, they didn't come to Paris to meet a sister and certainly they didn't come to plan a wedding.

Suspended

The phone rings again for the third time this morning. It's Regina; I've gotten two phone calls from my sisters this morning already telling me how happy they are about the family. This time it's Regina, she wants me and Walter to spend the day with them. By nine, we are at the restaurant in the girls' hotel having breakfast. The breakfast table is full with family, my family. Walter and Hellinher both speak French quite well and they place everyone's breakfast order. It doesn't matter what is ordered for any of us, we are all still too excited to eat. Breakfast lasted for two hours and Walter and I are asked to join them for an afternoon of site seeing. Instead, as our table is being cleared, Walter and I tell them that David and his wife Grace will arrive today and we need to meet them at our hotel when they get in around six. The squeals of happiness are signs of approval. Now that the excitement of hugging another sibling starts to settle over us, Walter and I raise the excitement level one more time by announcing the news of our wedding plans for the following day. Once the news is out, we switch form site seeing to wedding planning with only a day to get it done. Walter decides to leave all the planning to the women and tells us he will wait and meet David, Grace, and Ms. Blair and we could meet them when we return but the unbelieving looks on all four of our faces tells him that is not going to happen.

Before we leave Walter in the lobby, I kiss him and tell him we will see him around five. Each sister gives him a hug good-bye then walk out hand in hand like teenage best friends giggling and laughing and holding on to each other.

◆

Walter's suggestion was spot on. Our first stop was back to my hotel and the dress shop. A very helpful woman in her late forties who happens to be a wedding planner originally from New York City is the first one we speak to and the only one we need. By one o'clock, my entire wedding is planned along with a small reception in their private dining hall. Vickie finds a bridle shop in the middle of town where I find a beautiful pearl beaded wedding dress with a tight plunging neckline and the most *slimingest*, yes I just made up the word slimingest, waistline I have ever had on my body. I can't believe it's me in this dress. Fortunately, the dress needs little altering to it. The shop owner is a good friend of Vickie's. She says it will be ready by close of business tonight. My sisters are surprised and happy to be a part of and witnesses to my wedding. We have to pick numbers to see who would be my maid of honor and we said David could be Walter's best man.

We stop for a very late afternoon lunch at a sidewalk café and go over all the plans again to make sure Vickie hasn't forgotten anything, and of course, she hasn't. We only order drinks. We are so excited about David and Grace. Hellinher thinks we are close enough to the hotel that we could walk but Surely says she isn't in the walking mood so we compromise and walk two blocks and ride the last three blocks. I look at my watch and an enjoyable shiver runs through me at the very thought that I will be hugging my brother and his wife. Then a shiver that causes my body to jerk runs from my head to my toes and back again and is so noticeable, my sister Regina asks if I'm alright. All I can do is smile. How does a person put into words the gifts I've been given? Surely said last night that God has blessed our family to find each other and I think she could be right. This coming together of the brothers and sisters has a lot more to do with something that's bigger than all of us combined, something more than just who we are. I mean Nathan started the search before he died several years ago. Regina has been looking for about five years and Surely has been searching for almost two years. I have sat down at my computer off and on over the past several years in my tiny apartment and put the name of any family, friend or acquaintance I could think of who might have known our family in hopes that I would get a response. There was never any reply. I wasn't sure if they didn't want to be found or if they didn't want to ever know Syvon again.

Ten years ago, just after I left Aunt Joyce, Lawrence, and the boys, I was so lonely for someone to come into my life and stay. I began to think life just wasn't worth it. Standing at the shoreline for what felt like hours, I waited for the tide to come in and take me out with it. The waves were starting to crash the beach and I could feel the roughness of the water against my knees as the waves rushed in. I felt the soothing of the waters as it returned to the ocean. The night air was still thick with the heat from the last of the summer days but the water was so relaxing it forced me to relax and let go of some of the loneliness that I was holding onto. Finally, I heard the words of a kind man with a loving voice speak to me. I don't even know how long he had been there or when he even started speaking to me but his voice and words made me remember my Uncle Stew and how much he loved me. I heard the man standing next to me saying that life would get better, I just needed to know that everyday including that day was getting me closer to the day my life would become great and I would be very glad on that day that the waves didn't take me out with them. He told me I would look back and smile; he was right. He also asked me to remember to thank God for letting him meet me. I'm glad I remembered that part of that night, as well and so I do. I stop right in the middle of the streets of Paris and I look up and thank God for that man. Then I ask God to bless him to know that he was right. I'm still not sure where those words go but that man believed they will go to God. The man was right that night so he's probably right about God. Standing there looking up, I hear my sisters calling my name so I run a few steps to catch up with them.

While we wait to meet David, Regina and I sit nervously quiet for the first time since we met. Waiting is hard. Patience is something I've had to have all my life but today it feels like something I've never had to face before. I've folded a napkin so many times it's limp. Surely has unbraided one of her micro-braids and Hellinher

Chapter Forty-Seven

has doodled all of our names is ever way imaginable while Regina cleans every spot in my room. Walter finally suggests we wait downstairs like he and I did the night I met my sisters. The idea is met with agreement by all of us so we head for the elevators. The minute we get a few steps away from the door, we hear the phone ring in the room. We freeze first to make sure that it's our phone ringing. The phone rings again and we scramble for the key. Walter has it and opens the door and we all run for the phone. He grabs the receiver and shouts hello into.

"Hello, hello." Walter yells.

The voice on the other end responds and Walter's shoulders relax. He tells them we will wait in the room for them to come up then Walter hangs up the phone.

"Is it David," Surely asks quickly.

"Yeah, is it him, I mean them? Is it David and Grace?" Hellinher needs to know.

"Walter," is all I can say.

"Yes. It's them. They are on their way up right now." Walter says with relief.

I wonder which elevator they took; it's an awfully long wait for a knock at the door. Or perhaps Walter misunderstood what they really said. Maybe we are supposed to go down stairs. I'm about to ask Walter if he thinks we should go downstairs to see if we are to meet them there when the knock at the door vibrates in my ears.

CHAPTER 48

Truely and MaLyce are a little less tense today. Mark is doing better, much better than the doctors thought he would. The last medicine cocktail they gave him has helped Mark feel better, but MaLyce and Truely credit Mark's reprieve to the prayers their friends and church family has been sending up night and day. Four days ago, Mark was drifting into death, but now he is able to sit up and talk for a few minutes at a time. They don't want to exhaust him so Truely, MaLyce, Mitchell, and Winston talk with him every hour but only for a couple of minutes, then they force themselves to leave the room so he can rest.

Everyone knows that things could change at any moment so they are taking advantage of every good moment they have to rest, say some prayers of thanks and enjoy a little quiet time. Truely returns to work feeling better than he has in weeks. MaLyce spends two hours strung together at home and slips into a tub of bubbles with a glass of wine. The e-mail is on her mind. Someone is kind enough to offer a kidney to Mark; someone that none of them knows sent an e-mail offering to help Mark. This lady lost her husband because no one stepped up to help them in their time of need. She said she didn't want anyone to suffer like she had. The fact that she wasn't a close enough match didn't upset MaLyce and her family. They were just astounded that someone would do that.

As MaLyce enjoyed the bubbles around, her she let her mind run over that day so long ago when she and Truely made the agreement that neither of them would ever look for their families. They would be the first generation of family for their family line. She has hated that decision for the past three months. She has never said anything to Truely about the day they made that promise but she knows that he thinks of it as often as she does. After all, had they not planted themselves so strongly against finding any of them or responding to that letter and phone call they got almost three years ago, they might have that kidney Mark so desperately needs now. Neither she nor Truely remembers the man's name who called and they threw away the letter that had come to the house asking about MaLyce.

Now MaLyce is no longer relaxed. Her mind can't help but stay locked on the decisions of the past that may cost them their son's life today. Home alone she releases the stresses of the last several months with the tears she has kept locked away for just such a moment as this.

◆

Winston sits next to Mark's bed and watches his brother sleep. The thought of life without Mark is something Winston won't let himself settle with. As a matter-of-fact, he has started a web-site to search for his parents' families. Winston and his brothers have known since they were very young that their parents had severed all ties with their families but Winston believes this situation with his Mark's life is more than a time of forgive and forget; it's a time of need. Now is a time for help to hopefully save his brother's life. Winston hasn't said anything to Truely or MaLyce about launching the web-site this morning he's hoping for a positive response before someone sees it and tells his parents about it. With the unhappy thought of going against his parents' wishes, Winston says a prayer that God will have his unknown family find them and help, and he whispers a prayer for restoration for Mark while holding his brother's hand.

◆

Lynn and Barbara arrive first and ring the bell instead of using the key to enter their best friend's house. They knock because of the car in the driveway. As much as they knock and ring, no one comes to answer the door. Afraid there could be something more than just MaLyce sleeping, Lynn now puts the key into the lock and presses the lock lever down. Stepping in slowly, Lynn and Barbara call for MaLyce but they get no answer. The friends start to worry as they move through each room of this magnificent house a little concerned about want they might find. The formal dining room is Malyce's favorite room in the house and her friends agree. The room seems to always have an open invitation to everyone who looks into it and once you enter, it's hard to leave. At Lynn or Barbara's home, as with most homes, the kitchen is the gathering place in the home. At Rhonda's apartment it's the three season room and the family room is the gathering place at June's house, but here at Malyce's house it has always been the dining room. But today even though the dining room is calling they can't stay to visit. They must continue their search for life in the house. Moving forward they find nothing amiss on the first floor and head for the stairs with Lynn leading the way. Usually the paintings on the wall leading up the stairway catches Barbara's eyes; she loves the painting called, *The Baptism* and the *King's Throne* the best, but all four of the paintings are worth the time to meditate on. But right now Barbara pays no attention to any of the paintings. Her focus is on finding her friend and finding out why she isn't answering the door or them.

Reaching the top of the stairs both ladies stop and look down the hallway of this five bedroom, two and a half bath with a masterful master bedroom and bath which takes up the entire back of the upstairs of the house. When Truely and MaLyce bought the house and double lots, one on each side of the house, Truely had a vision for this once three bedroom property. He let no grass grow under his feet in giving MaLyce the house she wanted. They live in a great neighborhood but the house MaLyce wanted could only be found in a more upscale neighborhood which Truely couldn't afford back then so he and some friends got to work right away to get Truely and MaLyce the house of their dreams.

The small construction crew of Truely and his friends added an entire section to the back of the house giving the house a seventeen by twenty-three foot family room that emptied into an extremely spacious kitchen with sky lights and ceiling fans. One fan set in over the range so to pull the heat out of the kitchen when MaLyce cooks and the other is set in over the counter/island sink area to blow down air to help keep her cool as she prepared the meals. The entire kitchen is white with light oak wood trim and MaLyce has a leaf green color as her accent color because she loves the outdoors.

Above the family room and around the side of the house are the master bedroom and the master bath. The bedroom is sectioned into two parts, MaLyce can actually sit and watch television while Truely sleeps peacefully about fifteen feet away. Their bathroom is off the far side of the bedroom. Truely has two tubs that face the wall of windows overlooking the pond behind their house. He and MaLyce have shared a glass of wine; or rather, MaLyce has a glass of wine and Truely has a can of beer as they celebrate the important moments of their lives in their tubs. There is also a double shower and a double sink as well. MaLyce says she's glad there is only one toilet so she can have privacy sometimes.

Chapter Forty-Eight

The upstairs hallway feels as long as it looked in that poltergeist movie where the devil is in the kid's closet and the woman has to run down the hall to get to the kids bedroom. Lynn and Barbara move fearfully toward the master bedroom still calling Malyce's name. As Lynn's hand reaches for the door handle the ladies hold their breath. Fortunately, the door is partially open so they push it completely open and peer in. The bedroom is empty and still. There's a slight scent of lilac in the air; Malyce's favorite scent. She has the scent all through her house whenever possible. The ladies step into the bedroom and breathed a sigh of relief.

"Well, I guess she's not really home," Lynn says with a curious tone in her voice.

"Maybe we should check the basement," Barbara suggests as they turn to leave the bedroom.

"Maybe you should have checked the bathroom."

Both Lynn and Barbara scream and turn to see who it is speaking before they turn to run. Happy to see their friend and a bit ticked off that she scared them, all three of the ladies laugh and hug together.

"What are you two doing here," MaLyce asks her friends.

"We thought you might like to hang out this afternoon, you know, girl, like old times. Rhonda and June are on their way over. They are picking up something to eat and then they will be here. You know June has to get the kids settled before she can leave and Rhonda can't leave until she settles Louis with everything he thinks he needs," Barbara says with disdain in her tone.

"Let's not go there, ladies. She's only doing what she needs to keep her home peaceful. We can say whatever we want but they work and that's more than what we can say about others we know." Lynn reminds her two friends.

"You're right," MaLyce says turning back to her closet with her master bathroom on the other side of it.

Suspended

Lynn sits in the occasional chair that always looked a little more formal than occasional and Barbara lay across the bed as the women continue to talk. After a few minutes, Lynn and Barbara realize they are the only ones having the conversation. They call Malyce's name but get no answer so they go to the door of the closet to find her sitting at the mirror. Her face is blank and her eyes seem hollow. She's still holding her hair brush.

"MaLyce, honey, what's wrong? MaLyce, MaLyce , sweetie say something." Panic is starting to rise in Barbara's voice.

After a long minute, MaLyce says, "I wish Truely and I never made that agreement with each other," she says it without ever blinking an eye. She moved nothing but her lips to let out words that had eaten a hole into her soul so deep and quick that it oozes from every pour of her body like puss from an infected wound now.

"What agreement MaLyce? What are you talking about?" Barbara asks.

MaLyce sits paralyzed as she allows the puss to continue to seep from her lips. "When Truely and I first met and decided to get married, we also made an agreement with each other. We agreed that we would let the past stay in the past. We both hated our families back then and we didn't want to have anything to do with either side of the family so we agreed that our family line started with us. The boys have no grandparents, no aunts, no uncles, and no cousins. This house, this family, Truely and I are the beginning of this family. We felt we didn't need them, you know? We didn't know any of this would happen." MaLyce still doesn't flinch but tears run down her cheeks and onto her silk blouse causing huge tear stained shadows on her shirt.

CHAPTER 49

"Mercy have you heard from any of our sisters in the last couple of days," Honestly loves saying—*our sisters*. He doesn't say their names unless he is talking about only one of them. And he usually says *our brothers* when talking about one of the boys. He says he has waited all of his life to say it and for it to be true.

"No, none of them have called and today is Naturallee Joy's wedding. Boy, I wish we could be there," Mercy says with a smile on his face. He wanted to cater the bridal party dinner and the reception and to have the reception at Macy's but the plans were made quickly and before he knew about Naturallee and before she knew about him.

"Boy, that's going to be some wedding ceremony this spring. I'm glad she and Walter are going to repeat their vows this spring so all of us can be there assuming we can find Truely in time."

"Between Bailey and Walter's investigator he'll be found, and we will keep looking as well. Truely is the only missing piece of this family puzzle and you know what they say don't you, Mercy," Honestly teases as he get up from his favorite recliner.

"No, what's that, Honestly man, you always save the best for last and my twin, mine and your oldest brother is the best. That's why we have to find Truely last." Honestly slaps Mercy on his shoulder as he passes by on his way to the refrigerator for another beer.

"Hey, Honestly, bring me another one, too, please." Mercy thanks God often for his family; he loves them all. He and Honestly are becoming so close, Mercy can hardly contain his happiness sometimes. He loves all of his brothers and they all spend a great deal of time together but Mercy and Honestly get together more often. They enjoy the same things and they are able to share with each other more when it's just the two of them. For that Mercy is thankful.

"Here you go," Honestly nudges Mercy's shoulder and hands him the beer. Honestly slides onto the couch and grabs the television remote to look for the game. Even though it's only preseason, a basketball game is still a ball game and with football at its peak, the life of a sportsman is elevated to a point of frenzied excitement. The world can hand a man almost any problem to deal with and he can make the problem work out, at least through football and basketball season. Mercy and Honestly don't much care for baseball and neither of them liked hockey or soccer. Honestly likes to play golf and is pretty good at it. Each year, the university has an annual golf outing and Honestly has won the tournament seven of the last ten years. His trophies have prompted Mercy to ask his brother to teach him how to play. Tomorrow, after church Mercy gets his first lesson.

Honestly Sweet, Havesome Mercy, Ronald, Big, Man and Monkee have been attending the church Beverly attends but when David gets back from Paris they are planning to go and hear him speak for the first time. Big Man has told Mercy, Honestly, and Ronald how good David is but they want to hear for themselves. When David

Chapter Forty-Nine

and Grace get back along with Surely, Hellinher, Regina, and the newest sister they haven't met yet they are all going to attend service there together.

"A few months ago, none of us knew the others and weren't even sure any others even existed. Man we didn't know those we remembered were still alive but look at us now. Pretty soon ten of us will be gathered together celebrating a reunion for some of us and meeting others of us for the first time. Can you believe our lives, Honestly. Can you believe what's happened," Mercy's voice quivers at the end of his words as he gets up and walks to the window dropping his head to his chest.

Honestly gives no response but fully understands his brother's joy. He too, thinks about how life has come around and can't completely get his thoughts around the whole thing. In his very recent past, Honestly remembers his routine and rigid way of life. He remembers dinner out twice a week, one of those nights he'd add in a movie. He would only allow himself to drive to work those days to conserve fuel and to do his part to help rid the world of pollution. He recycles and he buys recycled products whenever possible. Honestly would skip his vacation time to work because he couldn't face life alone on vacation. That is, until he finally got up the nerve to meet Beverly. Then the night he planned to tell her about his feelings and ask her if she could possibly have those same feelings for him his plans were interrupted with the meeting of his brother Mercy and then the meeting of Ronald, and the girls. It took Honestly another three weeks to get up the nerve to tell Beverly how he felt about her. It only took Beverly three seconds to tell him she felt the same way. Now the family has two weddings to plan for. Finally, Honestly responds to Mercy's words with, "Man I hope we can find Truely soon. Then the family will be complete."

CHAPTER
50

It's been five days since Winston launched the web-site and only a few hits have been made to it, people looking for love or something but no one looking for family. He still hasn't told his parents. Every morning, Winston gets up afraid to say anything to Truely and MaLyce but once he gets to the hospital with Mark, he knows he is doing the right thing. Then he is prepared to face his parents if they find out what he has done. Winston just wants his brother to get better and live to grow old with him.

Tonight, before leaving the hospital, Winton tells Mark what he has done and Mark is happy about it but he agrees with Winston, they shouldn't tell Truely and MaLyce until there is a reason or need to say something. Winston also tells his brother that he wants everyone to come home tonight and have dinner together so that they can also have a family prayer for him. Mark agrees with his brother and can't believe how grown up and mature he is. Before leaving Marks' room, Winston and Mark have prayer together.

◆

Suspended

Truely and MaLyce are reluctant to leave Mark alone tonight but they understand they have other children and for the past two months, especially, Mitchell and Winston have been overlooked. MaLyce has asked her girlfriends to look in on Mark and Truely called his best friends Greg, Joey, and Clayton to ask that they stop by and check on Mark throughout the evening. Everyone has agreed so Truely and MaLyce drive home in a quiet car each with their own thoughts.

Truely wants to say something to MaLyce about finding their families but he, too, remembers the agreement they made years ago and he remembers the hurt and pain that took MaLyce years to get over. But he knows their son's life is on the line and they have to do something before they lose him. If they don't, Truely will never forgive himself for not trying everything he possibly could to save Marks life. Truely also realizes he may not feel the same way about the woman he loves because of their lack of trying. Ending his thoughts on the subject for now, Truely reaches over and squeezes Malyce's hand and that is the extent of his unspoken conversation to his wife the whole ride home.

◆

Mitchell leaves the doctor's office with a heavy weight lifted from his shoulders; he was afraid he was starting to suffer the same kidney problems as his twin brother Mark. Mitchell didn't want to worry the family so he's been seeing Dr. Morehead without his parents knowing about it. Walking to the elevator, Mitchell clinches his hands together and thanks God for it only being another one of those times when he and Mark share a pain or illness that only one of them really has. Like Mark, Mitchell has been feeling better but a few weeks ago, Mitchell was in such pain he made an emergency appointment with the doctor. Dr. Morehead understood completely and had all the necessary test ran in a matter of days. When he called

Chapter Fifty

Mitchell to come in and go over the results Dr. Morehead stayed late to meet with him. Tonight, after dinner and prayer, Mitchell will let his parents know what he's done.

◆

"Mark, how about we teach you how to play poker now. I hate chess and I stopped playing checkers when I was ten," Clayton says as he pulls a deck of cards from his jacket pocket. The gang is all here, all four of Malyce's girlfriends, Clayton, Joey, and Greg along with a few of Marks' closest friends who choose tonight to stop by to see him. Daniel's father brought Daniel and came up with him to say hello. Once he sees the crowd and the good spirit Mark is in he decides to stay for a while and help lift Mark's spirits. Brooke has just gotten home from school in Virginia and wants to see Mark. She and her best friend Madison Street have stopped by as well. Everyone has moved from Mark's hospital room down to the eighth floor sun room.

When they get to the sun room there is another couple there, concerned with their daughter's illness. They are discouraged and alone so Mark asks them to go and get their daughter and bring her to the sun room for a little fun. When they first brought her in, Delaney seemed sick and depressed but after a short while, she warms up and starts enjoying the gathering. Her parents are so appreciative and can't thank Mark and the others enough.

After a while, Lynn and the other girls suggest that Mark go back to his room and get some rest. The group promises that some form of the party will continue when he wakes up. Mark, feeling tired, makes no objection and goes back to his room with his entire entourage following him. After several minutes, each one drifts away quietly and within half an hour, Mark is asleep and only Lynn, Barbara, and Greg are left to watch over him.

◆

Suspended

Winston keeps the dinner conversation going, they even find that they can still laugh as a family. MaLyce didn't have time to really cook anything so she ordered pizza, Chinese, and chicken for dinner from everyone's favorite takeout place. She made a quick side salad and opened a can of baked beans and dinner was great.

While everyone is still enjoying the dinner atmosphere, Winston excuses himself from the table. He wants to check his web-site and to see if he has any replies to any e-mails, as well. Not wanting to go to his room to make a quick check of things, Winston goes to the den where the family computer is always on. He doesn't notice the silence in the dining room so Winston pulls up the web-site and then opens his e-mail. Before he can take a look Truely, MaLyce, and Mitchell come in wanting to start the prayer.

CHAPTER
51

"I thought we'd try our luck at finding Truely ourselves. Everyone is doing something and I feel like I need to try. So I've come up with this web search I want to do. Are you guys with me?" Honestly asks as he looks into the faces of Mercy, and Big Man and Ronald who arrived a short time ago.

"Of course, we're in. But I have to warn you, I got some real crazy stuff when I tried putting in Truely's name," Ronald says.

"I know. I tried just putting in his name before, too and I have no idea what that was I was looking at. But last night after I said my prayers, I got the strangest urge to try something new. And you want to know what's really weird," Honestly waits for one of them to respond with a *what*.

Mercy responds with, "What man? Tell us and let's get to it," his response comes with a bit of irritation in his voice.

"This," Honestly sits down to the computer and types in, *where is my brother Truely Grateful Peoples* and hits the send key. Honestly looks at his brothers and laughs, then they all laugh. But Honestly wants them to know that he thinks they have been making it too complicated, he believes simple is better. Instead of waiting for something strange to show up, they turn their attention back to the game that's on now.

◆

Truely and his family have just finished their prayers and are leaving the den. Winston is glad for the prayers but he is now wondering when they are leaving; he wants to get back to checking his e-mail. Truely spends a few extra minutes with Winston to tell him how proud he is that Winston called the family together for something they definitely needed. As Truely leaves the room, he hears the computer beep. Thinking he has left it on from earlier, he turns back to make sure he has closed the sites he has been on. Winston tells his dad that he will close it but Truely wants to do so himself. They stand face to face neither wanting the other to look at the computer. Winston has to step to the side and allow his father access to it.

When Truely raises the top to the laptop, Winston sees that it's his program that's running and someone has responded; Truely knows it too. Truly's not sure what kind of site it is and tells Winston not to go to sites that he and MaLyce have not approved. He tells Winston that he and MaLyce trust him and then starts to leave.

The word trust, when used by his parents, has always ripped to the very core of Winston. He has always felt like he lost his parents' trust when he was about eight years old. The family had gone to the beach with some friends and the older kids of the friends wanted to swim. Winston's parents told him he couldn't go in the water without them but because Winston wanted to stay at the beach and build a sand castle. They allowed him to stay with the twins but he had to promise not to go into the water until they came down to

Chapter Fifty-One

take him. MaLyce and Truely also had asked their friends to keep an eye on the boys. While his parents were talking to their friends, Winston walked right into the water and the waves took him out so quickly, no one had time to react. Truely had seen though and was in the water after Winston before he was taken too far out. Winston has never forgotten that time in his young life. It is that time in life that always washes away any excuse he has for going against what his parents have said. It's what stops him from letting his father leave the den now.

"Dad wait; I want you to see this with me." Winston feels a wave of stress come over him as he sits back down in front of the computer.

"See what, Winston? What sites have you been going to that you shouldn't have," Truely has a twinge of unhappiness in his voice.

"It's nothing like that dad. I know you and mom don't want to ever know your families but Mark needs a family member to save his life. I can't just sit there at his bedside night after night watching him waste away when all it could take is one relative we don't know yet. Dad, I'm sorry but I," Winston is crying as the words rush from his mouth.

Standing there, all Truely sees is his hurt little boy. Truely grabs his son and holds on to Winston until they both feel composed. Then Truely tells Winston that he understands and that everything will be alright.

"Dad, this e-mail could be the answer to our prayers; it could be what makes everything alright." Still composing himself, Winston tells Truely about the web-site and what he has been doing to find their family.

"I need time to tell your mother, but I have been doing the same thing, son. It was a mistake to make that agreement all those years ago and a bigger mistake to keep it. Then I complicated it by telling you boys that you had to go along with it. Adding fuel to an already ignited flame, I have taken too long, I think to start looking for any of them and it maybe costing us our family." Now Winston holds his father as they cry together. Away from the moment just outside of time, the world continues to spin but inside the moment, inside the den, time is standing still.

CHAPTER 52

They both simply stand and watch as the words on the computer sit on the screen. Then the picture comes into view and Winston feels strange looking at his father in a picture with other men that look a great deal like his dad and one man would have to be his dad. Who *else* could it be?

"Honestly. Honestly Sweet you're...you're...alive. You can't be. Syvon killed you and left your body in that basement. I saw her hit you; I saw you when you fell. She tried to get you up but you...you're alive. Oh my God, you're alive." Truely is so loud that Mitchell and MaLyce rush in to see what's going on.

"Truly, what's wrong," MaLyce demands of her husband but he is too elated to answer so she turns to her son.

"Winston, tell me what's happened. What's wrong with your father," again she is met with silence but Winston can move his arm to point to the computer screen.

Mitchell and MaLyce stand motionless as they, too, stare at what's on the computer.

"Is that you dad or is it my uncle, by chance," Mitchell asks.

"Truly, what's going on? Who are those men you're with and when did you have that picture taken an...,"

"It's Honestly, it has to be Honestly and my brothers I'm guessing. Can you believe this? You guys, this is my family-my brothers. I thought Honestly was dead. I saw her kill him; I'm sure of it. She told me she would kill me if I ever told anyone. I stayed with his body for what I thought was hours in that basement waiting for her to leave so I could get out before she killed me." Truely's voice is a mixture of joy and happiness overshadowed by bouts of sadness, pain, and regret all tearing at him at the same time.

"I never would have left him there all alone for her to come back and do whatever evil she could to him if I thought Honestly was still alive. I shouldn't have left him there." Truely is on the brink of tears and hysteria. MaLyce can see it. She grabs Truely's shoulders and yells into his face getting his attention.

"Honey, honey we need to put that away for right now. Syvon isn't here. She's hopefully dead so she can't hurt you or Honestly anymore. And you can't blame yourself for not staying there, that woman was insane and she would have killed you if you had stayed. If this is Honestly she didn't kill him like she thought she had. He got away and he's here now looking for you. You have to answer him." MaLyce tries to bring her husband back from that day in the basement but Truely can't shake the memory; not right away.

Winston and Mitchell are shocked at what they are seeing as well as what their parents are saying. Their father is unable to move past a moment in a basement and their family is sitting on the computer waiting for a response. Winston finally comes back to the present time at hand and sits down to reply to the message. He finds a family photo already on the computer to go with the message and he hits the send key and holds his breath.

Chapter Fifty-Two

MaLyce and Truely have left the den, leaving Mitchell and Winston more puzzled than when they first saw the picture.

◆

They were still yelling touchdown when the computer first beeped three minutes ago but Big Man hears it the second time. His mind was on Truely when he heard it so Big Man tells Honestly that it beeped but Honestly is into the game with Mercy so Big Man and Ronald take a look.

Moving his hand down the side of the screen, the computer comes up and so does the reply. Big Man hits the key and he and Ronald cheered louder than Honestly and Mercy do over the touchdown causing those two to rush to the computer to see what the excitement is about. Honestly and Mercy join in the cheers and forget about the game. After a few minutes they calm down and try to decide what to do next. Ronald notices a phone number at the end of the message. Moving on autopilot, Ronald picks up the phone and dials. He listens to the ring and then a young man says, "Hello, is this my Uncle Honestly," Ronald responds with, "No, it's your Uncle Ronald," and then he hears shouts of joy so loud Mercy, Honestly, and Big Man can hear it.

There is jubilation on both ends of the phone. After MaLyce gathers herself she takes the phone from Winston and talks for the first time with her brother-in-law, Ronald. Finally, Truely is able to take the receiver and talks with Mercy, Big Man and Ronald. Almost afraid to say his brother's name, Truely cautiously asks about Honestly. Ronald tells Truely to, "Hold on."

The three brothers have been watching how Honestly has morphed into a frightened man who can't wait to look over the side of a mountain. Ronald looks at Honestly and gives him the phone.

By the time Honestly takes the phone, tears are running down his face like a broken water faucet. The brothers hold their breath and wait.

Suspended

"Truely," Honestly's voice is shaky, "Truly, is this really you," Honestly waits for an answer. The brothers know that he gets the answer he's hoping for as the faucet turns into a rushing river and he falls into the chair.

◆

Truely is just over an hour away. Even though it's late, all five of the brothers, having waited a lifetime, can't wait any longer. The four of them, Honestly, Mercy, Ronald, and Big Man get into Big Man's F-150 truck and head south then west. The ride is quiet each man is to himself with his own thoughts to communicate with whatever memories they might have of a life they all want to forget.

"Honestly finally breaks the silence, "I haven't allowed myself to even think about the last time I saw Truely, that memory was far too painful. She," he says with disdain in his voice then says it again to reinforce his truest feelings, "She said she killed him. She even showed me the place where she put his body. When I woke from the beating that she gave me, Syvon took me to a small grave just past the cemetery with dirt piled on top of it. She said she did it because he had done something wrong and she hated him for it so she killed him. Then she looked down at me with those cold, deadly eyes of hers and told me I would probably wake up dead in the morning. I was only-- we were only nine at the time. With Truely already dead and no one there to help me, I ran. I didn't look back I just ran until I fell out. When I woke a few hours later, I ran again until I couldn't run anymore. The police picked me up after a few days and tried to get me tell them who I was, but I wouldn't tell them. I knew they would try to take me back to her. I also knew what she had already done to Truely with that hot water and they gave him back to her and I thought, now Truely's dead. I just kept my mouth shut. I went to foster care until I saw my picture on television. That night, I climbed out the window and left. I stayed on my own, living on the streets until I was taken in by a couple who wanted kids so bad they never asked me anything about my past and I never told them anything. I don't know how they did it but they enrolled me in school and got my birth certificate and all the documents I needed. They even got me a social security number. I was almost twelve when I met them. I spent ten years hating Syvon Peoples, but the Lewis' helped me to get past that. They were great people. They even encouraged me to keep my name until I was sure I wanted to change it. Once I got old enough to change my name, I realized the girls liked it, so I kept it. Plus I knew one day I would want to find Surely, Hellinher, and Mercy. I didn't know I had other brothers and sisters. All these years I thought Truely was dead at Syvon's hands."

When Honestly stops talking, they have crossed two county lines and are now pulling into the driveway of fifty-four forty-one Marriot Street. The brothers sit in the truck too nervous to get out. What they have all wanted so badly for so long is now before them and they are too scared to go in and get it. Fortunately, Winston and Mitchell aren't, they come out to meet them. The four brothers get out of the truck and stare at their nephews a while before the boys cry uncles and rush to them. More tears and emotion fill the driveway of the Peoples' home until Honestly looks up to see his brother and the other half of his life standing in front of him. Looking into Truely's face is like looking into a mirror, Honestly thinks. The men waste no time reaching for each other. Both thinking the other was dead for more than thirty years is more than either can take at the moment. No one tries to separate them. Instead, MaLyce and the boys lead the others into the house and give Truely and Honestly their private moment.

RESTORATION

CHAPTER 53

Married. I'm Mrs. Walter Mayfield of 4459 Overland Park East. Naturallee Joy Mayfield. I love the sound of it. I want to say it out loud all night but I'm sure the others are not as enchanted with the way it sounds as I am so I only say it when my husband is around. I don't know which sounds better my husband or Mrs. Walter Mayfield.

Vickie has got to be the best wedding planner in all of Paris; even the minister spoke English enough that Walter and I understood our wedding vows. Celebrating in the ballroom seemed too big so at the last minute Vickie was able to get the hotel to move it outside to their most beautiful floral garden. How she filled the garden with so many lilacs I don't know but the aroma, the colors, and the atmosphere, all of it is so much more than I thought I would have in an already beautiful place. The garden comes with a small orchestra and a continuous flow of wine. With the sunset upon us, the evening is perfect except for the fact that my brothers are not here but they will be present at the wedding this spring. Looking around the garden at my sisters, my husband and my good friend, Ms. Blair, I find my tears won't stop falling. Less than a year ago, I had no one to love and no one to love me. No one to see me fall and certainly no one who'd care if I showed up anywhere ever again. Remembering those words makes this time even sweeter for me. Now, here today, I'm married with some family and friends around me. I am happier than I thought I could ever be. I love Walter and I want him to be as happy as I am right now.

"Mrs. Mayfield, what are you thinking about," Walter comes up behind me and asks as he slides his arms around my waist. "Are you sure you're happy, Naturallee. This all happened so fast and you haven't begun to really live your own life. I," but I stop him from speaking,

"Walter, I'm not some naïve little girl who doesn't know a thing about life. I'm twenty seven years old as of last month and I know what I'm doing. I fell in love with you the first month I moved into the house with you. I should have allowed myself to let my feelings grow for you then but I was afraid. I was afraid because I'd never been in love before and I didn't know what it was. But I know now and I can't imagine loving anyone like I love you."

"Just promise me something; promise me that if your feelings change or you find someone more your own age you will allow yourself that happiness and not stay with me," I stop Walter again.

"Walter why are you so caught up with this age thing? And no, I won't promise you something like that. Making such a promise only suggests that what you are saying has some validity to it and it doesn't. Now this is the happiest day of my life and you are the man I love and will always love so stop trying to kill my joy. Please. Let's not talk like this on our wedding day of all days. Please!"

"Then can we talk about going upstairs to our room, Mrs. Mayfield," I like the look in Walter's eyes and I want to go but I don't want to leave our family and friends just yet.

Chapter Fifty-Three

"Isn't it a little soon to leave the reception though," I've forgotten about tonight and the things that go with it. Walter and I have lived together for almost a year but in separate rooms. Tonight, we will have to share the same room and that's the part I still feel a little unprepared for. I feel a little too young to take part in. I wonder if Walter knows it.

"No, it's never too soon to start your lives together," David has heard that much of the conversation and has sided with Walter.

What am I to do at this point? I have no choice. Walter and I tell everyone we are retiring for the night and then he leads me back into the hotel and then up to his room.

My sisters have been in here. I can tell. The room is set in a soft lilac color with the same soft scent. There are white rose pedals on the floor leading to the bedroom. There is a bottle of champagne on the table with strawberries and chocolate waiting to be eaten next to the champagne. I swallow hard and feel my hand start to slip out of Walter's but he tightens his grip as he leads me to the sofa. We don't talk or do anything else. We just sit; his arm around my shoulder and his head on the back of the sofa. His eyes are closed and his breathing relaxes and I think he has fallen asleep. I feel myself relax, as well. I snuggle in next to Walter and lay my head on his chest. I could hug and kiss this man for the rest of my life. I could stay right here for the rest of my life, as well. Thinking out loud I say just that and Walter lets me know he's not asleep.

"I could too, sweetheart or at least until it's time to eat," then Walter grabs my knee and I jump and move his hand.

"W-a-l-t-e-r I am s-o s-o-r-r-y, I didn't mean to do that. It was a reflex form a bad memory," I know I'm babbling but I want him to know I don't mean to push him away. I feel tears building up in my eyes and things are getting out of control. I'm drifting up, leaving the room, and leaving Walter. I'm afraid. I'm crying, and I'm afraid I've hurt Walter again. Things are moving and getting away from me. I can't stop it. Where is Walter? I need his help; but I'm too far away. Now the floor isn't there anymore and I feel like I'm going to faint.

"Naturallee, don't get upset. We've talked about it. I know. I understand. I forgot. I'm sorry." Walter has his arm around my shoulder again and I come back to him instantly. He is still talking but I can only hear his heart beating in his chest so I let go of the man with the one big eye and allow myself the safety of Walter's arms.

◆

When I wake I'm laying on the sofa still in my wedding dress. My head is on Walter's leg and his head is on the back of the sofa again and this time he is asleep. I think about waking him but I'm not sure. Sitting up, I look at Walter he looks so peaceful and so desirable. I want to kiss him and I do, lightly at first, then with more passion, with enough passion to wake him. Walter returns my kiss. Then he stops to look at me as if searching for answers to questions that haven't been asked yet. But I want to continue so I kiss him again with even more passion. Walter has his answer. Satisfied with my response, Walter leads me into the bedroom and then closes the door.

◆

It's after nine a.m. and Walter is still asleep and I'm just waking up. I see my wedding dress over on the chair and Walter's pants across my dress. I'm glad my wedding night was with Walter. He was so loving and patient with me. His tender touch was all I needed; it let me know it would be alright. No, his touch lets me know that everything will be great and it was, for me, I hope Walter feels the same way. I hope everything was good for Walter. He's had experience before with times like last night; I haven't. But I understand the joy of it now.

Chapter Fifty-Three

I want to kiss my husband until he wakes but this morning at four o'clock we were awake talking so maybe I will let him sleep. I start to slide off the bed but Walter's hand finds my arm and pulls me back into him. I'm in a place I don't ever want to leave. He offers me safety and happiness and I want to keep these gifts as long as I can.

We lay quietly at first, then Walter asks, "Are you happy, Naturallee, I mean are you really happy? Because I sure am," then he looks at me with his beautiful blue eyes and I slip into that place of contentment I go to whenever I look straight into his eyes.

"I never thought I could be this happy and I want to thank you Walter for being the biggest part of it." I have to kiss him again; I love Walter's mouth. I kiss his mouth and his eyes and his throat and his ears and I can't stop kissing my husband until Walter takes control of the moment and complies with my demands.

We leave our room for the first time the next day. I want to see my sisters, and David and Ms. Blair before they leave for the airport. Walter and I will be staying another two days. Walter says there is something we have to do before we leave Paris. We meet everyone for lunch and say our good-byes, at least good-bye until Walter and I get home. But before we can say our hello's my sisters are all telling me at once that our last and what we believe is the final sibling has been found. Truely Grateful was found by his twin brother, Honestly Sweet. The boys have all met each other and they can't wait to meet all of the girls and have all of us together in one room for what is sure to be the very first time in our lives.

Then I remember Syvon's safe and the letters to each of us inside.

I want, no, Walter and I need everyone to come to our house when we get back. Syvon has left some things for each of us and I want everyone to have as soon as possible. She was a horrible mother to all of us, but she tried to make amends before she died. We need to close that chapter of our lives and move on, but before we can completely close that door, we need to get everything out in the open so that we can leave it where it needs to be, in the past. Then we can move on with our lives together as brothers and sisters should. The girls said they would think about it but they could care less about what Syvon had left them and the boys probably felt the same way.

The afternoon is getting away from us and they have to leave or they will miss their flight. We all decide it will be better to say good-bye at the hotel instead of at the airport so with hugs and kisses all around, I watch my family pile into two taxies and pull away. I'm so glad Walter is here for this.

After spending the rest of the afternoon crying, I decide it's time to get it together so that Walter and I can have some fun before we turn in for the night. Maybe we could go out and get a quick dinner before it gets too late. But Walter is always thinking ahead and he has ordered room service and I'm glad.

CHAPTER 54

Winston and Mitchell want to share the good news with their brother, Mark. After a couple of hours of trying to adjust to what looks like two fathers in the same room, they head over to the hospital to tell Mark. Marks situation has been at such a grave point until recently that the hospital allows Mark visitors at any hour day or night.

"What kind of life has dad had? I mean what kind of mother was Syvon Peoples? Who could do those things to their own flesh and blood? Did mom say she tried to kill her own kids?" Winston cannot stop the words from pouring out of his mouth.

Uncle Honestly was on his own when he was nine years old. What happened to dad though, what do you think he did at nine years old?" The boys ride the rest of the way to the hospital in silence.

Mark is watching television and enjoying some cherry Jell-O and water.

Suspended

"What are you two lost souls doing out at this time of night," Mark asks with surprise in his voice.

"Man, we had to come and tell you. You'd never believe this stuff otherwise. I tell you I don't believe it and I was there and saw it all and heard it all, and I'm telling you, I still can't believe what's happened." Winston is still amazed at all that has gone on. "What, what, tell me what's going on and with who." Mark sits up a little higher in the bed.

Mitchell and Winston find places to sit, one on the heater and at the foot of Mark's bed, to tell Mark the story. All three of the boys are concerned for their father and very interested in getting to know their uncles. They spend two and a half hours discussing what little they know about their new family. Finally, the boys go home after Mark falls asleep.

CHAPTER 55

Home always feels good to return to but this time it feels even better. I am returning home as Walter's wife and not just a woman he's sharing the house with. The first thing I want to do is move Walter's things into my room. I never realized how lonely living alone was until I started living with him and now I realize how much happier life is when it's shared with someone you love.

Walter and I stayed in Paris a couple of extra days to finish up some important business that Walter had to take care of at Nathan's request. It was of course, things for Walter and me after we married but important, none the less. I found out that Vickie had already been expecting me; it was something Nathan had taken care of. Nathan had planned for us to stay in Paris for three weeks, just Walter and I, but with the unexpected surprise of my sisters our plans changed. Walter said he was sure that Nathan would agree with the way things were done. Our last couple of days, Walter and I did many of the things Nathan had hoped we would do just as he and

Syvon had done. The second to the last day we were in Paris, Walter took me to a beautiful apartment building just outside of town. The grounds were beautifully manicured, and the building had the perfect French look to it. I fell in love with it the minute I saw it. While I stood admiring everything Walter looked at me and asked if I wanted to keep it or if I wanted to sell it. It turns out that Nathan bought it for Syvon as a wedding gift and left it to Walter to give to me as a wedding gift from him and Syvon. We spent our last night in Paris in our apartment building. I had to ask Walter how wealthy was Nathan? The question simply made Walter laugh but he did tell me that I would be receiving a very large part of Nathan's estate. I would be receiving more than the original thirty seven million I was told about. And Walter told me that each sibling would receive more than I was originally told. We had to meet with a French lawyer to take care of the paperwork or at least get as much done as possible while we were there. Nathan was richer than I could imagine. Walter said he didn't have nearly as much money as Nathan had, but that he has enough to take care of us for the rest of our lives.

◆

On the airplane trip home, Walter and I make some big decisions; we both agree that moving into my bedroom is the better choice. We also agree that we want to keep our date night once a week. Walter says he wants to stop working at the firm full-time and maybe just do two days a week. He has always secretly wanted to travel. Nathan knew that about Walter? That's why to Walter's surprise, Nathan has made some traveling plans for me and Walter that Walter knew nothing about. It was nice to see Walter's face when the French attorney gave Walter the package from Nathan. Because Walter never liked traveling alone Nathan traveled a lot so that Walter wouldn't have to go alone.

We also plan to honeymoon someplace warm and sunny after

our big wedding at home in May. Where we go is up to Walter, I just want to be wherever he is. The first place we are going to go together he says is to church. We've discussed it extensively on the plane ride home and Walter believes it is what has made his life so good. It's what has gotten him through all of his tough times over the years, he says.

Because even though Walter and Nathan have always been best friends their childhoods were quite different. Walter's parents weren't well-to-do. Nathan's parents weren't well-to-do either, but Nathan's grandparents on his mother's side were. When they died, they left everything to their only child who was Nathan's mother. Then five years later after Nathan's grandparents died, his mother died in a car crash. Nathan's mother had secretly left control of her fortune to Walter's father because she knew of Nathan's father's indiscretions and wasteful spending habits. Nathan's mother wanted to make sure there would be money for Nathan as he grew up to give him the start he needed in life. When she died and the will was read, it tore the two men apart. But it also tore apart Walter's parents marriage because Walter's mother always thought, after the reading of the will, that there had been something between Nathan's mother and Walter's father. Walter was forced to live between parents and try to keep the peace. Finally, his father died and then his mother passed shortly after that. His brother died on the heels of their parents. By the time Walter was twenty-seven years old, he was alone. It may have been the reason why he married his first wife Elaine. When Mr. Mayfield, Walter's father, turned Nathan's inheritance over to him Nathan was twenty- five and had just buried his own father, Mr. Grey.

Walter was having a hard time paying for the last couple of years of school but Nathan loaned him the money. Once they both graduated, their professional relationship started and it strengthened their personal relationship more than it already was. They were in a three-way partnership with Carl's father but that only lasted a few years. Being on an airplane for that long I think made Walter talk about all sorts of things we had never talked about before.

CHAPTER 56

When Walter and I get into the house we don't stop walking until we get to my, our bedroom we are so tired we go straight upstairs to rest. Slipping out of shoes, coat, dress, pants and shirt we curl up together and sleep for the first four hours. When I wake Walter has his arm across my chest and his chin on my shoulder. He's close enough that I breathe in the air he breathes out. We share even the same air and I like it. I have started a brand new life at the request of a man I never knew and a mother I hadn't seen in almost twenty years. I want to thank God again for my life turning out as it has but I ask myself once more who is this God that I'm thanking? Why did Uncle Stew believe in him? Why is God so important to Walter. Important enough to Walter that he only allowed himself to fall in love with me because he had prayed about the entire living arrangement that Nathan made for us. Walter believes that God has put us together. He didn't mind the quick wedding in Paris because he was sure that God had blessed our union so whether we married in Paris five days ago or if we didn't marry for another five years. Once he prayed about it and got his answer, even his age has stopped bothering him now that we are actually married.

I like the way Walter does that. He turns to someone else; who he says knows it all, to make the decisions in his life. Walter says all he has to do is follow, and following is a lot easier than leading. I want to go to church with Walter. I'm interested in knowing a little something more about God. I want to know if Walter's God is the same God Uncle Stew knew. Yeah, I want to go so I can see what it is about God that makes my brothers and sisters feel the way they do about him, too. Oh, but I must go; the whole family will be there to hear Pastor Harris give the sermon. My brother, the preacher, there's got to be something special about God and I do need to know what that is. Besides that, everyone is coming here after church so that we can all get together for the first time in our lives. Then we can also get the envelopes Syvon has left for each of us in the safe that I found in my closet. Besides all of that, I will get to meet my brothers and sisters-in-law as well as my nieces and nephews. This is going to be great. Maybe get to meet God and the rest of my family.

I slide out from under Walter's arm and go to the closet to I open the safe. I'm not sure what different thing I think I will find when I open the safe but every envelope and piece of jewelry is still inside as well as everything else including Macho Man. The envelope that has my name on it is still here unopened, as well. I hadn't opened it for fear that it could have changed the course of things between me and Walter, and not for the better. I didn't want Syvon to interfere with my life. No, that's not entirely true; I didn't want Syvon to mess up my life, not ever again.

There's nothing in the safe that needs my attention; I'm not sure why I'm in here but I can't leave just yet. But I start to miss Walter so I return to the bedroom and see that Walter is still asleep. I sit in the chair to watch him sleep for a while before finally getting back in the bed and curling up next to him and fall asleep again.

◆

The chill in the air reminds me that winter still lingers. When my feet hit the carpet, I'm warmed by the plush carpeting. I've always loved living here in this house and I know we are home. Walter must have gotten up earlier because he's not in bed. But then I think I smell the coffee. Walter always makes it before he goes in to work, but I think it's Saturday and Walter doesn't work on Saturdays. Besides, he took several weeks off so that we could go to Florida and then France.

I need a hot shower to get myself going so I make my way into the bathroom. Walter has been in here; his toothbrush is next to mine and it makes me smile. I take a quicker shower than I thought I would because I want to see Walter, after all, this is our first morning together here in the house as husband and wife. Walter has told me he likes me in pastel colors so I find a soft lavender sweater to go with my jeans and slip quickly into both before making my way down stairs to see him.

I go straight to the kitchen to see Walter but he's not here instead Walter is sitting in the yard in the swing with his cup of coffee. He looks very relaxed and happy; I hope I have something to do with that. I head to the door then stop. What if Walter wants to be alone? I have to consider him in this marriage and not just me and what I want. What if he's out there so that he can be alone; I shouldn't interfere with that. I decide to wait in the house until he comes in. I sit at the counter and try to watch television.

It's a long ten minutes before Walter comes into the house to warm up his coffee. "Good morning, sweetheart. How did you sleep?" he asks as he walks over to give me my good morning kiss. "Why didn't you come out and join me? I've been saving you a seat next to me on the swing," he adds as he goes over to fill his coffee cup.

Suspended

"I didn't want to disturb you, you looked so peaceful out there and I didn't want to interrupt you," I tell him.

"Naturallee, I will always tell you when I don't want to be disturbed and that will never be when you're around," Walter tells me as he grabs my hand and asks me to join him on the swing. I think it's got to be wrong for any one person to be this happy, but how do you share this happiness with everyone? Can it be shared, happiness that is. I certainly hope so.

Walter and I spend the whole day together at the house. I talk with Surely and I spoke with her husband James for the very first time. Then I get a call from Mercy and Big Man. They tell me about Truely and what has happened with he and Honestly. They aren't sure that Truely will be able to make it tomorrow to church. Mercy said that Truely had a horribly ugly life with Syvon and he's having a hard time with the memories. Mercy, Big Man, and I talk for a while longer before I tell them I've got to feed my husband so I will see them in church in the morning. They say good-bye and we reluctantly hang up the phones.

I feel I should talk with Truely, maybe we all need to tell our stories of life at the hands of Syvon Peoples to make sure that we all can move on. I want to tell Truely what she made me endure at the hands of the man with the one-big-eye. I have listened to the stories of horror that my sisters have told me and Truely needs to know we all had unthinkable times with her. I was told that Syvon was exceptionally hateful to Truely though, so maybe he has more of a reason to hate Syvon than the rest of us. I do cringe at the thought of what she must have put him through.

CHAPTER 57

I don't remember Uncle Stew's church being quite this lively. The music and singing, the choir director alone is energized with a spirit that makes me want to get up out of my seat and sing, and I would if I knew the songs. I understand why Walter enjoys coming here. I feel great and David hasn't taken the pulpit yet. Sitting here, I think this place can make anyone feel better just being in the room. I hope Truely does come, I know he will feel better if he does.

We are all here; everyone but Truely. The service started about twenty minutes ago, so there is still time for him to get here. Truely did say that if they don't make it to the service he would come over to the house later. He said that he and MaLyce had someplace important to go before he could come to church. He wouldn't say when I asked him but we don't know each other well enough so I can't blame him for not wanting to tell me. I have finally hugged my brothers and I love the feel of family love.

Suspended

Monkee and Ronald are as different as night and day. Monkee is thin as paper but Ronald is a solid man with thick hands. They both have the Peoples green eyes. Monkee is a much darker man that Ronald and he wears his hair short. I'm sure he wears it so short because it is the typical black man's hair. It's dense and rough. Ronald's hair is much smoother and softer. It compliments his skin tone nicely. Big Man and David are like twins even though they are two parts of a threesome. Regina is a part of this trio. Honestly isn't a part of this set but he looks a lot like each of the brothers. It's funny, but Honestly looks like the original, the actual mold and the other brothers are spin-offs of him.

But Reverend Harris has come to the microphone and I turn my attention to him. He, too, has the energy that the choir director has. David's words are powerful and he delivers each word with a strength that comes from somewhere deep within him. I spent a couple of days with him and Grace in Paris and David never sounded like this. He sounds like a man possessed but I guess he is in a sense.

The room is electrified with all that is going on. Everyone whether white or black, Indian or Arabic and every other nationality, are in the same atmosphere here. There is no separation in the way they worship. I guess they all believe in what is printed on everything in the church; *it's all about the One we worship.* The words are printed everywhere. That and, *enjoy the worship then go out and do the work.* Walter told me this is something David had printed the week he got here. The people really relate to it. They want to live by the words. Walter has always lived by those words. I wonder if anyone here knows about the home Walter and Nathan had built in Florida and all they had to do getting the kids here. And the wing at the hospital, as well as all of the volunteering Walter does, all the volunteering Walter and Nathan both did. I wonder if any of them know all that he has done for me and my family. Do any of them know how much Walter believers in God and what God does?

Chapter Fifty-Seven

I want what Walter has with God. He says I can have the same relationship with God or I could have an even better one. I don't know how that could be possible but I am interested in finding out. I have always suspended myself to get away from my problems but Walter has always turned his problems over to God, he says. He has always trusted in God and things have always gone better for him. Even if things didn't go Walter's way, he always trusts that God will do the right thing for him. Walter has peace. When he thought that I was rejecting him before we went to Florida he was able to trust God with the outcome, and as it turned out I was the one on a mission to get to Walter and explain everything to him. He must have trusted God that I would do that.

Reverend Harris' topic this morning is about faith and he takes his text from the Book of Romans, he says and strange enough that was the same book that the preacher spoke from at Uncle Stew's funeral. He said Uncle Stew wanted all of us there to keep our faith in God no matter what. I wish now that I had remembered that.

The service ends an hour and a half after it started. In the middle of David's sermon Truely, his wife, MaLyce and two young men who I assume are two of their three sons slip in and sit right next to me and Walter. I only know it's Truely because I look over to see if Honestly is still sitting in front of us with Mercy and Ronald; he is. I know this identical face of Honestly's has to be Truely. It's almost scary how much they look alike. Watching them, they even move the same way at the same time. I think it kind of unnerves MaLyce, as well. Anyway, they got here in time for the last of what David is saying.

David introduces all of us to the church once he finished his sermon. He even tells everyone that Walter and I were the reason for his quick trip to Paris. He and Grace had gone over to witness our marriage. The people were completely surprised that Walter and I were married because they didn't know that Walter was dating anyone, they said. I think everyone congratulated us and wished us well.

345

Suspended

We stand around after the service and talk until David says good-bye to the last person. I don't think any of us knows why we are waiting but David doesn't seem to mind that we are. Walter and Mercy made arrangements for dinner at our house; Mercy prepared the meal. After David joins all of us on the parking lot, we pile into our cars and caravan our way to our house on Overland Park East.

Driving home, Walter and I talk about the fact that me and my siblings have all lived within a seventy mile radius of each other and never knew it. As a matter-of-fact, Truely has lived on Overland Park West which is just over nine miles from where Walter and I live now. Monkee lives about twenty miles away, and Big Man has done work for Walter's firm before while Surely, Mercy, and Hell-inher all live within a thirty minute drive of each other. Ronald has been living only a few miles away from them and Regina is still in the same state just a town away. We are all so close and we've all been so far away. And most of us never knew about the others.

Eight cars pull up with me and Walter and I couldn't be prouder. Truely, MaLyce, and the boys are with us. Inside the house there is so much happiness and laughter it's like we've known each other our entire lifetimes.

But then we start to settle in and some of us start to tell our story of hurt and pain. Stories that have more to them that any one person should have to endure. But the stories of life with Syvon are the worse. Maybe because she, being our mother and knowing that she did the things she did to each of us is what made it so hard for some of us to talk about. All of us weren't able to say all the things that happen to us when we lived with Syvon Peoples or in the foster homes and family members' homes we stayed in. When Truely spoke he said very little mostly confirming what Honestly said about the night Syvon thought she had killed her oldest twins.

Walter suggests that I give everyone the envelopes that Syvon has left for them. Now might be a good time so I go into the bedroom and get them. I hand them out without trying to get everyone's attention; there's so much talking I don't think they will hear me if I yell so I let the envelopes with their names on them do the yelling for me. As I give the last envelope to Regina, I realize that Syvon has put in parentheses the name Regina and I'm surprised.

"I know that none of you had a good life with Syvon but before she died she came to realize it, as well. She wanted to find all of you and let you know how badly she felt about how she treated each of you but by then, it was too late. Your mother died of cancer about four and a half years ago. My best friend for all but three years of my life was Nathan Grey. Nathan married your mother and helped her to get her life together. He had a house built for Syvon that is designed almost exactly like this one because he loved her and wanted her to be happy. Your mother was a sick woman and no one knew that until she and Nathan married. Nathan convinced Syvon to seek professional help and it was determined that Syvon suffered from mental illness. She had never been diagnosed. Once she was put on medication and she had a chance to think clearly she started to suffer emotional trauma due to the horrifying life she realized she gave to each of you and some of you more than others. She knew she could never apologize for what she has put you all through but she wanted to say something to each of you. That's what's inside your envelopes." Walter makes the announcement then looks to me but I know their pain so I can't say anything to soften the hurt we all feel because of Syvon Peoples. I simply smile at Walter and open my envelope hoping everyone will follow, and they do.

◆

A lot of silent time passes before David speaks, "She still knows how to shut us up doesn't she," he says without any emotion. Then the room is quiet again.

"I know none of us want to hear this because she was a horrible mother. I mean Syon use to put me in a room with a man who had one big eye that couldn't close or blink when I was about four or five. I would hear her say to the man's drug dealer cousin that I would like it once I got use to it. This man scared me to death the way he looked and because he would always put his scarred, scaly bent fingers on my leg and rub me. I couldn't scream because Syvon said she would kill me if I did and since she had already tried to kill me once I didn't scream when the drug dealer and his cousin came. Fortunately, he never did anything more than put his hand on my thigh but I was scared to death each time I was put into the room with him. I could hear Syvon and the drug man in the other room and I hated the whole thing. I hated her. There were other things she did to me that I don't want to get into right now but they were ugly things that I want to forget. And I know that my situation was bad but I also know that some of us had it worse than others." I feel the pain and see the hurt of each of my sibling as I continue speaking.

"I'm not asking any of you to forgive Syvon. That has to come in your own time if ever. But I am asking that you will help me. I don't really know this God like you seem to. I do know that with Him comes forgiveness and I want to learn more about Him. I am hoping each of you will help me to learn that and everything else you know about God. You guys have had the experience longer than I have. I was introduced to God by Uncle Stew but I was young and Uncle Stew died within the first two years of my being with him and Aunt Joyce, so I don't know that much. Walter has a great relationship with God and he has been generous enough to share with me. But Walter doesn't know the forgiveness side like I think all of us might have to learn and do. So I need your help not for Syvon but for me. I want to know God and I need to learn about Him the right way." I'm not sure where the words came from but I whisper a quick, "help me out with this," to someone. I think I said it to God.

"She's right," David says. "Naturallee has put some of the ugliness of her life on the table for all of us to see. That means she really wants to get rid of it. She wants to let it go and she is asking for our help to do that. She has told us she doesn't really know God and she wants to get to know Him as the God we say He is. We owe it to her to help and if Syvon gets forgiveness in the process then we are all the better for it. Let's not be Syvon Peoples who was actually diagnosed with mental illness. Let's be God's people and help a blood sister in need. And in the process we will, I'm sure, help ourselves," David says.

"I couldn't have said it better myself," Honestly states.

We agree to put the envelopes away and get to them later at a more private time. We try to get back to the place of joy we were at before the mood of the room changed. But there's a bit of a family dispute in the corner with Truely, MaLyce, and the boys.

"Today is not a day to argue," Honestly says as he pats Truely on his back.

"Dad, why can't we tell them now while everyone is here," the words are stressed as Mitchell says them.

"Because I said no," Truely stresses back through clinched teeth.

"Dad, please what if things change tomorrow for Mark, we need to say something now," Winston states the facts without hesitation ignoring his father's orders.

"Tell us what, Truly? What's Winston talking about?" Honestly needs to know what has his brother's family divided.

The room is quiet and all eyes are on Truely and Honestly as they stand face to face and for the first few seconds I don't even know which is which. For two men who have lived their entire adult lives apart they are one in the same person. I see Truely's jaw bone tighten and in the same instance, Honesty's jaw tightens too. Their hands go up to their forehead at the same time and the tension is released due to the laughter we all let out at the same time watching the brothers moving as one. They can't help it but they do the same thing so often, it's funny. But Honestly knows there is something bothering his brother and he wants to help. Honestly pulls Truely outside after we return to other conversations. I can tell it's something big but I don't go outside to interfere. Most of us have noticed they are in the yard discussing something but we have all decided to let the brothers handle it. MaLyce and the boys don't say anything to us and none of us ask them. We have enough other things to discuss. Besides, when they're ready they will tell us.

Finally, I notice the atmosphere outside has changed. My brothers are laughing at times and they have a more relaxed posture as they lay back in the chairs. Then Ronald and Mercy take a walk outside following David to join Truely and Honestly. Slowly Walter, Big Man, and Monkee make their way out pretending to discuss the landscaping until they deduce it is safe to join in the conversation. We sisters, including Beverly, MaLyce, Big Man's wife Crystal, and Monkee's fiancée, Diane are left inside with the husbands. It turns out that James treated Regina and Markus in their early years of needing counseling. Regina and Markus remembered James because he was able to get them past all of the hurt and pain in the beginning. Markus and Regina didn't want to let on that James had treated them and James says nothing either.

After a while the brothers outside, the brothers-in-law in the den, and the girls in the kitchen are asked to come outside. It seems Truely and his family want the rest of the family to know something important. Without hesitation we all make our way to the yard where the men who are waiting patiently.

Truly with his wife and sons at his side tells us about their other son Mark and the things they have been going through. He tells us that he originally started looking for us because they wanted a donor for Mark but now that he has found us he has a strange feeling about asking. He doesn't want us simply for a kidney for Mark he wants us as his family for life. Therefore he asks that we pray for Mark and his entire family. Truely says that they have had someone, a stranger to his family, volunteer already and he is sure there will be others.

Chapter Fifty-Seven

David chuckles before he tells Truely how he has no intention of praying that someone else will do for his family what he may be able to do. The rest of us feel the same way. We decide that we need to meet the whole family and since a part of our family isn't able to be here we are going to the family.

We go in and sit down to eat. Mercy has done a marvelous job on the baked chicken, wild rice, and mixed vegetables. The dessert of cherries and cream over baked apple crisp is something I can't eat very often but I eat more than I can hold today. We forgo coffee and conversation due to the lateness of the hour and pile back into the cars we came in and head over to Hope Memorial Hospital about twenty minutes back to town.

CHAPTER 58

Truely and MaLyce are so appreciative that the family wants to help they continue to thank us until Honestly threatens to go home if he or MaLyce says thank you again. There are so many of us in the hospital we have to take three elevators up to the eighth floor. Then we wait in the lounge while MaLyce and Truely go to Marks' room to get him. They want us to be a surprise to him so we wait and act as if we are strangers visiting other patients. We want to introduce ourselves as if we expect him to know us.

Our plans are foiled though when Mark comes in and the first face he sees is Honesty's, he does a double take then looks at his father.

"Uncle Honestly, is it really you? You look just like my dad. It has to be you." Honestly can only smile and hug Mark tightly. Then Marks catches a glimpse of two other sets of green eyes on the faces of black men and he knows they, too, are his uncles. Mark doesn't realize that the women in the room are his aunts so only his uncles introduce themselves to him. When his Uncle James, George, and Markus introduce themselves, Mark comments on their having common names and ask how is it that Syvon didn't name them something weird.

"That's because I only married into your family. I married your aunt Surely Fine," James says as he reaches for Surely.

"And I married your aunt Hellinher," George smiles and squeezes Hellinher's hand.

"But I was the luckiest," Markus states as he puts his arm around Regina, "Because I got to marry your aunt Regina."

Then everyone's eyes cross the room to Walter who is leaning on the window sill. It occurs to him all at once that it might be a good time to introduce him and me.

Clearing his throat, Walter stands up and scans the room for me. Then with a strong, sure voice Walter states, "Luck had nothing to do with it for me. I was blessed to be given this exquisite jewel, your aunt Naturallee Joy. Walter turns to Markus with a smile and says, "I knew you'd get caught up in the moment and forget. Can I have my five dollars, please," then Walter puts his hand out.

"That man will bet on anything given half the chance," Regina says playfully. "You lost, his introduction was so much better than, *but I was the luckiest,*" Regina says pouting her lips at Markus. "Now pay up," she continues to tease. Markus runs his hand into his pockets, finds a five dollar bill, and gives it to Walter.

Then the room explodes with laughter and shouts of joy. We're a family, together for the first time, shouts Honestly, while others are laughing and shouting at the realization that each and every one of us are here together. Finally.

"How did all of you find each other? I have been looking for any sign of family for the past three years. Have you all been living under the same rock," Mark let the words slide off his tongue naturally without regard for his parents' response.

"Man, I thought that was you who sent that e-mail about six

months ago when I posted that web-site. I thought at first, mom or dad had found the web-site and was trying to trace it back to me so I never responded again." Winston says.

"What are you talking about? What web-site? I never found a web-site and I certainly didn't respond to it," Mark wants Winston to know.

"The web-site that said, *could you be one of us*, and I put mom and dad's names on it with as much family history as I had found on the internet. The only reply I got was some flip answer like, *or could you be a part of me Truly.*" I thought it was mom so I didn't respond," Winston says and looks at his mother.

MaLyce throws her hands up and says it wasn't her, she never saw it. Then she looks suspiciously at Truely. He, too, says he never saw it. He has no idea what the boys are talking about.

"It was me," Regina says. Her face is serious and her words, flat. "I didn't know that you were serious because you signed the e-mail Truely Grateful, you didn't say your father's name was Truely Grateful. On the web-page you only stated that you were looking for your family. You said that MaLyce Miller was your mother and you were looking for both her family and your dad's family and that you'd be truely grateful if anyone who knew you would contact you. So I did hoping that if you were family and that you would reply since I called you Truely, but you never came back with anything. So I let it drop," Regina explained.

"That was why I thought it was mom or dad because of the Truely with the capital letter," Winston looked a bit hurt that the communication stopped at that point due to a misunderstanding on both ends.

"That happened because it wasn't the time for us to get together. But now is the time and we are all here now for more than just knowing each other," David says changing the atmosphere in the room. "We have some relatives that we haven't seen in a couple of decades and some we have never seen. But we have some that need all of our help and I'd like to start giving that help right now if we don't mind. Let's start with being thankful for the gift of finding family then we can ask for instruction on how to proceed. Next we will seek out the ways best for each of us to help and finally, we will pray for the coming together of it all to work for the good of God our Creator," David suggests with more of a strong order than a suggestion, that is what we will do.

And this is exactly what we do as we come together in a family circle holding hands tightly so that the family circle can't be broken while David leads us in prayer. Feeling the need to offer prayers as well, Surely, Honestly, Markus, Mitchell, Winston, and Walter all say a prayer, as well. Then we all start to celebrate again as if we all know that Mark is whole and healthy again. We laugh and hug and sing and dance as if life has just begun for us all, like we have been on this earth but not lived until this very moment. We celebrate life anew and although I don't understand it all, I am open to the movement inside of me and the excitement of the others. We empty the cart that has the pop and water bottles on it and we grab the candy, chips and pretzels from the table as well as all the fruit that is there and for the next hour we celebrate here in this hospital lounge with the family together at last.

Now I really know what it means to have family around. I look at each of my siblings and their families and I feel connected to something far bigger than I have ever been. Then I see Walter and I know that everything is good. My life has have direction and purpose because I intend to follow Him because Walter follows God and that's the direction I want to travel now. And I'm sure that after all of these years Walter isn't about to change his direction in life so I'll stay with him and get to know God and what He's all about.

CHAPTER
59

It's my wedding day again and the weather is beautiful. The sun is bright but not hot. The wind blows soft so the air is not still and the church has never looked so decorated before, not that I've seen. Everyone is here and my sisters and sisters-in-law are all helping me to get ready. I know that Walter and I are already married but I have the jitters like it is the first time Walter and I will be saying I do. In just forty minutes, I will be saying I still commit my life to Walter and I can hardly wait for that moment to happen.

I take a minute to look around the room at all of my sisters and I think about how blessed I really am. I look at MaLyce and I think back to the day Mark got his kidney. Most of us had been tested when they got the phone call that there was a perfect match and it was on its way to him. We wanted to say no, at first. We wanted to all get tested and use the best one of the family but David reminded us that was not the prayer we had prayed. We asked God to do the decision-making for us and this is the decision He has made. We were able to meet the family who had lost the child that Mark was being blessed by. The family lost their child because of negligence on the part of a woman who had been arrested for drunk driving twice and had no license when she hit that family's son.

Walter had his firm handle the case for the family pro bono. After suing the woman, it was found that she had half a million dollars in an out-of-state account as well as two additional homes and she was a silent partner in a tech startup company. She also had a life insurance policy with three hundred thousand dollars worth of cash value in it. When Walter's firm finished, the family that loss their child had just over three million dollars to start a foundation for families of victims of drunk drivers. Walter's firm also helped them to get the foundation stated.

Fortunately all of my family has been able to move past the days of Syvon Peoples and the terrible life we each had. Most of us have already forgiven her and moved on with our lives. We talk about our brother, Kane and our sister, Lovely Girl; we don't want to forget them. We also remind ourselves how blessed we all are to have found each other when we did. We make plans together and spend most weekends together at a different sibling's house each time.

Nathan was true to his word. He left each of my siblings three million dollars. But he left Truely and Honestly five million each. Those were Syvon's wishes. I received a check for so many millions of dollars. I can't begin to spend it all, to go with the house, the car, and all of the paintings in the house. It turns out the paintings were done by an up-and-coming new artist who died before she had her second showing. That artist was Syvon Peoples Grey. She painted the faceless mother and children to depict her life, the life she had wanted if she had known she was sick when she was younger and had all of us. Some of the paintings were promised to a gallery thirty days after we all received our envelopes. There were only five paintings not promised to the gallery so I gave them to different family members. I know I can see them whenever I want so why not let them have a part of our mother that was good.

It's time to go and meet Walter at the altar in our own church. Hellinher opens the door and Surely leads me to the arms of my brothers, Monkee and Ronald. They take me up the aisle to my brother, Mercy who walks me down the aisle to meet my oldest brother, Truely. The last steps are with Truely until I get to Walter. I see my brothers Honestly and Big Man, both are best men, standing there with Walter. Walter looks happy and I feel happy. I follow my sister, Surely down the aisle as she walks a number of steps behind Hellinher and Regina who walk with their husbands as escorts.

When I arrive at Walter's side, I can't stop smiling. I can't even tell you what Pastor Harris says to us but I agree to everything. The rest of the day is still a blur. My life stayed a blur right up to Honestly and Beverly's wedding in July, seven weeks later.

◆

During the seven weeks between our weddings, Walter and I vacationed in places I didn't know existed. Three different times we had family meet us where we were because Ronald, Mercy, and Monkee had never traveled outside at the state before and Big Man and Crystal wanted to do a three-day getaway. My sisters caught up with us in the Galapagos Islands just off the coast of Ecuador. This place is so beautiful. Walter and I spent an additional four days there. Finally, we return home and attend the wedding. I want to go again but Walter says he needs to rest up.

We stop traveling for a year. Once we start traveling again, we keep our trips to just three a year. Walter has retired and we get to spend all of our time together. I am so glad Nathan Grey met Syvon Peoples and married her. I am also glad that Walter Mayfield and Nathan Grey were best friends. I am even happier that Syvon felt so sorry for what she thought she had done to me that she wanted Nathan to do all he could to find me and I'm grateful that Walter followed Nathan's wishes to the letter.

After seven years, I feel even more love for Walter than I did the first time we said our wedding vows in Paris. As all of my brothers and sisters and my nieces and nephews stand around the grave site trying to comfort me I feel O.K. I know that Walter and I had a great life and I don't regret one moment of it.

◆

When I woke up at the beginning of this week I thought I would let Walter stay in bed and rest a little longer but the phone rang. It was Ms. Blair wanting to speak to Walter. I went back to the bedroom to wake him but he had died right after I got out of the bed. I don't believe he suffered. I do believe he enjoyed our life together as much as I did.

After the funeral and everyone leaves the house including all of my family I find that the house is so quiet I can hear a loud buzzing of stillness in my ears. Then I hear a voice speak to me and I'm not afraid. The voice is comforting and lets me know that I will be alright and that Walter is sleeping and I will be with him again one day.

I sincerely prayed that night for the first time since I lived with Uncle Stew. There has been something in the back of my mind that I haven't taken the time to let come forward. I think I'm afraid that if I do, whatever it is could bring me down and cause me to crash into a million tiny pieces. I'm not ready to do that just yet. But the memory wants out and I can't stop it from coming right now so I relent and allow my mind the freedom it seems to need.

Flashes from the past rush in and I see Uncle Stew in church on his knees praying. I can hear the minister praying as he stands behind the pulpit. Now Uncle Stew is at the dinner table praying again and I feel safe. I feel happy. There is trust in whoever it is that Uncle Stew says can protect and help me. I feel the presence of that some-

Chapter Fifty-Nine

one around me and I'm not afraid. I know it isn't Walter and I'm not afraid. In many ways this feels better than I ever felt with Walter. It doesn't change my love for him. As a matter-of-fact, I feel more love than I did before. I also feel a new love and this love I know will always be here with me. This love holds Walter's love for me with more love to it. I feel a new and real love that I have never felt before. It comes to me in prayer. I want to pray again, by myself. Then just as strongly as the memory and the feelings rush in they go, but I still want to pray, so I do. I pray and I feel safe and comforted. I let it all in. I understand now why my family loves this God. I know why Uncle Stew refused to let God go. I also understand what Walter saw in worshiping God. This is what I will do for the rest of my life. I will live for the love of God.

THE END

About the Author

Geraldine Davis

A grandmother of six, Geraldine had two dreams—graduating from college and releasing her first novel. In 2012 she accomplished both.

Davis graduated with honors from Owens Community College on May 4, with her associate degree in English Literature and on July 14th she celebrated the launch of her first novel, Suspended.

Davis is the primary caregiver of her six grandchildren: Aaryn Joshua, William, E.J., Autumn and twins Ebony and Christian. The children, whose ages range from 7 to 16, lives with her in Toledo, Ohio. She says, "they were a huge inspiration in my writing and going after my dreams even when others my age were thinking about retirement."

Suspended

To order additional copies of *Suspended* or other life changing resources from Zoë Life Publishing visit our web site at www.zoelifepub.com.

If God has placed a book idea in your heart or for special discounts for retail, ministry, education or missionary purposes you may also call or visit the Zoë Life Publishing web site visit at www.zoelifepub.com to find out more.

Zoë Life Publishing
P.O. Box 871066
Canton, MI 48187
(888) 400-4922
outreach@zoelifepub.com
www.zoelifepub.com